THE NINE ASSIGNMENTS

Glenda Winders

*For Tony and Lesley, who are not characters in this book
but who have taught me everything I know about sibling relationships*

ACKNOWLEDGEMENTS

Just about everyone I know has cheered me along during the writing of this novel, but there are a few groups and individuals to whom I am especially grateful. Those would be the San Diego Writing Women and my enormously supportive book groups in San Diego, California, and Eau Claire, Wisconsin. Extra-special thanks go to Carmen Zermeño for her close and sensitive reading of the manuscript and her insightful comments and suggestions; Jan Carroll, poet, friend and relentless editor; and Martin Stevens, my dear friend without whose constant encouragement and technical help this book would never have made it into print.

CHAPTER ONE

E xcept for the addresses, the two envelopes were identical. The
heavy stationery, called "Desert Haze" because its marbled,
off-white sheets in some lights appeared to be almost tan, was selected by Katherine Peterson, late wife of the also late senior partner at the law offices of Peterson, Horowitz, and MacDonald. She
thought it would not appear to be as stark and alarming as the
bleaker "Snowfall" would have been when it arrived in the mail,
sometimes bearing bad news, such as that the recipient had been
awarded only a token pittance in a great-aunt's will or joint custody
had yet again been denied. More often the envelopes contained a
statement for billable hours, and Katherine had believed that her
attention to the paper mitigated the sting, made it seem as if the
law firm were sending a friendly missive rather than whatever disappointment lay coiled and ready to strike inside.

In the return-address corner of the envelopes the initials of the
three partners, in a font called Edwardian Script, were entwined
in gold against a raised navy blue oval. One flowery, overwrought
arm of the *H* was linked to the *P* that came before it, while the other

grabbed on to the final *M* as if to keep it from sliding across the envelope and disappearing under the stamp. Katherine had also found postage meters to be hostile and impersonal, which meant that now a second generation of secretaries made trips to the post office during their lunch hours for sheets of stamps that could bear the image of anything except the American flag -- too nationalistic and confrontational, Katherine had believed. Beneath the logo the full name of the firm and its address in downtown Los Angeles were spelled out in no-nonsense black Times New Roman lettering. While the idea was to soften the arrival of a legal document, Katherine also wanted the recipient to be clear on where to send back any remuneration if that were required, which very often it was.

Early on a Saturday afternoon in May, the first of the envelopes slid through the rectangular brass-plated mail slot in one of a pair of heavy carved wooden doors whose provenance was believed to have been an early California mission. Today they lent drama – in the words of the interior designer who had procured them -- to the entrance of a Spanish-style white stucco and red-tile-roofed home that sat high on a cliff overlooking the Pacific Ocean in Malibu. It was one of a handful of similar homes designed in the 1950s by the late architect Archibald Hancock, who built first a home for himself and his third wife, Jada, and then homes for his five sons. All of the sons were older than Jada but willing to forgive their father his philandering proclivities and his betrayal of their mother and her successor for the privilege of having their own families ensconced in a high-toned neighborhood that, while easily accessible by way of streets that ran behind it, seemed to motorists speeding down the Pacific Coast Highway and swimmers on the beach beyond as if it were clinging to the hillside by dint of sheer willpower. Now Archibald was dead of old age, two of his sons gone, too -- the oldest one of cancer and the middle one in a motorcycle accident -- so that only three still owned the houses their father had created for them. It was to the address of the house formerly occupied by the ill-fated motorcyclist and his girlfriend that one of the envelopes had been addressed.

At the same moment the female letter carrier inserted the stack of mail containing the envelope into the slot, a small, thin Ecuadoran woman named Guadalupe, in gray sweatpants and a purple Lakers T-shirt, was pushing a dust mop over the parquet floor of the spacious foyer on the other side of the door. Earlier she had oiled the sculpted cherry arms of the identical twin antique settees situated invitingly on opposite sides of the area, although no one ever actually sat down on them. Then she plumped their red-and-gold-striped satin pillows. After that she polished the marble surface of a table in the center of the room and arranged an oversized bouquet of stargazer lilies in its middle since her employers were having an anniversary party that evening.

They had been married seven years. It wasn't a significant number, like five or fifteen or twenty-five, but they liked entertaining, and to further justify their self-indulgence, they told each other that, despite everything, they had a lot to celebrate, and it wasn't just about entertaining business associates and seeing what A-list Hollywood names they could attract. It was about their marriage. Really, it was.

The thick pile of mail, which had barely fit through the slot in one batch, landed with a soft "plop" on the floor, and then the individual pieces scattered across the glossy wood tiles. One caught in the fringe of the gray silk rug from China on which the marble-topped table was situated; another slid under a loveseat and came to a stop against the wall. Lupe propped the dust mop against the table and stooped over to pick up the letters and pat them back into an organized stack, larger pieces on the bottom, small ones on top. She inserted the legal-size envelope with the *PHM* monogram in its corner, unnoticed, into the middle of the pile where its size dictated it belonged and laid the letters on the table under the cascade of flowers.

Hours later, when Lupe had put away her cleaning supplies and changed into black pants and a white shirt so that she could help the caterer pass hors d'oeuvres, a tall blond woman in flowing turquoise silk pants and a sheer flowered blouse over a green satin camisole was making a last-minute inspection of the house to make sure everything was in order before her guests arrived. Her pink pedicured toes peeked out of silver high-heeled sandals and silver bangles jangled on her wrist. She frowned in annoyance when she saw where the mail had been placed. Lupe knew better. This might be where they expected to find the mail on a daily basis but not when they were entertaining. It should not be lined up with precision next to the flowers -- the first thing the guests would see when they arrived for the party -- as if she and Lawrence had given it thought and planned it that way, as if an insignificant pile of mail were part of their very thoughtfully arranged decor.

She picked up the pile and shuffled through it as she climbed the wide tiled staircase that led from the foyer to the second floor, her clacking silver heels now silenced by a thick white carpet runner. There were the usual bills she would put into the brown envelope that would go to their accountant, the junk mail that she'd leave on the upstairs hallway table for Lupe to recycle, and a couple of tasteful white envelopes addressed in calligraphy that she correctly guessed to be invitations. One was addressed just to her -- a baby shower at the Santa Monica Beach Club -- and the other was to them both, a retirement dinner for one of Lawrence's colleagues at the studio to be held at a co-worker's home in Beverly Hills. When she reached the top of the stairs, she turned into her bedroom and dropped those onto the white French provincial desk that sat next to the door, across the room from her lacy white bed, to be dealt with later. But one letter, addressed only to Lawrence and coming from a law firm, looked like it might be important. She walked through the marble-tiled bathroom that connected her more feminine boudoir to the darker, more disheveled room where Lawrence slept. Here she wound her way through the jumble of keyboards, computers, and shelves of sheet music and CDs that spilled over from the study adjoining it through yet another door. She considered opening the envelope but then realized she didn't really care who it was from or what it contained. Because of his work, Lawrence often got letters from lawyers, and it probably had nothing at all to do with her. Still, they didn't usually come to the house. She studied it again before she placed it upright on his computer keyboard to make sure he'd see it later, when the guests had gone, when the kitchen and dining room had been at least partially put back to order, when they had looked in on Dexter, given each other a chaste kiss on the cheek, and gone to their separate rooms to turn in.

Three days later, on the outskirts of Bedford, Indiana, a rural letter carrier, sitting in the middle of the front seat of his pickup so that he could both drive the truck and reach the mailboxes along the side of the road, pulled to a stop before a rusty wrought-iron post onto which was anchored a regulation rural mailbox. Its flag had been propped up to signify there was outgoing mail inside, and now he withdrew the three window envelopes, all of which appeared to be bills, and thrust them into a white postal service bin on the floorboard in front of the passenger seat. Then he reached into an identical bin on the seat next to him for a stack of catalogs and a sheaf of letters contained by a rubber band.

Not long after he had closed the mailbox and driven off, producing a cloud of dust when he left the dirt shoulder to once again gain footing on the pavement, a yellow school bus groaned to a stop at the gravel driveway next to the same mailbox. Its red lights were flashing, and its stop sign extended automatically when the driver opened the door to halt the scant bit of traffic behind it -- a panel truck from the electric company and a maroon Toyota sedan badly in need of a wash. Eleven-year-old Stephanie Chambers stepped off, clutching the heavy backpack she'd been holding on her lap during the ride home. It was still clearly navy blue, but it had seen better days. One zippered pocket was ripped off so far that it was useless, and a cup of hot chocolate spilled at a friend's house back in the winter had left a dark stain on the pack's front. She'd get a new one in August, when the back-to-school sales started, but for now this one had to do. How many times had she heard her parents say that money was tight, so there would be no point in asking for a new one this late in the year. Her straight brown hair was shoulder length and held back by a light blue ribbon that matched the sweater she'd worn that morning and that now threatened to tumble out of the unzipped top of the backpack. The tail of her white cotton shirt, so crisp and neat when she'd left the house, was only partially tucked into her fashionably threadbare jeans.

School would be out in just a few more weeks, and she wouldn't have to think about backpacks or schoolbooks for three months. There would only be lazy days of sleeping late and swimming in the pond and helping Dad around the farm and getting her calf ready to display at the county fair. And there'd be no more going to Shawswick Elementary School ever again. In the fall she'd go to the Stoneridge Middle School. She'd be let off first in the mornings and picked up last in the afternoons, finally one of what the Shawswick students called "the big kids." All of this was going through her mind as she turned back to wave at Michelle, the friend with whom she had been sitting, and then she reached toward the mailbox as the bus lurched into gear and lumbered away.

She loved the mail. When you lived in the country, it was a lifeline, especially in the summertime, when all of the other kids went to movies and the mall. The kids in the country just saw each other and helped out in the garden and watched television unless someone's mom was going into town and would be willing to give them a ride. Now she yanked open the dusty metal door and sifted through the contents: bills, seed catalogs, a newsletter from the Farm Bureau, a letter for her mom from some law firm in California and yes, there it was, pay dirt -- a lilac-scented envelope with pictures of the purple flowers spilling faintly behind the address, written in Carolyn's big, bold backhand. Six months ago she had answered a letter printed in the pen-pal section of the children's page in one of her dad's farming magazines. The girl was her age and lived in Beaver Dam, Wisconsin. Her hobbies were ice-skating, riding horses (she had her own, named Clipper) and watching movies. Her favorite foods were spaghetti and hot dogs with mustard but no relish. To Stephanie, she had seemed like a soul mate.

The very night the magazine came she had written a five-page response, hoping that her letter wouldn't be lost in a deluge of other letters from readers in Kansas or Illinois or Nebraska who would also undoubtedly be drawn to write to this magnificent girl. And apparently it hadn't because just a week later an answer came, and the letters had flown back and forth between them ever since. Sometimes they sent e-mails with short messages, like "Guess what! I got picked for our softball team" or "I got a D on a math test today. Major bummer." But they had agreed early on that they would confine their real correspondence to handwritten letters -- letters that would never be discovered in a parent's computer, that could be pored over in private, folded tightly and hidden in the flap of a notebook, and reread until they were memorized, that would contain their most private, innermost thoughts and that would never, ever, under any circumstances be shared with anyone else, even their best friends, even if they're staying over and telling secrets late at night. Stephanie often wrote back to Carolyn in her notebook during advisory period, so her letters were usually on lined paper, but Carolyn's were always scented and flowered -- sunflowers and lilies of the valley and now these lilacs. Once there had been strawberries.

When a letter came, Stephanie would do her chores and then her homework, and then she'd take it somewhere special -- maybe up into the sugar maple tree out in the pasture, maybe out to the rusted glider that had permanently been relegated to the junk heap behind the chicken coop. In the house where they lived before she would have closed her door and curled up on her bed with the sacred missive, but now that they'd moved, she had to share a room with her little sister, who might walk in at any moment and spoil her privacy. Danielle had just this year gotten good enough at reading cursive to make out what the letters said, and she loved to snatch them out of Stephanie's hand and run through the house reading sentences at random and shrieking in delight. By the time their mother intervened and got the letters back for her, the richness and magic of the experience would have been spoiled. Better to wait until just the right moment than to have it all ruined.

Her mother had a rule: "Housework, homework, fun!" she'd sing out when Stephanie would ask if she could watch television right after school or get off the bus at Michelle's house to hang out until dinner. The rule worked with both her and nine-year-old Danielle. They would dash through their work, emptying the wastebaskets into the trash bin, picking up their rooms, setting the table for supper and, for Stephanie, feeding her calf so that they could get on to their lessons and finally fun -- if it wasn't already bedtime. That way if they wasted their time, what they missed out on was fun, and there was no greater fun than reading a letter from Carolyn.

She ran down the lane, past her dad's dust-caked black pickup, around the house and through the flimsy screen door that banged shut behind her as she entered the kitchen. Her father, wearing overalls and a sweaty white T-shirt, was standing at the sink and gulping water from a tumbler, sweat darkening and matting down the wavy blond hair that peeked out from under a St. Louis Cardinals baseball cap.

"Hey, pumpkin," he said, wiping his mouth with the back of his hand when she came through the door. "How was school?"

"Good," she answered. She dropped the tattered backpack onto the floor next to the refrigerator and pulled open the door to retrieve a dish of butterscotch pudding left over from supper the night before. "I got an A on the language test, and Roger Morrison threw up at recess. His mom had to come and pick him up. Why are you home so early? Where's Mom?"

"She's working on the books at the store, and with Danielle home sick, somebody had to be here. I had some fences that needed repairing anyway, so I took the afternoon off. Anything good in the mail?"

"I got a letter from Carolyn."

"Who?"

"My pen pal, Daddy," she said in exasperation. How could he possibly not remember? "You know, from the *Country Farmer* magazine."

"Mmmm." He was looking out through the window over the sink at a sagging gate that also needed his attention. Every day it was something else that cost money. "Anything else?"

Stephanie shrugged.

"Some catalogs, some bills, a letter for Mom from California."

"Grandma's off on her trip, so it must be from her brother."

"I don't think so. It's from lawyers, and it looks official."

He took the letter from her, read the return address, and then turned it over, as if he expected the back flap to contain more information.

"Huh," he said. "You're right. It looks important. Leave it there on the counter next to the sink. She'll be home soon, and she'll see it when she comes in here to start supper."

CHAPTER TWO

"Our mother is certifiably crazy," Larry Langley said, smacking the pages in front of him with his knuckles and frowning in annoyance at exactly the same moment his sister laughed, shook her head affectionately and said, "Our mother is wonderful." Their comments were directed to Dennis MacDonald, but after their simultaneous outbursts, they snapped their heads toward one another, Gina Chambers's eyebrows shooting up disapprovingly at her brother's remark, and Larry scowling as if to let her know he thought she must be insane, too.

They were seated side by side, their legs crossed away from one another, in plush chrome office chairs covered with the red, blue, and green plaid of the MacDonald tartan across the desk from Dennis at the law firm of Peterson, Horowitz and MacDonald in Los Angeles. Dennis's back was to a window overlooking a smoggy downtown, and it would have been hard to see his face, backlit as it was by the late afternoon sun reflecting off the orange haze, except that, knowing this, he had installed wooden Venetian blinds that were now tilted against the glare behind him. At this moment he was leaning in toward them, his hands making a steeple like the church in the children's rhyme, waiting for them to read through the identical copies of a single-spaced two-page document he had just handed to each of them. The decor in his small office also included a blue-and-white striped sofa in the navy from the plaid on the chairs, a crowded bookshelf with paperbacks and file folders crammed into the spaces on top of the law books, and a red Turkish carpet with hints of gold and the same blue in the pattern. A massive mahogany desk that was stacked with books and papers hid the beginnings of a paunch, although he was still reasonably fit and with only the inkling of a bald spot starting to encroach on what had been a thick mane of sandy hair. A pair of rectangular tortoiseshell reading glasses sat near the end of his nose, and now he peered first at one of them and then the other inquisitively over the rims.

When he had first talked to them about their mother's plans, Gina had wondered just how close his relationship to her was. He seemed to know a lot more about her -- and them -- than would have been necessary for a simple legal transaction. Why should he know when Anita Langley's birthday was and that her favorite color combination was terra cotta with deep turquoise blue, and yet these facts had made their way naturally into the conversation. Gina also guessed that Anita had had a hand in decorating the office even before Dennis pointed it out.

Larry, who finished reading first, plucked idly at the crease in his khaki pants and made a circle in the air with the toe of his Italian loafer while he waited for Gina to finish reading. He wore no socks and a black T-shirt under an olive jacket -- the uniform of a young studio executive, although Gina did not yet realize this. She just thought he looked like he'd foolishly spent way too much money on his clothes and his haircut.

Larry looked more like their mother than she did. His spiky dark brown hair, now rendered almost black with the gel that maintained its calculated rumple, was much darker than Anita's strawberry blonde, but the bone structure and wide-set liquid brown eyes were unmistakably his mother's. When the two of them were together and someone commented on this fact, they always responded with the same joke: "You're telling me I look like a man?" Anita would say, and Larry would follow up with, "Hey, do you think I look like a girl?"

He did not resemble Gina in any way, and no one would have guessed they were even related. He was as tall and lanky as Gina was petite, her build the only clue that she was her mother's daughter, and now she was also plump. At six two, he had been the star center of his high school basketball team, and his dad's dream had been that he would play in college. But the scholarships had gone to players who were six seven and six eight, and the polite form letter from San Diego State only gave him an excuse, a way to break it to his dad that what he really wanted to do was play music. He'd lived at home and gone half-heartedly to community college classes, but then he'd dropped out after the second year, much to Anita's and Jay's disappointment, and moved to Los Angeles.

"Do you know how many wannabe garage bands there are in LA?" his father had said, his voice rising with every word, the night Larry announced his plans over dinner. They were sitting out on the patio in the twilight, eating chicken that Jay had barbecued on the grill. "Have you not seen the specials on the news about homeless teenagers who move to L.A., every single one of them thinking they're a star? Do you want to wait tables or park cars for the rest of your life? My God, it's a cliché. My son is choosing to be a cliché." His mother had stared down at her plate, bit her lip, and said quietly, "Oh, honey, no." Larry didn't know then or ever which of them she was talking to.

"I just want to try it for a couple of years. Maybe not even that long. I just want to see what I can do. I'd hate it if I got to be an old man and worked in an office somewhere and hadn't ever tried."

He saw his father's face darken. "I'm not talking about you, Dad. You're doing what you want to do, what you're good at, and that's what I want for myself. I just want to see if this is for me." Then, trying to lighten the moment, he said to his mother, "Hey, Mom, it's your fault. You're the one who dragged me to piano lessons and made me practice." And then, when nobody laughed or spoke, "Wouldn't you rather I do this now, while I'm single? Someday I'll probably get married and have kids, and then if I haven't been able to make it, I'll get a real job. I'll work in an insurance office or become a CPA."

"Not without a college education you won't," Jay thundered.

"Then I'll go back to school. College will always be there, Dad. You don't have to be any certain age to get a degree. You're always reading in the paper about people in their seventies who get their bachelor's, but you don't hear about people in their seventies who get their first recording contracts."

"Where will you live?" Anita asked, and with her use of the future tense rather than the conditional he knew the tide had begun to turn, that if he could persuade her that this was a good idea, she would help him convince his father. He was twenty years old, and he didn't need his parents' permission, but still he worried about letting them down, and had come to this table without an appetite, knowing what lay ahead of them.

"I met a guy, Billy, when we played at the battle of the bands at the Del Mar fairgrounds a couple of weeks ago. The keyboardist in his band got sick and didn't show. Billy plays bass guitar." He added this parenthetically, enthusiastically, as if somehow knowing a bass guitarist would make a difference to Anita and Jay and sway them immediately to his point of view. "I sat in with them for a couple of sets, and they liked what I did. A couple of weeks after that their guy quit the band altogether, so now they want me to play with them full time. Billy says I can stay at his place until we see how it goes."

"What about the band here?" Jay asked, his tone freighted with judgment. "Aren't you letting down the guys you've been playing with all through high school?" Maybe calling on his sense of loyalty to the band would bring Larry around, even if the boy couldn't see the train wreck ahead in his own future.

Larry shook his head.

"They know what this means, Dad. That's the way things work in the music business. It's the break we all hope for. If one of them had gone, I would have understood, and they do, too. They're cool with it."

Anita shot Jay an amused glance, her lips pressed together to stifle a laugh at Larry's casual use of the phrase "music business." Playing in each other's garages and for the occasional party or competition hardly qualified as "business." When they did get paid, which was seldom, the fee barely covered the costs of getting to the venue. But she would support his decision. How could she not? He was right: she had set all of this in motion when she had bought a used upright piano and found a teacher in the yellow pages. And how could she, of all people, squelch someone's dream of making a living in the arts, using their natural talent to do the thing they loved most? Jay would be the practical one. He would fight this one to the end, willing Larry to get a law degree from Berkeley or an MBA from Wharton. She wouldn't argue with Jay in front of Larry, but she would give her blessing -- silently or otherwise -- to this wish of her son's to see where this path could take him. He was right about something else, too. There would always be time in the future to do something different if this one didn't lead where he wanted to go.

The chain of events that followed hadn't been exactly what Larry thought would happen, but in the long run it all turned out better than he could have hoped, especially now that he did have a wife and a child. The band had never become famous, but they made a living playing at dances and parties, and one of those parties had been at the home of an executive at Morrison Pictures, itself a new, young indie filmmaking company. One of the executives was only thirty-five, and he liked the music. When the band took a break and he came over to the table where they were eating barbecued chicken and drinking Cokes to compliment them, he and Larry had started talking about soundtracks, Larry's favorite part of going to the movies. He could name all the songs and who sang them or the classical pieces and who composed them, and he always stayed through all of the credits to see if he'd been right. More often than not he had ideas about how it could have been better, noting that Chopin's "Prelude in E Minor" might have fit better behind the scene where the woman leaves the man, turning to walk away into the rainy night, than Elton John's "Your Song," which was exactly what he said to the executive that day about the studio's most recent release.

The executive said they had an opening for an assistant to their music supervisor and would he be interested in applying. Larry wasn't sure exactly what a music supervisor did, but after the interview he knew it was the right job for him and that he'd get it, and he did. In the beginning he only researched the pieces of music that Harvey Okerblom might eventually use. He'd read the script, sometimes hang around the set, and when the session was over, watch the dailies. Then he'd listen to hundreds of songs and pull the CDs or the sheet music, sometimes staying up all night to find just the right piece, or he'd make notes and hum a few bars until Harvey recognized what he was talking about. It didn't even feel like work, and it amazed him that he was actually paid for doing it. He always gave Harvey several choices, but more and more often Larry's first recommendations were the one they stayed with and that directors agreed to use, often using the words "brilliant" and "genius" when they read the list he had provided. On a few occasions he actually wrote bits of background music when what he heard in his head didn't match what was already available.

His job also involved filing sheet music, alphabetizing CDs and making the obligatory phone calls to legal offices to obtain the rights to use the songs. This part wasn't so interesting, but he just chalked it up as part of the deal. What mattered was that his days were filled with music, and when Harvey left to go to a bigger studio, there had been no question that Larry would move up to the top spot. By then Morrison Pictures had grown, too, and his income had increased so dramatically that when offers came from Warner Brothers and Dreamworks, he could afford to turn them down. A soundtrack he had created had landed an Academy Award nomination a couple of years ago, but he had yet to actually win the big prize. He still sat in occasionally with the band, still played late at night on the electronic keyboard he kept in his bedroom, using the earphones so he didn't wake Dexter or disturb Marqueeta, while the shiny black Yamaha grand sat silent in the living room downstairs. Marqueeta found his playing to be loud and distracting and said it caused her to have migraines, but the decorator had sold her on the idea that the piano was a "design element." Lupe was the only person who ever touched it and then only to dust.

After a string of apartments followed Billy's in Hollywood, Larry had bought a condo in Santa Monica, where he could work at home and bring dates back without having to coordinate with a roommate. Eventually he met Marqueeta, who had been the public relations representative for one of the actors in a movie he was working on, at a wrap party, and not long after that, she moved in. After they were married and Dexter arrived two years later, they started a search for a bigger place that ended the day they found the house in the Malibu Hills.

Sitting next to her brother now, Gina wore a black dress with a matching jacket that had white piping around the edges. It was too warm and out of season, really, for June in California, but it was the only thing she had that seemed appropriate for meeting with her mother's lawyer. She also wore pantyhose and black patent leather pumps, which now felt matronly and out of place in the casual atmosphere that permeated this city. She looked like she was going to a funeral, or at least to church, when what she wanted was to look like the women she'd seen at the hotel and in the lobby of this building -- thin, wearing filmy, brightly colored shirts layered over plain white T-shirts or shimmering tank tops that peeked out just where the cleavage was about to begin, rendering them appropriate for work but still the tiniest bit sexy. Little purses hung on long straps all the way down to their thighs and their backless high heels slapped against the soles of their pampered bare feet. But how was she to know? The only person who might have told her differently was her sister-in-law, and that wasn't likely to happen. She hadn't even seen Marqueeta in the seven years since Larry's wedding. They exchanged occasional e-mails, mostly about what the children would like for their birthdays, and there were the obligatory Christmas gifts -- gourmet fruit baskets with festive bows tied around them and wine cradled in satin-lined boxes from Larry and Marqueeta, and, for a while, fudge from a Lawrence County candy maker that she shipped to them in a holiday box with a snow-covered Christmas tree and the words "Back home again in Indiana" on the lid. The gifts, until they stopped on her side, had been sufficient to keep up the illusion that they weren't actually estranged but not enough to indicate that they actually knew each other. Even in the best of times there had never been books by favorite authors or ties and scarves in colors to match a particular jacket or gag gifts meant to recall the memory of a good time together.

She uncrossed her legs and then crossed them again, this time pointing in Larry's direction, but his long legs were still angled away from her, and he was surreptitiously checking messages on his cell phone. She still clutched the purse that matched her shoes and then, realizing that she was broadcasting her nervousness and wanting to match Larry's relaxed poise, she dropped it to the floor next to her chair, where it landed with a too-loud thud. A tube of lipstick fell out and rolled under Dennis's desk.

"Sorry," she said with a grimace, leaning over to retrieve it and stashing it back into the bag. Larry was struck again at how much she looked like the man in the picture he had seen once in Anita's studio, his blond hair hanging to his shoulders, his eyes partially closed, that same apologetic smile -- as if he knew when the picture was taken that he would disappoint the woman who would save it -- and printed across the bottom of this black-and-white glossy publicity shot the name Davey Calhoun. He had been a musician, too, the lead guitarist in a band called Trieste. The photograph was on top of a thin stack of yellowed and crumbling newspaper and magazine reviews that raved about his talent, but his story had been tragic. The headline on the final clipping, dated March 22, 1974, was Rock Musician Dead in Drug Overdose. He had already left Anita and their baby girl, and she had already married Jay. He had left his band, too, in a ridiculous argument, also documented in the clippings, over which hotel to stay in the one time they had played in London, and they had gone on to respectable record-ing success while he played clubs and then sank into obscurity. Shopping mall nostalgia tours and wedding receptions might have been in his future except that he didn't have a future. Anita's name didn't appear in the article, and there was no mention of his leav-ing behind a little girl.

"I've known your mother for several years," Dennis said now in the Scottish accent that caught Gina by surprise every time he spoke, "and I would say you're both right. She is a little crazy, but in the most wonderful way. You've got to admit that what she has done here is certainly creative."

What he didn't tell them was that he loved their mother. He had taken her to dinner not long after he became her attorney, and when their relationship became more than professional, he handed her contracts off to another partner so that he could spend more time with her without any question of impropriety. Eventually he asked her to marry him, but just when he thought the time was right and was positive she would say yes, she had said no.

"Oh, Denny," she had said when the conversation went in that direction over a late drink one night. It had been a summer evening, and they were sitting outside the restaurant on a deck overlooking the water in Puerto Vallarta, where she had come with him for a weekend seminar on estate planning. She had looked especially lovely that night, he remembered, her coral satin dress cut low enough to reveal a hint of the breasts he loved to fondle, tendrils falling gently against her cheeks from the knot into which she had twisted her hair, her ears glittering with the diamond earrings he had given to her for her birthday. For some reason he remembered that the palm trees that leaned out over the water had been wrapped in tiny white lights, and even now when he saw trees decorated like that for the holidays, he felt a stab of regret. He had known the moment he heard the sad, sorry tone in her voice that the answer was no and that now he had lost what part of her he did have. From here on out their relationship would revert back to the lawyer-client formality where they had started, back to before the Sunday mornings of crossword puzzles and coffee in bed, the walks along the beach in La Jolla, where Anita had moved after Jay died and she began to make real money, the plays and movies and art galleries, and one vacation to Hawaii that her children assumed she had taken with a girlfriend.

"You know, I've been everything you can be on a legal document," she had said that night, laughing a little nervously, wrapping her fingers around his clenched hands in the middle of the table in an effort to lighten the mood. "I've been single, married, separated, divorced, and now widowed. I think I'm ready to just be me."

"I'd never get in the way of your independence," he'd said, probably too desperately, hoping this reassurance would change her mind. "I know how important your work is to you. I'd never interfere with that. And besides, I'm busy, too. It's not like I'd be lurking about underfoot and expecting to be entertained."

Anita's rise to the fame and money she enjoyed now was as unlikely as her son's. When she had met and married Davey Calhoun, she had been an art student at San Diego State. Despite being married and pregnant -- the timing so close that even she couldn't be quite sure which came first -- she finished college, but the bohemian career in oil painting that she had imagined couldn't support an aspiring musician and a baby girl, and she had gone to work for an interior design firm. She'd never regretted that detour, she was quick to tell anyone who heard her story and clucked sympathetically. It had taught her about a whole new area of beauty that she hadn't even considered before. She had learned, she would tell them passionately, that a house, a room, even just a slice of a room, could bring joy to the people who lived there, that a plant placed on just the right table and that table placed on just the right rug -- from Iran or New Mexico, depending on the rest of the decor -- under just the right mirror that reflected just the right bookshelves, their volumes carefully arranged to appear as if they had been tossed there by afterthought, a candlestick and a bowl of fruit on top, a statue of a seated Buddha to keep books from falling over -- that was art, too, dynamic art that people lived with every day and changed with the seasons and photographed to send to their relatives and came home to. One of her clients had confided to her that she had decided against asking for a divorce because it would have meant leaving the uniquely beautiful home Anita had helped her put together. Anita didn't know if that was good or bad for the woman -- she had never met the husband -- but she was secretly pleased because it spoke well of her ability to do her job.

The rest had come later, after Larry and Gina had left home and she had time to get out her paints, often on Sunday afternoons while Jay watched sports on television or played golf with his friends. She started with landscapes but quickly realized that it was rooms she had come to love -- rooms, with their carpets and fireplaces and statuary, their tables and cushions and photographs. She also changed her medium to watercolor. The canvases she needed for oils were big and bulky and expensive, and she was just doing this for fun and giving her pieces away as gifts, so there was no chance of recovering her costs. These smaller pictures allowed her to narrow the focus and concentrate on one area at a time -- a comfortable-looking easy chair covered in paisley under a yellow puddle of light spilling from a red satin lampshade, a book lying open on a plump blue cushion, a cup of tea on the polished wood table beside it. Or the corner of an elegant French chair, covered in olive green satin brocade, sitting on the corner of an Asian rug while beyond an open door beckoned to a plant-studded patio where a table was set for lunch, a low, informal arrangement of red carnations and white daisies at its center. For their annual Christmas card she added festively decorated trees, cats curled up on rugs, rich-looking copper-colored balls spilling across a mantelpiece that had been draped in teal velvet and studded with pine boughs.

When a friend who knew a gallery owner had suggested that she display some of her pictures in a holiday show, she had at first been reluctant, laughing and calling herself an amateur, but then her pieces had sold out. She had only taken twelve, and after the first day of the three-day show, the owner had asked for more. When the holidays were over, he had offered to represent Anita's work on a permanent basis. The real upturn in her fortunes happened when she joined forces with a company that sold prints in art shops all over the country, and her "Hints of Home" prints -- which sold for low prices like $29.95, but there were thousands of them -- became books, greeting cards, place-mats, and coffee mugs, and finally wallpapers and fabric de-signs. By then Jay had died, and she had filled the long, lonely evenings and weekends with work that began to pay off as soon as she turned it in. And now an English publisher was funding her travel for the next year to paint vignettes of houses -- homely fishermen's cottages in Northern Ireland, adobe haciendas in New Mexico, royal palaces in Thailand. To play on her trade-mark, the book would be titled "Hints of Home from around the World."

"It is important to your mother that the two of you remain close," Dennis said now. "Or, maybe better put, to get back to the relationship she feels you once had but that has been lost. She re-alizes, of course, that you have different lifestyles and live far away from each other in different parts of the country and never see each other."

"Isn't that pretty typical?" Larry interrupted. "Isn't it normal to grow apart as you grow up? I don't know very many people who are tight with their siblings. I think Mom's old-fashioned ideas come from a time when people stayed where they grew up and saw all the relatives every Sunday for dinner, like she did. No offense, Gina, but I think we're doing fine. You've got your life and your friends in Indiana, and I've got mine here. You know I'd be there for you if you ever needed me."

Gina shot him a "You're kidding, right?" look, and he said, "Well, I would be now. That was before ... that was when ..."

"I don't think this is the time or place to talk about that," Gina said. "It's ancient history now, and the damage is done, but you can see why I can't take you very seriously when you say you'd be there for me. That's just too rich."

Dennis looked quizzically, uncomfortably from Larry to Gina and back, and when no one seemed willing to explain what they were talking about, he went on.

"As you know, your mother is an only child. She had a lonely childhood, and she says she was even lonelier as an adult when she had to move her mother, against her wishes, out of the house she had shared with your grandfather before he died and into an assisted-living facility. As I understand it, she also had to make the decision by herself to stop the medications when her mother was in a coma and then immediately turn around and make all of the funeral plans without anybody's help. She tells me she wants to make certain neither of you ever has to face anything like that."

"That's what I'm saying," Larry said. "Gina and I would always help each other in situations like that, but to jump through all these hoops just to try and make us buddies is ridiculous."

"Your mother wants to begin sharing her money with you now," Dennis went on, as if Larry hadn't spoken. "Gina, she knows that you and your husband have had some money problems, and now that she is in a good financial position, she wants to help you, but she also wants to be fair and share her wealth equally, even though she realizes, of course, Larry, that you don't need her help. As part of the arrangement, she has created these nine assignments for the two of you to do together. She selected nine because the Chinese believe nine is the most perfect number."

"Ah, yes, we're in our Chinese period these days, aren't we?" Larry said, his voice laced with scorn.

Anita had raised her children as Catholics, had even given them the names of saints, as the church required, but once they had grown up she had become disenchanted with the church's attitudes toward birth control and abortion and then angry when the stories about the abuse of children had begun to leak out. During a trip to Bali she had discovered Hinduism, and after that she had lit incense to various gods each evening and started the next morning by placing a plate filled with flower petals on the front porch so that evil spirits wouldn't come through the door and disturb her work. She had brought back multicolored batik pillows and scattered them like confetti onto sofas and chairs and beds throughout the house.

"Yes, I do realize I'm not really a Hindu," she had responded when Larry had questioned her zeal during a trip to San Diego for a weekend when he saw the new trappings for the first time. "But they have such a better outlook on things than we do. They believe so strongly in karma that they never harm anyone or steal anything for fear of being reincarnated as something they don't want to be. How can you not like that?" This time it was she who had had annoyance in her voice. How could someone who worked in music, who lifted a film from an ordinary story to a soul-stirring experience, possess such a singular lack of imagination and sense of adventure?

A trip to Istanbul had yielded the blue and white tiles she had mounted and framed for the wall in her dining room, each one of them representing a bird or a flower since the Islamic faith forbade the artistic rendering of deities. After that trip she began what passed for her prayers with "Bisma'allah." Most recently she had been to Hong Kong by request of a wealthy industrialist to paint pictures of the rooms in his house on Victoria Peak, and after that trip a jade dragon had appeared on her coffee table and she had started doing tai chi each morning before she began her work. She also quoted Lao Tsu whenever it served to make her point in a conversation.

"This could get expensive," Gina said when she looked up from the pages Dennis had provided. "I flat don't have the money to do all this. You just said that Mom knows Steve and I are having money problems. We lost our farm, for God's sake." She paused and purposely did not look at her brother. "I can't be coming out here to spend time with Larry and Marqueeta," she flipped angrily at the page with an index finger as her brother had earlier, "or flying off to some foreign city or spending a week at Mom's cabin. It all sounds great, but it costs money."

"Your mother will cover all the costs, just like she did for your trip out here," Dennis said. "That won't be a problem."

"Well, she bought me a plane ticket," Gina said, correcting him. "I don't mean to seem ungrateful for that, but she's not paying for my hotel in Santa Monica at $300 a night or my meals or the cab I had to take to get here or the cab I took from the airport and the one I'll take back to the airport when I leave tomorrow morning."

"I believe," Dennis said, looking uncomfortable, stopping and then starting again, "I believe your mother thought, that is, assumed, you'd be staying with Larry. It didn't occur to her that a hotel or meals or cabs would be necessary."

Now it was Larry's turn to look uncomfortable.

"I'm sorry, Gina," he said, "but when I got the letter, I didn't know what this was all about any more than you did. I've been busy at work, and I really didn't think about where you'd be staying while you were here. Marqueeta should have called you, and we could have made some plans."

"I'm not Marqueeta's sister, am I?" she asked pointedly.

"And anyway," Dennis went on quickly, "not all of the items on the list cost money. Look at number nine: Make a scrapbook of your adventures together. Or number eight: List ten things you like about your sibling. Those things cost almost nothing."

"Jesus, what are we, twelve?" Larry said, again clearly irritated. "This is the kind of crap you do at summer camp -- or marriage counseling." This last he said quietly, as an afterthought that he didn't intend for anyone else to hear.

"Is something wrong with Mom?" Gina asked Dennis suddenly. His comments about her mother having to care for her parents had just soaked in. "Has she found out she's sick? Because it just occurred to me that all of this interest in having us do things together because she doesn't want us to be alone when she's gone might be because she knows something." Having thought about this now, she scooted closer to the edge of her chair and turned to face her brother, her voice rising, almost in a panic. "Do you know something, Larry?"

"You can relax on that score," Dennis reassured her, chuckling. "Nothing is wrong with your mother. In fact, she told me she's had more fun putting these plans together than just about anything else she's ever done, and she thinks you're going to have fun with them, too. She's counting on it. Your mom loves her work, and she loved Jay, but more than anything else she loves the two of you, and this is really important to her."

"Then why didn't she just talk to us about it directly?" Larry asked. "Why all the cloak and dagger, lawyers and documents and Gina having to fly out here for this meeting? If she loves us so much, which, of course, I do realize she does, why doesn't she do all of this stuff with us? Wouldn't that be more 'fun,' if that's one of the points of this exercise?"

"She did actually consider that," Dennis said, "but she thinks having her with you would muddy the waters, so to speak. She wants you to interact with one another, just for these short periods of time, on your own, without her there to run interference. When it's all over, she says all of you will get together and celebrate. And the reason for my involvement is that she knew you would resist, and she didn't want you to have that option."

"Can we talk to her about all of this?" Gina asked.

"Of course. She's traveling with a laptop, as you know, and she's expecting e-mails from you after this meeting. I think she'll get a kick out of hearing about your progress."

"Do we have to do the assignments in order?" Gina asked. "I mean, is there a reason we're supposed to go to a foreign city before we work in her studio?"

"Only the first one," Dennis replied. "She knows you're both busy, and she wants you to make whatever plans your schedules allow. But she definitely wants you to make the foreign trip first."

"And how long do we have to get all our little projects completed?" Larry asked in the condescending tone that said he still thought the whole thing was ridiculous.

"She'd like for you to be finished by the time she gets back from this trip." He consulted a calendar on his desk. "She's been gone since January, and she plans to be back to have Christmas with you. That means you still have six or seven months to accomplish everything she wants you to do. I don't really think you'll have any trouble doing that. You'll notice that not every item involves travel, and some of them you'll be able to do in an afternoon -- like making the list of things you like about your sibling and exchanging them. How long could that take?"

Gina's derisive snort didn't escape either of the men, even though she covered her mouth as if she had instead coughed and looked down into her lap in an attempt to hide the expression she knew was on her face. At the moment she couldn't think of one good thing to say about her brother, and she didn't know enough about him to begin to come up with nine more.

"And 'Create a scrapbook of these activities.' You'll be doing that as you go along."

"What if we said no?" Larry asked. "What if we just said this is crazy and we're not going to do it? Would she donate her money to charity and be done with us? I find that hard to believe."

"Oh, no. Your mother would never wash her hands of you. She's crazy about both of you. That's the whole point. The only difference would be that you would have to wait until she's dead to realize your inheritances. If you fulfill her assignments, she'll start gifting it to you at the rate of $14,000 per year for each member of your family, which is what the IRS allows without charging big penalties. It's not so much to ask for that much return on your investment."

"So I'd get $42,000 per year and Gina would get $56,000. Is that how it would work?" Larry asked.

"Exactly. Unless, of course, you and your wife decide to have another child."

"I don't think that's going to happen," Larry said, more to himself than to Dennis, "and I don't really need the money now. I'm not interested, nor do I have the time, in jumping through these ridiculous hoops. I'm a very busy person. I'd just as soon have Mom enjoy her money now and pass it down to Dexter at some point in the future."

"Ah, but your sister does need the money," Dennis said, "and that's the major issue. Your mother wants to know what the two of you would be willing to do to help each other."

"I'm not a charity case," Gina said, the anger that flared directed now toward Dennis. "It's true Steve and I don't have the kind of money Larry does, but we get by just fine. And as far as an inheritance, I agree with Larry. I'd rather have Mom stick around and spend it on herself. She's earned it, and I don't need it badly enough to inconvenience … anyone."

Again she avoided looking at her brother, but there was no question about to whom this remark was directed.

"This sounds like the plot of a bad made-for-TV movie," Larry said.

"Or a murder mystery," Gina said bitterly.

"To repeat," Dennis said in frustration, "your mother wants you to help each other. It's not just about you as individuals, and it's not just about the money." He looked at his watch. "It's up to the two of you, but for now you'll have to excuse me. We've run over the time I had allotted, and I've got another client waiting."

Outside his office, they walked down the marble hallway together toward the elevator.

"Look, Gina," Larry started haltingly. "I'm sorry we didn't ask you to stay with us. That was stupid on my part. I just wasn't thinking. I travel all the time for work, and I'm so used to my assistant making my hotel reservations. I just didn't think. It wasn't a slight on purpose."

"It's all right," she said, though it clearly wasn't. "My hotel in Santa Monica is nice, and I can walk right down to the beach from my little patio. That's a real treat for me."

Neither of them mentioned that she could have enjoyed the same amenity at Larry's house.

"And I'm busy at work, and I've got issues at home. You know, Marqueeta's got problems ..."

She was curious about what those problems were, but now didn't feel like the right time to ask. His quickening gait and constant glances at his watch told her he was antsy and eager to get away.

"Really, Larry. I'm good. I would like to have met my nephew while I was here, but if we -- you -- decide to carry out all of these plans, I'll get a chance to."

"Of course we're going to do the idiotic projects," he said, as if there had never been any question. He fumbled in his pocket for his wallet and flipped through its contents.

"I thought I had a new picture of Dex, but I guess I never got around to putting it in here."

The only picture he had was the same one that had come in last year's Christmas card and was now secured under a magnet of the Eiffel Tower -- a gift from friends who went to Paris for their anniversary -- on the front of Gina's refrigerator back home. He put the wallet back into his pocket.

"All right," he said, blowing air out between his lips as if he were exasperated, "I guess we need to start making some plans. When you do you leave?"

"Don't do me any favors, bro."

"No, seriously ..."

"I've got a seven a.m. flight from LAX, so I'll be up and out really early."

He pulled the cell phone out of his pocket and pecked at the numbers.

"Let me just give Marqueeta a call, and maybe we can pick up some dinner together somewhere."

"That would be a start," Gina said and instantly regretted her tone. Larry was at least making an attempt to be civil. "I'd like that," she tacked on feebly.

But Marqueeta reminded him that they already had plans for the evening. They were meeting friends at the beach club for a birthday dinner. In fact, the sitter had just arrived, and she was just about to leave to meet him there. She thought he'd already be on his way. Even standing away from Larry, Gina could hear her sister-in-law's voice growing shrill with anxiety.

"I completely forgot about that. Well, maybe I can at least give Gina a ride to her hotel?"

Gina heard the request for permission in the question mark at the end of his sentence, but on the other end of the line Marqueeta reminded him that he had promised to pick up the gift -- the silver pen set that was being engraved -- that they planned to give to the honoree.

"I feel like a real shit," he said to his sister. "Ordinarily it would be no problem to drop you in Santa Monica on my way home, but I've got to go to this jewelry store and pick up some present, and it's in the other direction, and I'm already going to be late."

"It's no problem, really," she said. She had spotted a line of cabs outside a hotel across the street -- another ride her mother hadn't figured in when she arranged the expenses for this visit -- and was already turning away from him.

"I'll call you about the plans," he said.

"Right," she called back over her shoulder with a wave of the hand that wasn't carrying the handbag.

He had planned to watch her into a cab -- he could at least do that much -- but the light turned red so that she had to wait before she could cross the street. He looked at his watch again. He really was going to be late, and Marqueeta wasn't going to be happy. When his sister turned around to give him a last wave, he was already walking away.

CHAPTER THREE

From the wedding pictures on the coffee table Anita Langley had fashioned from an antique mahogany library table (it would have been bad feng shui to put them on the mantelpiece like most other people did, the belief being that the souls of the people pictured could vanish right up the chimney), no one would guess that not all the figures in them had been quite as happy on the day they were taken as they appeared. In the silver filigreed frame, inscribed "Lawrence and Marqueeta, May 19, 2008," the couple's families are posed with the Golden Gate Bridge in the distance behind them. The wedding was yet to take place in a synagogue in another part of the city that had no such spectacular view of the bridge and would be followed immediately with a formal dinner at the Fairmont Hotel. But the photographer -- the same one who persuaded them to do the pictures in black and white for a hipper and more sophisticated look -- knew of a patio at a different hotel that would give them just the view that would set their wedding photos apart from everyone else's and make them the envy of all their friends. So the very taking of the pictures would have started everyone off on the wrong foot -- if they hadn't already been sharp and testy with one another over a hundred other little annoyances and hurts. Larry, not yet the force at the studio that he would later become, worried about the expense, even though Marqueeta's parents were footing the bill and Marqueeta's mother chirpily, gratingly repeated in a saccharine voice that sounded as if she were talking to an infant that money was not an issue when her baby girl was getting married.

Marqueeta's father grumbled throughout the picture-taking session about the inconvenience, not to mention the utter ludicrousness, the sheer lunacy of hauling all of them through traffic to take pictures that would make it seem as if the wedding had taken place somewhere that it had not. Anita, who hoped that as the mother of the groom she would have some say in the wedding plans, had not. Now she was irritated that in order to catch the sunlight coming through the heavy Romanesque columns at just the particular angle to create the shadows the photographer had in mind they had to take the pictures in mid-afternoon when the candlelight ceremony wouldn't take place until 7:00 that evening. Their formal clothes would be rumpled from the extra ride in the car. The upswept hairdos, stiffened with clouds of hairspray, would be mussed by the wind, coming loose in sticky clumps from the forest of hairpins meant to secure them rather than in natural-looking wisps that might actually have seemed spontaneous and pretty. The mascara would have melted into dark pools beneath the eyes of the bride and the bridesmaids to be mopped up carefully with tissues and cotton balls just before the ceremony, rendering the expense of the makeup professional who had tended to them all earlier in the day for naught. In the pictures, though, their hair is sleek, their eyes darkly lidded, their cheekbones highlighted to make their faces appear thin and glamorous, their lips perfectly outlined and with a pronounced Cupid's bow that would have been smudged or eaten off long before the ceremony began.

Larry's brother-in-law, Steve Chambers, remained silent while the pictures were being taken for the benefit of his wife, the groom's sister, but earlier in their hotel room he had exploded in frustration.

"Jesus fucking Christ," he had yelled, pacing the bedroom in his white boxer shorts, his blond curls still wet from the shower. "Who do these people think they are, Bill fucking Gates? No, wait, if Bill Gates had been stupid enough to pour all this money down a sewer hole just for the sake of what other people might think, he wouldn't be one of the richest men on the planet."

His face was red and his voice louder and an octave higher than usual, but Gina knew that if he got it out of his system here, he would be better company when it was time for the events he was railing against to actually happen.

"A fleet of limousines, for Christ's sake, a *fleet* of limousines. For what? To drag all of our sorry asses from pillar to post, to some hotel where the wedding won't even be, wear us all out, keep the kids up late at a reception that will go into the night and then dump us back out at a hotel we can't afford, where we now find out we have to spend an extra night and pay another $200 so we can go to a brunch the next day to watch a couple of spoiled, self-centered brats open up a bunch of useless, overpriced crap that will tarnish before their first anniversary and wind up in a yard sale somewhere after the inevitable divorce."

He threw himself into an armchair and began furiously pulling on the black socks that had come as part of his rented tuxedo ensemble.

"Shhh, honey," Gina said, nodding her head toward Stephanie, who had just emerged from the bathroom. "I know, I know."

She had enough anxieties of her own over this whole situation, and she'd been feeling like she could throw up ever since breakfast. But if she told him the truth -- that she'd grown apart from her brother, didn't even know him anymore, and would rather be just about anywhere besides this hotel in San Francisco -- she would only fuel Steve's agitation and wind him up even more than he already was. She didn't want to talk about Larry or his fiancée or the wedding or any of it. She just wanted to get through the day and go home.

Danielle, who had just turned two, played with a pink plastic dog and a bright green terrycloth frog in the crib the hotel had provided after three phone calls to the front desk the night they arrived. Stephanie, at four, tugged on the ivory satin slip that stretched across her mother's rounded post-pregnancy hips and whined to be able to put on the dress she would wear later that day for the pictures and then, later still, when she would walk down the aisle in front of the bride, sprinkling rose petals on the white runner as they had practiced at home. Gina had made an aisle of striped and frayed bath towels that started in the kitchen and went through the dining room and down the hallway to the living room so that Stephanie could practice with an Easter basket filled with daisy petals. She wasn't crazy about the woman Larry was marrying, but he was her brother, and he had asked his niece to be the flower girl at his wedding, and if for no other reason, Gina wanted this day to be perfect.

If asked, she would have said she loved her brother, and then that sentence would trail off to the inevitable "but": "But he can be a real pain in the ass," "But he's not the brother I used to know" or "But he's the golden boy who always got by with murder. Just ask my mom how special he is." Secretly -- late at night, after sex, spooning with her bottom curled against Steve and him just awake enough to mumble the occasional "uh-huh" against her hair -- she made outright fun of Larry's fiancée. Most of her jokes centered on Marqueeta's being too thin. Maybe this was a defense of her own weight, which had ballooned after her children were born and hadn't yet been done away with. A pile of Lean Cuisine and Weight Watchers frozen dinners darkened the freezer side of the refrigerator, but still the needle on the scale landed each morning with disheartening dependability on 150.

Because it rhymed, the name she called her soon-to-be sister-in-law -- and which, because she had used it so often, she had come dangerously close to calling her to her face at the groom's dinner the night before -- was Parakeeta, sometimes shortened to "Keeta" or "Para." This last one had come up after a barbecue at some friends' house when she had had a little too much to drink and come home punchy. "Para," she'd giggled as she fell backward onto their bed. "Like half, or almost. You know, like paralegal -- almost a legal, I mean lawyer. I mean almost a person."

Besides her instinctive dislike of the bride -- what she knew of her at all, considering that they had only met once, briefly, when she and Steve had gone back to San Diego for her step-father's funeral -- Gina had other issues with this overpriced circus of a wedding. Larry knew they were having money problems, knew they couldn't afford to fly four people from Indianapolis -- well, three, since by trading off holding Danielle on their laps for four hours they had saved the price of one fare -- and then stay in this overpriced hotel. And that didn't count the tuxedo Steve had had to rent to be an usher and the $200 dress for Stephanie, which Marqueeta and her mother had picked out at a Saks Fifth Avenue store but didn't offer to pay for. On this her feelings were mixed. She wanted Stephanie to be in the wedding, and Stephanie was adorable in the dress -- "a confection," Marqueeta's mother had proclaimed, pointing to the way its pale pink taffeta skirt fell from a belt fashioned of white embroidered rosebuds. But Larry knew even then that the farm was in jeopardy. He knew this would be a setback for them.

"Wasn't there something your mother could have done to stop all this crap?" Steve asked her now.

"No," Gina said softly, "there wasn't. She tried when they started making wedding plans. She told them she thought they were spending too much money and inconveniencing a whole lot of people. She even added up what the cost would be for everyone who had to fly in and stay at this hotel. She offered to have the ceremony in San Diego. She's got that nice patio, and one of her good friends is a caterer. She talked to them about how much they could save if they had 50 people instead of 200, but Keeta and her mother wouldn't have any of it. Mom said she doesn't think they even heard her. All Keeta could think of was how they could release doves at the end of the service and how they could incorporate a hot-air balloon into the day. Fortunately Larry put the kibosh on the balloon, but there will be doves."

"I hope every single one of them poops on their limousine as they fly out of their cage or whatever the hell they're supposed to do."

Stephanie giggled and said to her oblivious sister, "Daddy said 'poop.'"

In the dramatic, envy-producing black-and-whites that resulted from the photo shoot, no one could hear Marqueeta's shrill, almost hysterical voice barking orders at the bridal party and rolling her eyes if they failed to take their places immediately and exactly as the photographer had instructed. No one could hear her murmur, "Undisciplined little brat" when she learned that Stephanie had spilled fruit punch onto the sleeve of the expensive dress -- punch that was only offered because the photographer was late in arriving and Stephanie had been bored and hungry and needed to be distracted. The box of punch and a tiny bag of pretzels left over from the airplane were all Gina could produce from the diaper bag. No one could tell that the bride's father had made a pass at the groom's recently widowed mother.

Larry and Marqueeta, are of course, in the center of the photo, looking delighted to be married, even though they weren't yet and wouldn't be for five more hours. Marqueeta's parents stand next to their only child, her mother radiant in a pearl-gray satin floor-length suit, her tuxedoed father's false proud-looking smile not revealing that he could not wait to get a Scotch in his hand and would, in the bar of this unfamiliar, unrelated hotel, as soon as the pictures were finished. He would, in fact, drink so many scotches throughout the afternoon that by the time of the actual ceremony he would be tipsy (his wife's word, by way of explanation at the reception, by which time she had cast the entire episode as hysterically funny) and would weave and bump into the bride repeatedly as he walked her down the aisle.

On the other side of Larry are first his mother, wearing a full-skirted dress embroidered around the scoop neckline that she had brought home from a trip to Mexico. That it had been bright red had been an issue, too. The bride and her mother thought that since the groom's father had died only nine months before, it would be appropriate for his mother to appear in the black of traditional mourning, and they had seen just the dress for her, also at Saks. But Anita had said no. She had worn black to Jay's funeral -- could, in fact, have pulled that same dress from the back of her closet and made it work again very nicely for today -- but after that she had decided to celebrate life: Jay's, her own, her children's, life in general.

"I've just found out how short life can be," she told her children the morning after the funeral when she appeared at breakfast in a yellow T-shirt, white Capri pants, and sandals bedecked with colored glass cut to look like gems. "I'm not going to waste a minute of it looking like a reminder of death. Jay would hate that, and so would I if I were the one who had died and he had gone around moping."

She had repeated the sentiment to Marqueeta's mother, Sylvia, when she had called to tell her that the same gorgeous black sheath they had found in San Francisco was available in her size at a San Diego Saks and they had put it on hold for her. From the smiles in the photo, no one would ever know that Sylvia had immediately telephoned Marqueeta at her apartment and sobbed about how this beatnik, this, this over-aged hippie was threatening to ruin the entire wedding, that Marqueeta cried so hard that her mother insisted on picking her up and taking her out to lunch at an expensive restaurant on Nob Hill. After sharing a bottle of wine, they had consoled each other that at least the pictures would be in black and white.

Beyond Anita is Gina, who, holding Danielle in her left arm and touching Stephanie affectionately with her right hand, would never know the "tsks" that passed between Marqueeta and Sylvia about her weight and how much nicer the photos would have been if everyone had been in shape. Maybe it was because she had waited so long to have children, they speculated. And that hunk of a husband! How did she hang on to him with a body like that? When this question arose, they inevitably arched their eyebrows knowingly at one another. Gina must be doing something to keep him at home. Did they even have gyms out there in Indiana? Couldn't she at least take a walk around the hayfield and work some of that baby weight off?

Stephanie had been strategically positioned on that side of the photo so that the punch-stained sleeve could be successfully hidden behind her mother's skirt. She is smiling broadly, so proud of her dress, the biggest event of her young life just hours ahead. And unlike everyone else in her family, she thinks Marqueeta is wonderful. She loves her long, blond hair and the jangle of the bracelets she wears. She thinks the woman who will soon be her new aunt looks just like a princess. Her father, standing in the gap behind her mother and her grandmother, is smiling, too. To let his wife know that despite his frustration he is still crazy about her, he has just pinched her bottom, and she is grinning like she has won the lottery.

The other frame on Anita's coffee table is less ostentatious. It is green-stained wood, purchased by the bride, along with several others just like it that she gave as Christmas gifts that year, at a Target store. There is no inscription, but Anita remembers the day like it was yesterday, November 30, 1996. It was the Thanksgiving weekend, and the ever-practical Gina planned it so that nobody had to take off too much time from work or miss too many days of school. The people in that photo seem more relaxed than their filigreed doubles, but there had been drama surrounding that wedding, too.

Gina, who had always been good at math and as early as fifth grade loved doing her homework and said it was just like working a puzzle, had won an engineering scholarship to Purdue University in West Lafayette, Indiana, where she had met Steve Chambers, an agriculture major. They had gotten engaged in their senior year and married two years after graduation, when they were sure they could be financially independent. Steve's parents had given him 40 acres of land adjacent to their farm near Bedford as a graduation gift, and he and his three brothers had built a house on it -- three bedrooms, two baths, a dining room, a wraparound porch -- with money he had saved from working summers through high school and college in the stone quarries. Gina had moved to Indianapolis, where she had been recruited to work for the engineering division of Meyercorp, a large construction company that built housing developments. It wasn't the bridges and skyscrapers she had imagined, but the pay was enough money so that her real life with Steve could begin -- to move to the house in Bedford and start a family and work with contractors and architects whose projects would make a difference, when her time would be her own.

Since they both lived in Indiana now and so did Steve's large family and most of their friends from college, it seemed logical to have the wedding there, but Gina's family had been disappointed.

"Honey, your high school friends and all of our family are in San Diego," her mother had said when she and Steve called to tell them about their plans. "And, no offense, Steve, but if the bride's family is going to pay for the wedding, shouldn't we get to have a say in where it's going to be?"

"You don't have to pay, Mrs. Langley," Steve broke in from the kitchen extension at his parents' house. "Gina and I have that covered. And anyway, it won't be expensive. We live in a small town and go to a small church. My mom and her friends will cook for the reception. It'll probably just be something like a potluck with cake and punch in the church basement after the ceremony. And we don't plan to have a big crowd -- my family, whoever can come from your family, a few neighbors and a few friends from college. We're looking at probably seventy tops."

And so the California contingent had boarded a plane in the dark early hours of the Friday after Thanksgiving and headed east. This time it was Jay, the bride's stepfather, who had grumbled in the car on the way to the airport about its being the busiest travel weekend of the year. When they had arrived in Indianapolis, he had grumbled again, this time about its being colder than a witch's tit. The pilot had announced as they were landing that it was 31 degrees and sleeting.

"Why the hell didn't they decide to get married in Alaska?" he muttered to his wife while they waited for the suitcases filled with their wedding attire to arrive on the carousel. "It wouldn't have been any colder than this." Like her daughter would twelve years later, she said nothing, not wanting to agitate her husband even further, and, besides, she had worries of her own. Watching the other passengers who had deplaned with them, she realized she should have packed sweaters and boots. Unless they had a chance to go shopping, he and Larry would complain about what they were wearing for the entire weekend.

"How long do you think Gina's going to be able to stand it out here in the sticks after living her whole life in California anyway?" he said, but before Anita could answer, Gina, who had gotten to the airport later than she expected because of the weather, spotted them in the crowd and came rushing over, her cheeks reddened by the cold, her eyes sparkling with happiness and excitement, her blond curls tumbling from beneath a green knit ski cap, to hug them and help them with their bags, which had just that moment arrived.

They had wanted to stay at a hotel, but Steve's parents, Sid and Maryanne, wouldn't hear of it. It had taken three hours on treacherous roads to get to the farm from the airport for lunch, and they said they were not going to let their new family go out into that mess again. Sid offered beers all around while Maryanne reallocated her family's bedrooms.

"Mike can move in with Sam, and we've got a rollaway bed somewhere down in the basement that we'll get out for Steve. That way Gina can have Steve's room to herself." She said this with a straight face, even though Gina had already left her job and moved into Steve's house, even though she had been on the pill since they had started dating sophomore year. "That leaves Warren's room for the two of you, and we'll make Larry a bed right out here on the sofa."

Larry gave his mother a pleading look, but she shook her head ever so slightly. "We have to make this work," she telegraphed to him with her pursed lips. "These people are right. After the wedding tomorrow, we will all be family."

All of them, plus Steve's older brother, Warren, and his wife, Cindy, and four-month-old baby boy, Charles, made up the party for the groom's dinner, which Maryanne had cooked with Cindy's help. The actual wedding rehearsal had been called off because of the weather, but no one seemed worried, especially not the unflappable Gina. Instead they sat down directly, without the emollient of a real cocktail, at 5:30 in the afternoon, to ham encased in pineapple rings and cherries, scalloped potatoes, corn, green beans, deviled eggs, and a cherry molded Jell-O salad studded with fruit cocktail -- Steve's favorite, according to his mother. For dessert there was a homemade chocolate cake with vanilla icing and a lopsided pink heart, inside which Cindy had shakily written with a frosting tube "Steve and Gina Forever."

Anita had packed dressy clothes for the occasion -- a maroon silk pants suit for herself, gray wool pants and navy blazers for Larry and Jay, but they seemed inappropriate and out of place here, where no one else changed and all of the men were wearing jeans. So they remained in their wrinkled and wadded travel clothes, as if that were exactly what they'd planned, as if each of them wouldn't have traded everything they owned for the hot force of a good hotel shower.

By morning the rain and sleet were over, but the forecast called for more bad weather. Sid took Larry and Jay outside to show them around the farm while the women made breakfast. He wore overalls and a red plaid shirt from which peeked the waffled neck and sleeves of his long underwear. He offered Larry and Jay woolen jackets from hooks just inside the mudroom door, but they simultaneously said they were fine and went off into the cold in jeans and the blazers they hadn't worn the night before, their sockless feet slipped into their Topsiders. The sky was still overcast, and the trees, resplendent in reds and golds as recently as two weeks ago, were now cold, black, and bare, their thin branches reaching up to the metal-gray heavens as if to ask what had happened and to beg for the return of their colorful apparel. A worn-out tractor sat entrenched in mud that had frozen overnight just outside the barn, which, itself, looked as if a good stiff wind would blow it right over. An advertisement for chewing tobacco had been painted on the side facing the blacktopped road years ago, but now the red package and black and white letters had been absorbed by the weathered gray of the boards to which they had been applied and were too faded to read.

When they had eaten breakfast -- a real farm breakfast, Maryanne bragged to them, that included homemade biscuits and gravy along with the eggs and bacon -- they loaded their suitcases into Gina's car for the trip just down the road to the new house, her house, where they would get dressed for the wedding this afternoon and spend the night before leaving the next day and going home. Gina and Steve would leave directly after the reception in the church basement so they could get at least part way to Chicago, where they'd spend a three-day honeymoon, before it got dark.

Back at the farmhouse, Sid dried the steaming dishes as Maryanne washed them, rinsed them in a sink filled with hot water and bleach, and then stacked them in the drainer on the counter.

"Talk about the city mouse and the country mouse," he said to his wife, with a deep chuckle.

Despite her determination to fit in, Anita had committed her first faux pas the night before when she asked what wine they'd be serving with the ham and if she could pour it. In fact, Maryanne had made a big pitcher of sweetened iced tea to have with the meal. They had, however, chilled two bottles of champagne for a toast. Anita noted without meaning to that it was a grocery store brand that she always avoided, but she appreciated the effort. When she said, "Where could I find the flutes?" Sam, Steve's fourteen-year-old brother, said, "Cool! Is somebody going to play music?"

This picture has more people in it than Larry and Marqueeta's simply because Steve comes from a bigger family, and it looks a bit off-kilter because the bride and groom are not in the middle. Try as he might, the local photographer, an elderly man who had taken the senior class pictures of every Chambers boy and their mother, couldn't work out a plan in which Gina and Steve didn't end up too far to the left. Ultimately he shrugged his shoulders and said, "Well, we'll just have to make do with what we've got." Looking at Gina and Larry, he joked, "Your mom and dad just needed to have more kids!"

Gina laughed. Everything delighted her today. Larry scowled and Anita smiled politely. She was used to this by now, and it would have been irrelevant to respond to his comment, made with no more serious intention than to fill the time while he fiddled with his tripod, that Gina was the product of a previous relationship. But Jay never thought it was funny. He would have liked a bigger family, more children of his own besides Larry, and while Anita had been willing, too, and while they had never used birth control once in their marriage, it hadn't happened.

And so there is Jay on one end and Sid on the other, both men turned and facing slightly in, like two cusps of a horizontal partial moon, guarding the people who stand inside their protective half-circle, for whom they are jointly responsible. Anita stands next to Jay and reaches across herself to hold his right hand with her left one. In the photo this pose looks a little awkward, but at the time it had been exactly the right thing to do. He had been out of his element with these people, in this place, but he had come through for Gina when her real father, her biological father anyway, had long ago disappeared from their lives and subsequently died. She was grateful to him for that and for marrying her even though she had a two-year-old and for being as good a dad to Gina as he was to Larry, even though there were times during the middle-school years when he had often roared, albeit affectionately, "Can't we send this child to boarding school?" and "I'm taking the next bus to Mexico."

He would rather have been working out at the gym or hitting golf balls at the driving range than slogging through the mud to examine a new section of barbed-wire fence, rather have been consulting with one of his clients at the brokerage firm than helping out with farm chores, but he had done the right things, said the right things, even embracing Sid as they left that morning, saying how much he'd enjoyed feeding the pigs -- it had been the first time in his life.

There are no tuxedoes in this photograph. All of the men are wearing suits, and since this picture is, ironically, in color, it's obvious that they were not coordinated, that none of them had known what the other was wearing until they turned up at the church that day to run through the ceremony just once a few minutes before it actually began. Jay's suit is black -- he would actually have preferred the anonymity of identical tuxedoes that would have spared him the need to discuss what he'd wear and shop for it, and a black suit was as close as he could get. Larry is in the charcoal gray suit he had gotten for high school graduation the year before, Steve in navy blue, and Warren in brown. Sam and Mike are in light blue and tan, respectively, regardless of the season and a day that had turned off bitterly cold, despite the pale, watery sun, which had remained behind the clouds all morning and only made a brief appearance just as the ceremony ended.

"Like a good omen!" Gina had cried when she and Steve walked out of the church under a hail of ecologically correct birdseed and looked up at the sky, oblivious to any of the issues, thinking only that she had the most wonderful big family in the world, and this was the happiest day of her life.

CHAPTER FOUR

It wasn't Larry who called two weeks later but his assistant, Piper Cummings, who left a voice-mail message that said she was calling on behalf of Lawrence Langley to coordinate schedules. Her voice was chilly and clipped, almost mechanical. If she knew she was calling Larry's sister, it apparently didn't matter to her. Gina imagined her as one of the skinny young women she had seen in L.A., probably eating yogurt and soda crackers for lunch and flashing a toe ring from sandals that tied up around her calves and looked as if they had formerly belonged to Roman soldiers.

"That is so typical," Gina said to Steve when she had listened to the message. She dropped the canvas bag of groceries she had carried in from the car onto the oil-cloth-covered kitchen table, pushed the repeat button, and wrote the number onto a pad Steve handed her from the nearby counter. "I'm glad I was out when she called. *Lawrence* needs to know he's not the only one who's busy. He'd probably send an assistant on this trip for him if he could."

She shrugged out of the soggy green fleece jacket she was wearing. A late spring rain had caught her without an umbrella, and her hair was plastered to her head and dripping onto the floor where she stood. Steve hung the jacket over a drying rack in the adjoining laundry room and wiped up the puddle with a paper towel.

"So was the call about making plans for the trip?" he asked her. They had talked about the list endlessly, often far into the night, since she had gotten back from Los Angeles.

"Yes. I'll be interested to see where he has in mind to go. We have to spend at least three days in a foreign city together, and we have to cross water. It can't be in Canada or Mexico, and it can't be anyplace where either of us has been before -- not that that's a problem for me. When it comes to picking a foreign city where I've never been, the field is pretty much wide open."

She had e-mailed with her mother, who was in Thailand, to ask questions about the project as soon as she'd gotten home. The original notes had only specified a foreign city, but in her messages Anita made more specific demands.

"It's about time you finally have a passport," she told her daughter. She had asked Gina to join her on several trips, but Gina had always said, mildly annoyed, that she couldn't leave Steve and the girls and her job at the store to go trotting around the globe. Did her mother know anything at all about her life? Didn't she remember what it was like to have two children?

"Stephanie and Danielle are old enough now that they can spare you for a few days, and I know Maryann would be thrilled to help out," Anita wrote. "I want you to go someplace wonderful. If I know your brother, he will try to link the trip up with work, and I want his attention to be on you -- and yours on him, of course. His studio does a lot of filming in Canada, and it would be like him to try and do work while he was away, so that's out. And you've both been to Mexico as teenagers, so you can't go there. And anyway, that would be too easy, especially for Larry, and it's dangerous there now. I want you to explore someplace new to both of you.

Larry has traveled more than you have, and I don't want him to be in a city that's familiar to him so that he dictates everything you do. I think the trip should involve flying over water." She had put a happy-face emoticon after the Xs and Os and the "Love, Mom" that ended her message.

"How's an assistant going to arrange that?" Gina said now to Steve. "We have to figure out where we're going and when. I haven't gotten the passport yet, and it's going to be the height of summer by the time we can put something together, so airfare and hotels are going to be expensive and hard to get. I don't think Mom thought some of her ideas through. She might be able to pick up and leave any time she wants to, but I can't, and certainly his royal highness, studio executive par excellence Sir Lawrence, can't."

"You know I can take care of the girls whenever you can get away," he reminded her.

"Yes, but they're going to be out of school, and ..."

"And your mom's right. My mom and dad would love to have some time with them. Call your brother and get this thing squared away. Do you know what we could do with $56,000?"

"I know what we could have done," she said, frowning and shaking her head sadly. "Talk about too little, too late."

She lifted a bag of potatoes, some carrots, and a package of chicken pieces out of the grocery bag and turned on the water in the sink. She'd had a dentist appointment after she'd left the store, and dinner was going to be late. Danielle came down the stairs into the kitchen now, dressed in pink shorts and a white T-shirt with a red heart appliquéd onto its front.

Gina had begun scrubbing carrots, and now she rinsed one off under the faucet and handed it to her daughter. Danielle took the carrot and headed for the living room, where Stephanie was watching a movie.

"Thanks, Mom," she said as she left, her sandy ponytail swinging.

"I wish money wasn't even part of the deal," Gina said now, picking up where she had left off with Steve. "If I was ever to go away with my brother, I'd like to think it was because we both wanted to, like that's ever going to happen. I hate it that we're virtually -- no, literally -- being blackmailed by our own mother. I wish I could tell them both what to do with this whole thing and that I'm not interested. Except that I am. Some of the assignments are a little hokey, but I have to admit that going away to a foreign city with someone else paying the bill is kind of exciting. If only I were going with you instead of Larry, it would be perfect. Some brother. He's Stephanie and Danielle's uncle, and they wouldn't know him if he walked into this room. They were so little the last time -- the only time -- they ever saw him."

Steve had been sitting at the table absently turning the pages of a farm magazine while he listened. Now he moved behind her and wrapped his arms around her while she continued to wash and peel.

"I wish I could be giving you nice things," he said into her hair. "I wish I could be whisking you off to some exciting place, just the two of us." There was genuine regret in his voice, and Gina was instantly sorry for her complaining. She dried her hands and turned around to face him.

"We're not about things," she said. "We never have been. All that really matters is right here in this house. We knew there would be sacrifices when we made the choices we made, but look how well the girls are doing, even now that I'm working part-time at the store. Danny wasn't doing well at the beginning of the year, but I've been here to help her with her homework, and look how she has really turned her grades around."

"But you're used to nice things, you grew up in a nice house ...."

"Right. And if I had been willing to stay with Meyercorp, to leave you and the girls and our home and this town and everything we've built up together at the store, we could have a bigger house and nicer things that I could occasionally come and visit. We made a choice to do what's best for the family, and we agreed that living in a smaller house and my working part-time and having less money is worth it to all of us. When the girls are in college we'll talk about my getting a job and us taking trips together. My mom has discovered this great career later in life. Maybe I can, too."

She punctuated this last with a quick but heartfelt kiss and then turned quickly back to the carrots in the sink. She wasn't quite as cheerful about giving up her own work as she led Steve to believe, but she did mean everything she'd said.

"I'm just trying to find the silver lining in this ridiculous game we're about to play. Knowing what else we could do with the money the trip will cost, I need to adjust my attitude and try to make the most of the experience if my mom is going to force me to do it -- and pay for it."

"I know," he said quietly. They had talked before about the irony of his having been to South America twice on Farm Bureau exchange trips, and he didn't much care if he ever left the farm. She, on the other hand, had talked the whole time they were dating about how she someday wanted to see the world. On their first date, long before they knew they would end up together, she had told him she didn't want to get married until she had traveled to every continent. Not long after that she had realized that a pile of plane tickets and passport stamps from all over the world couldn't match up to Steve -- Steve who went to her classes and took notes for her when she had the flu, who planned the picnic in the woods where he would propose, who made her laugh when one difficult semester kept her out of Phi Beta Kappa.

She dredged the chicken with flour and dropped the pieces into olive oil that had been heating on the stove. She arranged the potatoes, onions, and carrots in a glass baking dish, poured in some chicken broth from a carton in the refrigerator, and placed the browned pieces on top before she slid the pan into the oven.

While she worked she imagined calling Larry at home right then and there to tell him to talk to her directly and not foist her off onto someone else like just another item to be checked off the list in his so-busy day-planner. But the sad fact was, she didn't feel comfortable calling her own brother's house. What if Marqueeta answered? What if he did? What would she say to either one of them, really?

In the morning, after Steve left for the store, she fidgeted and watched the clock until business hours arrived on the West Coast and Larry and his assistant might be in the office. And then she hesitated, not wanting to seem too eager. Good grief, to quote Larry, what was she -- twelve? Why should she worry about what time she called him and where? She hadn't felt this way since she was in high school and waiting for a boyfriend to call or calling him, her pulse pounding, hoping with all her heart that no one would be home and not knowing what she'd say if he answered. Even before money had clouded the picture, when had she and Larry gotten so out of sync with each other? When had she stopped knowing her own brother?

When they were kids, all he wanted to do was tag along after her. How many times had she ordered him out of her room when her girlfriends were over? Once, when two of her friends were spending the night, they had all thrown pillows at him when he tried to come into the room after they were in their pajamas, and she had called out, "Mom, please get my moronic pervert of a brother out of my room." She must have been about fifteen at the time, which would have made him eleven. "Hey," he'd cried, putting his hands up in front of his face to ward off the shower of ruffled pink missiles, "all I want to do is hang out with you guys." She'd felt a protective pang of sympathy for him, but she had an image to maintain, so she chased him away so the other girls wouldn't think she was some kind of dork who didn't have anything better to do than play with her little brother. Another time she had been roller-skating on the sidewalk on the way to the park near where they had lived when she shot across a crack in one of the slabs and fell and twisted her ankle. Larry had run all the way home -- only three blocks, but it seemed like a long way since she was nine at the time and he would have been only five -- to fetch their mother. When he came back, he was crying harder than she was, and he carried the skates while Anita carried her daughter, sniffling and wiping his nose on the shoulder of his striped T-shirt the whole way home.

When had she stopped being the cool older sister and become a stranger he hadn't even thought to invite to his home when he knew she was coming to town? Did it happen when she left for college, or was it later, when she married Steve? Things had already changed between them when the family came to Indiana for the wedding. For the first time she could remember, she hadn't been able to think of much to say to him. She had sent him a few letters from college, and in the beginning he had answered. She still had the handful of letters he had written to her on lined notebook paper when he was bored in one of his classes. She knew this because that's the way he started the letters: "I'm sitting here in algebra class bored out of my mind and thought I'd write you a letter ..." After he'd graduated from high school, that had ended. Maybe then his life had filled up, and he hadn't needed to resort to writing to his sister when there was nothing better to do.

She remembered hugging him awkwardly when she met her family at the airport and that night at the groom's dinner, so humble by California standards, she had asked him ridiculous questions like if he'd seen any of her friends around town and how was band practice going. It was as if he wasn't even related to her anymore, as if she were talking to someone else's younger brother, just filling up dialogue balloons with meaningless words like a poorly conceived comic-book character. He had grown up and become a man, and maybe that was it. Maybe it was as simple as her being female and his being male, and maybe she was overthinking the whole thing. Probably their lives just grew apart. That happened to everybody -- just like Larry had said in the lawyer's office -- didn't it? Since he'd gotten his fancy job and married Marqueeta, he had become even more distant, and asking him for money certainly hadn't helped matters, either. But she had been desperate. There was nothing else she could think to do.

"Enough!" she said aloud, even though she was alone in the kitchen, but still she didn't make a move toward the telephone. She stacked the cereal bowls from breakfast into the dishwasher and ran the dust mop under the table where the crumbs from last night's chocolate cake and this morning's toast lay scattered on the linoleum floor. She could hear the girls' footsteps above her and the water running in the shower. It would be a perfect time to call. Still, before she did she took the precautions of making a comforting cup of tea and writing down the names of the cities and dates she'd been thinking about on the pad where she usually made grocery lists so she wouldn't forget them if she got flustered. Then she punched in the numbers on the telephone. A glance at the clock confirmed that she had dawdled away twenty-three minutes so that she would be calling at an odd time instead of on the hour, as if she'd been waiting for just the right moment to arrive. It would seem more like she'd been busy all morning and just that minute gotten to it and hadn't been waiting anxiously since the alarm went off at 6:00 to return the call.

First there was the phone tree: "Hello. You have reached the offices of Morrison Pictures. If you know your party's extension, please enter it now."

She punched in the 2973 that Piper Cummings had left in her call-back message. What kind of a too-cute name was "Piper," anyway? She was no doubt a wannabe actress and it wasn't her real name at all. After two rings an impatient-sounding voice picked up and without a greeting barked, "Piper Cummings."

"It's Regina Chambers," she said. "I'm Larry ... Lawrence Langley's sister. You called my house yesterday, but I was out."

"Oh, yes." The tone softened slightly. "Good. Let me get Lawrence's calendar up on the screen so we can get some dates penciled in."

Gina had her calendar out, too, and she smiled to think how different it must be from Larry's. Hers was the one they had given away last Christmas at the store. The pictures were scenes of Indiana throughout the seasons -- the Indiana Dunes in the spring, the sun warming the ripples in the piled sand; Spring Mill State Park in summer, a spray of water coming off the wheel that still ground corn but now just for tourists; the reds and yellows of the leaves in Brown County in autumn; and snowy Monument Circle in Indianapolis decked out in colorful lights for the holiday season. On the top of each page was printed "Chambers Farm and Feed." She could literally pencil things in onto the white squares of her calendar, but Piper would need to type in the event and then delete it again if Larry didn't approve.

"OK, we've got the week of July 9 open. How does that sound?"

She sounded like she was booking a dental appointment instead of a potentially life-altering adventure. But Piper couldn't know that making these plans had kept Gina awake most of the night wondering what they would talk about for three whole days and if they would have separate rooms or bunk in together as they had when they were kids. She wanted her own space, a place to be alone and take off her makeup, to collapse on the bed in her bathrobe and call home to tell Steve about the day. Would Piper be making all of these arrangements, and what would Larry tell her his preferences would be? And when it was all over, would they somehow magically be closer, or would they bore each other numb and never want to see each other again once these obligations were over? Would they be worse off when they got back than they were before they left? Why had their mother made this the first exercise? One of the assignments was to make a creative project honoring the other sibling. Why couldn't they have done this first to get accustomed to being in each other's lives again and then moved on to spending actual time together when they were a little more comfortable with each other? Or why couldn't they do the one that required spending time in each other's homes first? She would have liked to have Larry at her house so that Steve could be around to help her talk to him. They were very different, but they were both men, and maybe if Steve talked to Larry about cars or computers or machinery it would take the attention off her and the glaring, painful fact that she had nothing in common with her brother, not one word to say to him.

"Mrs. Chambers?"

"I'm sorry," Gina said. "I was just consulting my own calendar. Part of the problem is that I only applied for my passport a couple of weeks ago. They say it could take up to six weeks."

"It never takes as long as they say," Piper said with an air of knowing confidence, "but just to be sure, what about the week of the 23rd?"

"Has Larry told you that we don't know where we're going yet?" she asked.

"Um, yes, but he's got some ideas in mind. We'll get to that in a minute."

Gina's temper flared. Here was another example of Larry being self-important and her being the country bumpkin who hadn't been farther away from home than back to California for her stepfather's funeral and Larry's wedding. After that, with Anita on her own, it made more sense for her to buy one plane ticket to Indianapolis than for Gina to buy four to San Diego, and they couldn't have afforded it anyway. In the seven years since his wedding she had not seen Larry again.

But how could she be angry when she had made a list, too, and July 23 was the first date she had written down. Beneath the dates there were five cities: London, Paris, Rome, Nassau, Berlin.

"The week of the 23rd is good," she said, "and I've got some ideas about where we can go, too. What are his?"

"He actually wants to talk to you about them himself. If you can hold for a minute, I'll grab him. He's just down the hall working in editing."

She said this as if Gina were familiar with the studio's layout, as another sister might have been.

A recorded message loop came on the line, repeating an ad for a new Morrison movie, a futuristic western, complete with music -- undoubtedly of Larry's choosing or creation -- and the video-game sounds of weapons firing. Each time the ad finished with a mechanical voice saying, "Where past and future dangers meet in the present," and then a chirpy female voice that reminded the caller to remain on the line since the call was important to them.

"Hey, Gina." Larry picked up in the middle of the sixth go-around of the advertisement. By this time she had it memorized. He sounded pleasant, like he actually wanted to talk to her.

"Hi, Larry. So, where are we going?" Before he answered, she added, "I've got some ideas, if you don't." She was too cheerful, talking too fast, but maybe if she spoke up first she'd have a chance of going where she wanted to go before Larry took charge and railroaded her to do what he wanted.

"I've got some ideas, too," he said, "but let's hear yours first."

This sounded promising. Maybe she had underestimated him. She read off the list.

"I was thinking maybe Vancouver," he said when she had finished, as if she had not even spoken. "We're doing a picture there next year, and I'd like to get a feel for the city."

Maybe she didn't know her brother anymore, but their mother obviously did.

"Mom says no Canada or Mexico."

"Why?"

"Mexico because we've both already been there and Canada because Mom doesn't want you to combine work with our trip."

"We film a lot in Toronto, but I've never been to Vancouver."

"She specifically said no Canada and no work. Period. And anyway she says we have to cross water."

"I think Mom's getting daffy in her old age," he said, "or senile and controlling. It's like she's some bizarre puppeteer pulling the strings of our lives."

"It is what it is," Gina told him. "I've been e-mailing with her, and I don't think there's anything wrong with her, but I do think she's having a good time batting us around like a cat with a stuffed mouse. What about London? I've always wanted to go there."

"Yeah, I've been e-mailing with her, too, but she didn't mention these rules. The thing is, I've been to London several times. I wouldn't mind going back, though. Why is that a problem anyway?"

"She doesn't want one of us deciding what we're going to do. She wants us to explore and decide on things together."

She didn't add that Anita's concern was only that Larry might take charge, but then it occurred to her that she didn't know what the e-mail exchanges with him had included. Maybe Anita had worried that she would be a bossy older sister. Larry had accused her of that more than once when they were growing up.

"We always have to do what you want to do," he must have said on a thousand occasions, and she always responded, "That's because I'm older and I have better ideas."

She read the rest of her list to him. He had been to all of the cities except Nassau, and he was planning to take Marqueeta on a cruise that would stop there for her birthday.

"She'd kill me if I went without her before then," he said, and Gina read in the finality of his tone that there would be no further discussion about the Bahamas.

"So what's on your list?"

"Sydney, Hong Kong and Tokyo. I guess you can tell I live on the West Coast. You think Europe, I think the other direction."

"Hong Kong," she blurted out without thinking. Their mother loved China, so she would definitely think her money was being well-spent. Hadn't they joked in Dennis MacDonald's office that she was in her Chinese period? Maybe they would come back doing tai chi and celebrating Chinese New Year and redecorating their homes with mirrors and chimes and crystals like she had.

"You sound pretty certain that that's where you want to go," he said, and in his laugh she heard the ghost of his fifteen-year-old self."

"I am."

She hadn't been, though. Despite her dream of traveling around the world, now the idea of actually going so far away without her family was frightening. She wished she hadn't blurted out her choice so quickly, but if she'd had time to think about it, she might have chickened out altogether. And once she'd said it, she liked the idea more, liked thinking the words, liked the feel of the hard consonants in her mouth. She would enjoy saying things to her friends like "I can't come to a meeting that week because I'll be in Hong Kong" and "I'll call you as soon as I get back from Hong Kong."

"That sounds good to me, but that's a long way to go for three days. Let's plan to stay for five."

Immediately she regretted her choice. Now there would be two extra days to fill with forced conversation.

"I have to be back for corporate meetings the following week, but I could stay away until the 29th, and Mom's allocated enough money that we should be able to cover a hotel for a couple of extra nights." He said all this like he was thinking out loud. Then he tuned back to her frequency. "OK, I'll get Piper to make the arrangements for both of us. I'll leave from here, but I'll have her book you out of Chicago. Oh, and one more thing, I'm going to upgrade to business class at my own expense. Do you want to do that, too?"

"No," she said quickly. There was no thinking about the answer to this question.

"Look, Gina, I could help you with this."

She could hear the embarrassment in his voice, his realization that he had raised the awkward, ugly specter of money between them once again. He must have known how pathetic this offer sounded in light of what had been at risk -- and lost -- when he said no before. "I've got all kinds of frequent-flyer miles. It wouldn't be any big deal."

"No," she said again. "Have Piper e-mail the itinerary to me. I'll see you in Hong Kong."

CHAPTER FIVE

The best itinerary Piper had been able to find was a Southwest flight with a stop in Phoenix that delivered Gina to LAX to connect with the very same Cathay Pacific flight Larry would be taking. In the three and a half hours between the time her plane had landed at 5:00 p.m. and their flight would begin boarding at 8:30 she had taken the shuttle to the international terminal, finished the book she was reading on the flight out and bought another one, along with a *Los Angeles Times*, at a newsstand. She had sat alone in an airport bar and treated herself to a glass of wine, lifting the glass into the air and silently toasting her world-traveling self, hoping that bravado would overwhelm the anxiety that had taken possession of her stomach and crowded out any thought of food. She'd walked through the duty-free shop and then gone through security much earlier than she needed to, but the line had been long, and she didn't want any last-minute problems to screw up this trip. On the other side, she slipped her feet back into the new brown flats she had bought for the trip, put on the navy cardigan she had shed for its ride through the X-ray machine, and bought a bottle of water to put into her carry-on bag.

Her luggage was new, too -- red canvas with brown leather trim. When Steve had brought in the old maroon hard-sided suitcase she had taken to college and they had used for their Chicago honeymoon from the attic over the garage, she sensed the wave of embarrassment she would feel claiming it from a carousel and handing it to a cab driver in an unknown city. Larry, she was sure, would have his slacks and jackets folded neatly into a leather garment bag or tucked into a piece of designer luggage with his initials engraved onto a discreet brass plate next to the handle. When she had opened it to look inside, the smell of mildew -- years of damp and cold alternating with hot and humid during which the suitcase had never been opened -- was the sharp, pungent permission she needed to spend $175 on an "expandable upright" and another $100 for its matching carry-on "satchel."

Now the satchel and the brown leather handbag that roughly matched the color of its trim were tucked under the plastic seat while she worked the *Times* crossword puzzle, alternately glancing at her watch and looking up every few minutes to scan in every direction from which Larry might appear. It was 8:15, and the desk at the gate was already busy. A tall, elegant Korean woman in a green uniform clicked on a microphone and read the names of standby passengers who could be accommodated on the flight. At the end of the announcement she said boarding would begin shortly.

Gina looked at her watch again. Where the hell was he, and if he didn't show up, what was she supposed to do then? This was so typical. How many times when they were kids had he kept the whole family hanging, wondering if he'd show up on time for dinner or be ready when they were about to leave for an important event. On the day she had graduated from high school he had been playing basketball at a friend's house and showed up to get into the shower after she and her mother and Jay were ready to go. She had been pacing the floor, the text of her valedictory speech tucked into an outside pocket of her purse, the underarms of the new white dress she'd wear under her robe already ruined with nervous perspiration.

"Why's everybody so uptight?" he'd said, taking his time as he went upstairs to the bathroom. "I said I'd be here and I'm here. We've got lots of time. Chill, okay?"

They did get to the school auditorium in time, but just barely. She had hoped to see her friends' dresses before they gowned up, to sit in her seat and look over the speech one last time before she had to give it, but no. Even though it was her big day, they had all operated, as usual, on Larry time. And Jay, as usual, had let Larry get by with it. He had been a good dad to her and hadn't shown any favoritism in granting favors or giving gifts, but when she and her brother got into it, he nearly always took Larry's side. Becoming a parent herself had helped her forgive him. She couldn't imagine loving a stepchild with the intensity she felt for her own flesh and blood.

Now she dug in her purse for her cell phone to see if she'd missed a call or a text. She hadn't. She'd call him. She sighed audibly. Just like always, he was the one who screwed up, and she was the one who fixed it. There was a history of that scenario, too, like when he had asked two girls to the eighth-grade dance and she had been the one to find a date for the one he had decided to abandon.

And then, scanning the list of contacts in her phone, she realized she didn't know his number. She had the number for Shawswick Elementary School, the numbers of three baby-sitters, and the wholesalers with whom they did business at the store programmed into her phone, but she didn't know her own brother's number. After they'd decided on Hong Kong, Piper had made all of the plans, and she hadn't talked to him directly again. Piper probably thought she had covered everything, but she had omitted one important piece of information. It wasn't her fault, of course. She would naturally have assumed that a normal brother and sister would already know one another's cell-phone numbers. Now, at this hour on a Saturday evening, there would be no point in calling the office. She did have his home number in the tattered address book she'd brought along so she could send postcards, but that would mean dealing with Marqueeta, and her guess was that Keeta would already not be too happy about Larry's taking what amounted to a holiday and leaving her behind. And if Larry was still home, there would be no hope of his getting here in time to take this plane. No, she'd wait a few minutes more before she panicked. At least she'd had the sense to e-mail her number to him, so maybe he would call her.

When the woman at the desk said into the microphone that they'd begin boarding first and business class, Gina took a last opportunity to use the ladies' room she'd passed on her way to the gate. When she came back out, there was still no sign of Larry. The long line of coach-class passengers had begun to form and snaked out into the concourse. A stooped, balding man in a long trench coat and glasses with big frames disappeared into the first- and business-class entryway. Just after him, a woman with short blond hair in tight black pants and high heels urged along a bored-looking teenage girl in jeans who shuffled behind her with ear buds isolating her from the riffraff. Gina couldn't actually see them under the girl's thick mop of curly red hair, but she saw the cord that attached to something in her pocket and split into two parts just below the neckline of her long-sleeved black T-shirt. The woman with her wore sunglasses even though it was dark outside, and in the midst of her worry about Larry, Gina wondered if she were a celebrity.

"We're ready to begin general boarding now," the uniformed woman said into her microphone.

What should she do? She walked out into the concourse and looked anxiously in both directions. The line at the desk had thinned down to only a couple who were trying to have their seats changed so they could sit together. She took a place behind them and waited, still scanning, still checking her watch, which had only moved two minutes since the last time she looked.

"Could I help you?" the woman asked when the couple had been satisfied and left to join the line.

"I need to find out if my brother has checked in," she said. "We're supposed to be on this flight together, but ..."

"I'm sorry," the woman interrupted, smiling apologetically as if she actually were. "We're restricted by privacy laws from revealing the contents of our passenger list. Why don't you try calling him on his cell phone?"

"I would," Gina said, "but I don't have his number."

"I thought you said he was your brother."

"Yes, but we're not close. It's a long story."

"But you're taking a trip together?"

"Yes, well, at least we're supposed to. I know it sounds crazy, but yes we are. I was supposed to meet him here, but I haven't seen him, and if he doesn't show, I probably won't go, either."

The woman was dubious now.

"All I can suggest is that you look for him once you're on board. Do you know what seat he's in?"

"No, somewhere in business class."

"Oh, well, then, you don't have to wait through the line. You can board through the business class jetway and look for him right now."

"Except that I'm not in business class."

"But you're traveling together?"

"I told you it was a long story," Gina said. "Thanks for trying to help."

She walked to the end of the line, her eyes riveted on the business-class entry, and began moving toward the coach door behind the other passengers. Finally it was her turn to hand her boarding pass to the gate attendant and walk into the jetway.

She was the last person onto the plane, and a flight attendant was already giving the talk over the loudspeaker about how they needed to put their carry-ons into the overhead compartments and take their seats immediately since they were ready to close the door. Another attendant greeted the last of the passengers.

"I need to find my brother before you close the door," Gina said to her, "because if he's not on this plane, I shouldn't be, either."

"What seat number is he in?" the woman asked, frowning in concern and taking Gina's boarding pass to read as if she expected the answer would be there.

"I don't know," Gina said, "he's somewhere in business class. As you can see, I'm in coach."

"Well, the privacy laws ..."

"Yes, I know," Gina said, hearing her own voice rising against her will. "Could you just go into business class, check for Lawrence Langley and get his permission to tell me he's here. If he's not, there's no reason for me to go to Hong Kong."

"I will check," the woman said, "but I'll have to ask you to take your seat. We've got to get ready for takeoff."

"But that's what I'm saying ..." Gina began.

"You sit down, I check for your brother, that's the deal," the woman said. She was smiling but firm.

Gina walked through the galley and down the far aisle as the flight attendant had indicated. Thanks to Larry, she was so late that now she'd have to ask her seatmates to move so that she could get to her window seat. In the brief phone call and e-mail exchanges she'd had with Piper the one thing she had specifically asked for was a window seat. There wouldn't be much to see when they were out over the ocean, but she had been reading about Hong Kong since they'd started planning the trip, and when they landed tomorrow she wanted to be able to see the tall buildings and the busy harbor from the first possible moment -- unless, of course, Larry wasn't on the plane and she got off and didn't fly to Hong Kong at all.

But inconveniencing the chubby woman with a frizzy gray perm and the dark-haired, sulky child, who looked to be about ten, turned out not to be an option.

"I'm sorry to bother you, but I have the window seat," she said.

"Oh, I know," said the woman. "But I was hoping you wouldn't mind if my nephew took it instead. I think he'll sleep most of the flight, and it'll be easier for him if he can put his pillow up against the window."

"I actually asked specifically for the window," Gina said. "It's my first overseas flight."

"It's his, too," the woman said, stiffening now. "I'm guessing you don't have children of your own or you'd know how important it is that he sleep during this flight."

"Yes, I do have ..."

"You're going to have to take your seat, ma'am. We're about to close the door," said a third flight attendant, this one male. While he talked he used both hands to close the bins over her head.

"You can't close the door," she said frantically, nearly in tears now.

"What?" he said, soberly and giving her his full attention.

"I'm waiting for another flight attendant to check and see if ..."

Just then a crackle announced that the loudspeaker had been turned on again.

"Ladies and gentlemen, the door has now been closed, and we must ask you to put away all electronic devices ..."

She sank into her seat, the tears coming despite her efforts to stanch them. The flight attendant knelt by her aisle seat and talked to her in the tone he must have saved for children and mentally unstable adults.

"Look, ma'am, we're about to take off here. You need to tell me exactly what the problem is."

"I'm supposed to be taking this trip with my brother," she said, opening her handbag and fishing for a tissue. "But I didn't see him get on the plane, and I don't have his cell number, so I can't call him. If he's not on the plane, then I shouldn't be going, either."

"He's your brother and you don't know his cell number?" he began. But then, mercifully, before she had to explain for a third time, the flight attendant to whom she had originally spoken fairly ran down the aisle, nodding her head and smiling brightly.

"Yes, he's here," she said over the head of her still-kneeling colleague. "He's in seat 14-A. He can't come back here now because we're about to take off, but he says he'll come and talk to you during the flight."

The magnitude of her relief was unreasonable. She felt like crying again for pure joy -- that her trip hadn't been spoiled, yes, but she also felt the long-dormant mixed emotions of being a big sister charged with looking after her little brother and not knowing where he was, the same primal fear she'd felt when she'd once lost track of Danielle in a department store.

And then, just as quickly, relief turned to anger. While she was anxiously watching for him and worrying that he wouldn't make the flight, he'd probably been sipping champagne and looking at the menu of dinner choices they could bring him later, if the movies were to be believed. A name she had called him as a child and not thought of for years floated to the surface of her mind.

"Boogerhead," she said aloud. She had once been sent to her room without dinner for calling him that name in anger and frustration, when he had gotten his way yet again, but no one was here to punish her now.

"Boogerhead, boogerhead, boogerhead!" she said, more ever more forcefully.

"What?" The woman next to her in the middle seat frowned and pulled away from her.

"Nothing. Sorry, I was just thinking out loud."

The woman had taken advantage of Gina's interaction with the flight attendants to further ensconce her nephew in the window seat. He had taken off his shoes and wrapped up in a blanket. A DVD player and a vinyl envelope of disks waited in his lap for the proper altitude, and a pillow was wedged between his seat and the window so that he could go to sleep when he had eaten his dinner. A bottle of water, a coloring book and a big box of crayons had been shoved into the pocket on the back of the seat in front of him. His aunt had obviously counted on Gina's thinking that asking him to move would be more trouble than it was worth, and it had worked.

"It's OK," Gina reasoned with herself, trying to quell her disappointment. "It'll be easier for me to go to the bathroom, and if Larry comes back here, I'll be able to talk to him more easily. A lot of people actually ask for the aisle seats."

She looked toward the window and realized she could see beyond the child, even without having the seat by the window. As they began to taxi, she saw other airplanes, a catering truck, a police car, the lights inside the terminal disappearing behind them as they rolled past. She would just as easily be able to watch their approach to Hong Kong. Everything would be all right.

Dinner was over. She had chosen the pasta option over the beef. The pasty noodles in a pink sauce had come with a dinner roll, a cellophane packet of grated Parmesan cheese, an iceberg lettuce salad with a few shredded carrots and a wedge of tasteless tomato, and a square of chocolate cake that was frozen in the middle. She had sprung the $7 for a miniature bottle of generic white wine, of which she had drunk only half. The boy was asleep, his DVD player balanced on the tray table and continuing to show an animated movie despite having lost its audience. His aunt had gone to sleep, too, after slamming down the window shade and explaining to Gina that she wanted to make sure the light in the morning didn't disturb his sleep. She snored lightly, and her head bobbed like a bud on a stem. Each time she veered into Gina's territory and bumped into her shoulder, she jolted awake, muttered "Sorry" with hostility, as if Gina had been the one to invade her space, and resumed flipping through the *People* magazine that crumpled into her lap when she dozed off again.

Gina finished the *Times* puzzle and took the new paperback she'd bought at the airport out of her satchel. She had just started the third chapter when a man once again knelt in the aisle by her seat. This time it was Larry.

"Hey, Sis," he said, keeping his voice low in deference to the sleeping passengers around them. "The adventure begins, huh?"

"Well, well," she said, turning the book upside down in her lap, "so glad you could make it." She hated the sarcasm she could hear in her own voice, but nobody ever made charming Prince Larry pay for his selfishness and disregard of other people's needs.

"I told you I'd be here, and here I am," he said, flashing the smile that always ensured forgiveness. "If something had come up, I would have called."

"Well, it was for sure I wasn't going to call you. When I tried to I realized that neither you nor your oh-so-professional assistant had bothered to give me your number."

"I would have called you if there had been a problem."

Either her hostility hadn't registered or he chose to ignore it. "For future reference, here's my business card. It has all of my numbers on it. You can always reach me, day or night."

This was how he always wiggled out of trouble. He would anticipate what you'd be mad about and then be prepared to pacify you so that then it seemed like you'd been the one who was being unreasonable. There were plenty of examples of that in her memory, too. She took the card from him and slipped it into her book to serve as a bookmark. Then she closed the book and turned as much as she could in her cramped seat to face him.

"How did you even get on the plane?" she asked him. "I got to the gate early, and I watched for you the whole time."

"I did get here late," he admitted. "I had a meeting at the studio that went longer that I thought it would, and then I still had to go home and pick up my suitcase. I thought Marqueeta would have it packed, but there were some problems with that. Anyway, I had a driver from the studio drop me off. He knows this town like the back of his hand, and he took shortcuts I didn't even know existed. By the time I got here, they were into general boarding. I got right on. I looked around for you, but I didn't see you."

"But you got on the plane anyway?" she asked in disbelief. He must have arrived and boarded in the few moments while she was in the restroom.

"What if I hadn't been here? Didn't you wonder where I was?"

"I figured you'd already boarded. I guess I had a little more faith in you than you did in me."

"But what if I hadn't been here? What if my plane from Indianapolis had been delayed? The fact is, there was a thunderstorm predicted for this afternoon, and that could very well have happened. What if it had been something out of my control?"

He sucked in his cheeks and looked away as if at some far point in the distance, as if he were carefully considering her question.

"Hmm. Then I guess I would have called you as soon as I got to Hong Kong and figured out how to get you over there with me. The airline would have taken care of you and put you on the next flight. The latest you would have been would be a day behind me. Originally we didn't think we'd be flying together anyway, did we? It was just a happy coincidence that we wound up on the same plane. Chill out, Sis. None of that happened. We're here now and everything's good."

He stood up and stretched his arms over his head.

"I'm going to go back and see if I can get some shut-eye so I'll be ready to roll when we land."

"I've done a lot of reading about Hong Kong," she said now, wanting to end their conversation on a positive note, "and I've got lots of ideas about things we can do."

"I'm sure you do," he said, and she couldn't tell whether he meant it or was being sarcastic. Before she could ask, he walked away.

She pulled the flimsy cotton blanket around her and tried to position her head so that she could sleep. There hadn't been a pillow on her seat when she boarded, and in all the worry over Larry she hadn't thought to look around for a spare. When she'd finally asked for one, the flight attendant said they were all taken.

"Boogerhead," she thought to herself now, not wanting to bring the snoring aunt to consciousness. "Boogerhead, boogerhead, boogerhead."

CHAPTER SIX

The first thing Gina did in Hong Kong was sleep. After a head-bobbing night of trying to get comfortable in the narrow confines of the airplane seat, of turning away from the aunt, who appropriated the armrest for herself, and then back because her leg had fallen asleep, only to bump shoulders with her seatmate, startling them both awake, all she could think about was the smooth white sheets of a hotel-room bed. Before they had landed on Monday morning, the flight attendant had insisted, against the aunt's protests, that the little boy open his window shade for the landing, and secretly delighted, Gina had leaned ever so slightly across the aunt to catch a glimpse of the shards of tall buildings spiking upward around the busy harbor.

Piper had booked them at the Peninsula Hotel, and Gina knew from the guidebook she had read exhaustively -- and that even now was tucked conveniently into a side pocket of the satchel -- that it was way more expensive than she could have afforded on her own.

"I know Mom's paying for this," she said when they were settled in the backseat of the cab that sped through streets crowded with cars and buses, "but I don't think we should be taking advantage of her and just throwing her money away."

"I knew you'd worry about that, big sister," he said, an irritated sigh just behind his words even though he smiled at her. "We each have a small single room, and I e-mailed with Mom before Piper booked them. That's where she stayed when she was working for the guy here, and that's where she wants us to stay. She says we'll have an excellent view of the harbor."

The harbor view turned out, purely by chance, Gina had to admit, only to be Larry's, while her room, on the same floor but the opposite side of the hotel, looked out over the crowded backside of Kowloon. The buildings, many of them dingy and vacant, were crowded closely together and looked dirty, tired, and useless when she awoke hours later and opened the curtains to look outside. Except for the mountains that lay far beyond them, there was not a sprig of green that she could see.

Larry had had a good night's sleep comfortably reclined in his business-class seat, followed by a full hot omelet breakfast and gourmet coffee an hour before landing, so he spent the morning working out in the hotel's gym and then taking a walk along the harbor and down to the ferry landing. By the time he met his sister in the hotel lobby at noon, he had also organized the rest of their day.

"I've hired a driver and a guide for us," he said.

"Without consulting me?" Gina flared. She could feel the same flash of anger, the heat in her cheeks that she'd felt when they were kids and Larry made a plan that included her without first asking. He might be four years younger, but that didn't stop him from taking charge of situations where he had no business interfering, like the time he invited three of his friends to her thirteenth birthday party without asking. And, as usual, their father had convinced their mother to go right along with it. That year she'd wanted a '50s-era theme, with her girlfriends all wearing poodle skirts and putting their hair up in ponytails and a pink and white heart-shaped ice cream cake for dessert, and her mother had said that was a great idea. But once Larry invited boys, she had said that would be fun, too, and changed the theme to clowns and the cake to chocolate as cheerfully as if she thought that's what Gina had wanted all along. Gina had gone to her room in tears when she found out, and later her mother had come in to talk to her about the value of being flexible and sharing and how her brother was more important to her than any group of girlfriends would ever be. She still remembered that as the worst birthday of her life, with her nine-year-old brother and his weenie friends making fart and boob jokes and her friends rolling their eyes and finally holing up in her bedroom with the door locked while the boys hammered away outside. Anita, always wearing her rose-colored glasses, must have heard all the clamor from the kitchen where she was getting the refreshments ready and interpreted it as just kids having fun.

"Well, yeah," he said now. "I thought you'd be pleased."

That was typical, too. It was what he'd always said when Gina had tearfully told on him and he'd been busted. Somehow he always came off as the helpful, thoughtful brother and she the ungrateful sister who just wanted to have her own way.

"Well, I have some ideas, too," she said. She pulled the guidebook out of her purse and took from it a list she'd made on hotel stationery after her shower. "And they don't involve the expense of a guide."

"Mom allowed some money for sightseeing, you knew that," he said, exasperated. "But if we should go over the allotted amount, I'll pay for it. I just thought that since we're only here for five days, we should maximize every minute and not spend half our time groping around trying to find things by looking at maps and signs that are written in Chinese. And I figured you were sleeping. I didn't want to wake you up to ask your permission for something that I thought would be a great surprise."

He had put emphasis on the word "permission."

"You don't need my permission for anything, Larry," she said, her voice deadly calm now. "But you travel all the time, and this trip is about the most exciting thing I've ever done, so I'd like to have some say about how I spend my time while I'm here. And anyway, if the whole point is for us to get to know each other again, we might have talked about what we were going to do while we're here. You don't even know me anymore, so I don't know how you can presume to imagine what might interest me."

"Come down off the ledge, Gina," he said, his level but irritated tone matching hers. "I didn't have any idea it would upset you like this. It's only for this afternoon. You'll have plenty of opportunities to get your way while we're here."

They were still standing by the elevators where they had agreed to meet, and now a fresh carload of people arrived so that they had to move out of the way so the group could emerge into the lobby.

"It's not about having my way," she said through gritted teeth. "It's about trying to do what Mom had in mind for us to do."

"I think your anger at me is more about the farm than about seeing Hong Kong," he said as they walked past the registration desk and toward the door that led out to Salisbury Road. She whipped her head around to glare at him. "Well, come on, that's the elephant in the room, so we might as well talk about it and get it out in the open so it doesn't ruin our whole time here. I'm sorry about the farm, Gina, and I know I let you down, and I guess I thought that maybe showing you a really good time here would be a way to …"

"I lost my home, Larry," she interrupted, stopping abruptly and turning to face him. "It was the house my husband and his brothers built with their own hands on his parents' land, the land they gave him when he graduated from college. It was the house I went home to after my wedding. My little girls used to have rooms of their own, and now they have to share. Did you really think you could make that up to me by showing me a 'good time'? Are you serious?"

"No, I didn't mean that. It was a poor choice of words. I know nothing could make up for that, but … " He filled his cheeks with air and let it escape through his pursed lips in frustration. "I just wanted us both to have a good time. That's all. And I thought cramming everything we could into these five days would be a start."

"Would you at least look at my list? There are some things I really want to see while I'm here."

"Yes, of course. The guy's going to pick us up at one. I told him we'd catch some lunch around here and meet him out front. He knows we just got in this morning and will probably be jet-lagged, so it's going to be an easy afternoon."

Instead of leaving the hotel, they turned back to one of the restaurants just off the lobby, where Larry deftly ate a plate of vegetables and rice with chopsticks while Gina used a fork, but she would be damned if she would comment on his accomplishment. She couldn't imagine when or how he had mastered using them, but here again was an example of Larry being cool and cosmopolitan while she was the country cousin. While they ate she showed him the list she had made -- Wong Tai Sin temple, Hong Kong Park, Stanley Market, Victoria Peak, the giant Buddha on Lantau Island, the Tai-O fishing village -- and he showed her the printout of suggestions he had gotten from the tour company, which included everything except the fishing village.

The guide arrived with a driver he introduced as Daniel in a black Mercedes promptly at 1:00. The guide spoke British English as well as Cantonese and introduced himself as Jiang.

"We have a very good program for you this afternoon," he said to Gina when Larry introduced her, "and I've got ideas for the other days, as well."

"One of the things my sister especially wants to see is the Tai-O fishing village," Larry said as they settled into the back seat of the car. And then, because he knew without looking at her that she would interpret his comment as somehow putting the blame for changing the plans on her or making her seem unreasonable, he added, "We both do."

"I'd like to see a real Chinese junk, too," Gina said, and Larry added, "Yeah, me, too."

Their first stop was Victoria Peak, where they took the funicular past luxury homes to the top and stepped out onto a viewing area that allowed them to see all of the city from its top. Jiang pointed out the convention center, the Bank of China tower designed by I. M. Pei, and a tall round building with a swimming pool on its roof.

"The business in that building wasn't going well," Jiang explained, "so they brought in a geomancer who said it looked too much like a cigarette. They put a swimming pool on top to put out the fire. I don't think anyone actually swims there, though. Chinese call this practice feng shui. I think you have it in America, too, yes?"

"Yes," Gina said, smiling now at the memory of the crystal that hung in the doorway between her mother's bedroom and bathroom so that her energy wouldn't be sucked down the drains of the tub or the sink or flushed away through the toilet. Late afternoons the sun came through the western window and shattered pieces of light across the floor, ceiling, and walls. "Our mother came here a couple of years ago to do some work, and now she practices it in her home."

"They say it brings good luck," Jiang said, shrugging his shoulders as if to say you couldn't prove it by him. "Would you like for me to show you more examples later?"

Larry looked at Gina, whose eyes had come to life with interest in what Jiang was saying. He couldn't have cared less about feng shui. It sounded like so much silly superstition to him, but neither did he want to be saddled for five days with someone who was spoiled and petulant, who took offense and found fault in everything he said. He could afford to cave on his own interests if something, anything, would make Gina smile.

They took the funicular back down and climbed once again into the Mercedes. For the next hour they drove through the city streets while Jiang pointed out famous buildings and statues and hotels. Picking up on Gina's interest in feng shui, he asked Daniel to make a stop at the Hong Kong and Shanghai Bank so he could point out the bronze lion statues that stood outside the front door to guard the building.

"The Japanese took them away during World War II to melt them down for bullets, and the bank had some troubles," Jiang said. "But then the bomb fell on Hiroshima and the war ended. After the war the lions were found again. The Japanese hadn't melted them, after all, and when they were returned, the bank prospered again." He pointed now to the Pei building. "These two banks compete," he told them. "The sharp corners of the Bank of China are said to cut into the Hong Kong and Shanghai building, but look at its roof."

A crane perched atop the roof was idle but appeared ready to lift something heavy.

"When they put a crane up there to do some work, they realized it looked like a canon firing at the Pei building, so they left it."

"You've got to be kidding," Larry said. In this city of rich, sophisticated people, this hub of international banking and technology, people actually believed that something that looked like a canon -- not even a real one -- could protect one building from another whose sharp corners threatened to cut into it? He couldn't believe that his mother bought into this stuff and that now Gina was asking questions and saying yes when Jiang asked if they wanted to see more examples of this silliness.

"No, I'm not," Jiang said now, seeming a little offended although he prefaced every story he told them with the caveat that he didn't necessarily believe in it. "Some companies put mirrors up to reflect bad energy away. People do that in their homes, too, if they have problems with their neighbors."

Back in the car they drove past cemeteries where the graves were auspiciously positioned on hillsides with good views of the water and to an apartment building that had one whole section missing so that the mythical dragon rumored to live in the hillside behind it could make its way to the water for a drink and thus not become angry and hurt the people in its path. By the time the tour was over, Larry was the one bunched into a corner of the backseat with his arms folded and a scowl on his face.

"Here's my suggestion," Jiang said, overly cheerfully, obviously sensing that Larry hadn't fully enjoyed the afternoon. He looked at his watch. "It's nearly six o'clock. Why don't we drop you here? You can find a good restaurant for dinner and then walk through the night markets. After that take the Star Ferry back to the Kowloon side. The ferry terminal is very near your hotel. You can walk from there."

Larry gave Gina a questioning look. He wouldn't make the mistake of consenting to anything without her input again.

"You look tired," he said.

"Of course I'm tired. I didn't sleep the night away in business class. But I also don't want to waste a whole evening of our time here. A walk sounds nice, and we don't have to make it a late night."

Larry paid Jiang and handed Daniel a sizable tip through the window.

"Now, about tomorrow ..." Jiang began brightly.

"You've given us a great overview," Larry said, "but from now on we won't be needing a guide." And then, looking at Gina for her approval, "I think we'd like to explore on our own."

They ate dinner in a Chinese cafe where they could sit outside and watch as darkness fell and the neon-lit street around them took on a different personality from what they had seen all afternoon. The men in black suits talking on cell phones and women carrying briefcases, their high heels digging determinedly into the pavement, gave way to a younger crowd of girls in shiny dresses and bright red lipstick, boys in black pants and T-shirts and sneakers, their expressions impassive, earbuds blocking out the noise around them.

When Gina and Larry had finished eating, they joined the throng that was moving in the direction of the ferry terminal. Back on the Kowloon side, they walked past their hotel and up Nathan Road in search of the night market Jiang had mentioned. The streets, which had been filled with traffic when Daniel had driven down them earlier in the day, were now blocked off and filled with stalls whose proprietors hawked every variety of trinket. The high, tinny sound of Chinese music pumped into the crowd from a portable CD player, turned up as loud as it would go, on a table in one of the booths. A trestle table just outside it was filled with what were obviously pirated movies and music CDs. The smells of fried fish and roasted chicken lay on the smoke that clouded the air. Gina stopped to look at a rack of knockoff designer handbags and then moved on to where a young woman with a long black braid sat on the corner of a blanket that was loaded with brass Buddha figures of all sizes, chopsticks made of plastic and ebony, and live birds in bamboo cages. She knelt to pick up a small Buddha and examine it.

"I've got to get some things to take home to Steve and the girls while I'm here," she said to Larry, who had stopped next to her. She stood again to show him the statue. "I think Stephanie might like something like this. It's exotic. I'm sure she's never seen anything like it."

"Don't shop here," he said under his breath. "This stuff is all junk. I talked to the concierge at the hotel, and he gave me the card of a store that carries quality stuff. He said they have porcelain bowls, carpets, brass figures -- just about anything you'd want -- and they ship so you don't have to worry about hauling it home and going through customs with it."

"You still don't get it, do you, Larry?" she said, shaking her head to underscore her disbelief while she opened her purse and took out her wallet to pay for the Buddha. "I lost my home." She said these words slowly, stretching them out for emphasis, and then she looked Larry squarely in the face and said them again. "Lost. My. Home."

CHAPTER SEVEN

When the ferry tied up at Lantau Island, they realized they'd probably made a mistake by coming in the morning. At 10:00 the fog still lay thick and heavy over the boats moored at the landing and the nearby shops and houses, rendering photographs impossible. The giant Buddha -- the biggest in the world, according to the guidebook -- that Gina had placed at the top of her list of things to see disappeared in the mist and was almost completely invisible. Nonetheless, they climbed the stairs up to its base and took some close-up photos of the smaller statues that encircled it. Then they asked a monk who was tending to nearby plants to take a picture of them together to put into the scrapbook they would make when all of the other assignments had been fulfilled. Their too-wide smiles spoke embarrassingly of their discomfort at standing so close to one another, and the truth was that they could have been on the beach near Larry's house or in the pasture behind Gina's for all the story the murky prints would tell.

"We'll take more when the sun comes out. This won't be the only chance," Larry said, and Gina nodded her head, smiled briefly, and said, "Sure."

When the aroma of food being cooked by the monks began to mingle with the vapors, they decided to have an early lunch at the monastery and then move on to the fishing village.

"Sure you don't mind vegetarian?" Larry asked her as he set his tray down across from hers on the long communal table and lifted first one long leg and then the other over the bench beside it.

"No, of course not. I love vegetables and rice, and this is a curry, which I also love."

"I thought maybe, with living on a farm and all, you had become a big meat eater."

"I do eat meat, but I also eat a lot of other things. I'm not just one big walking cliché, Larry. I do more with my life than shoo the chickens with my apron and slop the hogs."

"You have chickens and pigs?"

"Jesus, Larry, I was being sarcastic. We -- well, the farm -- has a few chickens for eggs and about thirty head of cattle -- Herefords. What I'm saying is that just because I live on a farm in the Midwest doesn't mean I'm a yokel. I do have a college education, you know."

"Oh, yes, big sister. I do know." Now he was the one with the edge of resentment in his voice. "You're the brainy engineer, and I'm the community college dropout."

"Can you just for one moment get over yourself?" she said, smacking her spoon down so hard in her bowl that grains of rice flew up in a shower and rained down on her tray. It was not the first time he had made biting remarks about her degree. "Who's got the big-deal job and the fancy house in Malibu and the studio driver who drops him off at the airport? Who can upgrade to business class and hire private tour guides and ship expensive porcelain bowls thousands of miles without even giving it a thought? Let me tell you, it's not this college-educated engineer."

"But that's your choice. You're not working right now because of your kids, right?"

"That's why I'm not working in my field, yes. I do have to work, though. I help Steve out at the store."

Again the elephant in the room reared on its hind legs between them and roared. The unasked questions and withheld explanations lay suspended between them so palpably that Gina almost felt she could touch them.

Suddenly she was glad for the fog that still swirled around them, glad for the mist that seemed to wrap their words in white, filmy cotton and muffle them so that their sharp edges couldn't cut so deeply. Larry obviously felt it, too, because instead of looking away nervously or changing the subject he asked the question they'd been tiptoeing around since their first meeting in Dennis MacDonald's office. Yesterday, in the glare of the bright sun and grit of the city, the crush of crowds on sidewalks so dense that it moved them along in whatever direction it was going, neither of them would have said these things. But today, in this obliterating, confessional murk, it was possible.

"Tell me what happened, Gina," he said softly, invitingly. "I know it had something to do with farm subsidies and a drought and the bank, but I obviously don't know the whole story."

"I'll answer your questions if you'll tell me why you wouldn't help us," she said, glad he had finally addressed the subject but consciously having to work -- in vain, as it turned out -- to keep her lip and chin from quivering, her voice steady even as she felt it beginning to crack. She was as determined not to cry as she was not to let the ripple of caustic anger that lay permanently just below the surface of everything she said to him bubble up and corrode the fragile relationship they were beginning to rekindle. This was the conversation she'd been waiting with dread and longing to have with him, the conversation that would determine their future with one another, and she couldn't think of a better setting than here in this quiet, sacred place with the sun just beginning to burn through the fog as if finally to shed light onto a subject that had been off-limits, alluded to with hostility and then shoved back into the dark for too long.

"Deal," he said. "You first."

"I don't know where to start," she said. "There were just lots of things that went wrong all at the same time."

The subject that lurked behind her consciousness, the guilt that she suffered daily -- had it been the right decision or not? -- the words that ran through her brain like a gerbil on a wheel when she was helping customers at the store, driving in her car to take the girls to the dentist's office, trying to fall asleep at night, now abandoned her. They chipped at her constantly, like handfuls of pebbles, leaving tiny dents and wounds that one by one weren't significant but taken as a whole, day after day, year in, year out, were exhausting and finally devastating. But she hadn't ever thought about how she'd organize them if a chance to talk to Larry arose. She had always assumed it wouldn't.

"The biggest issue," she said finally, "was that Steve's parents were having money problems, too."

"But what would that have to do with you?" Larry interrupted. "I thought they gave the land to Steve for college graduation." He pointed his chopsticks at her, as if to use them to poke holes in what she had to say.

"Well, yes, they did, but what they gave him was permission to build on land that was still mortgaged. They didn't ever give him a deed or anything like that. They just told him he could build there and they'd keep up the payments to the bank for the whole farm. Then, eventually, when it was all paid for, they'd give him the deed for his 40 acres."

"So he went ahead and built on land that wasn't really his or his parents'?"

Gina fought the urge to snap at him. Why couldn't he just for once shut up and listen to her?

"Sure. Why not? That's the way it usually happens. Back then their credit was good, and they were making a living by farming. Steve didn't have any trouble getting the building permit."

"What about his brothers? Did their parents offer them land to build on, too?"

"Yes, but nobody had yet. Warren is the only one older than Steve, and he and Cindy wanted to live in town. He teaches at the high school and didn't have any interest in farming. The other boys did, but it never happened."

"So why were the parents -- I can't remember their names -- having problems?"

"Sid and Maryanne. And as I said, there were lots of issues. Farmers all across the Midwest were in trouble. Some of them were so desperate they even committed suicide. Steve and I actually worried about Sid. The farm had been his whole life, but he's also a big family guy. He wouldn't have done something like that to Maryanne and the boys."

"And these issues were …?"

"Government subsidies dried up. We couldn't kid ourselves that selling the actual corn and soybeans was paying the bills. And then, as if on cue, in came a big corporation with an offer to buy up everything for miles around. We didn't have a chance against them. Once they come in, they can mass-produce everything -- irrigation, machinery, seeds -- and sell for less. Everybody around us was selling to get out from under their debts. We were the last holdouts, but even working together, Sid and Steve couldn't make enough money to keep up the payments. Maryanne got a job working in the cafeteria at the school where Warren teaches, but you can imagine what that pays. She didn't have anything more than a high school diploma, and she'd stayed at home to raise her kids, so she hadn't put together a resume for twenty years."

"So that left you," Larry said. He seemed determined to shift the responsibility for their loss from his shoulders to hers, but she wouldn't let him.

"And you," she said, softly, almost inaudibly, but looking him straight in the eyes.

"OK, here's where I always get lost."

"Always?" she said, cocking her head to one side and arching an eyebrow in disbelief. "Like this actually comes up?"

"Yes, always. You may not believe me, but I've thought about this a lot since it happened. I feel awful about it."

Not awful enough to actually help, she thought, although she didn't say it. Instead, she said, "What part don't you understand?"

"Not to sound cold and insensitive, but wasn't it Sid's problem more than yours and Steve's?"

"Well, sure. His name was on the mortgage papers, but we lived on the same land and worked it as a family. If he lost, we lost."

"But here's what I still don't get, and don't get mad, Sis. I'm just trying to understand. You do have a college degree, and you were making good money when you worked in Indianapolis, right?"

"As good as an engineer right out of college can make working for a housing developer in the Midwest, yes."

"So it seems to me that you were the one person in the family who had the potential to make the big bucks, and yet you weren't willing to do it. So, correct me if I'm wrong, it seems like the one you should be mad at is yourself."

"You think I'm not? Do you really think that doesn't eat at me every day?" her cheeks were pink with temper, even though she kept her voice down. The tables had filled with other people having lunch who wouldn't want to listen in as they aired this pile of dirty family laundry.

"So why didn't you do it? You must have known then that you were the one who had the solution."

"Part, Larry. I had part of the solution. You've got to realize that we're talking about a lot of money here. And it wasn't just the bank getting ready to foreclose. There was machinery -- we'd already had a tractor repossessed -- and there were bills for seeds and fertilizer, and Sid and Maryanne's roof needed to be replaced. It was overwhelming. So yes, I went back to my company in Indianapolis and inquired about getting a job. They actually had one and would have been happy to have me back, but it wouldn't pay enough to cover everything that needed to be covered."

"Your in-laws didn't expect you to cover their debts, too, did they?"

"No, bless their hearts, they were willing to carve off just our 40 acres if we could find a way to make the payments, but for Steve and me it was all or nothing. Either we found a way to save his parents' investment and their home, or we went, too."

"That was noble of you," Larry said, and she could hear in the edge to his voice that by "noble" he meant "stupid."

"It wasn't just about that, Larry. It had more to do with simple economics. Steve and his dad farmed together, and the whole farm was 600 acres. We couldn't have lasted against the corporation very long with just 40, even if we could have paid the bills."

"So what you were asking me for was money to pay for people I barely knew -- had only met once and couldn't remember the names of?"

"They're my family, Larry. Yes, I was asking you to help save me and my family. In the few months I had to work with I could have made about half of what it would have taken to make us productive again."

"Productive?" Larry interrupted again. "Didn't you just say that the government subsidies were gone and you couldn't make it work?"

"We had a plan. We were going to turn the farm into a stable where we could give lessons and people could board their horses. There's no place around Bedford that does that, but there are people who have horses and would like to get out from under the expense of maintaining them themselves. There are also people from Chicago and Indianapolis and Louisville who have homes in the country that they come to on weekends, and they could have horses for their kids and grandchildren without having to worry about maintaining them when they're not here. We did a feasibility study and wrote a business plan to show the bank if we could get everything else worked out. We could have done it if you had lent us the money. It would have meant either a killer commute for me or getting someplace in the city to stay, both of which would also have added to the expenses. And it would have meant leaving my girls. They were just little things then, and that would have killed me, but Maryanne was willing to take care of them while I was away and I was willing to do it if it meant saving all of our livelihoods. But then you said no, and after that there was no point in my going back to work. I would have made part of the money we needed, but there was no hope of getting it all in time."

She felt herself beginning to tear up, so she took a long drink of water and looked off into the trees while she waited for the urge to cry to subside.

"You didn't tell me all of this then. You just said you needed the money."

"I had this weird expectation that you might call me and we'd talk about it, but you didn't. You just wrote a letter saying the money was tied up and unavailable, whatever that meant. It was like a goddamn form letter." She had memorized the exact wording of his short letter without meaning to, had read it over and over in disbelief before collapsing at the kitchen table and sobbing with the realization that her life was about to change in ways she would have given anything to prevent. She angrily fought the tears she felt coming again now. "If I had explained all the circumstances, would your money have magically become available? I don't think so."

"You never wrote back at all after that. You even stopped sending Christmas cards." He didn't mention that the fudge to which he looked forward every December also stopped arriving.

"It wasn't just the money, Larry. The truth is that a small ugly part of me was almost relieved because once I knew the situation was hopeless, there was no point in leaving my family. I had done everything I could -- contacted my old boss and my rich brother -- and I still couldn't make it work out. But I got big points from Steve's family. They thought I was some kind of saint. What bugged me was how little you seemed to care. Can you imagine how hard it was to ask my little brother for money? I knew you'd think that with my education I should be able to help support my family. Writing that letter to you almost killed me, and it was even worse on Steve. He didn't want me to do it at first, but you were our only hope. I finally convinced him to let me write to you, but his pride was destroyed." When Larry didn't speak, she went on. "A phone call would have been nice. A 'Hey, Sis, what's happening out there?' Or 'Hey, Sis, is there anything else I could do to help?' Or 'Hey, Sis, I can't help, but I'm sorry you're in this bad spot and I'm thinking about you.'"

"But you're OK now, aren't you? I mean, you still live on a farm, right? And you have the store in town. It sounds like you came out of it all right."

She shook her head and smiled sadly at his cluelessness.

"I guess it depends on how you define 'all right.' Yes, we have a roof over our heads, and Steve has a job."

"But the store has your name on it."

"We're part owners. The other partner is silent. He's a banker in town whose business partner in the store had died. He had adult children, but they weren't interested in running the store. He got interested in us when we were trying to sort everything out and helped us get started, but he's not involved in the day-to-day operation. When the farm was sold Sid made sure that we took the amount our 40 acres would have brought in the deal. That helped, too, but most of the money came from George Ferguson, the banker. He wanted Steve's name on it because Steve is the farmer. He knows everybody around here, and people trust him. The store had been there for a long time, but the previous owner had died, and his children lived out of state and weren't much interested, so it wasn't very successful. We've done better, but with farming changing and the big companies doing a lot of it and buying their seeds and equipment from big suppliers and big-box stores taking over, I don't know how long that's going to last. There's already a big home-improvement store going up on the outskirts of town."

"But you're living on a farm still, right?"

"We are tenant farmers, Larry," she said through gritted teeth. "Do you have any idea what that means to a man whose family has been in farming his whole life?"

"I'm not sure I know what it means, period."

"Remember I mentioned the wealthy city families who keep farms where they can go for weekends? That's where we live. The farm is just 50 acres, but there are two houses on it -- a big, beautiful one with five bedrooms and a state-of-the-art kitchen, and a two-bedroom cottage where the caretaker lives. I'll let you guess which one we live in. It's a small enough operation that Steve can handle the day-to-day chores and still manage the store. In return, we live there rent-free. We also get eggs and milk, and when we butcher, we get a freezer full of meat. The owner is a software manufacturer who grew up not far from Bedford and is just a few years older than we are. He and his wife entertain quite a bit when they come down from Chicago, and when they do they often hire me to help cook and serve. When I do that they pay me a little extra."

Larry closed his eyes and rubbed the bridge of his nose with both of his hands. He thought about the parties he and Marqueeta had hosted, about Lupe weaving through the living room carrying a silver tray loaded with tiny bundles of chicken and disks of bruschetta and offering them to pretentious guests who were too immersed in hearing themselves talk to even look at her as they plucked off one of the morsels or waved her away with an impatient "Not now."

"I told you the truth," he said finally. "My money was -- is -- tied up. It was all invested, and there would have been huge penalties involved if I had cashed out before the maturity dates. And some of my money is in real estate -- a couple of rental properties near the campus in Santa Barbara. I don't sit around with piles of money stacked up on my desk as you seem to think. And I have my own obligations, you know. I also have a mortgage and a son who goes to a private preschool and will someday go to college. And Marqueeta has issues that have to be addressed, and that involves medical bills and extra help around the house."

"Issues?"

Now that he had brought it up, she felt more comfortable asking, but he brushed away her question with a flip of his hand as if he were shooing away an insect -- or a server with a tray full of appetizers in which he had no interest.

"I don't want to get into that now. We've got enough other stuff to talk about. If we're going to do these assignments, you'll be spending time with her at some point and she can tell you about herself. You may think I'm a scoundrel, but at least I don't gossip about my wife behind her back."

"Sorr-ee" she said. "You're the one who brought it up. I would never have pried into your personal life."

She put emphasis on the words "personal life," emphasizing the fact that her having just deposited her most personal problems and secrets in her brother's lap still didn't earn her a place in his inner circle. The dig landed squarely on its target, but Larry chose to ignore it.

"Why didn't you ask Mom for money?"

"Oh, my God. Steve would never have allowed that. And besides, all that happened before she'd become well-known and made her money. It's ironic, isn't it, that now she turns out to be the one who does actually have the money and wants to give me some, but I still have to go through you to get it. I so wish it didn't matter, that I could tell her I don't want her money and drop out of this ridiculous little program altogether."

"You know, you could have picked up the phone and called me, too. Last I checked the telephone signals worked in both directions."

"Right, and beg some more? No, thank you. It was all I could do to write that letter, and when I took it out to the mailbox, I stood there for about fifteen minutes, putting it in, taking it out again, trying to make up my mind whether to put up the flag to have it taken away." She looked off in the distance, her jaw set, and shook her head in frustration. "Look, you're right," she said finally. "We are OK. We make a living, and we're healthy, and we have each other and our beautiful girls. That's all anybody needs. Neither one of us is really about owning a bunch of stuff."

Now the Malibu house and the business-class ticket, the expensive clothes and porcelain bowls and household help lay between them, as surely as if they had materialized on this remote Chinese hillside.

"Let's get out of here and go to the fishing village," Larry said.

She was glad to go. The lunch crowd had picked up, and people waiting for seats were hovering near their table, politely nodding at their half-eaten plates. And besides, the moment had passed. They had eaten lunch without tasting it and spent the whole time talking about something that was just as cloudy and obscure now as it had been before they began.

They spent the afternoon meandering through the narrow streets of Tai-O, each determined to maintain the fiction that they had come here by choice, that they were ordinary tourists who had come over from Hong Kong for the day, that the person they were with wasn't the last person on Earth they would have chosen as a companion. By now the sun was blazing overhead and the temperature had risen so that Gina took off the bright red sweater she'd been wearing earlier and tied it around her waist.

The houses built on stilts over the tidal flats were just as they had appeared in the photographs she'd seen in the guidebook. Rickety steps led down to faded yellow and blue rowboats that sat on wet sand now but would rise with the tide when it came in later. Bent and rusted television antennas still sprouted from some of the roofs. Laundry fluttered from flimsy rails around the make-shift decks of others.

For lack of conversation, Gina pulled the guidebook out of her purse and began quoting from it to fill in the awkward silences as they walked.

"This village has been here for more than 500 years," she read. "Some of the same families have been here that whole time. They're the descendants of the people who first settled Hong Kong."

"It looks like some of the houses have been here the whole time, too," Larry cracked, his own attempt at humor in the hope of salvaging the afternoon, but Gina ignored him and remained unsmiling. People making the best of their lives in shabby homes didn't seem like a laughing matter to her, but she didn't want to re-open the conversation that had gone so badly up at the monastery. Let him go through life thinking everybody lived in a mansion at Malibu, that a caretaker's cottage was the house of her dreams. What did she care?

In the center of the village the smell of fish mingled with the incense that wafted from a red-tile-roofed temple and makeshift altars along the uneven sidewalk. A woman wearing a woven straw sun hat sat among a cluster of clear plastic tubs filled with live fish that swam and flopped in the water. In open stalls, dried fish hung from the ceiling and waited in plastic bags for the customers who would take them home for dinner. On side streets the clatter of mah-jongg tiles permeated people's conversations and the music that drifted out of homes and shops whose doors were propped open to create a breeze and alleviate the heat inside.

"I'm ready to go back whenever you are," Gina said abruptly. They had walked the length of the village, and the ferry landing was in view.

Larry splayed his hands in the air.

"Whatever you want. You're the one who wanted to come here. I'm just along for the ride."

"You know, if there was something you'd rather be doing, you didn't have to come out here with me. We're not joined at the hip, you know."

"That's not what I meant, Gina, and you know it. Stop looking for ways to be offended and trying to make an argument out of everything I say. All I meant was that I'm willing to go back whenever you want. If you want to stay longer, that's fine, too, and if you want to go back now, I'm ready. That's all."

On the ferry back to Hong Kong Larry walked around the deck and had a cup of coffee at the snack bar while Gina sat inside the cabin and flipped again through the guidebook. Once the ferry was tied up, they walked down the gangplank together but silently, and at the door to the hotel Gina said, "You know, Larry, I think I'm just going to have dinner sent to my room and stay in for the evening. It's been a big day, and I think maybe I'm a little jet-lagged. Tomorrow will be better."

"Like you said, we're not joined at the hip. That's fine with me. I'll probably have a little something to eat and then go out to see if ..."

And then they heard their mother's shriek of pleasure.

"There you are! My darlings!" Anita rushed toward them, the silk tail of her long red tunic waving behind her black pants, her finger marking the page of the book she had been reading while she waited for them.

"Mom?" Gina said. For a moment, out of context, she almost hadn't recognized her own mother. "This is sure a surprise."

Anita laughed and hugged them both at once, so happy to see them and full of delight at surprising them that she didn't notice they were partially blocking the entrance and a bellman with a trolley filled with suitcases was politely waiting to get around them. Larry steered them away from the door, and Anita led them back to the sofa where she had been reading and where her backpack and some shopping bags still waited for her.

"What are you doing here, Mom?" Larry asked as they walked.

Anita sat down and patted the cushions on either side of her for Gina and Larry to sit down.

"What do you think I'm doing? I came to see the two of you."

"Dennis MacDonald told us you were working in Thailand," Gina said.

"I was until about a month ago. I'm in Shanghai now, and I'll be there for two more weeks. I couldn't believe it when I found out you'd picked Hong Kong for your foreign adventure, and the timing was perfect. Of course I had to come. It also gave me a chance to visit my friend, Mr. Wu. He's putting me up in his guesthouse overnight. My English publisher still keeps an office here from before the handover, so I'll have a meeting with his people in the morning and fly back tomorrow afternoon. Now, tell me everything. Isn't this the most fabulous city in the world? Are you having an absolute ball? Tell me everything you've done so far, everything."

She looked from Gina's scowl to Larry's eyebrows, arched in resignation, and then her expectant smile faded.

"Oh, dear," she said. "What's happened? What's wrong?"

"Everything's fine, Mom, really ..." Larry began.

"You're right. It is a wonderful city, and ..." Gina said.

They had both started talking at once and too fast, neither of them wanting to hurt their mother's feelings, neither willing to take on the burden of responsibility for the trip's not working out exactly as she would have wanted, to tell her that her idea had been a waste of their time and her money.

"I hear a giant 'but' in both of your voices," Anita said, again turning her head to look from one to the other.

"I know you came up with this idea with the best of intentions," Larry said, "but you have to admit your plan has some flaws. Gina and I aren't little kids anymore. You can't send us off on a scavenger hunt and expect to make us best friends. And the whole idea of tying the outcome to money is, well, I don't know how else to say it, blackmail."

"Ah, but I never mentioned anything about the outcome," she said, raising a finger in the air to make her point. "All I ask is that you do the assignments. You may very well still be squabbling and bickering like toddlers when they're all done. That's not the point."

"We're very different people, Mom," Gina chimed in. This was at least one subject on which they all could agree. "We haven't lived in the same city for years. We don't really know each other's families. We hadn't even seen each other since Larry's wedding seven years ago. We're fine, but we're never going to be six and ten again. You've just got to accept that we are who we are, who you brought us up to be."

"I didn't bring either of you up to cut your sibling out of your life," Anita said softly. She avoided looking at either one of them by focusing on a gold and celadon porcelain ring she twisted around one of her fingers. "You know how important that is to me. Each of you has something so precious, and you can't see it for … I don't know what. The forest for the trees. I'll never understand it."

How many times had they heard this speech when they were children, sometimes even punctuated with Anita's very genuine tears. From the separate rooms where they had been sent in punishment for fighting or treating one another badly they each thought she had been the lucky one. She'd never had to share her toys or her space or her parents' affection, never been embarrassed by a lame sibling's obnoxious behavior.

When Gina had written the letter asking Larry for money, she had asked him not to share her problems with their mother. "It's difficult enough to come with my hat in hand to you, and Mom has enough to contend with now that Jay is gone," she had written to her brother. "Please keep this letter just between us." She certainly wasn't going to bring it up now just to explain why she and Larry were at odds.

Anita stood up and gathered a lightweight black shawl around her shoulders.

"I've made reservations for us at my favorite Hunan restaurant over in Central," she said, choosing to ignore their previous conversation as if it had never happened. "In the United States you typically get Szechwan or Cantonese or Mandarin. I think Hunan cuisine is a great change. Let's go have a nice dinner and catch up. I'm only here for this one night."

CHAPTER EIGHT

Dinner was over, and the previously crowded restaurant had begun to clear out. The din of clattering china and conversation was subsiding, the chairs pushed into the tables that had already been set with fresh white linen and clean dishes in anticipation of tomorrow's lunchtime buffet. A plate of virtually untouched almond cookies sat in the middle of their table, and they were sipping green tea poured into red mosaic porcelain cups from a pot that had just been refreshed for the third time. The evening had been easier than any of them had thought it would be. Watching her mother and Larry gracefully handling their food with chopsticks, Gina had decided to try, and after a few false starts easily picked up bits of meat and vegetables, although the rice rolled back onto the plate with frustrating regularity that eventually drove her back to her fork.

"If I had to eat with these all the time, I wouldn't have a weight problem," she said.

She laughed, but being in a city where most of the people were slim and then seeing her trim mother had made her self-conscious about her size. When she got home, she promised herself, she'd get serious about a diet. Since Danielle had been born she had excused the extra pounds to herself as post-baby fat, but now that the baby was nine, it sounded ridiculous -- even to her.

Anita was full of stories about her work -- the statues of Buddha in the homes in Thailand, the jade dragons in Shanghai that she could draw in her sleep, what a gracious host Mr. Wu had been, and the artful way he had framed the paintings she had done of his home and hung them in his foyer. And there were other neutral topics, too. Gina brought out an envelope that contained school pictures of Stephanie and Danielle and felt a stab of homesickness as she laid them out of the table for her mother and brother to see. Since their meeting in Los Angeles, Larry had also added a new studio-quality black-and-white photo of three-year-old Dexter taken at his pricey preschool to his wallet.

"He's your child, but I can see Marqueeta, too," Gina said.

He had his father's spiky dark hair and his mother's glassy light eyes, which Gina recalled were the green of cat's-eye marbles.

There were also a lot of shared childhood memories on which they could draw for topics that didn't seem on the surface as if they would lead to an argument. Seeing Gina's picture of her daughters in swimming suits had reminded Anita of a family vacation to a cabin at Lake Arrowhead in the San Bernardino Mountains when Gina and Larry had been about their ages. The place had obviously won Anita's heart because years later she surprised her children by telling them she and Jay had bought it.

"Wow, there's a trip I'd like to forget!" Gina said. "Talk about the vacation from hell."

"You're kidding, right?" Larry said in disbelief. "That was the best summer ever. Remember that kid from across the lake who used to come over and play with me? What was his name?"

"Bobby," Gina said, remembering him as if she had seen him yesterday and wasn't very happy about it. "Bobby Gonzalez. What a little brat."

"He was not. He taught me how to fish that summer, and I remember that his dad played the guitar. You remember how they'd come over to our side, and we'd make a campfire and roast marshmallows and sing."

"He was a little punk who chased me with every living creature he could find. He put a lizard in my bed one day, and he was always catching worms and that garter snake that he tried to put down my shirt."

"He liked you, Sis," Larry said. "Don't you know by now that's how little boys show their affection?"

"I just remember that I didn't like him."

"Ah, but you did like his older brother, as I recall," Anita said. "What was his name?"

"Rudy," Gina said. The name popped out of her mouth so fast that it startled even her.

"Yes, that's right," Anita said, warming to the memories. "Roberto and Rudolfo. Their father came from Mexico City, but their mother was from San Francisco. They were both good-looking boys. How old were you two then?"

"I was twelve and Larry was eight," Gina said. Rudy had been thirteen.

The recollections were indelible in her mind -- the sweetness of a first kiss behind the cabin while the mothers collected the plates and cups they'd used during the campfire and the fathers folded up the lawn chairs and replaced them under the striped awning that protected the front stoop. Her curling up on the top bunk while Larry snored and farted below. Unable to sleep, she had watched the moon move across the sky through the curtainless window, willing morning to come and with it the hope of seeing Rudy again.

But the next day a new family arrived in a minivan that pulled a boat behind it and moved into the cabin three doors down from the Gonzalezes. For the rest of the week Rudy stayed on his side of the lake. Gina waved to him once when he went past on water skis behind the new family's boat, but either he didn't see her or he pretended not to. A girl with a blond ponytail sat in the back of the boat, turned around in her seat to spot him. Gina could hear her shrieks of laughter even now -- at what? What had been so funny? The night before the Langleys left to go back to San Diego the Gonzalezes came over for one last campfire and brought the other family with them. They were Mr. and Mrs. Wright, and their daughter, their only child, was Karen. Karen Wright. Such an innocent, nondescript name for a girl who had the potential to do so much damage. Gina remembered that she had worn a silver ring with a pink stone in it on her middle finger. It had flashed in the firelight when she had tucked her arm through Rudy's and said, "Feel like taking a walk?" The two of them had gotten up and wandered away from the rest of the group, leaving Gina with the grown-ups while Bobby and Larry chased each other through the dark trees, periodically coming back to the circle to threaten her with insects and snakes, either real or imagined.

"Ah, young love," she heard Rudy's mother say to Mrs. Wright. "I remember my first summer romance, don't you? There's nothing like it ever again."

The next morning Gina awakened to her first period and a crop of zits on her chin, and when she went with her mother to the general store to buy sanitary napkins, Rudy, who was there picking up bait with his father, said, "Hey, kid. What's that on your chin?"

"I remember you were mooning around about him, but he only came over to our place a couple of times," Anita said now.

"He liked that other girl, the blonde. What was her name, Sis? Do you remember?"

"Uh, no," Gina said. Even now she found it too distasteful to say, and anyway, it was embarrassing to so clearly remember so insignificant an event that was now long disappeared into the past. "And I wasn't mooning."

"She was hot, whatever her name was," Larry said. "I was still too young to care about girls, but I remember thinking how pretty she was. That was just a great week."

"It's the Rashomon effect," Gina said.

"The what, honey?" Her mother leaned toward her across the table and turned an ear in her direction as if she hadn't quite heard.

"The Rashomon effect. It describes the role of subjectivity on perception."

"Ah, and out comes Miss College Girl to impress Mom with her vast stores of wisdom," Larry drawled.

"Don't be an idiot," Gina said, glancing at him but still focused on her mother. "It means that for every person who witnesses an event there will be a different story because we all bring our own experiences to bear on whatever happens to us."

"Then why couldn't you just have said that?" The smirk lingered in Larry's voice.

"Because there's a name for it. I figured you were both familiar with it."

"As you'll recall, I didn't finish coll-ege," he drew out the word, taunting her as a playground bully might have, "but how about this? Two weeks ago I had lunch with Cameron Diaz."

"Nobody cares, Larry," Gina snapped. The words came out before she could stop them and were sharper than she had intended.

"Gina!" her mother said, looking at her with the same disapproving expression she had used throughout Gina's childhood, like the day she had been trying to spin one of grandmother's plates on a stick and broken it and when she had tried to dress their snarling cat up in doll clothes with disastrous results.

"He's just trying to one-up me, as he has done every time I've made a positive accomplishment in my whole life. I will not apologize just because I have a better vocabulary than he has. And what does that have to do with movie stars? Larry works at a movie studio in Hollywood. He sees movie stars every day of his life. Big deal."

Anita still refused to let the friction that sparked between brother and sister ruin the one evening she could spend with them.

"It doesn't have to make any sense," she said, smiling now and reaching over the pat Gina's hand. "You two have always been competitive, but I think that's normal. That much I do understand about siblings. Remember the time you picked all of the flowers in the backyard and made a bouquet for me?" She was looking at Larry now, and then she turned to Gina. "And then you went to the house next door and picked all of theirs? Johnson, I think their name was, but they didn't have any children, and they were snippy and kept to themselves. Dad and I ended up buying them some new plants to keep the peace in the neighborhood. We thought it was adorable, but they didn't see the humor."

"I never knew that," Gina said, smiling nostalgically now, a crisis momentarily averted, "but I do remember the bouquet. I could hardly carry it in both of my hands. I knew I shouldn't have done it, but I didn't care. I'd seen how happy Larry's flowers made you, and I wanted to make you that happy, too."

Once again she felt a stab of homesickness, remembering a Mother's Day when Stephanie and Danielle had made breakfast while she and Steve still slept and trailed cereal, toast crumbs, and milk all the way up the stairs to their room in their determination to serve it to her in bed.

"And don't forget the beds!" Anita looked at each of them in pointed mock admonition. They looked at each other and frowned, not remembering. "Gina, you were in high school, and we bought you a new bed, don't you remember?"

"Oh, I remember the bed. I was fifteen when I finally graduated out of the princess canopy bed I'd had since I was seven. But I don't remember any problem about it."

"That's because you didn't know about most of it. Larry, you had a meltdown because you thought she was getting something you weren't getting, so that night, while you spent the night with a friend, a surprise new bed appeared in your bedroom."

"Oh, sure, I remember that," he said now, smiling at the memory. "It was a twin bed with a rocket ship and planets on the spread."

"What neither of you realized was that it was Gina's old princess bed. We took off the canopy and spray-painted the headboard bright blue that night after Gina went to bed, and Dad bought the new bedding at Target the next morning as soon as they opened. He brought home doughnuts as a cover in case either of you wondered why he had gone out so early on a Sunday morning. He stashed it all in the garage until he was sure you hadn't come home yet and Gina was otherwise occupied, and when he found out the coast was clear, we ran upstairs and made up the bed."

She was laughing now at the memory of the fast one she and Jay had put over on the kids, at using her blow dryer to make the paint dry faster and running around the ends of the bed, bumping into each other awkwardly like characters in a flickery old black-and-white movie to get it made before their trick was discovered. Gina laughed, too, but Larry's smile had disappeared.

"So you and Dad tricked me," he said. "That explains why it was a twin. I wanted a double bed, but I didn't say anything when I got home that morning was because you were both so excited about the rocket ship bedspread."

"Oh, Larry, come on," Anita said. "We spoiled you by even doing that much. We shouldn't have rewarded that kind of behavior at all. I hope you know that now that you're a parent. And anyway, you eventually got a bigger bed, too, after Gina went off to college."

"Yeah, I inherited her bed again. She always got new, and I always got hand-me-downs."

"That's just the curse of being a second child," Gina said, more to break the mounting tension than to make a point. She poured the last of the green tea into her cup and reached for a cookie. "You can ask Danielle about that. She'll tell you the same thing. She seldom gets anything that hasn't been Stephanie's first."

"And what about all the musical equipment that came later -- guitars, electronic keyboards, amplifiers?" Anita asked. Was she reminiscing or trying to justify the decisions she and Jay had made? "You weren't exactly mistreated."

"I think in a lot of ways the second kid gets a better deal," Gina chimed in. "I may have gotten insignificant things like a new bed first, but after I was out of the house you were essentially an only child when it came to getting things that really mattered."

"Still." Larry wasn't convinced. "I think it had more to do with the fact that you and Dad were constantly overcompensating her for the fact that her father had left her and then died. Poor, tragic Gina."

"I don't even remember my father," Gina snapped, looking as if she were going to come across the table at him. "I was a baby when he and Mom split up. What I do remember is that you got a car when you were sixteen -- I didn't -- and you got all of the musical equipment you wanted and you got to go to Washington, D.C., on your class trip. I'll trade you a bed for all of that any day. The fact is, you were always Dad's favorite because you were his biological child. I figured that out when Mom told me I wasn't, and it was just something I had to live with. If I had tantrums, I got sent to my room. When you had tantrums, you got what you wanted." Her cheeks were blotched with red and her eyes were steely with anger.

Anita's good humor disappeared as if they had only imagined it, and she covered her face with her hands, a gesture of frustration they both remembered from growing up.

"I think you're right. This was a bad idea," she said after a moment. She uncovered her face and folded her hands on the table in front of her as a diplomat might have at a multinational meeting. "You two don't deserve to have a sibling, and I can't create love where there isn't any."

"Oh, Mom, cut it out," Larry said. Now he was irritated. "Don't be so melodramatic. Of course I love Gina. You don't ever have to worry about that."

"I think what Mom had in mind was that we might actually grow to like each other," Gina said. Her voice had softened since her earlier outburst, but there was still an edge to it.

"Yes, well, both," Anita said. "I have such wonderful memories of the two of you playing together as children. Do you remember the day you cooked up a magic act and scared the wits out of me when I thought you were going to try to saw Gina in half? Or the time the two of you decided to cook dinner for Dad and me and made that ghastly spaghetti out of a box? We ate every bite. You were so cute in your long frilly aprons and serving water out of the wine glasses. I guess I had the fantasy that the two of you could get that back, that you could have fun together again. Mainly I just wanted to reacquaint you with one another. Maybe if you didn't live so far apart, this gulf wouldn't have opened between you. But I shouldn't have tied it to money. That was a mistake. Maybe I'd just read too many books and seen too many movies about people doing things to earn their inheritances. I thought it would be fun for you. But the fact is that I meant to give you the money anyway. I've been so lucky with the way my work has gone in the last few years, and I'd rather have you benefit from it now, while you have young families and need it, than someday in the distant future when you have money of your own. I'm going to start doing that anyway, but you don't have to do anything to earn it. Just forget about my silly assignments, go back home and get on with your lives."

Her voice quavered, and they could tell she was on the verge of tears.

Larry ignored that she had just let them off the hook, and then he let out the same sigh of resignation he'd used a million times as a teenager. "Look, Mom, there's something you need to know that will explain why Gina is so angry with me." He turned to look at his sister. "I'm going to tell her. It's ridiculous that she doesn't know."

"What?" barked Gina. The word rang out like a single report from a pistol, a single staccato note played on a perfectly tuned concert piano. A busboy clearing a nearby table snapped his head around to look at them, startled, as if the word had literally hit him in the back.

"What are you talking about?" Anita asked. Her question was less distilled but no less panicky. "Is something wrong?"

"Larry ..." this time Gina fairly growled in warning.

"No, Gina, if Mom wants us all to be some kind of big happy family, she needs to know what is going on and we need to talk about things out in the open instead of keeping secrets from each other. Mom, Gina and Steve had awful financial problems a few years ago. She asked me for money, but what I had was tied up in investments and my own obligations. I turned her down, and they lost the farm."

"You lost the farm?" Now Anita was the one whose shrill raised voice caused the busboy to look again in their direction and frown. "You told me you and Sid and Maryanne had decided to sell to that big farming conglomerate."

"Nice, Larry. Real nice. I specifically told you I didn't want to bring Mom into this. Steve will die when he finds out she knows. So much for bonding with my brother. I ask you to keep one secret, and you can't even do that." She shook her head at him in anger. "Yes. We did, Mom, I told you the truth about that. What I didn't tell you was that it was forced on us. We didn't choose it. We had hoped to hang on to our 40 acres and open a stable where people could board their horses. Meyercorp offered me my job back, and if I'd taken it and Larry could have lent us some money, we could have done it. But he couldn't because of his money being 'tied up.'" She rolled her eyes and made quotation marks with her fingers in the air so they would both know she still didn't buy the story.

"Why didn't you come to me?" Anita asked, her voice plaintive, filled with grief for her daughter.

"Your work hadn't really taken off at that point, so I thought Larry was my best shot, and besides, Steve didn't want you to know. It's still a sore spot with him. He's an old-fashioned kind of guy. Not being able to support his family is a real mark of shame to him."

"But it sounds like you live in a nice place now."

"We're tenant farmers, Mom. That means Steve got a job managing someone else's farm for him in exchange for rent. The house is tiny, but it's OK. We're doing fine." She glared at her brother while she spoke.

"And you have the store."

"Yes, we are part owners of the store, but there's a big home-improvement store going up that's supposed to open next spring. We won't be able to compete with their prices, and that will be that."

"The point in telling you, Mom, was so that you'd know what this money will mean to Gina. I didn't have any evil ulterior motive." Now he was looking sourly at his sister. He knew there was more to the story but that it wasn't his to tell.

"But you never went back to work."

"I am working. I help Steve at the store and I do occasional freelance projects. But no. I'm not working full-time for an engineering firm, if that's what you mean. I would have done it to save the farm, but when Larry turned me down and Steve and I realized that wasn't going to happen, we decided my time was better spent at home. Going back to my old job would have meant moving back to the city for five days of the week or driving three hours a day. Maryanne was willing to help out with the girls, but I didn't want to be away from them that much. Childhood is short enough as it is. And anyway, with me doing the books and helping out around the store, we were able to do with two less employees, so that helped out there."

"But it hasn't been all that successful, is that what I'm hearing?" said Anita, who had relaxed in her chair but now sprang back up to the table.

"Well, yeah. Think about it, Mom. The small family farm industry has been on the decline for the last decade or more, and the economy hasn't come back like we hoped it would, at least where we live. People just buy what they absolutely have to have. We run ridiculous sales on patio furniture and kitchen faucets, sales that mean we wouldn't make a dime, and still nobody buys. They buy enough feed for their animals and enough plants for their kitchen gardens and enough lumber to add a bedroom when what they really hoped they'd be doing was moving up to a bigger house and maybe more land. And then you've got the big discount stores that have come in and ruined locally owned businesses since we've been there."

"What would you do if ...?" Anita asked, realizing she didn't even know the right question to ask and stunned over how out of touch with her daughter's life she had become. There was a price to pay for the new life she'd made for herself, for trotting around the globe doing exactly as she pleased. She'd change that when this project was finished.

Gina shrugged her shoulders.

"We still have the dream of buying some land of our own and opening a stable. The girls love horses, and it's something we could all do together. As they get older, they could give riding lessons and help take care of the animals."

"I can help this time," Anita said, animated with purpose. "I'll call my accountant tomorrow and have money wired to your bank."

"Mom, please," Gina said. She was suddenly exhausted and just wanted this conversation to be over and this evening to end. "If you want to give us some money because you're giving some to Larry, fine. I gratefully accept. I'm not too proud to take something that would give my family a boost. But let's not borrow trouble. I promise if the store goes under, you'll be the first person I'll call. And now, I'm calling it a night."

She stood up abruptly, retrieved her handbag from where it had been hanging across the back of her chair and slung it over her shoulder.

"Wait a minute," Larry said. "I think we're all ready to go. We might as well go back together."

"I don't think so, Larry," Gina said. She moved around the table to embrace her mother. "You stay here and see Mom back to Mr. Wu's house. I'm going to grab a cab back to the ferry landing and turn in. Mom, thank you for dinner. Thank you for this trip. Thank you for the money, and thank you for what you tried to do. I just think … well, never mind what I think. It's wonderful to see you, and when your project is over I hope you'll come out to Bedford so we can have a good visit. The girls miss you."

"So, OK, what about tomorrow?" Larry asked. He stood quickly and grabbed her arm."Do you want to meet for breakfast? We haven't really made any plans."

"You know, Larry, I think I'd like a day on my own." She narrowed her eyes and tightened her mouth, as if she were thinking hard about this decision. "I need to shop for some souvenirs to take home for Steve and the kids, and there are a couple of other things I'd like to do that probably wouldn't interest you. Why don't we just plan to meet up for dinner somewhere."

She turned without waiting for his answer and walked through the restaurant and out onto the sidewalk, hot and crowded even this late in the evening. She moved quickly, as if he had actually moved to follow her and she were afraid he might catch up.

The weather the next day was an exact copy of the one before it. When Larry got up for his early morning run, the harbor was still shrouded in fog. Gina, eating a breakfast she'd had sent up by room service for fear she'd run into her brother in the coffee shop, watched the sun break through the mist out her not-so-scenic window.

Later, figuring that however Larry had decided to spend the day, he would already be doing it, she ferried back to Central Hong Kong and took a cab to Stanley and spent the rest of the day poking through the shops and stalls in the market. She had Steve's name done in Chinese by a calligrapher and found a doll in a red silk dress for Danielle. Then she came across a shop filled with colorful silk clothing and settled on a pair of aqua silk pajamas for Stephanie. Wouldn't that be all right? Or would Danielle wish she had pajamas and Stephanie a doll? Wasn't Stephanie too old for dolls? Did girls ever get too old for dolls? Would this someday come up in a dinner conversation when they were grown-up and estranged, Stephanie living in one part of the world and Danielle in another. Would they get together only occasionally, maybe every few years and only then because their mother expected it, plotted it, and would what they said to one another be laced with sarcasm, barbed with anger and disappointment? Would they be so out of sync with one another's lives that they would have to struggle to come up with something to talk about? Would they look at pictures of each other's families and milk them for substance until they had analyzed every centimeter, discussed clothing and haircuts and relative size until all they could do was put them back into their wallets in stunned, awkward silence?

"This is crazy," she said aloud to no one. Nevertheless, she bought a second pair of pajamas, these in gold, and retraced her steps to the toy shop, where she bought a doll identical to the one she had purchased from the same saleswoman an hour earlier, except that this one's dress was bright blue. Then she sat down at an outdoor cafe and had a cup of tea before she cabbed back to the hotel.

As she expected, the message light on her telephone was blinking.

"It's Lar," the voice said, chipper, as if nothing untoward had happened at dinner last night. "Looking forward to dinner and hearing about your day. Call me."

What she wanted was a bubble bath and a bowl of noodles. If the game was over and the money their mother was going to give them no longer attached to the assignments, why bother with the charade of spending time together the last two days? They didn't have anything in common, couldn't possibly be interested in seeing the same things. The trip to Lantau Island and the monastery and the fishing village had obviously been an indulgence for Larry when what he would rather have been doing was ... . She had no idea. She tossed her shopping bags onto the bed, and one of the dolls rolled out onto the duvet, its red silk dress a glittery slash on the landscape of pristine white. She sat down on the edge of the bed, picked up the doll and studied it for several minutes. Its smiling Chinese face and straight black hair somehow conjured up the peachy, freckled faces of Stephanie and Danielle. Then she sighed, poked the doll back into the bag and punched the number of Larry's room into the telephone.

Larry was seated at the bar, nursing what looked like a Manhattan, when she walked into the restaurant. He was watching for her and waved his arm to get her attention when she appeared.

"Our table will be ready in about ten minutes," he said, and he stood up to give her his seat, both of the adjacent stools already having been taken. She shook her head.

"I'm good," she said. "Go ahead and sit down."

But he didn't, so now both of them stood awkwardly by one empty chair. Gina ordered a glass of red wine.

"So, tell me about your day," Larry asked. He made no mention of the previous night's turmoil, so she decided she wouldn't, either.

"I just went to Stanley Market," she told him. "I had hoped to do some other things, but there's more there to see than I thought -- shops and stalls in every direction, and I wanted to take some things home for the girls."

"What did you end up getting?"

"A doll and some silk pajamas for each of them, and then I found a guy who did names in Chinese calligraphy, and that's what I'm taking for Steve. What about you?"

"I had a good day, too," he said, thinking for a moment and then nodding his head as if affirming to himself that what he had said was true. "Yeah, it was really good. I had a run in the morning, and then I shipped a jade Buddha home to Marqueeta, and I got measured for a couple of suits. You know they're famous for that here, right? They'll be ready tomorrow afternoon, so I'll be able to take them with me on the plane on Friday."

"Sounds good."

"But that wasn't the best part. I actually did some work." His sister shot him a critical look over the rim of her wine glass. "Hey, I get that Mom didn't want me to do work because it would take time away from us being together, but once you booted me out and we weren't together anyway, I figured all bets were off."

Gina shrugged her shoulders. "Fair enough," she said.

"So while I was running I got to thinking that there are a lot of possibilities here for shooting movies, so after breakfast I went back out with my camera and just walked and walked and took pictures that I can take back to the studio. You know, there are hillsides, and parks and hiking trails, and they're right up against skyscraper buildings and traffic and the harbor. And then I started to think about my end of things -- how if we ever did do a film here, we'd need music. So I went to some music stores and loaded up on Chinese CDs. Man, I love their instruments -- the gongs, the wooden drums."

He had become more excited while he talked than she had seen him this whole trip. He used his hands to describe a gong in the air and then tapped on an imaginary drum so convincingly that Gina expected it to appear on the empty bar stool between them.

"Well, then, see, it sounds like you had a better day without me than you would have with me."

"It wasn't about you at all, Sis," he said. He might not have been so brave except that he saw the maitre d' come up behind her and knew that their table was ready.

"So what about tomorrow?" he asked when they were settled at their table and a waiter had taken their order. He removed the bottle of white wine from an ice bucket beside the table and poured first into Gina's glass and then his. "Despite Mom's not requiring us to do her little projects, I'd like to spend the day with you, if you're willing, I mean, after last night."

Ah. So he hadn't forgotten.

"Speaking of last night," she said, "did you get Mom safely delivered back to Victoria Peak?"

"Yeah," he said, the word superimposed over a chuckle.

"What's so funny?"

"I think she and Mr. Wu might have a little thing going on," he said. "He was wearing a silk bathrobe and waiting up for her. We had a nightcap while I was there, and he was pleasant enough to me, but I got the feeling he couldn't wait for me to go."

"And how did Mom seem?"

"You know Mom. She loves everybody, so it's hard to tell, but she did hug him and give him a kiss on the cheek when we got there. He kept raving about the paintings she did of his house, which I'm sure she loved hearing."

"She said she was staying in his guesthouse."

"Well, maybe that's where she thought she was going to stay. I think he might have had other ideas."

"Well, she's a grown woman, and she's been alone for a while. A good tumble between the sheets might not be a bad thing for her."

"Yeah, I know. I just ... I don't know. It just seems odd to think of her with anyone other than Dad."

"It is what it is. She's got to play the hand she's been dealt."

"Sure," he said. And then deliberately changing the subject, "You said you didn't get everything you wanted to do done today. What's left on your list? We can do it tomorrow."

"Hong Kong Park, for one thing, but I'm guessing you went there today."

"Nope. I ran past it this morning and thought about going in, but then I remembered that you said there was a zoo there and a museum you wanted to see."

"It's a museum of teapots, Larry," she said, looking at him dubiously. "How interested can you be in that?"

"I told you. I got my stuff done today. What else?"

"The guidebook says the locals go there every morning to do tai chi. So I wouldn't mind getting an early start and seeing that."

"Done. What else?"

"I still haven't ridden in a junk. I thought I'd do that this afternoon, but the time just got away from me. And there's a floating restaurant in Aberdeen Harbor. Maybe lunch or dinner there."

"I've heard that's a big tourist rip-off. They say the food's not all that great."

"In case you hadn't noticed, I am a tourist, Larry. I've never been here before, and I want to see all the stuff I've read about. I'm not like you. I don't need to do all the trendy things so that I can go back home and drop the names of everyplace I've been."

"Hey, simmer down, slugger," he said.

"Well, really, Larry. I know that you go to all the cool places in LA and everyplace you travel." She fanned her hands upward to indicate that the very restaurant they were in proved her point. "I just don't need that."

Larry refused to be sucked into another argument.

"Floating restaurant it is," he said.

They were silent during the ride to the airport in a Peninsula limousine on Friday morning, both actively looking out the windows, each capturing last memories to take home. Then, as they rolled their suitcases toward the airline's ticket counter, Larry steered her to the business-class line.

"I know this is going to make you mad," he said, "but I upgraded you to business." He held up a hand to ward off the hostility he knew was coming. She had already opened her mouth to start talking, and her eyes had gone from pleasant to angry as quickly as if she had switched them like channels. "I have lots of airline miles from my credit cards," he went on. "It didn't cost me or Mom a dime, and I've got lots of miles left for anything else I want to do, so get off your high horse and stop being so defensive about everything. That huge chip you are determined to keep carrying around on your shoulder gets old and tiresome."

"OK, if it didn't cost anything …"

"Right. And now you can be comfortable for the ride over so you won't be exhausted when you get home. We'll have a nice lunch and get some sleep, and the next thing you know, we'll be landing in L.A."

She did exactly as he said. First there was a glass of champagne before takeoff and after that hot towels and a menu of such attractive options that she had trouble choosing. She polished off both the shrimp alfredo and the fruit-filled meringue that followed, had a cup of tea, and then pulled down her window shade, wrapped up in a blanket, reclined the seat, and went to sleep.

Six hours later she awoke and climbed over Larry to go to the bathroom. Back at her seat and wide awake, she drank half a bottle of water and flipped open the inflight magazine. Beside her Larry pecked on his laptop computer, and she could see that the name of the file he had open was "Treatment." Around the ear buds attached to his phone she could hear the high-pitched sounds of the

Chinese music. Then abruptly he pulled them out, turned to her, and said, "I think we should do the rest of the assignments."

"Yeah, so do I," she said. And then, suddenly drowsy again, she reclined her seat and went back to sleep.

CHAPTER NINE

Anita would forever be grateful to the hospice nurses and volunteers who came to the house at the end of Jay's illness. Without them she would have been forced to move him to a nursing home, and while she hadn't had a reason to go to one in years and had been told how much they had improved, she was determined that Jay's life would not end in such a place. She still carried the memory of her own ten-year-old self going to visit her grandfather in a linoleum-floored, green-walled facility that smelled sharply of urine and bleach. The people there, Grandpa Sol included, sat in wheelchairs in the hallways outside their bedrooms for the greater part of the day. Some of the healthier ones thumbed through magazines or worked crossword puzzles out of the newspaper, but most of them stared into space, looking at their pasts, perhaps, or maybe at nothing.

At first, clutching her mother's hand in fear, she had believed they were all looking at her, but as she moved past them, trying to find Grandpa in the lineup, she realized their eyes never moved. Once she and her mother had passed, whatever had been in their line of vision before it was momentarily blocked came back into view.

Yes, of course things had changed in the fifty years since then. The laws governing such places were stricter, the buildings cleaner, the nurses kinder, the medicines more effective, the community rooms filled with people playing Scrabble or learning French or how to edit photos on a computer, but she still couldn't imagine Jay in his bathrobe, eating pudding and being pushed around by strangers -- well-meaning volunteers who talked to their charges in a sing-song voice as if they were babies, saying everything too loudly because they assumed everyone was deaf. The memory was still fresh of her mother gripping her arm with a leather-gloved hand and whispering from beneath the witchy veil of her hat, shiny with black feathers, her breath sharp with the aroma of spearmint chewing gum, "Promise me you'll never put me in a place like this."

It had never been clear to Anita just why her mother had agreed to this living arrangement for her own father if she was so dead-set against it for herself, but then she had siblings, a brother and a sister, and when people had siblings they made difficult decisions like that in groups. No one person had to shoulder the guilt and blame all by themselves as she would have if she'd locked Jay away in an institution where she didn't have to face his deterioration -- the once healthy body, the quick wit, the sense of invincibility disappearing bit by bit, day by day. One day he could feed himself, the next day he couldn't. One day he could get to the bathroom with the walker the hospice people had brought over, the next she had to help him with a bedpan.

Each morning a nurse would arrive to help her give Jay a bath and feed him and monitor his medications, and then later in the day a volunteer would stop by to get her grocery list or take her place by Jay's bedside if she needed to go out to an appointment. She had cut back her hours, but she still went into the office a couple of times a week to check on her clients' projects. Some days she took advantage of this respite time to take a walk or guiltily go to lunch with a friend. There was her own health to consider, the nurses kept reminding her. She couldn't take good care of Jay if she got sick herself.

But as much as she appreciated these people, these literal angels of mercy, she wasn't sure she agreed with everything they said -- that he could hear and understand everything she murmured to him, even once he was in a coma, that he was waiting for Larry to come and say goodbye before he would let go, that once Larry arrived they should reassure him it was all right to leave, that they would be fine, that he should follow the light and be released from the illness that had ruined him.

Gina had volunteered to come out and help, but Anita had discouraged her, had even played down the seriousness of Jay's situation when they talked on the phone so that she wouldn't set her own life aside to come to the aid of her mother. The girls were babies then, and she was helping Steve out on the farm from early in the morning to late at night. Still, she always sounded positive when her mother called -- her stories full of images of herself on a tractor, herself stacking bales of hay in the barn or scattering corn to a barnyard filled with scratching, clucking chickens. It wasn't the future Anita had envisioned for her daughter. Gina had such talent in math and science and drawing. She could have joined a big firm in San Francisco or Chicago and made a fortune, but this was what she had chosen, and she seemed happy. The truth was that the older Anita got, the more Gina's decisions made sense to her. At the very end of Jay's life, when she and the nurses who now stayed with her around the clock sat by his bed and wondered if another breath would come, she finally told Gina how bad off he was. She had held the phone to Jay's ear just in case -- hoping that the nurses were right -- and Gina had tearfully told him what a good dad he had been to her, how much she loved him, and that she would be there soon, although by the time she finally arrived, the plane having been diverted to Los Angeles because of fog -- he was gone.

Larry came on weekends and sat with her, talking cheerfully to his unresponsive father, telling him funny stories about work and promising to take up golf so they could play together once Jay was well again, tears running down his face the whole time he was pretending to laugh about an assistant who laid down the wrong tracks for a movie and had Tony Bennett crooning "I'll Be Seeing You" while on the screen one car chased another along narrow Highway 1 through Big Sur, eventually skidding off the road and plummeting over a cliff and into the sea.

Anita had felt relief when Jay had gone into a coma and she knew the end was near and then instantly guilty for her selfishness. But it had been release for him, too. In the early days after his diagnosis, he had railed against it, and even when he had become unconscious, he had tossed restlessly in bed, kicking off the blankets and tearing at the buttons on his pajamas. "He's fighting it," one of the nurses had whispered, which had done nothing to calm her anxiety. It had not been at all like the movies, where peaceful men in striped pajamas and neat, well-made beds slipped away as if they were only dropping off for a brief nap.

Larry had been with her when the last breath finally came, but they hadn't been with Jay. They hadn't left the house for two days, and the hospice volunteer had suggested they go out for an hour to get a bite to eat. They had stopped at the closest place they could find, a Mexican diner near the house in Clairemont, and their plates of enchiladas had just been served when Larry's cell phone rang. They left the food untouched and raced the mile back home, but it was over.

"They choose their time," the volunteer, Rosa, had assured her, putting her arms around Anita and letting her sob into her shoulder even though they had only just met that day, the roster of volunteers having changed with a new week. "He was probably waiting for you to leave. They do that sometimes. They don't want their loved ones to have the last breath as their final memory."

Rosa had told Anita and Larry to take their time, that they could have as long as they wanted with Jay before she called the funeral home to send over a hearse. As she walked away from them she stretched out her fingers to admire a manicure she'd had that morning. As helpful and caring as she had been, this was not her husband who had died. For Rosa, another job had ended, and there was paperwork to be done before she could go home for the day. She left them alone beside the hospital bed that had been set up in the living room and disappeared into the kitchen, where she put a pot of coffee on before she sat down at the table to fill out the forms on her clipboard.

Anita and Larry sat by the bedside, holding hands, Larry weeping openly, Anita feeling numb. She didn't need the time with Jay's body that Rosa had thought she should take. The fact was that Jay had really been gone for a long time now, and this cooling, hardening body before her that looked like the marble effigies she had seen in European churches was no more her husband than the lamp that sat by the side of the bed and illuminated his immobile face.

When Rosa came back into the room with mugs of hot coffee, Anita said she should go ahead and call the funeral home. It was nearly eight o'clock, and she didn't want these people to have to work into the night.

We look different in different mirrors, different lights, different colors, Anita thought. In the peach-painted, incandescent-lit bathroom her makeup had looked perfect, the reflection of her hair thick and shiny in the mirror on the medicine cabinet. Now, in the bright, sunlit bedroom, her hair seemed dull and the wrinkles around her eyes prominent, the crepe of her neck obvious above the V-neck of the black blouse she was wearing underneath a charcoal suit. Downstairs, in the mirror over the washing machine in the utility room where she checked herself one last time each morning before opening the garage door and heading off to work, she knew she would look good, the shadows beneath her cheekbones making her face look thinner than it was, the gray in her dark brown hair virtually disappearing.

But she couldn't look in that mirror now because people had arrived for the reception, and she had just these few moments stolen for herself to freshen up and steel herself to go down and greet them, accept their hugs, listen to their murmured condolences, thank them for coming, smile bravely, offer them a glass of wine. And today, of all days, if she looked worn and exhausted and old, she would be forgiven. In the weeks and months to come, she could look forward to being told how much better she looked, how healthy, how much younger than her years. She knew this because she had said it herself to other women who had lost their husbands after cataclysmic illnesses, and every single time it had been true.

What a meaningless, inane thing to be thinking about, she chided herself. Today was not about her and how she looked to the group of neighbors and friends and colleagues collecting around the buffet table in the dining room. Today was about Jay, only Jay. And yet, in some ways the ceremony she had just planned and attended was also about her. It was the threshold of a frightening new life without a partner who would climb up on a ladder to change a lightbulb and sit beside her in theaters and make plans with her for vacations or improvements to the house. When they had found out he was sick, they had just the week before decided to renovate the master bathroom. The night before he was diagnosed, they had stood together in the doorway and talked about moving the bathtub under the window where she could watch the stars while she soaked in her bedtime bubble bath. Now the meetings with the contractor, the choice of shower head, the selection of floor tiles would fall to her, and she would lie awake in the small hours of morning worrying over her decisions rather than curling into the warmth of Jay's arms contentedly to whisper about them.

She was lucky to have her children, of course. That was comforting, even if their connection was mostly by telephone and e-mail. It had been wonderful having them both here for the past few days and today, walking into the chapel holding both their hands, sitting in the front row between them, reaching around Larry to clasp the hands of Jay's brother, Charles, and his wife, Lorraine. Sitting between Gina and Larry, having them both in her realm, even for a short while, would be the high point in this otherwise dismal experience, the stripe of color that would permeate the warp and weft of black on black that would forever characterize this day.

Even eight years later, sitting in the Shanghai airport and waiting for a flight to Sydney, these memories were still fresh and raw, had never been far from her mind since Jay had been gone. And she realized now that it was on the day of Jay's funeral that her passion for mending the relationship between Gina and Larry had been born. She had seen the dissension even then, and that was long before everything else had happened, before the crisis that she hadn't even been aware existed had completely estranged them.

She had first noticed it the night Gina had gotten in. The flight had been delayed, and Gina had taken a cab to the house, arriving after Larry had gone to bed in the room that had once been his and was now the guest room. Anita had long ago turned Gina's bedroom into Jay's home office since the room that had previously served that purpose was smaller and had more light, thus making it a perfect studio for her. Tonight she had made up the pullout sofa in the living room, and Gina had gone directly to bed, even refusing the cocoa she had offered, more out of nostalgia than any idea that her daughter would need the warm milk to help her get to sleep. In the morning, Larry had worn pajama bottoms and a T-shirt into the kitchen for breakfast and arrived yawning and stretching, asking what there was to eat. Gina had slept poorly, the metal support bar beneath the sofa bed's mattress digging into her back all night, she said, and she had gotten up before dawn to fold up her bed, start the coffee, and drive her mother's car to the patisserie for fresh croissants. En route back to the house, she had stopped at a market for fresh pineapple, cantaloupe, and strawberries, and the bounty now lay perfectly arranged on one of their mother's crystal platters. Larry popped a strawberry into his mouth and said could he have some eggs, and that had been the beginning. It was like they were children again, and neither one of them could seem to say anything that didn't irritate the other.

"I got up early to get all this food for us," Gina said. "Surely you don't expect Mom to cook for you."

"That's great, Sis," Larry had countered. "But I'm a growing boy. I can't live on that frou-frou stuff alone."

They were determined to make this awful time easier for their mother, but every subject that came up seemed fraught with potential for yet another argument. When Larry tripped over Gina's suitcase and swore under his breath, she heard him from two rooms away and yelled that she wasn't lucky enough to have a room of her own at their mother's house, as he did. In the car on the way to the Unitarian church to meet with the minister Anita had asked to conduct the service, Gina brought up the subject of Bible readings and prayer. Since she'd married Steve, she had gone to his family's Methodist church and become more religious than she had been as a child. She had brought a hymnal with her so that she could suggest some music, and she'd called ahead to the Methodist church closest to Anita's house to check on the availability of the chapel there.

"Geez, Gina. Way to move in and take over," Larry said from the backseat, where he was crouched with his Walkman. "If you'd given it any thought, you'd know Mom would already have plans of her own."

"It's all right," Anita said, taking her hand off the steering wheel to pat Gina's arm. "I appreciate anything either of you wants to do, but I'm trying to concentrate on what Dad would have liked, and he wasn't very religious. I thought we'd just do some poetry readings and classical music and ask a few of his friends to speak. The minister will really just be there to tie all of that together. He'll do some spiritual readings, but they won't be from any particular denomination. Dad always thought religion was at the root of all the world's problems. Every time we'd watch the news and see Arabs and Jews fighting each other in the Middle East or Catholics and Protestants in Ireland, he'd sing the line from "Imagine" about what a better place the world would be if we didn't have religion. Knowing that, I think it would be an insult to him to have a Christian service and sing hymns and pray to God or Allah or anybody."

"Whatever," Gina said, clearly disagreeing.

"She's done this her whole life," Larry piped up again, yanking the headphones off his head to indicate he was now totally engaged in the conversation. "She makes all these plans without consulting anybody, and then she's mad if you aren't all appreciative and grateful and you don't do things her way."

"That is so not true," Gina said, whipping her head around to face him over the back of her seat. "I'm just trying to take some of the pressure off of Mom."

"Oh, right, and that's what you were doing this morning when you went out and got breakfast without asking anybody what they wanted." Then he looked toward the back of his mother's head. "She's done this for as long as I can remember, Mom. Don't you remember when I was in high school and she cleaned my room to surprise me." He made quotation marks in the air around "surprise." "She did a bunch of laundry and shrunk my best Led Zepplin T-shirt, and she rearranged my closet and the CDs on my shelves. Then when I got mad and told her to keep away from my stuff, she got back at me by telling you about the Playboy magazines she had found under my mattress. What was she doing looking under my mattress anyway? But you told me to be nice and that she was only trying to be 'helpful.'" Again the quotation marks in the air. "That was just pure and simple bullshit." Now that he lived on his own in L.A. and had a job, he sometimes exerted his independence by swearing in front of Anita, and she, not wanting to be characterized as old-fashioned and uptight, let it pass. "All she wanted was an excuse to dig around in my room and then get thanked for it."

"Get over yourself," Gina said, "like I'd have any interest in the crap you had in there anyway." She turned back around to look out the front window, signaling that he was dismissed and the conversation was over.

"I can't believe either of you still remembers that," Anita said. "I do, but only because both of you were in such a state about it, both of you wanting me to punish the other. I actually thought you were both right. Gina, you shouldn't have gone into his room without permission, and Larry, you should have appreciated her effort for what it was. She spent a whole Saturday toiling away in there while you were ... where? I don't remember."

"Band camp."

"Ah, yes, band camp," Gina said now. "Geeks on parade."

"Yes, and now look who has a job in the music business and who's living the life out on Old MacDonald's farm."

"Mom ...," Gina began through gritted teeth, but they had arrived at the church, and Anita had pulled into a parking space marked "Visitor."

"Not now," she said wearily. "Not today."

Then there had been Larry's wedding, but they were all tense then. It wasn't just Larry and Gina. Sylvia had reigned like a lace-encrusted harpy, and Marqueeta had cried and melted down every time something didn't go her way like a spoiled child. Anita still hadn't quite forgiven the snarky remarks she'd made to poor little Stephanie just because she'd gotten punch on her dress and that only because she was starving and the wedding party was spending the afternoon traipsing all over God knew where taking pictures and sweltering.

And now Hong Kong. They'd had a good time. Despite their set-to in the restaurant, she could tell that. Among their digs and barbs was also laughter, and good memories had bubbled up to surface along with the bad ones -- the two of them dressed as a pilgrim and an Indian in homemade costumes of their own devising, Gina in an old black blouse of Anita's that she covered with a kitchen apron and topped off with an old-fashioned sunbonnet from the dress-up box, complaining that she had wanted to be the Indian, Larry with a pink-striped bath towel wrapped around his waist and colored-paper feathers stuck into one of Gina's headbands. The Easter when the neighbor's dog ate all the eggs they had colored and hidden, the day Gina had run right out of her fifth-grade class without permission and through the building to the first-grade wing when someone told her Larry had fallen off the monkey bars.

How, with all that rich history, all the pictures of them clutching one another's hands and smiling at the camera, looking like they were so happy they just about couldn't hold it, how did people lose that? Anita's best friend, Noreen, had had a falling-out with her sister years ago, and they had reconnected at their mother's funeral when they realized neither of them could remember what the argument had been about. Even Jay. Besides Charles, who lived in San Diego and played golf with him most weekends, there was another brother, Ed, who had taken a job in Michigan and moved away, never to return. When the Christmas cards from him and his wife arrived, Anita would say to Jay, "You know, we should invite them to come out," or "Why don't we go to Michigan sometime and see them? I've never been there, and I'd love to go to Mackinac Island." He would shrug and say, "Yeah," but nothing would come of it. "Is there something wrong between the two of you?" she finally asked him, and he'd said, "No, but he's got his life and I've got mine. Let's just leave it alone." Ed had sent the biggest bouquet of flowers at the funeral with a note that said business kept him from getting away.

What happens, she wondered. When do they stop seeing each other as best friends and become enemies? Is it pure jealousy over their parents' affection? Obviously it's not gender since sisters drifted apart from sisters and men from men. Can they point to a day when the other person gets on their nerves to the point where it's unbearable and secret giggles turn to shrieks of anger and disgust? Now, of course, Larry and Gina had this money issue between them that she hadn't known about until this trip, and that didn't help, but what had caused Gina, that day back in junior high, to start referring to Larry as her half-brother? She and Jay had never talked to her about the logistics of their family tree, had referred to them as brother and sister since the day she brought Larry home from the hospital. But Gina had obviously been watching, paying attention when they hadn't realized it, had learned on the playground before Anita had a chance to tell her where babies came from and figured out that if she was born in 1966 and Anita and Jay married in 1968 -- the framed wedding certificate hanging above the chest of drawers in their bedroom daily proof -- then something didn't add up. She had asked her teacher to explain it, and the teacher, thankfully, had called Anita, who only then had told her about Davey Calhoun and how, while he was what was called her biological father, Jay was the man who loved her and took care of her. He was her real daddy. After that Gina introduced Larry as her half-brother and referred to him that way even at odd times that embarrassed everyone. Once, when Larry and some friends had been playing guitars in the garage, an indignant neighbor had rung the doorbell and said, "I need to speak with your mother. Your brother plays his music much too loudly. I can't hear my own television set over it." Gina had deliberately sidestepped the point and explained, "He's not actually my brother. He's my half-brother. My mother had me with another husband. He was a rock star." Anita had run up behind her and gently, smilingly pushed her out of the way, but the damage had been done; the information had served to make the family seem weirder than they actually were, and the prudish neighbor had never warmed up to them the whole time he lived across the back fence from them. She and Jay had tried to explain that they were a family and that it wasn't necessary to share their business with strangers, but Gina had dug in her heels and referred to Larry as her half-brother for as long as she lived at home. Anita wondered if she still did, or if, more importantly, she thought of him that way -- her not-quite brother, her brother, sort of.

The funny thing was that in so many ways they were so much alike. The negative qualities they constantly accused one another of having were exactly the same ones they had themselves. They each accused the other of moving in and taking charge, being bossy, manipulating situations to produce the outcome most beneficial to them. Yes, Gina had wanted prayers and religion at Jay's funeral, but hadn't Larry wanted his band to play? But she had held to her determination to have a service Jay would have appreciated and not made a joke about later. She believed she had succeeded, and knowing that helped her get to sleep at night in the early days after his death, but she knew that her children were disappointed, would have done it differently. She could hear the discussion Gina would have had back home with Steve and Larry with Marqueeta, who would soon be a member of the family. She could hear them itemizing how it might have been better.

The scene in the restaurant had been disappointing, and she had realized with embarrassment how foolish she had been to tie the money she planned to give them anyway to a silly game. But just now they had sent a text message from the Los Angeles airport saying they had decided to do the assignments anyway, and she'd felt hopeful again. They would work out the details, they told her, and then they would all be together to celebrate finishing them at Christmas.

Well, good, she thought as she poked her cell phone back into the pocket on the outside of her handbag. At least they would have that. There were things she needed to discuss with them, stories she wanted to tell them, facts they needed to know, but she wanted them to know each other and appreciate each other first, wanted them to have a real connection -- not just in terms of bank accounts or someday planning her funeral together.

The gate agent announced her flight, and she gathered up her carry-on bag and the book at which she'd been staring while she thought. Yes, at the cabin, when her trip and all the work were finished, when the assignments were done, then they'd talk.

CHAPTER TEN

Gina reached an arm out from under the sheet to silence the blat-blat-blat of the digital alarm clock on her bedside table that read 6:00 a.m. Steve put an arm around her and pulled her closer to him.

"Not yet," he mumbled, still not fully awake. But the early morning sun was already lightening the east window, which reminded Gina that they had not even closed the curtains last night. Not only that, but she and Steve were both naked. They had not let that happen since the morning three-year-old Stephanie had wandered into their room and, seeing only her father, asked, "Where's Mommy?" He had said she was in the bathroom, and that if Stephanie would go back to bed, he'd make sure she came in to check on her as soon as she was finished. The moment lost to the surprise intrusion, Steve had rolled off his wife, and she had gone to the bathroom, flushed the toilet without using it, and padded down the hall to Stephanie's room as if it were any other morning and nothing unusual had just happened. After that they tried closing their door, but then they worried that they couldn't hear her -- and later Danielle -- if she woke up and needed them. Eventually they fell into the habit of closing the bedroom door when they made love and then opening it afterward, after they had put back on the pajamas that had been stripped off unceremoniously and flung to some other part of the room.

But this morning the blue-and-white wedding ring quilt her mother-in-law had made for her bridal shower lay in a soft, thick heap on the floor at the end of their bed, and the short blue cotton nightie she had worn to bed was draped across the radio that sat on the nightstand on Steve's side of the bed. His gray-and-white striped pajama bottoms made a lump under the sheet that Gina now located with her toes and kicked to his side of the bed.

The plane home from L.A. had been delayed, and by the time the flight that was supposed to land in Indianapolis at eight had landed at midnight and they had collected her suitcase and driven home to Bedford, it was nearly three. The girls had both slept in the car all the way home, had barely awakened when their parents unfastened their seatbelts and herded them into the house and up the stairs to their bedroom. Gina had helped them slip off their tennis shoes and socks and covered them with sheets against the cool that she hoped would settle over the house before the sun came up and it was soon stifling again. They would sleep later today and wonder for a moment when they woke up why they were still in the shorts and T-shirts they had worn for the trip to the airport.

Steve had carried her suitcase to their bedroom, and Gina had followed with the matching carry-on. She had hoped to show him his name in Chinese and was digging through the satchel to find it when he came up behind her and wrapped his arms around her, causing her to abandon the search in favor of his affectionate welcome. Now she snuggled against him just long enough for a kiss that said yes, I remember. Yes, it was lovely. But no, there's no time to do it again.

What she thought as she crossed the bare wood floor toward the bureau drawer where she kept her shorts and T-shirts was how happy she was to be home. She should feel tired, but instead she felt completely alive. Maybe it was the difference in time zones -- she would not have had any idea what time it was in Hong Kong if she hadn't put off resetting her watch, as if that would somehow extend the holiday -- or maybe it was the hours of sleep she had had in the business class cabin and the catnaps she had been able to catch once the plane to Indianapolis had taken off -- cramped in coach like Cinderella in her pumpkin though she was.

The altercations with Larry notwithstanding, she had loved the trip to Hong Kong. It had been another world from what she was used to. She felt like she had been opened up somehow, like a dark, musty box spread out on the warm grass so that the sun could at last permeate each of its shadowy corners and reveal its exotic secrets. Parts of her own mind that hadn't yet been explored -- or that had been otherwise occupied since college -- were now filled with colors and smells and sounds she'd never realized existed -- the reds and golds of the dresses in Stanley Market, the greens of jade dragons in the window of the expensive store where Larry had gone back to shop, the smells of fish at Tai-O, the incense at the Buddhist monastery, the gongs and drums at the temple where they had gone after the tea museum and before taking the junk with the bright red sail out to the flashy, neon-encrusted floating restaurant. She wanted to show Steve and the girls her pictures and give them their presents, but there would be time for that later. For now what she wanted most in the world was to drink a cup of coffee in Lindsay Faraday's kitchen. She texted to make sure her friend was up. There would be plenty of time before she had to be back when the girls woke up and Steve had to leave for the store.

After she made sure he was awake, she tiptoed down the hallway to the stairs and then, slipping her feet into flip-flops, out the front door. Standing on the porch, she was aware again of the sense of being new inside herself. She noticed things she'd never noticed before -- the drops of dew that clung to the serrated leaves on the rose bush, the ground fog that lingered in the yard between the house and the barn, the sweet, delicate scent of the honeysuckle that vined over the trellis at the end of the porch and mingled in the mist with the rich, visceral smell of manure from the nearby pasture. If someone from China came here, is this what they would take away with them? Would they go back home feeling as if they had been pried open and filled to overflowing with the green of rolling hills, the gray of the weathered wood that fenced in the tiny patch of front yard, the annoyed cries of blue jays as they chased each other from their favorite branches?

She backed the Jeep Cherokee around the barn and drove slowly up the lane, then turned onto the main road. It was still early enough that few of her neighbors would be out yet, and her sense of a private cultural epiphany could continue. They would all be up, maybe wave to her from their windows if they happened to see her go by, but they would be busy with their own children, their own breakfasts, the animals that needed to be fed, and many of them -- just like Steve -- would be getting ready to go to a job in town, even though it was Saturday, even though they were farmers who in better times would have been climbing onto their green and yellow John Deere tractors for a day in the fields or putting up bean poles out in the garden.

It would be another scorcher. As soon as she got back home she would close the windows and doors to trap the cool night air, and that would keep the house comfortable until noon, when she'd open them again and set up a fan in a screened doorway to create a cross-draft. The main house, vacant now with its owners in Chicago -- had central air.

The house where they had lived before had had it, too, and while they were always careful to keep the electric bill down as much as they could in the summer, they had been comfortable.

Now there were nights when they couldn't get to sleep because of the heat, and that would only get worse as the summer wore on. By August the girls would be begging to camp out on the porch and she and Steve would give in, mostly so they would have an excuse to sleep out there, too.

She tried to crowd thoughts of the other house out of her mind so they didn't ruin this perfect morning. She tried not to remember that the girls each had a room -- Stephanie's buttercup yellow, Danielle's bright pink -- tried not to think about the utility room with the ironing board built into the wall and space enough for a folding table, tried not to remember the dining room where Steve's whole family could gather on holidays and the den where company could sleep on a fold-out sofa and the extra bathroom where they could use the toilet or take a shower without having to wade through puddles of the family's wet towels on the floor or look at themselves in the mirror through the splatters from Steve's shaving cream.

There was no point, nothing to be gained in remembering the other house, and it only fueled her negative feelings about Larry, whose contribution could have meant she would still live there -- big-deal Hollywood Larry, Larry who had surprised her by hiring the junk with the red sail when he found out the ferries to the restaurant were ugly and crowded, who had sacrificed his frequent-flyer points so that she could rest on the plane and come home to this beautiful morning.

Lindsay was watching for her from the kitchen window and waving with as much energy as a child. Then she ran out to Gina's car and yanked the door open before Gina could turn off the ignition. She was wearing khaki shorts and a white T-shirt. She hadn't thought about shoes when she dashed outside in her enthusiasm to greet her friend, and now she tiptoed gingerly over the gravel surface of her driveway and back into the house, saying "Ow, ow, ow" as she hobbled along.

Gina and Lindsay had become instant friends when they had both played on a softball team the summer after Gina and Steve's wedding. Lindsay had been a lab technician at the hospital in town when she'd met Kevin, who'd had an emergency appendectomy and had to have blood drawn. Kevin's dream had been very much like Steve's, and after they married Lindsay gave up her job with the romantic notion of the two of them and their future children living off the land.

The dream ended just five years into their marriage when the tractor Kevin was driving dropped a wheel into a ditch he hadn't seen, causing it to flip and him to be pinned under it for hours. Since he often stayed out in the fields well after sunset, Lindsay hadn't gone looking for him until it was pitch dark. Even then she had called a neighbor for help since she couldn't leave three-year-old Casey alone. When the neighbor made his terrible discovery, he had called the sheriff, who said he guessed Kevin would have died quickly and there was no reason for the guilt and remorse that immediately seized her.

It had taken a full year for Lindsay to smile again. In that time she had gone back to work, leaving Casey at the hospital day-care center, where she could visit him during her breaks and at lunchtime. When she was at home, she wanted the two of them to be alone. She planted a garden and canned vegetables and played her guitar. Besides Casey, the only people she ever wanted around were her husband's son from a previous marriage, also named Kevin and called Deuce, now a teenager, and Gina. When Gina's life had taken a downward turn, Lindsay had been the only friend she had wanted to see, too. They were yoked by disaster, a sorority of two, each of whom thought she knew -- almost, but not quite -- what it felt like to be the other. When Gina grew frustrated because Steve didn't want to go out with her to the movies or didn't put his mud-caked jeans into the washing machine, she caught herself and remembered gratefully that she had him, he was alive, he wasn't Kevin.

Eventually the light had come back into Lindsay's dark brown eyes, and today her wide, friendly mouth was smiling like it might break. Her legs and arms were tan from being outside in her garden, her light brown hair streaked with what looked like gold ribbons, and to anyone who didn't know her story, she would look like the picture of good health and happiness.

"So, world-traveling girl," she said as she poured coffee into two mugs with bright yellow daisies painted on the sides, "how was the trip, and how did you get along with your fancy brother?"

"It was good," Gina said. She was still high on whatever had gotten into her this morning. "It was wonderful, in fact. I'll show you pictures I took after I have time to sort through them. I saw so many things that I've only read about in books. It sounds corny, but I feel like my whole life changed."

"Well, of course it did! And your brother?"

Gina winced playfully.

"He's still my brother. We had words a couple of times, but he also redeemed himself. He did everything I wanted to do, and on the way home he used his frequent-flyer miles to upgrade me to business class."

"Really! He is fancy," Lindsay said as she blew steam away from her coffee.

"It was just like the movies. And our mom even showed up and surprised us, so we got to have dinner with her one night."

"Wow! How's her book coming?"

"Really well, I think. Larry and I also think she might have been having a little thing with the Chinese guy who was putting her up. She had done some paintings for him another time, and when he heard she was flying in for a couple of days, he offered to let her stay in his guesthouse. Larry took her back there after we had dinner, and he got the distinct impression that Mr. Wu was eager for him to leave so the games could begin. I say if it makes her happy, she should go for it."

"Absolutely. So you could get a stepfather at your age!"

"Correction. I've had a stepfather most of my life. Mr. Wu would be my second, except that Mom has said she doesn't plan to marry again."

"Oh, right. I keep forgetting that your biological father was some kind of rock star."

"I don't know about star, but he played in a band. It seems like he got all the bad stuff that goes with that life and none of the fame and money. But Larry was Jay's biological child, so he's really only my half-brother."

"Do you think he'll ever come out here, or is he too Hollywood to mingle with us country bumpkins?"

"One of my mom's assignments for us involves our families spending time at each other's houses. And since we have to get all this done before Christmas, I'm guessing you'll meet him and Marqueeta sometime before too long."

"Cool," said Lindsay. She glanced at her watch. "And now I've got to roll Casey out of bed and get to the hospital."

When Gina got back home, Steve was dressed, now all business, working at the kitchen table and ready to leave for the store. The lover she'd left behind an hour ago had vanished as completely as if he had climbed into his truck and driven away. The flimsy screen door flapped shut behind her and he looked up from his laptop.

"It's going to be a hot one today," she said. "The thermometer says 80, and it's not even eight o'clock yet."

Steve was wearing a white T-shirt beneath the blue denim shirt with his name stitched over the pocket that he would peel off sometime before noon. He motioned her over to look at the screen.

"You should find this interesting," he said and pointed to a column of numbers. The site he had up was their bank account, and the most recent deposit was for $56,000. "It looks like your money was wired in just this morning."

"Mom's in Sydney. She must have done this as soon as she got there. Wow. She said this was what she was going to do. I guess she did it."

"And she's planning to do this every year?"

"That's what she says."

"And she's giving Larry the same?"

"He gets $42,000. It has something to do with taxes. She can give each person $14,000 a year, and he only has three people in his family."

"And he's OK with that?"

"I guess so," she said, shrugging her shoulders. "It is what it is. He and Keeta can have another baby if it's worth it to them, but I don't think they really need money. He seems to make a bundle. The whole time we were in Hong Kong he was buying presents to send home and hiring drivers and upgrading this and that. I don't think we need to worry about old Lar."

"My, aren't we feeling feisty this morning!"

"That's what happens when you keep a girl up so late," she said, and she squeezed his shoulders and kissed him before turning away to get a cereal bowl out of the cabinet.

"Well, when you get a chance, there's also an e-mail from 'old Lar' that you'll probably want to read. He's got the rest of the assignments all planned out."

"I'm sure he does. He's definitely Mr. I'll Take Charge."

"Just read it. You might be surprised."

In fact, she forgot all about the message until the middle of the afternoon when she came back to the computer to send a message of her own to their accountant.

"As you can see, I'm up very early," Larry began. "Guess I'm still on HK time. How about you? I'm glad you agree that we should go ahead and do Mom's assignments. I talked to her more after you left the restaurant the other night, and for whatever nutty reason, they seem to be important to her. If you've looked at your bank account this morning, you've probably made the same discovery I have. She's held up her part of the bargain, and she's not making us do ours, but I know she's happy that we're going to.

"I know that with caring for the farm and running the store and having two kids, time to get away is a problem for you, so I've been looking at the rest of the assignments and trying to figure out how we could double up on some of them and get this thing knocked out quickly. We need to organize Mom's studio, and you and your family need to spend time at my house. Could you come out in August? If you fly out alone, you and I could drive down to San Diego and spend a couple of days doing whatever it is we're supposed to do in Mom's house. Steve and the girls could join us in L.A. when we're finished. We could figure out then when my family could come to your house, and maybe you could find someplace for us to do the volunteer work while I'm there. That just leaves the list of good qualities and the creative project, which we have to do on our own anyway, and the scrapbook, which we can do online and then take to the cabin when Mom gets back in December.

"If you have a better idea, I'm open to anything. Just want to get some plans on the calendar. Now that I've seen pictures of Stephanie and Danielle, I'm looking forward to having them here to meet Dex. Love, Larry."

She pulled a surprised face. "Huh," she said aloud. "Love." Then she hit the reply button and started typing.

"I'll have to talk to Steve, but I think he could get away toward the end of August. Yes, we got the money this morning, too, and, like you, that makes me want to get the other assignments planned. It's the least we can do to show Mom how much we appreciate what she's doing. I don't know what your schedule is like, but I'm hoping you can come out here in the fall. October would be best. The leaves will be beautiful, and we can carve pumpkins and take Dexter for a ride on the tractor.

"I volunteer once a month at a homeless shelter in town. It's run jointly by all the churches, and several of us in my church take turns making food and spending the night. When we get a date set, I'll put us on the calendar. More later after I talk to Steve."

She hit send and then picked up the phone and punched in the speed-dial number for Steve's cell phone.

CHAPTER ELEVEN

G ina's first impression of her mother's house was the sharp medicinal odor that attacked her sinuses and that even after they'd opened the windows and propped open the doors still seemed to numb her lips.

"What *is* that?" she asked her brother when he turned his key in the lock and pushed the door ahead so that she could step inside before him. "What does she keep in here?"

"Paint," he said, laughing. "It's usually not this bad because when she's here she keeps the windows open, but the place has been locked up since she left in April."

"Doesn't she have anyone coming in to water the plants or feed the goldfish or something?"

"Just me. I told her I'd come down every few weeks while she was away to check on things, but I've been so busy at work and then with the trip to Hong Kong and things at home, I haven't been here in almost a month. As to plants, they're all silk, and there aren't any pets. When she started traveling more, she streamlined her whole life so it would be easier to get away."

By now Gina knew better than to ask what the "things at home" were. While she was in California she hoped to figure that out for herself. Larry had picked her up at LAX, and they had driven in the heat of the August morning straight down Interstate 5 to San Diego, so she still hadn't yet seen Marqueeta.

"What about her mail?"

"She has it all forwarded to me. I go through it and send the bills to Dennis MacDonald so he can pay them. The personal stuff I put in an envelope and send to her every couple of weeks."

"I didn't realize you and Mom were so tight."

She felt a twinge of jealousy now of a different kind. Her dad may have had a good reason for preferring Larry to her, but did her mother, too? She and Anita had been close when she was a little girl, but once she'd gone to Indiana for college and then gotten married and had her children, they had drifted apart. Her mother had come to visit at least once a year in the beginning, but her visits had been less frequent in the last couple of years. When she did come, she always brought gifts from foreign cities, always making sure to pay for gas and picking up the tab at restaurants, always gave her daughter a wad of twenty-dollar bills before she left, but they didn't sit at the kitchen table talking about the real substance of their lives far into the night. If she had been comfortable telling her mother about their financial situation, maybe it would have turned out differently. Maybe she could have helped them. Maybe Jay had left her some money that she could have lent them, even before her work became popular and her name became a household word like Laura Ashley's had once been. Maybe. Like the roads leading to Rome, every situation reminded her of what she had lost.

"She loves me most," he joked, and then, seeing that she wasn't laughing, quickly added, "Oh, come on, Gina. Lighten up. I have an advantage. I live in the same state. You, on the other hand, are what we out here call a GU -- geographically undesirable. That's what guys say when they decide not to date a woman who lives on the other side of L.A. because it's too far to drive. You live too far away to be useful."

She let this comment slide without a retort, her mind already busy elsewhere.

"I've never even been to this house, let alone having my own key. Geez, I'm trying to remember how long she's lived here."

"Well, Dad died in 2007. It was a couple of years after that that her artwork really started to sell and a couple of years after that when she felt like she could move here. Probably about four years."

"It's small."

She was moving from one piece of furniture to another, exploring her surroundings like a cat evaluating the home of a questionable new owner, plumping cushions, picking up a small glass sculpture and turning it over in her hand, opening the shades that had kept the house dark and cool since her mother had closed them almost five months ago. The light that now flooded the living room revealed a space that looked exactly like one Anita might have painted. Asian carpets overlapped one another beneath eclectic carved tables and a sofa covered in paisley brocade. Against one wall floor-to-ceiling bookshelves were filled to capacity with hardcover volumes, the space above them crammed with paperbacks, the remaining lip of shelf filled with mementoes of her travels -- a cowbell from Switzerland, a stone carving from Tanzania, and a miniature *retablo* from Peru with a patch of tiny potato-paste flowers blooming inside its partially opened doors. Paintings in ornate gilt frames, hung salon style, as close together as they could fit, covered the opposite wall above the spinet piano that had replaced the larger used upright on which Larry had learned to play.

The framed pictures from both of their weddings sat on a coffee table, and photos of their children clustered on an eigthteenth-century French desk under the window that faced the quiet, shade-dappled street. At the end of the room, closest to the kitchen, was a small teak dining table that would seat four. Gina wondered what had become of the beat-up mahogany veneer set with all the leaves that they'd grown up on, the table that would extend to seat twelve on holidays, when they trolled the house for the mismatched chairs and borrowed extras from the neighbors to accommodate the annual mix of relatives and friends and acquaintances who had nowhere else to go. Twin crystal candlesticks sat on this one instead of the bowl filled with apples, oranges, and bananas she remembered from childhood, and the deep red and cream striped satin seats showed no signs of chocolate milk or spilled oatmeal.

"It's a cottage," Larry said. "That's how it was advertised, but you've got to remember it's in La Jolla, California. I think she paid a million three for it."

Gina flushed with the familiar sickening wash of jealousy and anger. The year before her mother assembled this jewel box of a house in one of the country's most expensive neighborhoods and had a key made for her brother, she had been packing the cartons that she and Steve would load into his pickup and drive away from their home. The house she lived in now wasn't much bigger than this one, and there were four of them instead of just one. But her mother hadn't known how much she needed money, she reminded herself, and that was her own fault.

"I don't think she would have done it if Dad had still been alive," Larry went on. "Once she started making money, they would probably have moved from the old house, but it wouldn't have been here, and it wouldn't look like this."

"But it's the road not taken, isn't it? If Dad had been alive, would any of it have happened? Would she have concentrated on painting? Would she have put her work out there, or would it have just been a hobby, and would she and Dad be retired now, living in a condo on a golf course and going on cruises?"

Despite the brighter light, she shivered.

She moved now beyond the living room to the galley-like kitchen, a small, cozy room with flagstones on the floor where a person cooking a meal could reach from the refrigerator to the stove and the sink almost without having to move. Copper pots hung, arranged by increasing size, over a terra-cotta-tiled counter on which rested a wine rack filled mostly with reds from Italy and whites from New Zealand. The back wall over the sink consisted entirely of small windowpanes through which she could see a small garden lushly crowded with a profusion of rusty yellow and orange daylilies, bright blue agapanthus and smoky-foliaged lavender. Two teak chairs with forest-green cushions and a table clustered around a low chiminea on a tiled patio that was shaded now by a tower of bright red and pale pink intertwined bougainvillea growing on a nearby trellis.

"Somebody must come by and do the yard. It's gorgeous."

"Yeah, Eduardo. She's had him ever since she moved here. I think he does most of the houses around here. I've met him a couple of times."

She turned and walked through a doorway into what had been intended as a second bedroom and was now her mother's studio.

"Wow."

"I know." Larry looked in over her shoulder. "It's a mess. We've got our work cut out for us. No wonder she made this one of the assignments."

"No, I mean, just ... wow."

The wall of windows continued across this side of the house, and late-morning sun edged under the woven-wood shades as Gina rolled them up. A skylight overhead had already dropped a square pool of illumination directly beneath it and rendered the room secretly cheerful even when the shades had been down. Partially finished paintings were propped on two floor easels -- one a bowl of lemons on a red checked tablecloth, the other a pot of irises on a table by a mustard yellow sofa -- and a table easel sat naked on a broad oak worktable in the middle of the room, its sturdy wooden tripod legs open, a backing board waiting for the piece of 300-pound cold-pressed paper and heavy wet pigment that her mother would transform into a work of art. The old desk that Gina remembered from Jay's study in the Clairemont house was shoved up into a corner opposite the windows and covered with file folders and envelopes. Above it clippings from magazines -- photographs of lamps, pillows, daisies, a rusty wheelbarrow, a basket of peaches that Anita might like to incorporate into a painting -- and snapshots of her own work were thumb-tacked to a cork bulletin board. The same two-drawer filing cabinet Anita had used since they were children sat next to the desk, a jar filled with brushes on top, the sable bristles of the flat ones and their round counterparts pointing expectantly toward the ceiling.

Next to the filing cabinet was a low chest with five shallow drawers. When Gina pulled the top ones open, she saw a jumble of paint tubes in no particular order. While Anita had obviously once arranged them by color, inserting them carefully into the metal slots designed for that purpose, now there was no organization -- ultramarine, cadmium red, emerald, and benzamida lemon in one drawer, alizarin, indigo, and burnt sienna in another. The two drawers closest to the floor contained blocks of blank watercolor paper.

An old bookcase, once purchased at an unfinished furniture store and painted pink for Gina's room, sagged under books about art -- *Art in the Western World, A Compendium of Nineteenth Century Art, The English School, How to Mix Colors, The Use of Shadow, Drawing for Beginners.* Three unopened cardboard boxes labeled with the return address of Anita's publisher were stacked up against it. The floor, the same flagstone as the kitchen, was spattered with flecks of paint. Their mother had apparently forgotten to empty the last jar of water she used before she left, because there it still sat, a putrid slosh of gray with a foul tinge of green.

Gina forced herself to move from there to the short hallway that led to a tiny old-fashioned bathroom where a claw-foot bathtub perched on octagonal tiles opposite a pedestal sink and a commode with a wooden seat and lid. Cream and red towels, exactly the colors of the stripes on the dining room chairs, hung from a functional chrome towel bar. A second doorway connected it to her mother's bedroom, also small, with space for little more than a queen-size bed and a chest of drawers on which the wedding picture of her and Jay still sat as it had in the other house. This room was less carefully appointed than the living room but impeccably neat. Gina remembered her mother telling her during one of her visits to Indiana that she had had trouble sleeping since Jay's death and that the fewer distractions she had in her bedroom, the more comfortable she felt. The bed was covered with a simple aqua-colored duvet and two pillows in cases edged with white crochet. A Tuscan tapestry draped over a bronze rod forgave the fact that there was no headboard and protected Anita from the danger a heavier framed object might have posed in case of an earthquake. The paintings of flowers displayed in a group of three on the front wall were her own, the familiar capital *A* scrawled in pencil across each of their bottom right-hand corners.

"Mom told me once that she didn't like distractions in her bedroom," Gina said to Larry now. He had followed her from room to room, also picking up items that interested him, straightening pictures, using the toe of his Italian leather loafer to kick the fringe out from where it had been accidentally folded underneath a rug. It was like being a child again, he thought, but also like being in an exotic foreign country where their mother, with a life of her own that only peripherally touched theirs, was the lone and sovereign inhabitant.

"It's weird being here," Larry said. "It kind of reminds me of when Mom and Dad went out for the evening and left us alone. You remember that? It always seemed like we could get by with murder, but we never could figure out what to do first. I remember smoking one of Dad's cigarettes back before he quit and you tottering around the house in Mom's high heels."

"I do remember those times, but as I recall we usually tired of being wicked pretty early and ended up making popcorn and watching a movie and wondering how long it would be until they got back."

"And fighting over what movie to watch."

"Well, yes, that, too."

Gina was already making her way back down the hallway to the studio and said this last over her shoulder.

"So what is it exactly that she expects us to do?" she asked Larry. "Do you have any idea? I wouldn't know where to start."

"The stuff that's sitting out will be easy enough."

As if to prove his point, he picked up the jar of brackish water and carried it to the kitchen, where he poured its contents down the sink, rinsed it out and turned it upside down on the drain board to dry.

"There! That's one job done. And the paint will be easy enough to put into some kind of order by color. I'm thinking it's the papers that will be hard."

"You think she wants us going through her private papers?"

"I think that must be the main thing she wants us to go through. In her grand scheme of assignments to help us get to know each other, I can't imagine that she would have us come down here just to dust and vacuum. And her paintings don't need to be catalogued. Her studio may be a pigsty, but she's careful about keeping track of her work."

"She should. That's where her big bucks come from." Again Gina heard the edge in her own voice, and Larry chose to ignore it.

"There's really not much of her stuff here to deal with anyway. It usually goes out the door to the gallery or off to a publisher the minute the paint's dry. No, I don't think it's that. I get the idea there's something else here that she wants us to discover."

"OK, Frank Hardy, then there's only one way to find out."

Larry carried in Gina's suitcase and the overnight bag he had packed, and they both changed into jeans and T-shirts.

"You can have Mom's room," Larry had said, rolling her red bag to a stop in the doorway to the hall. "I'll take the couch."

"Thanks," Gina said. After the episode when she had come home for Jay's funeral, she felt like he owed her a little comfort. "I only regret that you won't get to experience the bar under the mattress on her old pullout sofa. What ever happened to that? For that matter, what ever happened to all of the stuff from the old house that she didn't bring here?"

"I took a couple of things from my old room for Dex. Everything else got donated to St. Vincent de Paul's."

"Once a Catholic, always a Catholic, huh? Feng shui period or not?"

"I guess so."

They worked without stopping for a solid four hours. As Larry had suggested, they did the easy jobs first. Gina headed straight for the paint drawers and began laying the tubes out in rows of color families on the nearby worktable. Larry emptied the trash and swept then mopped the floor. He positioned the easels against one wall so they'd have more room to move around the room as they did their work. Then he stopped by the desk and looked at the piles of paper in exasperation.

"It's hard to know what to keep and what to toss," he said. "She's an artist. Anything could be an inspiration."

Gina tucked tubes of lamp black and Chinese white into the last slots in the third drawer and pushed it closed. Then she began to investigate the contents of the top drawer of the filing cabinet.

"Jesus," she said. "Look at this stuff. It's not even in folders. It's just crammed into these drawers, and it's all kinds of stuff -- phone bill receipts, her resume from when she worked for the design firm, tax papers, sympathy cards from Dad's funeral."

"OK, then let's start making piles. Chances are with some of this stuff if we toss it, she'll never miss it. We'll pick up some file folders when we knock off for dinner."

"At least if we do it together, if we make a mistake and throw away something important, we can both share the blame," Gina said.

He pulled over the trash bin he had just emptied and began tossing papers into it, starting with little slips of outdated grocery store coupons and big manila envelopes that had contained insurance papers and maps.

"That's not a bad idea," he said. He pulled the white bench that had flanked the worktable closer to the desk so they could both sit down. "Have a seat, co-conspirator. And maybe if we both look at everything, we won't make any mistakes that are too serious."

"Besides," she said, "if there is some hidden gem we're supposed to find, I want to see it, too."

"Who knows?" he said. He was shaking his head at the jumble in the drawer. "I'd be very surprised to find any gems here, but whatever. Let's just get it done."

It took three hours to go through the top drawer. At the end of that time the trash can was heavy with paper that Larry carried outside to the recycling bin. On the worktable yellow post-it notes identified the remaining stacks as legal, household, Gina (greeting cards and letters), Larry (also greeting cards and letters), business and general correspondence. All that remained in the bottom of the drawer were some paperclips, a few rusted staples, and tiny yellowed triangles of crumbling paper.

"I'm starving," Gina said, looking at her watch. It was nearly four. They hadn't stopped for lunch, and all she'd had to eat all day was a muffin she'd bought at the Indianapolis airport and a cup of orange juice and some stagnant coffee on the plane.

"Yeah, you must be whipped, too. It's three hours later in your head. What time did you have to get up?"

"Four, my time, which was one here."

"Let's knock off and go get some dinner. We can buy the file folders while we're out, too, and get some of this stuff put back away."

"I'm not really dressed for dinner." She swept her hands along her jeans and dirty T-shirt to demonstrate like a fashion model might have on a runway.

"You're just fine for what I have in mind. Let's get something from a takeout place and walk to the beach."

"That sounds wonderful. I just need a couple of minutes to wash up."

Forty-five minutes later Gina sat by her brother's side on one of their mother's Navajo blankets, her toes buried in sand, a plastic carton of chicken tikka masala and rice balanced on her lap. Larry had opted for the vindaloo when they stopped at Bombay Palace. They had had an Indian beer while they waited for their food to be ready, and now they were chasing their spicy meals with bottled water. The sun was still bright and only beginning to inch toward the west. A bank of clouds gathering on the horizon would obscure the sunset that was still more than two hours away. The beach was in transition -- mothers gathering up buckets and shovels and delivering the news to unhappy toddlers that it was time to go home, after-work surfers in shiny black wet suits running eagerly across the sand and into the water with their boards under their arms.

During the three-block walk from the restaurant they had used up all available conversation about Indian food -- where they'd first had it, what they liked, Stephanie liked it but Danielle didn't yet, Dexter was too young to try it. Then while they spread out their blanket and laid out the food they worked their way through talk about the beach. It must be great to live there, Gina said, and Larry told her yes, but mildew and rust and salt damage were problems, and there were whole overcast days when the marine layer that came in overnight never dissipated. And then there was awkward silence. Gina could think of anecdotes about the girls that would probably bore Larry; he might have mentioned a technical problem he was having at work, but she wouldn't even understand what he was talking about. Without the props of their mother's home and studio, they once again ran out of anything to say.

Eventually Larry gave up trying to come up with idle chit-chat and lay back on his elbows. Gina watched as the surfers beyond them drifted idly on momentarily quiet water and waited for a wave.

"So what's the plan for tonight?" she asked him finally.

"I don't know. You want to knock off and go to a movie or something?"

"That sounds like a lot more fun that sorting through more of Mom's detritus, but ..."

"Detritus?" He said the word with a deriding, questioning drawl, as if she had just said something ridiculous.

"Stuff, little brother. Junk. Shit, you would call it. Now, as I was saying, yes, a movie would be fun, but I'm only here for a few days, and part of it is supposed to be spent with Marqueeta at your house. And I'm also dying to meet my nephew. I think we should buy the folders and work on that second drawer. We've still got the desk to go through, and the bookcase needs to be straightened up. If we get some of that done tonight, we should be able to finish in the morning and head back to L.A. tomorrow afternoon."

He shrugged his shoulders. "Sounds like a plan. Let's do it."

They walked back to the restaurant to pick up Larry's car and drove to an office supply store. Back in the studio, Gina wiped out the file drawer with a damp cloth and arranged the stacks they had made into neatly labeled folders that filled three-quarters of the top drawer. Then she pulled open the bottom drawer, which was stuffed so full with papers that it was difficult to release. The contents had jelled into a yellow block that smelled of dust and age.

"This stuff looks older," she told her brother. "I think when she got the filing cabinet, she must have started with the bottom and just worked her way up. Some filing system."

While she began prying off the top layer, Larry pulled open one of the desk drawers to reveal scotch tape, a stapler, pencils, and pens. Another contained stationery, greeting cards, and stamps.

"Nothing of importance here," he said. "If there's something she wants us to see, it must be in that drawer."

They fell back into the same routine they had used earlier in the day. Gina examined a paper, held it up for Larry to see and then put it either into the trash or onto the appropriate filing pile. Then Larry did the same thing. Sometimes they had a brief discussion about whatever it was. As long as they had a common goal, conversation came easily. It was in the blank spaces where there was no work to do, no meal to discuss, no beach to admire that the silence fell heavily between them and they realized again how little they knew about one another's lives. In this way they worked through copies of Jay's death certificates, a letter from the Bank of America inviting Anita to the opening of a new branch three years ago, receipts from having the house painted just before she had moved in.

"For somebody who seems to have her life so under control, she sure is a slob when it comes to managing her papers," Larry grumbled. He had just tossed a brochure about a trip to Hawaii into the trash bin. Beneath it was a photograph of Anita with Dennis McDonald, both with leis around their necks.

"Interesting!" he said, holding it up and giving her a knowing smile.

"But I thought she went to Hawaii with a girlfriend." Then the lightbulb turned on. "She just said 'friend,' and I assumed it was a woman. So maybe Mr. Wu wasn't her first. Geez, she's got a whole life I didn't know about."

While she spoke she continued digging through the pile. "Hmmm," she said. "Look at this." She was holding up a bulging brown envelope from which she had withdrawn a piece of drawing paper folded twice into a square. Inside, in childish blue crayoned letters, Larry had written, "Mommy and Daddy, please come to my school play."

"Huh," he said, taking it from her. "That was when I played Jack Sprat. It was third grade. We were acting out a bunch of nursery rhymes." He couldn't help smiling at the memory of his own little self grasping the crayon in chubby hands and coloring the invitation for his parents.

"I remember that," Gina said. "You were taller and skinnier than anybody in your class, so you were the perfect kid for the part."

"Who was the girl who played my wife?" he asked now, his eyes squeezed shut as he tried to recall a name he hadn't sought for more than thirty years. She had moved away in fifth grade, and he'd never thought about her again until now. "She was skinny, too, and they put a pillow inside her dress to make her look fat."

"I remember that! It was so funny. Her skinny little arms and legs stuck out of this stuffed, plump little body. She looked like a giant insect. You would have thought the teacher could have found somebody more suited to the part."

"There was a chubbier little girl in the class. Her name I do remember: Rita Parker. She was absolutely the obvious choice, but that's exactly why Mrs. Romero couldn't pick her."

"Didn't she grow up to be an actress, though? I thought I remembered seeing her name somewhere."

"Yeah, that's the irony. She's turned heavy into an art form, and she's a great character actress. She's been in a couple of our movies, and I've seen her once or twice around the studio. We talked about that program once. She ended up playing Little Bo Peep."

The rest of the envelope contained similar mementoes from their childhoods -- childish drawings, some with names, some that neither could remember drawing but obviously had. There was Gina's certificate of achievement for getting perfect spelling scores for all of third grade and another for getting a perfect score on the states and capitals test in the fifth, Larry's red ribbon from winning second place in a middle-school swim team relay, a program from senior night at Larry's last high school basketball game, a note from the principal congratulating Gina's parents on her getting the scholarship to Purdue, a ribbon with a tiny piece of paper -- "Regina's prom" -- attached with a straight pin that drew a startled cry when she stuck herself pulling it from the envelope, a note Larry had left at some point -- "Going to practice and having dinner at Jeremy's."

"It's funny that she kept all this," Gina said, tenderness in her voice. "I have an envelope -- well, a box really -- just like this at home for the girls' papers. I hate to throw any of their schoolwork away, but you can't keep everything. I try to choose the very best ones or the ones that mean the most. What about you? Do you keep the things Dexter makes?"

"You know he's only in preschool, right?"

"Yes, but I'll bet he's already finger-painting and drawing and gluing bits of colored paper onto something. They all do that."

"I don't know. Marqueeta shows me that stuff, but then it disappears."

"I bet she's got a box or a folder somewhere. I can just about promise you that."

"Hey, aren't we supposed to be taking pictures of everything we do?" he asked, clearly happy to change the subject.

"Oh, God, yes. I forgot all about that," she said, standing up and stretching. They'd been working for more than three hours, and for most of that time she had sat on the plank bench hunched over the low drawer. Darkness had fallen, and they'd turned on the lights so they could keep on working. "I've got a camera in my suitcase. I'll go get it. Too bad you already threw away that gunk in her water jar. That would have been a good shot."

"Oh, I think we've got plenty here to prove our point," he said, and he laughed. It was the laugh Gina remembered from years ago, as if it had been uncorked from a bottle or released from the folds of the delicate papers they'd been sorting, as if it belonged only to her and to childhood and wouldn't be heard again outside of these walls and this time once the sun came up again and they finished their work and locked their mother's door behind them. Even at his most pleasant, she hadn't heard him actually laugh out loud since he'd been a child.

When she returned with the camera, they posed for silly pictures of each other.

"If we have to make a scrapbook we might as well make it worth looking through," Larry said.

Gina picked up the bin and poured the papers they had discarded over her lap and looked exasperated, her arms in the air, her legs sprawled, as if she were totally immobilized by the weight of this responsibility. Larry pressed the end of a brush to his lips and gazed thoughtfully at the empty tabletop easel, pretending to ponder an invisible picture. Gina held a document from the drawer and studied it in mock alarm. Eventually they balanced the camera on a stack of books on the worktable, set the timer and sat down on chairs next to each other with the filing cabinet and the desk in the background, each of them holding up a drawing from the envelope. Larry had started to put his arm around Gina but then thought better of it and gripped his drawing with both hands as a proud child might, causing Gina, beside him, to copy his idea. Without discussing it, they both smiled at their mother as if she were in the room and taking the picture herself.

When the flash had gone off and they had looked to make sure the picture was good, Gina suddenly realized she was exhausted.

"You know what, I'm whipped," she said.

"You've had a day, but you've really been a trouper," he said. He waved his arm in the direction of the paint cabinet and the file drawers. "We've gotten a lot done."

"Yes, but there's still a lot to go. I was hoping we could get back to L.A. tomorrow afternoon."

"I think we can. There's not that much more to do. You can finish the filing cabinet. I'll straighten up the closet."

"Oh, God. I didn't even think about the closet. What's in there?"

"It isn't as bad as you'd think." He opened the door, pulled the string to illuminate the pantry-like space, and stepped inside to look around. "It's mostly just props. She's got vases and old books and silk flowers and an antique globe in here, and there are some more brushes and odds and ends," he called out. "I don't think there's any sorting or thinking to do really."

"OK, good. Then I'm going to bed."

"How about a quick nightcap before you head off?"

She started to decline and then realized her brother was seeking out her company and didn't want her to go to bed just yet. She could practically feel the cool sheets and soft pillows, but how many nights were she and her brother alone in their mother's house with nothing else to do besides savor whatever memories had made the move to these four walls, with no spouses, no children, no jobs, nothing to distract them and call them back to their own responsibilities.

"Sure," she said. "Does she have amaretto?"

He fumbled around in a narrow credenza that flanked the dining table and housed Anita's small liquor supply.

"Um, yes, she does. And I'll have a brandy."

He pulled out the two bottles and set them on the table. Then he retrieved two snifters from a different compartment and poured amber liquids into both. He handed one to her and clinked it with his own.

"Here's to you, Sis," he said.

She smiled and responded, "And to you."

He took a sip and then set his glass down on the coffee table behind the wedding pictures. Then he flipped open the lid of Anita's piano and, still standing, began to pick out scales with one hand. Then he slid onto the bench and began playing with both hands. It was as if he couldn't help himself, as if the mere act of touching the instrument had lured him in, the siren's call too compelling to be denied. He started with "Fur Elise" and a couple of other classical pieces Gina didn't recognize, then swung into a medley of standards that included "Embraceable You," "Don't Get Around Much Anymore," and "Blue Moon." Gina slipped off her shoes and stretched out on the sofa to listen. How many times had she yelled at him, her other hand covering the mouthpiece of the telephone receiver, to stop banging on the piano and give her some peace? How many times had she marched to wherever their mother was and demanded that he have a set practice time and that it not go beyond the hour a day required by his teacher because he was driving her crazy. But it had all led to this, and now he was a real musician who was giving her a private, privileged concert, a lullaby, a soundtrack of her life. Eventually he played "Through the Eyes of Love," which he knew was her favorite. By this time her eyes were closed and she was drifting off to sleep, but still she smiled.

When he had finished he stood up and gave her legs a nudge with his now shoeless toe.

"Hey, you, sleepyhead," he said. "Get out of here. You're on my bed."

"Thanks," she said. "That was nice, really nice."

She stood slowly, yawning, and headed off in the direction of the hallway that led to the bedroom, but instead of going in, she turned left and went back to the studio. She flipped on the overhead light and surveyed the work they had done, pushing in the bottom file drawer with her foot so that neither of them would trip over it in the morning. Then she paused by the pink bookcase and read through the titles. Among the art books were a few novels, a guidebook to the birds of California, and a book of maps of San Diego streets. These were the functional books -- the ones her mother would pull out and refer to while she worked or when she was taking a break from painting. The pretty books, the leatherbound sets and old classics, were arranged more artfully in the living room. And then she saw it, a big, flat oversized book lying on its side with other books resting on top of it: *How to Draw Buildings: Notes on Perspective.* She knelt and tugged at it, pushing at the volumes on top of it with her other hand to keep them in place. Then she laid it out on the worktable and opened it, moving the bench back into place and sliding onto it as Larry had the piano bench, as eager to leaf through the pages as he had been to touch the keys.

"Hey, I thought you were going to bed," Larry said now, appearing in the door that led to the kitchen. "I just came in here to turn out the light. I didn't realize you were still up."

"Look what I found," she said, her eyes shining, her smile barely containing her excitement.

She closed the book so that he could read the title, marking her place with her finger, and then opened it again.

"It's a book about drawing perspectives," he said, frowning. "I honestly can't think of anything more boring."

This time she was the one who laughed.

"Of course you can't," she said. "This is my thing, like music is yours. And this book is really special."

She stroked it unconsciously as she might have a cat stretched out lazily before her on the table.

"This is the book that got me interested in engineering. I always liked to draw, and when Mom was doing interior design work, I was always looking through her books and watching her make her sample boards. Do you remember those? When she used to draw pictures of the rooms and then put little bits of fabric and carpet and paint chips next to them to give the client an idea of what the finished room would look like? I loved that. One day she had this book out because she was working on a hotel lobby and she needed to look something up. She left it out when she was finished, and I picked it up and started looking at the pictures. Suddenly everything in my head came together. I was good at math and I loved to draw. Bingo. I've still got some of my early architectural drawings at home somewhere. I must only have been ten or eleven at the time, but it was like I had fallen in love. For a while after that all I did whenever I had any free time was draw pictures of buildings -- pictures from real life, pictures from photographs, pictures from my imagination. When I was bored at school I drew pictures of little buildings in the margins of my notebooks."

"With Mom being a designer and you liking to draw buildings, it seems like the logical choice would have been to be an architect."

"I probably still could. I've certainly had my share of drafting classes. But I also loved numbers and math, and I wanted to make my buildings work. I didn't want them to be just pictures on a page or little scale models. I wanted to figure out what it would take for bridges to carry cars over water or floors to hold hundreds of people working in offices. I wanted my buildings to be full of life. I wanted them to breathe. Engineering just took everything a step farther."

She turned back to the book.

"I had honestly forgotten about this book, but when I saw it tonight, it all came back to me. I wonder if Mom would mind if I took it home with me. I'd love to show the girls. They'll soon be about the age that I was when I first saw it."

"We'll take it with us tomorrow and send Mom an e-mail from my house. I can't imagine she'd mind if it's that important to you, especially if you just want to borrow it. And now I'm going to bed. See you in the morning."

He retraced his steps back into the living room, and she could hear him pulling out blankets and pillows from the shelf in the coat closet. Then she turned out the light and walked down the hall to her mother's bedroom, clutching the book to her chest as if someone were trying to take it away from her.

In the morning Gina woke up before her brother. Her first instinct was to go out in search of coffee, croissants, and fruit for their breakfast, but then she remembered that this was exactly what she had done when she had come back for her stepfather's funeral and that Larry hadn't appreciated her effort. The familiar annoyance with her brother tugged at her mind but was quickly replaced with something much more pleasant. She pulled on the jeans and T-shirt she had worn the day before -- there would be time for a shower later, when they had finished their work. Then she tiptoed out into the hallway. Larry was still asleep on the sofa, snoring softly, the satin edge of the ivory blanket rising and falling with his breath. They had left the shades up overnight, and soon pale yellow-gray light would wake him up if she didn't put them down. She slipped into the living room, tugged on the cord and let them fall slowly and silently, protecting Larry from light that would awaken him before he was ready to get up.

What time was it, anyway? The sky was gray and overcast, but she knew that sometimes the sun didn't break through the cloud layer until midday. A glance at the digital clock on the microwave told her it was only 6:13. Good. There was time.

Larry finally emerged from the house, barefoot and still wearing the briefs and T-shirt in which he had slept, just after 9:30. The sky was still murky, but a sliver of blue was visible and a pale, watery suggestion of sunshine was beginning to warm the backyard. Gina stood before an easel, facing him, a palette loaded with paint in one hand and a brush in the other. When she heard the door open, she turned to face him, smiling in pure delight.

"Good morning!" she practically sang out.

"What are you doing out here?" While he spoke he walked toward her and then around to the other side of the easel, where he could see that she had nearly finished a painting of the garden, a perfect miniature of the scene in which he was standing. There were the chairs with the green cushions and the bougainvillea cascading down from the trellis. She had even duplicated the stray blossoms that had broken loose and now dappled the patio tiles like red and pink confetti. Behind it all was the house, every tiny windowpane and roof tile represented, next to a tangled green mass from which emerged the agapanthus and lavender and lilies. She had added a bright blue coffee cup and an opened book with a bright orange cover turned upside down on the little table.

"Gina, my God, this is incredible," Larry said. He moved even closer for a better look. "This is as good as the stuff Mom does. I had no idea you could do this."

"Neither did I," she said, almost giggling. "I mean, I knew I used to be able to do it, but I haven't picked up a paintbrush for years, other than to play around with the kids when they were little. And when I was working in Indianapolis, sometimes I'd throw a little watercolor onto my presentations -- a bush or a tree here, a person walking through a plaza there. I'd forgotten how much fun it is. No wonder Mom seems so happy. She gets to do this for a living -- and now travel around the world to do it."

She pressed a brush loaded with deep purple onto the patio under the bougainvillea arch to create a perfect puddle of shadow. Next she dipped her brush into a jar of water -- the very jar he had emptied last night -- and used it to lighten the cerulean blue sky she had created overhead. Then she stepped back and said, "There. I think that's it."

"I'm not kidding, Gina. I'm dumbfounded," Larry said. "You should do something with that."

"I'm going to," she answered, laughing. "I'm going to leave it on this easel as a surprise for Mom when she gets home. Despite having to go through all of her old crap, I've had a really good time here. I'd never have time to do this with two kids and a husband at home and my work at the store."

She gestured toward the painting, and her eyes lingered as if she, too, couldn't quite stand to take her eyes off it. Then, as if awakening from a trance, she said, "Well, we can't stay out here all day. We've got work to do." She started to pick up the easel to carry it back into the studio, but Larry pulled it away from her. She followed him with the water jar in one hand and her palette and brush in the other.

There was nothing in the house for breakfast, so Larry dressed and went out, returning fifteen minutes later with a bag containing two coffees and two muffins. After they'd eaten, they again took up their posts at the filing cabinet, and again they found nothing remarkable -- yellowed newspaper reviews of shows in which Anita had exhibited her paintings, a few letters from friends, more of their childish artwork and school papers. Eventually they reached the photo of Davey Calhoun that Larry had seen one other time before.

"Here's that picture of your dad," he said now, holding it up. "Have you ever seen it before?"

"Yes, and don't call him my dad. He may have been the sperm donor, but Jay Langley was my dad as much as he was yours." She took the photograph from his hand and stared at it thoughtfully. "The sum total of what I know about this man is this picture and the clipping of his obituary that's here somewhere and the little speech Mom gave me when I figured out that the dates of her and Jay's wedding and my birthday didn't add up. That must have been a talk she'd been dreading my whole life."

Larry had just located the newspaper piece and handed it to her.

"What did she say to you?"

"Not very much, really. And when I say 'speech,' that's what I mean. She had obviously rehearsed it. She was holding a dish towel when she told me, and she had squeezed it into a tiny little ball before she finished. She just said that she had been married another time before she met Dad and that they had had a baby that was me and then they had gotten divorced and he had later died. Then she asked me if I had any questions, and that was that. I remember that she practically fled from my room when it was over."

"Did you?"

"Did I what?"

"Have any questions?"

"No, not really. It was a shock of course, but what else was there to know? I had a great dad, Jay, and this other guy had been sort of famous for a little while, so that seemed kinda cool."

"You look exactly like him."

"And you look exactly like Mom. Funny. To be perfectly honest, I think the only negative effect the revelation had on me was that I was aware then that you were Jay's child and I wasn't, and I started seeing the ways he obviously favored you that I hadn't noticed before."

"Like what?"

"Oh, now I think it might just have been that you were a boy and I was a girl. I used to be jealous when he took you to the driving range with him or when he went to watch your basketball practices, but I don't think that had anything to do with excluding me. Looking back, I see that he came to my stuff for me, too. I do think that if he could only have saved one of us from a burning building it would have been you, but that's only to be expected."

"And I always thought he spoiled you because he felt sorry for you."

"Well, there you are, then. When did they tell you I wasn't really your sister?"

"Gina, you are my sister. At the very least, you're my half-sister. We do have the same mom, remember. But the funny thing is, I think Dad was telling me at the same time Mom was telling you. I think I was about eight, so that would have made you twelve. Obviously they knew we'd talk, so they had to tell us both. He took me out to the garage on the pretext of fixing something on my bicycle. I don't think he ever looked at me directly the whole time he was talking to me. He kept fiddling with my bike, but there wasn't anything wrong with it."

"Weird. Parents get weird ideas in their minds. Do we do that?"

He laughed again. "I hope not, but ask Dexter when he's a teenager and he may have a different opinion."

"I'm sure my girls do now."

While she spoke she slipped the picture and clipping into a new folder that she labeled "Davey Calhoun."

"The clipping doesn't even mention Mom or me, but he was her husband and my biological father, so I think he deserves his own folder."

By the time they finished the drawer, they had added a faded marriage license, a postcard from New York, and a snapshot of Anita and Davey together, maybe on their wedding day, his arm around her, a long-since-changed skyline of San Diego in the background but familiar enough to indicate that they had been on Coronado Island when it was taken. Larry wiped out the drawer while Gina arranged the file folders alphabetically and then they were done. They spent another half-hour washing the shelves in the closet and replacing the props Anita sometimes used in her paintings. Then they tackled the papers on the desk, filing them into the proper folders, too. At last Larry slid the bench back under the worktable and stood back, crossing his arms and leaning against the doorjamb that led to the kitchen to survey their handiwork.

"I think we did it, Sis," he said, "but we never did find any startling revelations."

"I know. I'm a little disappointed, too, but at least we're done. And now ..." she turned and ran from the room, calling behind her, "dibs on the first shower."

CHAPTER TWELVE

"It's weird, isn't it, I mean the way your mom planned this whole thing to get you and Larry to do stuff together," Marqueeta said. Against Gina's protests, her sister-in-law had insisted on struggling with her suitcase over the uneven stone path that led to the guesthouse, leaving Gina feeling helpless but free to look out over the ocean and marvel at this place where her brother lived and the view to which he and Marqueeta woke up every single morning of their lives.

"I'm an only child, like your mom, and I'm telling you, if I had a brother or a sister, no one would have to bribe me to do things with them. I'd probably drive them crazy wanting to be around them so much." She laughed, a high, nervous whinny that caused Gina, walking behind her, to grimace and think yes, that might very well be the case.

Larry had dropped her off at his house and gone on to the office. The new movie was in post-production, he explained apologetically, and after being away for two days, he was sure she'd understand that he needed to get some work done before he came back for dinner. Nothing like throwing me in the deep end of the pool, Gina had thought but didn't say. But then, Marqueeta, wearing chocolate-brown shorts and a turquoise T-shirt and running shoes, had run down the Spanish-tiled steps toward the circular driveway where Larry had pulled up, smiling welcomingly as if it were her own long-lost sister who was arriving.

"I mean, I've never heard of anything like it, except in movies," she went on now. "Remember in the movie *It's a Mad, Mad, Mad, Mad World,* when all of the people were racing against time to get to the money first? It reminds me a little bit of that."

Gina suspected that Keeta was as anxious and eager to make a good impression as she was, so she listened silently to her sister-in-law's incessant prattle. In the few moments they had been together, this was her third comparison of a real-life situation to a movie. Did everyone out here think like that, especially if they were involved in the filmmaking business? Was life here just one big issue of *People* magazine?

"I hesitate to use the word 'weird' about my own mother," Gina said now, feeling suddenly protective and loyal, "but unusual, yes. Definitely unusual." She smiled so that Marqueeta would know she wasn't being critical. "And apparently it's not a bribe. It was about the money in the beginning, and I hated that. Larry and I have been out of touch for a long time, but he's still my brother, well, half-brother. You know that whole story. Anyway, it puts a really bad taste in my mouth to think I am doing things with him just to get money, and I hated it that Mom was kind of blackmailing us in a way, or bribing us, like you said. After she got mad at us and said we didn't have to do the assignments, it actually started to seem like they might be fun." Then she laughed. "I guess that probably goes back to our childhood, too, you know, ganging up on your parents."

"I wouldn't know about that," Marqueeta said, putting a key into the slot under an antique bronze doorknob. "But the money's nice. You've got to admit that. I'm trying to think what we might do with our $42,000. I think I might see a new car in my future, or we might do some remodeling or take a trip to Europe. We'll just have to see."

Gina wanted to hiss at her that she and Steve did not have the luxury of such a dilemma, that their money had gone directly into the bank as a hedge against any of a number of calamities potentially waiting to befall them -- the store going under, the Stevensons deciding to sell the farm so that they'd have to find another place to live and start paying rent. Even in the best of circumstances they'd eventually need it for the girls' college tuition. If Anita kept her promise and gave them $56,000 a year for the years between now and when Stephanie went away to school, they could still fall short.

Fortunately, just then Keeta opened the door and went inside with the suitcase. She was chattering now about the guesthouse, giving Gina instructions about how the shower and coffeemaker worked and pointing out the amenities as if she were the manager of a high-end hotel. Indeed, the place could have passed for a casita at a five-star resort. There were two bedrooms joined by a sitting room, a bathroom, and a kitchenette. In the bedroom with the queen-size bed there was a bouquet of fresh yellow roses on the dresser and two sets of fluffy, new-looking ivory towels folded on the bureau. A box of expensive chocolates and several shiny new magazines lay on the coffee table in the sitting room, and in the bedroom that contained two twin beds hung a banner that read "Welcome, Stephy and Danny." Stephanie had never been called "Stephy" in her life, Gina mused, but she appreciated the effort. When the girls arrived, she'd head Stephanie off and caution her not to laugh when she saw the sign in the bedroom. The bedspreads had sparkly pink and green fairies embroidered all over them and unicorns appliqued onto the pillowcases.

"For the mother of a little boy, you certainly know something about girls," Gina said, running her hand over one of the spreads to feel the bumpy glittered wings. "They will love this room. They'll never want to go home."

Marqueeta opened the closet door and pointed to two sets of Batman bedding and two sets of plaid sheets and plain white duvets on the shelf.

"We're prepared for whoever comes," she said proudly. "Boys, girls, or adults. We're all set."

"It must be nice," Gina said before she could stop herself, and immediately she saw the hurt look on Marqueeta's face.

"I'm sorry," she said. "I guess it looks like I'm showing off. I just meant that it isn't like I'm especially intuitive or anything. I just want people to be comfortable when they stay with us, no matter who it is."

Gina wished she could suck the words back in and return them to the dark place from which they had slunk out, more as if they came from a petulant adolescent than from a grown woman.

"No, I'm the one who's sorry," she said. "I didn't mean to sound sarcastic. It really must be great to have so many nice things. Larry has probably told you that Steve and I have had some financial difficulties in the past few years, so we're happy to have one set of sheets and blankets. That's all."

Marqueeta shook her head and looked puzzled, and Gina knew instantly that Larry had not shared any of this information with his wife, either when the letter asking for money had arrived or in the recent past, when he had come home from Hong Kong full of the talks he and his mother and sister had had there, or now, when the two of them must have had some kind of discussion, made some kind of plans as they got ready for this visit. Talk about weird. Didn't they communicate at all? Were these the "issues" and "problems" to which Larry was constantly alluding without any explanation? What were they walking in to?

"Forget I said anything," she said breezily to Marqueeta. "We're going to be fine. Now, when do I get to meet my nephew?"

The cloud lifted from Marqueeta's face as quickly as it had settled there, and she looked at the oversized watch on her thin wrist.

"I think Lupe picks him up around four, so he'll be here in about an hour," she said.

"Ah, so it's an afternoon preschool?" Gina asked. Stephanie had gone to a morning preschool the whole year she was four, but by the time it was Danielle's turn, there hadn't been enough money to send her, and Gina had taught her the alphabet, numbers, and printing her name at home.

"Oh, no, it's morning. Larry drops him off on his way to the studio at eight-thirty. The school also provides lunch and day care, so he stays there until four."

"Wow. That's a long day for a little guy. He's three, right? He must be exhausted when he gets home."

"Yeah, but Lupe has a bunch of kids of her own, so she knows how to take care of him. She gives him a snack and keeps him entertained until Larry gets home, and then he takes over."

Gina felt her eyes widen in surprise and then quickly narrowed them to hide the judgment she felt, but it was too late. Either Marqueeta had seen her expression, or she knew she had reason to be defensive.

"You probably think I'm a bad mom and that I should be making his meals and playing games with him, and sometimes I do. But sometimes I'm just not up to it. I have ... issues. I'm sure Larry has told you all about that."

"No, that's all he's ever said. Just 'issues.' Aren't you well? I'm sorry."

"I'm manic-depressive. I have good days and bad. But I'm on medication, so the chances are good I won't fly into a million pieces and hurt anybody or destroy anything while you're here."

Again, Gina felt her eyebrows shoot skyward of their own accord.

"That was a little joke," Marqueeta said. "Look, I was about to go for a walk. I go every day about this time. It helps me keep in shape, but it also clears out my head. Why don't you go with me? I think it would help you relax."

Dinner was over. Lupe had served a marinated shrimp dish from her native Ecuador and then left for the night while they were finishing the ice cream that followed. The shrimp had been too spicy for Dexter, who cried until the woman replaced it with a pile of chicken nuggets on a plate shaped like a football and stirred him up a glass of strawberry-flavored milk. Larry had given him a bath and Gina had helped, using the plastic boats and fish in the bathtub to distract him while Larry shampooed his dark hair and rinsed it. As Gina carried him, wrapped in a fluffy blue towel with a duck's bill protruding over his forehead, down the hallway to his room, he had pointed to the door of the frilly boudoir and said, "Mommy's room." Then, before they turned into his own rodeo-themed chamber, he motioned down the hall.

"That's Daddy's room," he said sleepily, and Gina thought that whatever went on in this household even a three-year-old could pick up on its strangeness.

"Leave it to kids to give away the family secrets, huh?" Larry asked her. He was walking behind them, carrying Dexter's play clothes and shoes.

She read him a story while Larry listened, then Marqueeta came in to say goodnight and give him a kiss before she went to bed at 9:00.

"Once I take my medication, I'm not good for anything," she said, and this time Gina realized she was not making a joke. "I'll see you in the morning." She fluttered her fingers in a wave and then disappeared into her room and closed the door. The unmistakable click of the lock was deafening.

Now Gina and Larry were wrapped in blankets side by side in lounge chairs on the deck. Despite its being August and the day having been hot, the marine layer that had rolled in from the ocean had brought with it dampness and cold. Larry had produced a glass of amaretto for her and set the bottle down on the table between their chairs. He was sipping what looked like the same brandy he'd had the night before at their mother's house. For a long while they were silent. There was a lot to talk about, but Gina didn't know how to begin, and she didn't want to ask questions that would start an argument or make Larry think she was prying. Still, he was the one who kept talking about "issues," and Marqueeta had used that word, too. Apparently Larry was having the same thoughts and must have been trying to figure out how to broach the subject as she had.

"So did Marqueeta tell you about her illness?" he asked.

"She told me she was manic-depressive and that she has good days and bad. That's all. She was busy showing me the guesthouse, so she didn't go into detail. I'm not sure exactly what that involves. I mean, I've been depressed, but never to the point where I needed medication."

"It goes a lot deeper with her than just temporary sadness. It's organic, something in her makeup that just talking to a counselor won't help. The shrinks put her on medicine that evens out her moods, but if they don't get the dosage just right she goes manic. She flies high for a few days, makes plans, goes shopping, starts projects, sees her friends, and then, just as quickly she goes dark and has to stay in bed for a day. When that happens she feels like nobody cares about her, like she's a failure at being a wife and a parent, that she ruins everything she touches." He sighed deeply. "She talks about suicide, but so far she's never actually attempted it."

"Oh, my God!" Gina turned to face him so quickly that some of her drink sloshed out onto her blanket. She mopped it up with one of the paper cocktail napkins Larry had brought out with the liqueurs. It was embossed with a large gold *L*. "Wow. I had no idea."

"Yeah, see, you're not the only one with problems. Mine are different, and thank God I have the financial wherewithal to manage them, but my brain is ready to explode at any given time, just like yours must be."

"I had no idea. When she said, 'medication,' ... "

"She also has night terrors. The things that just make her depressed in the daytime horrify her if she wakes up and thinks about them in the night. The doctor she's seeing now has given her some sleeping pills, but she has to take a low dose. She's so thin and susceptible to medication that if she actually took enough to keep everything under control, she'd turn into a zombie. With Dex to take care of, she can't afford to sleep her life away."

"But she said he goes to preschool and day care all day, and then Lupe takes care of him and then you do."

"That's her putting herself down, something else that comes with her illness. She's a great mom. She's crazy about him, but she knows her limitations, and she'd rather have him someplace where she knows he's getting good care than at home where something could happen to him that would be her fault. Fatigue also sets her off, and for the last few days she's been in a tailspin about your visit. She wanted to buy the groceries herself and make up the beds in the guesthouse and pick up the flowers. Usually Lupe would do all of that, but she wanted to make sure everything was perfect. That worries me a little bit. I hope she can hold it together until Steve and the girls get here tomorrow."

"I hate to think our visit would cause her to be sick," Gina said. "If it does, what should we do? How can we help? Should I call Steve right now and tell him not to come?"

"No, no. Nothing like that. I think having you all here will be good for her. It's just that that very level of activity could push her over the edge. The best thing to do is carry on like nothing has happened. Thanks to Lupe, our lives go right on ticking away, and if you didn't know better, you wouldn't notice anything was wrong. She keeps food on the table and laundry done and Dexter happy. When Marqueeta has a bad day, she goes into action canceling her appointments and making her comfortable and checking on her to make sure she doesn't hurt herself."

Gina couldn't imagine dealing with a crippling condition that would send her to bed and dull her life with Steve and the girls. Again a deep sigh emanated from beneath the blanket in the chair next to her.

"There's more. There was also a traumatic event in her life that her psychiatrist says undoubtedly contributed to her condition."

He was quiet again. Gina wondered if she should ask what the event was, but she thought better of it and sat silently and waited. Larry drained his glass and then sat up to pour more brandy into it and fortify himself for what was to come next.

"She was beaten and sexually abused as a child."

He slumped against the back of his deck chair as if uttering the sentence had exhausted him. It had been so freighted with anger and sadness that it must have been an effort to even conjure up the words. Now they flamed up between the two of them as if they had been written with Fourth of July sparklers, the blazing memory of the letters hanging for a moment on the damp night air before it dissipated.

"Oh, Larry. God, I'm sorry. Who? For God's sake, who did this to her? Were they found? I hope somebody's rotting in jail for this."

Her eyes filled with tears. Obviously she had been unfair to Marqueeta, and she couldn't help but think of her own daughters, their smooth, fresh faces, their sturdy legs and gangly arms that had turned deep brown over the summer. Suddenly she couldn't wait until they got there. She had been bluffing when she'd suggested calling Steve to cancel their trip. All she could think about was seeing them tomorrow and holding them close to her and tucking them into the fairy-and-unicorn beds where she could hear them breathing from just across the sitting room.

"No," Larry said. "The culprit was her father."

"Evan?" she practically shrieked, sitting bolt upright, and he frantically shushed her.

"No, no of course not. There's more you don't know about Marqueeta. There's just never been a good time to tell you. Evan and Sylvia adopted her. They aren't her biological parents."

"Does Mom know this?" The words popped out before she could stop them. She didn't know why it was important, but she desperately needed to know.

"She does now, but I only told her a couple of years ago. It was a night something like tonight. Everybody else was in bed. Dex was still just a baby, and Marqueeta had turned in early, like she usually does. I knew Mom didn't care much for her, and I wanted to explain why she is the way she is, but I had been waiting for the chance to explain it without any distractions or interruptions. It's not something you bring up in idle conversation."

"No, I guess not. So what happened? How did the Cohens get her?"

"She was seven when it happened. A relative of her biological mother's, a cousin I think, had been visiting, and Marqueeta's mother had given her a key to their apartment so she could come and go whenever she wanted. She'd gone out to a movie one afternoon while Marqueeta's mother was at work. Marqueeta's dad didn't have a job at the time, so he stayed home to baby-sit. The cousin didn't like the movie, so she left early and came home. She could hear Marqueeta screaming and crying from the hallway, and when she let herself in, she saw that the door to Marqueeta's bedroom was closed. Her father had obviously heard the key in the lock, and when he came out to see who it was he was threading his belt through the loops in his pants. I can see that scene as clearly as if I'd been there, and I've never even seen a picture of the guy. Anyway, Marqueeta was hysterical. The woman grabbed her up and ran with her. She drove to the supermarket where Marqueeta's mother was a checker and tried to explain what had happened, but her mother wouldn't hear it. She claimed the cousin had a thing for her husband and was making up a story to get back at him because he didn't return the advances she made while the mother was at work. She told her to go get her things and then clear out. The cousin called the police, but of course the father denied everything and the mother stood by her man, you might say. She never would accuse him, never would even admit that anything had happened. He had obviously threatened Marqueeta, and she was too young and terrified to understand what had happened, let alone talk about it. Then just a couple of months later she had to go to the school nurse when she fell off the monkey bars on the playground, and the nurse saw bruises and knew as soon as she saw her what had been going on. She called the social services people, and they took her away from her parents and placed her in a foster home. The doctor who examined her said she had not actually been raped. From what Marqueeta was able to tell him, he put together the father was touching her inappropriately, and when she told him to stop, he took off his belt and let her have it. Obviously it happened more than once. Anyway, the father just disappeared, vanished into thin air, so he never was prosecuted, and the mother blamed Marqueeta for chasing him away and never warmed up to her or wanted her back."

"How do you know all of that? How could a child remember all of those details?"

Again the tears that this time spilled over and dripped down her cheeks and off her chin. She blew her nose on the cocktail napkin, mentally calculating that if it was eleven now and her girls would arrive at three tomorrow afternoon, she would see them in sixteen hours.

"The cousin couldn't take her, but she kept in touch with Marqueeta all the way up until Dexter was born. She sent a little present -- a homemade quilt that we still have. Then we got word that she had died. She had actually become pretty close to Sylvia, and one time when Sylvia came down to visit she told me the whole story. I tried to mention it to Marqueeta, but she got so agitated, it wasn't worth it, so we've never actually had a conversation about it."

"So when did Evan and Sylvia enter the picture?"

"The mother surrendered custody to the foster parents, but they already had a houseful of kids themselves, so an adoption agency became involved. Sylvia couldn't have children of her own, and they adopted Marqueeta when she was nine. They had hoped for a baby, but when the social worker told them Marqueeta's story, they wanted to meet her. They fell in love with her and that was that."

"Well, that much, at least, was a happy ending."

"Yes and no. I appreciate what they did for Marqueeta, but they're not my favorite people. Evan's a womanizing lush, and Sylvia's a social climber who spends her days shopping and her nights going to charity benefits, but they love their daughter. Evan's never around much, but Sylvia adores her, which in some ways just adds to the problems. She goes ballistic any time Marqueeta has an episode. She's never learned to just go with it like I have."

"That explains a lot of things that happened at your wedding."

His chuckle was tinged with bitterness, or was it just sadness? She couldn't tell.

"Yes, I guess it does."

"Sylvia was a real shrew when Mom wanted to wear that red dress from Mexico, and Marqueeta was in a frenzy, too. And then Marqueeta went to pieces and was yelling at Stephanie because she got punch on her sleeve."

"You have quite a memory, Sis. Don't you ever let anything go?"

"My mom and my daughter were both upset, so I got it from both sides. Of course I remember."

"Marqueeta had gone off her meds not long before the wedding because she wanted to get pregnant. We'd been living together for a while, and one of the reasons we decided to make it legal was because we were ready to have a child. The problem was that when she's not on medication, she comes unglued fairly easily, and one of the manifestations of coming unglued is not being able to deal with unexpected events or disappointments. She gets in her mind that something is going to be a certain way -- like Mom is going to wear a black dress or Stephanie is going to look perfect in her little pink dress -- and if anything happens to change that, even if it's something that insignificant, it can send her into a downward spiral. Sylvia's no help. With Evan being out of the picture half the time, she poured all of her love and attention into her daughter so that Marqueeta is admittedly spoiled, and when you expect everything to be handed to you on a silver platter and then it's not, or the silver platter is a little bit tarnished and doesn't look exactly the way you thought it would, all shiny and bright, you can spend half of your life being depressed. So she's got three strikes against her -- a clinically diagnosed disease, a violent past, and parents who have never come to grips with what's wrong with her."

The clouds that loomed over them, the blankets that encased them, the warm afterglow of the alcohol all combined to make the mood intimate enough that she felt she could ask the question that truly wasn't any of her business.

"So that's why you have separate bedrooms?"

"Yep." The word started somewhere deep within him and ended with the p sounding like a cork that had just exploded from a champagne bottle.

"I'm so sorry. I can't imagine. Steve and I are such snugglers. I can't imagine being married and sleeping alone."

"I didn't know most of this stuff until after we were married. I guess a suspicious person would say she tricked me into marriage, but I see it for what it really was. She loved me -- she still does -- and she thought she could endure it to make me happy and to get pregnant. When we were dating she stayed at my place most of the time, and she was pretty good at faking it. The sex was pretty frequent and pretty good. I think she was trying really hard, but it must have been awful for her. Looking back now I can see there were clues, but I was crazy about her, and I felt like I was ready to get married." He laughed softly. "And truth be told, I was jealous of you."

"Me? Good lord, why?"

"Because you had it -- the marriage, the family. Mom was always talking about Stephanie and then Danielle and how she looked forward to when I got married and had kids. Anyway, the thing was that Marqueeta wanted it, too, but now I see that it was in a childish way. She kind of got stuck back there at four or six when she was playing with paper dolls and teddy bears. Her idea of marriage was wearing a pretty white dress and having a big party, and her idea of motherhood was decorating a nursery and dressing her baby up in cute outfits. We hired Lupe right after Dex was born, and I don't know what we would have done without her. When he would cry or spit up or have a dirty diaper, Marqueeta would hand him over to one of us with this look on her face like she was genuinely puzzled and couldn't figure out how it had happened. And as for sex, she finally admitted that doing what it took to land me and then get the baby she wanted was a nightmare for her. There had never been anyone else. Sometimes I wish she'd had a whole string of boyfriends so that there would be some buffer between what happened in her childhood and the awful thing her husband was asking her to do. She'd been in therapy, of course. Evan and Sylvia saw to that because they knew her history, but I think all of the effort went into healing her from those events and not into preparing her for a healthy adult relationship."

"So what do you do? Is there anyone else?"

"Nah. She indulges me a couple of times a year, sometimes when she's had a good day or we've had a nice evening out and we're feeling especially close. Sometimes it's after we've had too much to drink, so I always feel like a shit afterward. I know what must be going through her head the whole time. She never, uh, finishes, if you know what I mean, and it usually sets off an episode. She always says it won't and she wants so much to please me, but it always does, so then I feel like a shit again. And yes, I've had a couple of flings when I've been out of town on film locations, and then I feel like an even bigger shit. It's not worth it."

"Does she have any idea what ever happened to her biological parents?"

"Sylvia kept track of them. To her credit, she's always told Marqueeta if she ever wanted to seek out a relationship with her mother, she'd support it, but Marqueeta was adamant that she didn't. Then just a couple of years ago, we heard that her mother had died in a car accident. The father never was heard of again, and that's part of the reason Marqueeta has night terrors. She thinks he could still be out there. And maybe he is, but, believe me, he doesn't want to have anything to do with her. She could still have him prosecuted, and I'd kill him with my bare hands if he ever showed up."

"You do know that you have an airtight case for a divorce or an annulment. I hate to say it, but surely you've thought about it, too."

"I can't say I haven't, Gina. But here's the thing, I do love her. I don't know what that says about me and what kind of a wimp of a man I am, but when she's good, she's really good. We have fun, we play with Dex, we laugh. We both love our house. She put it all together herself with just a little help from an interior designer. Even Mom says what a good job she did."

Gina recalled the twin white sofas that sank into thick white carpeting in the living room and faced the windows that overlooked the sea, the brass telescope trained on the horizon, the state-of-the-art kitchen she had seen during her tour earlier in the day. In the master bathroom a flower-bedecked trompe l'oeil arbor covered one whole wall, with stray vines and blossoms growing on across the ceiling. She assumed their mother must have helped out with that part of the project.

Larry punched the stem of his watch and the dial illuminated. It was nearly midnight.

"I've got to get to bed, Sis."

"What time do you go to work?"

"Usually nine, but tomorrow I'm going in early so I can knock off when Steve and the girls get here. You can sleep as late as you want. Just let Lupe know what you want for breakfast when you're ready. Depending on traffic, I should be back here with your family between four and five."

He stood up and began folding his blanket.

"I really appreciate your telling me all this, Larry," Gina said. "I just wish I'd known before. Things between us might have been different."

"It's tough," Larry said. "I say this without any self-pity because I made a commitment that I mean to keep. But it's lonely, you know? She doesn't have many friends, and we don't have any real couple friends. We entertain a lot, but it's mostly work-related people who come over. She's fine at first, but then she scares people away. I don't blame them for not wanting to come around after they've seen one of her episodes."

"I certainly wouldn't have been so hard on Keeta," Gina said, her voice almost a whisper.

The derogatory nickname slipped out before she could stop it, but instead of being offended, Larry chuckled.

"That's cute," he said. "She'll like that."

He stowed their blankets in a trunk at the edge of the deck and picked up the two bottles to return to the liquor cabinet in the house. Gina started to follow him with the glasses, but he waved her away.

"Lupe will get those first thing in the morning," he said. "You go get some sleep, and tomorrow night we'll do this again. It'll be good to have Steve here with us."

Will it ever, Gina thought to herself as she went down the steps that led to the flagstone path and disappeared into the night.

CHAPTER THIRTEEN

When Gina rolled over and looked at the digital clock on the bedside table in the guest cottage, the red numerals read 6:17. Damn. So much for the chance to sleep late. She slid out of bed and crossed the room to pull on the cord that raised the expensive honeycomb blinds. Outside dawn was just breaking, and thanks to the marine layer that still lingered from the night before, it would be hours before any sunlight would have reached her window and awakened her naturally. Despite this being her third full day in California, she was still waking up on Indiana time. It would be 9:17 in Bedford. Steve and the girls would already be up and driving to Indianapolis to catch their plane. She thought of calling Steve's cell phone to make sure they were on their way but then thought better of the idea. If he'd had any trouble getting Stephanie and Danielle packed and dressed, he'd be frazzled and in no mood to chat with her, and she would spend the rest of the day worried about their getting to where they needed to be on time. And if all had gone well, they'd be in the car, and she didn't want to distract Steve while he was driving. He talked and texted too much on his phone in the car as it was, and her fear when he called her, sometimes just to alert her that he had left the store and was headed home for supper, was that she would hear a sickening crash and know that at the moment everything changed forever she was the one on the phone talking to him about something trivial. She for sure wouldn't risk that when the girls were in the car along with him.

Instead, she wrapped herself in the thick white chenille robe that hung on a hook in the bathroom and switched on the coffee-maker. When the coffee was ready, she poured herself a cup and stepped, barefoot, outside onto the deck, a comfortable miniature of the one at the big house where she and Larry had sat last night. The fog that had encased them still swirled between her and the sky, and seagulls shrieked in the distance as they dived through the mist. This was what she had wanted last spring when she came to California to meet with Larry and Dennis MacDonald -- to be in her brother's house, enjoying the sea, restored to her rightful place as a part of her own family. She nestled down into the canvas chaise, propped her coffee cup on her plump chenille chest, closed her eyes and smiled.

Just after seven she heard the sound of a car arriving that would be Lupe's faded red Ford pickup. She was ready for breakfast, but she didn't feel comfortable with the idea of having a servant, and she would not ask the woman for special favors. She'd walk up to the house, still in her robe, and join the rest of the family. She would fit in and not be a guest. She'd even ask Lupe if she could help out.

But when she pushed open the door that led off the deck to the kitchen, she knew immediately that her dream of a cozy family breakfast had been just that. The entire room was in motion. Lupe, her expression troubled, moved so quickly around the kitchen that Gina backed up against the wall to stay out of her way. First she stirred oatmeal that bubbled on the stove, then she retrieved a carton of eggs from the refrigerator and cracked three into a frying pan. Next she pulled a banana from a stalk on a wooden hook and sliced it with machinelike precision into a bowl on a tray that looked to be headed for a bedroom. Dexter sat in his highchair crying and pounding the tray with his spoon. Larry fairly ran into the room, a jacket dangling from one shoulder as he attempted to grab it with his other arm. Gina suddenly felt conspicuous and out of place and wished she were back on the deck at the guesthouse.

"Good morning," Larry said as he moved past her in the direction of the coffeemaker without actually looking at her. "How'd you sleep?" But he didn't stop moving, and she sensed he didn't expect -- or want or have time for -- an answer to his question. He seemed more like the Larry she had come to dislike -- abrupt, self-important, above the needs and concerns of the people around him -- than the brother with whom she had been sharing confidences just hours before. Without waiting for her to speak, he said to Lupe, "Nothing for me this morning. I've got to get out of here. I'm late already."

"You've got to have something, Mr. Larry," the woman said. "You can't go to work on an empty stomach. I'm making you something you can eat in the car."

As if on cue, two halves of an English muffin popped up from the toaster. She deftly spread both sides with butter and slid one of the now-fried eggs between them. She wrapped the whole thing in a napkin and dropped it into a small paper bag along with an apple from a glass fruit bowl that sat on the island.

"You're an angel," Larry said to her. "Thank you. Is Dexter ready to go?"

Lupe frowned and shook her head.

"He poured the cereal and fruit onto the floor, and I just got it cleaned up. He said he wanted oatmeal. It's ready now, but it's still hot."

"Jesus!" Larry said. He pushed up the sleeve of his jacket and consulted his watch. "Can you take him to preschool, Lupe? I've got so much to get done today, and I have to leave early to get to the airport. If I wait for him to eat, I'm going to hit traffic."

Her face clouded and she pointed to the tray to which she had just added a plate with two eggs on it.

"I've got to take this up for Miss Marqueeta."

They both looked questioningly at Gina, who froze at the thought of driving a strange car on a Los Angeles freeway. Then it occurred to Larry that his sister didn't know what was going on.

"Marqueeta isn't well today," he said simply. "I told you last night that sometimes big events and lots of excitement push her over the edge. I was afraid this would happen. She'll come around later, but she's going to have to stay in bed this morning. I'm sorry. She had planned to take you shopping and out to lunch down in the village."

"Don't take him to preschool," she blurted. Larry and Lupe both looked at her like she was speaking a foreign language.

"What do you mean?" Larry asked impatiently. "Of course he's going to preschool. That's his routine. It's what he does every day."

"I'd like to spend the time with him, and I don't think missing a day of preschool will keep him out of Harvard."

A child his age shouldn't even be in preschool and daycare, she thought without saying it aloud. He should be at home with his mother.

"He's a handful," Larry said doubtfully, and Lupe nodded her head in regretful assent. "And Marqueeta really needs the peace and quiet to rest if she's going to be able to take part in the rest of the weekend."

"I'll take him down to the cottage and entertain him there," she said. "I'll eat breakfast with him, and then I'll take him back with me. Maybe Lupe can help me pick out a few toys and books. We'll be fine. It'll be a chance for us to get to know each other."

"Well," Larry looked anxiously again at his watch and then back at her. "It would certainly solve a huge problem and make my day go better."

"Excellent. Then it's settled. Aunt Gina and little Dexie are going to have some quality time together."

That hadn't been as idyllic as she'd hoped, either. After Larry left, Dexter also refused the oatmeal with raisins that Lupe had prepared, and she was about to make toast for him when Gina said, "Look, Dexter, Lupe has already made you two lovely breakfasts. If you don't eat the oatmeal, there won't be anything until lunchtime."

Lupe looked anxious. Clearly this wasn't the way these situations were handled around here. Dexter took one bite and then pushed it away. Gina lifted him out of his highchair and said as cheerfully as she could muster, "OK then. You've made your choice. Let's go have a good time." The boy puckered up and looked mournfully at Lupe, who chose that moment to go to the playroom and look for toys.

Back at the guesthouse, while Gina quickly dressed in jeans and pulled her hair into a ponytail, Dexter was again petulant, asking for his daddy and then saying he wanted Lupe. He played with the toy computer she had brought down, answering the questions it asked him -- do dogs bark or quack, are roses red or green, can trucks fly, yes or no -- until he got an answer wrong and the thing made a buzzing sound and a snippy female voice said, "You'll have to try again. Better luck next time." He pushed the whole contraption violently across the sitting room floor, and it came to a crashing halt when it hit the bricks at the edge of the hearth.

"That's not the way we treat our nice things," Gina said. She was thinking of Stephanie and Danielle and how skimpy the Christmas tree had been for the past few years, how they cared for the few toys they did have so lovingly it was almost pathetic, knowing that if those were broken or lost, there wouldn't be replacements. One night Danielle had left her precious collection of paper dolls on the front porch and a thunderstorm had come up overnight and ruined them. The sound of Danny's racking sobs still haunted her. She had tried to make it up with a book of bridal paper dolls squeezed out of the grocery budget and purchased at Target, and Danny had been appreciative and played with them half-heartedly for a couple of days, but the other box had contained Princess Diana and Patty's Prom Night and Tracy Goes to College. The idea of her throwing it across a room in anger was laughable -- and now sad.

Next she pulled a fire engine out of the shopping bag Lupe had provided, but the batteries were low, and instead of shrieking and wailing, the siren made weak and intermittent "peeps." Dexter gave it a kick and pulled a long face, looking at her sullenly, daring her to punish him.

"That's it, kid, we're out of here," Gina said to him. While she picked up the toys and returned them to the bag, he stood by the door that would lead back to his house and tugged on the doorknob.

"We're not going that way. Your mommy is asleep, and we want to let her rest. We're going to the beach."

His eyes widened in disbelief. He obviously hadn't expected his bad behavior to result in such a reward. Gina picked up the phone and punched the intercom button that connected her with the house.

"I'm taking Dexter down to the beach," she said. "I didn't want you to worry. We'll be back by noon for lunch."

She smeared both of their arms, legs, and faces with sunscreen and jammed the hat Lupe had provided down over Dexter's dark curls. She sent him to the bathroom even when he said he didn't have to, gave him a drink of water, and they set off.

"I want a snack before we go," he whined.

"Nope. Remember when you didn't eat the cereal or the oat-meal Lupe made for you? If you had, you could be having a snack right now. But that's not the choice you made. We'll only be at the beach for a little while, and when we get back, it will almost be time for lunch."

The day before she had spotted the rusty gate that opened from the fence on the back side of Larry's property. Now she removed the heavy chain loop that secured it to the fencepost, pushed back dry, stiff weeds and brush that were taller than Dexter, and cleared the way so that he could slip through and onto the path that twisted and turned down the scrubby hillside until it reached the Pacific Coast Highway. There they walked down the steps into a dank pedestrian subway and emerged on the other side of the road. A pale trace of sunlight was beginning to penetrate the mist, but the wind was brisk and chilly, and except for a white-haired couple taking a walk and two barefoot teenagers in wet suits toting surfboards, the beach was empty. That would change, she was sure, but for now it was theirs.

She spread out the blanket she had brought from the guesthouse while Dexter ran to the surf, stopping just short of the water and waiting for it to roll up and lick his toes. Then he giggled, and the sound reverberated in her mind as fine crystal might if it shattered and dispersed into color and music. She had heard him talk, whine, and cry, but this was the first time she had heard him laugh. She wanted him to do it again, so she joined him on the packed, wet sand and waited with him as the waves receded and then came back again to cover their feet with foam. Again and again he shrieked with laughter, as if he had never played this game before and every return of the gentle waves was a totally new surprise.

Eventually he tired of the game and looked around for something else to do. Gina pulled a plastic bucket and shovel out of her bag, one of two from the guesthouse that had obviously been provided for Stephanie and Danielle. Dexter sat down right where he had been standing and began digging a hole. Gina joined him, shaping the mounds of sand he was excavating into a crude box-like castle with two wobbly turrets. Then she told him what a moat was, and he dug one around the structure, to keep the bad guys out, he said.

"What bad guys?" Gina asked him. "I don't see any bad guys here."

He looked quizzically at her.

"Pirates, a-course," he said.

When new waves encroached on their kingdom, she took Dexter by the hand and walked with him down the beach toward a pile of kelp she had spotted earlier.

"Do you know what this is?" she asked him. He frowned, too darkly for the situation, she thought, and shook his head. "It's kelp. It's a plant that grows in the ocean." She knelt and splayed some of the flat leaves across her palm for him to see. He touched them gingerly, as if he were afraid they might bite him. "It's just a plant, honey," she said, "like grass or flowers."

Then she pointed to one of the rubbery gas bladders and said, "Watch this." She jumped on it hard and squashed it open with her foot. "It feels funny on your feet," she told him. "Try it."

He approached one of the pods with trepidation and tapped at it so lightly with his foot that nothing happened.

"Stomp!" Gina cried over the wind that had picked up. "Give it all you've got."

This time it opened, and once he'd felt the power of the wet explosion under his foot, he wanted to try it again and then again until all of the pods he could find in the soggy mass were flattened, squealing with joy at the newfound sensation. Then he looked up at her beaming, obviously proud of himself for what he had accomplished.

"You know what, buddy, it's time for us to get back. Lupe is going to have our lunch ready, and I've got a surprise for you."

"What is it?" Again the suspicious look from beneath his long, dark eyelashes.

"You'll see. Let's go."

When they got back to the cottage, Lupe brought down a tray that held a peanut butter and jelly sandwich cut into triangles, carrot sticks, and milk for Dexter, a Caesar salad and a bottle of sparkling water for her. A tiny dish contained alternating slices of lemon and lime, and the small plate next to it held a roll and an artful curl of butter. She set the tray down on the coffee table in the sitting room as she might have if she'd been working in room service at a five-star hotel.

"Wow!" Gina said. "Thanks, Lupe. This is better than a restaurant."

The woman smiled and bobbed her head shyly in acknowledgment of the praise.

"Can I get you anything else, Miss Gina?"

"No, this is more than enough. I think we're fine, don't you, Dex?"

She wanted to ask about Keeta but decided against doing it in front of Dexter, who was frowning again.

"Where's the surprise?"

Lupe raised her eyebrows at Gina, shook her head ever so slightly, and turned to leave.

"The surprise is that we're not going to eat our lunch in here. We're going to have a picnic outside."

"That's all?" His lower lip came out, an automatic reaction she could see he had practiced for so long that he didn't even realize it was happening.

She couldn't believe what an ungrateful little twit he was. She looked at her watch. Almost one. The plane would be landing in less than two hours, and then Stephanie and Danielle would be here. She had never missed them so much. The longer she was with her nephew, the more they seemed like perfect children in comparison. Still she couldn't be angry with Dexter. He was three, and if he was spoiled and difficult, it was what his parents had taught him to be. Too many expensive electronic toys that he was too young to understand and operate, too many days with a hired caregiver instead of his own mother, too many nights of being put to bed by a harried, preoccupied father while his mother took her medicine and locked her door.

"No, that isn't exactly all," Gina said. She recalled that there were two toy horses in the bag of toys Lupe had assembled. "We're going to pretend to be cowboys. We're out on the range, and we've been herding our cattle. Now we're going to tie up our horses and eat our lunch, except cowboys would call it 'grub.'"

The distrustful frown deepened.

"Come on. I'll show you."

She collected the toy horses and handed them to Dexter.

"You carry these," she said, "and I'll bring the tray."

She had left the beach blanket hanging over the railing along the deck. Now she retrieved it and laid it out on the patch of grass just where the hillside began to slope down toward the gate they had passed through earlier. The fog had disappeared, and the sun, high overhead, rendered the sea a deep teal blue and warmed the scrubby grass beneath them. The sky was cloudless. Dexter set the horses down on the blanket.

"No, pardner," Gina said, affecting a deep voice to sound as masculine as possible. "We can't have our horses eating our grub. Let's tie them up by that tree over yonder."

She galloped one plastic horse over to a nearby tree stump and provided him with a meal of crushed leaves from a coastal sage bush. Then she signaled for Dexter to bring over the other one, which he did purposefully, copying his aunt in pretending the horse was galloping toward its food. When she asked him what his horse was going to eat, he assembled a tiny pile of sticks. Then they returned to their blanket and their own lunch, for which they were both by now starving.

"I don't like ..." Dexter began, frowning at his sandwich, but before he could finish, Gina interrupted, "Better eat up. I think Lupe has some nice snacks planned for when your cousins get here, and it would be a shame to miss them."

He ate two of the triangles and a carrot before he spoke again, and then it was to ask what herding cattle meant and then if cowboys slept outside with the cows. She could tell that he was becoming drowsy, so when they had finished eating, she piled their dishes back onto the tray and led him back to the cottage. Then she suggested he lie down for a bit on one of the girls' twin beds.

"Stephanie and Danielle are so excited to meet you, and you may be staying up a little late tonight, so I think it's a good idea if you have a little rest. I might do the same thing."

Instead, however, she retrieved the box she had filled with paint at her mother's house and one of the pieces of expensive 300-pound paper she had filched and returned to the deck to try and capture the idyllic blue panorama before her. She sketched the coastline and the occasional red tile rooftops along the highway that stretched to the north and mixed paints to try and achieve the exact color of the water. Cerulean was too aqua, cobalt and ultramarine too bright. A touch of hooker's green and a drop of lemon yellow, and there it was. She added more water to make the tips of the waves the pale, icy green they became as they broke and collapsed on the shiny raw sienna sand. She didn't hear the door open or the footsteps that approached her.

"What are you doing, Aunt Gina?" His hair was mussed, and he was rubbing one eye with his fist. He stood beside her and looked at what she had done.

"I'm painting a picture. You're so lucky to live in such a beautiful place, and I want to remember what it looks like when I go back home to my house in Indiana."

"Can I paint, too?"

She looked at the few expensive sheets of paper she had brought, the two sable brushes, the tin of high-quality pigments. This spoiled child wouldn't have a clue about what to do with them, and she was on the verge of saying no when he looked at her frankly, his eyes wide, and said, "Please?" What price tag could she put on building a relationship, however fragile and intermittent, with Larry's son?

"OK, come and sit here beside me. There's room for both of us."

She scooted to the end of the bench to make room for him. Then she laid out a piece of Anita's precious $8-a-sheet cold-pressed paper. She positioned the paint box and water jar between them. Dexter grabbed a paintbrush and dipped it into the water immediately.

"There are a few things you want to think about before you start," she cautioned him, gently putting a hand on his arm before he could reach the paints. "Like, what do you think you'll paint?"

"I already know," he said with confidence. "It's a surprise."

"That's fine, but we need to keep the paints nice so we can use them over and over. Each time you change colors, you'll need to rinse out your brush. And then you'll need to tap the brush on the edge of the jar so that you don't get too much on the next color. If you do, the colors won't be very bright and your picture won't be as pretty. Right?" He nodded his head vigorously. "This is Grandma Anita's special art paper, so think about where you want to put things and what colors you want them to be. We don't have a lot of extra paper to play with."

She made a mental note. This Christmas, along with the reinstated fudge, there would be paints and a pad of heavy watercolor paper for Dex.

For the next several minutes she worked on her own painting, just glancing over occasionally to check Dexter's progress and make sure the paints in the palette weren't being ruined. He worked intently, biting his lower lip as he did, gripping the brush so tightly that his small, chubby fingers were white, religiously observing her rules about the water. He painted first a long dark-brown oval with four sticks under it and a circle at one end that was obviously meant to be a head. Then he washed out his brush, dipped it into the burnt sienna and painted a similar figure next to the first one. Some green grass sprouted underneath his horses and a blue sky predictably followed, with a sun occupying the upper right-hand corner, as he must have learned in preschool. Finally, he drew two circles near the horses' heads and filled them with orange and green dots.

"There!" he said with finality, plopping his brush into the water and holding up his picture for her to see. Again the proud smile that would have brightened the day if it weren't already sun-spangled and brilliant. She had learned with her own children never to ask what a picture was. She still remembered Stephanie's desperate tears when she hadn't recognized the portrait of Steve's parents' old dog, Wally, that she had painted at age four.

"Tell me about your picture," she said, more tactfully this time. She laid her own paintbrush down to let him know she was paying full attention.

"It's our horses!" he sang out. "See, that one's yours and this one's mine."

"Beautiful!" she exclaimed, and realized as the word came out that she meant it. "Now tell me about the orange and green dots."

"That's their grub," he said, "like we had for lunch." And he laughed again with the tinkling crystal laugh that made her want to say one funny thing to him after another. He had said "grub" more deliberately and loudly than the other words, letting her know he enjoyed learning this new word. "Can I have another piece, please?"

Again the price of the pages ran momentarily across her brain and then disappeared.

"Sure," she said. "But just one more, so think hard about what you want to paint."

"I already know," he said.

Again they painted in silence. She mixed a terra-cotta red for the rooftops and a watery reservoir of ultramarine and purple that she planned to use for the point where the sea disappeared at the horizon. This time she was so engrossed in her own work that she didn't pay any attention to what Dexter was doing until he finished and held up his paper, and this time she knew immediately what his picture was about. A tall stick figure and a smaller one stood side by side on an amorphous pile of green, yellow, and brown. Their feet were huge in proportion to their bodies, their smiles filling up most of their faces.

"It's us," she said, and the smile inside her was as big as the one on the paper.

"We're jumping up and down on the kelp!" he said excitedly. "See?"

"I do see. This is great. Do you think I could take it home with me so that I can remember what a good time we've had today?"

His frown returned, but ever so slightly.

"Yeah, I guess so, but first I want to show my mom."

He didn't have long to wait because just then the doorbell buzzed and Marqueeta stepped inside the cottage.

"Yoo-hoo," she called. "Anybody home?"

"Out here," Gina called, and Dexter simultaneously cried, "Mommy, Mommy, look what I painted!"

Marqueeta picked up the paintings and appeared to study them.

"What are they?" she said, and then after Dexter, crestfallen, explained them, she said, "They're good, honey," and them laid them aside.

"We've had a great day, haven't we, Dex?" Gina said in an effort to salvage his good mood. "We've built sand castles and jumped on piles of kelp at the beach, and we played cowboys and horses while we ate our lunch, and since then we've been painting pictures."

"We call each other 'pardner,' don't we, Aunt Gina?" Dexter chimed in and again laughed his musical laugh.

"That all sounds like fun," Marqueeta said, making a face aside to Gina that indicated it absolutely did not, "but now I want to play with Aunt Gina, and Lupe needs your help in the house."

"Awww," Dexter complained.

"Why don't you take your pictures to show her, and you can tell her all of the things you and Aunt Gina did this morning."

With that encouragement he grabbed the papers and set off in a run through the door and up the path.

"Play?" Gina asked, curious about what the two of them could possibly have in common that would seem like fun.

"I was hoping you'd be up to take another walk with me. I realized yesterday how much more fun my walk was with someone to talk to."

"So you walk every day?"

"Yes. It was my psychiatrist's idea. He said being outside in sunshine and nature would help my spirits, and it does. And honestly, now that I'm in the habit, I miss it on days when I'm too busy to fit it in."

"So you must be feeling better."

"Yeah. I'm sorry about ruining the morning. I wanted to take you shopping in the village and out to lunch. Sometimes the things I get most excited about and look forward to most are the very ones that wind me up and spoil everything."

"You know what? I wouldn't have traded my morning with Dex for anything, but a walk now sounds great."

Fifteen minutes later they were walking along the streets of Malibu with Marqueeta pointing and interrupting their conversation with the names of the movie stars whose homes they were passing.

"This was a great idea," Gina said. "What a great way to see this place. You'd miss a lot of this just driving through on the highway."

"Well, I admit I had some ulterior motives. I wanted to get a chance to talk to you by myself. Besides, Lupe's making a big dinner for tonight, so if we walk off lunch, we'll be able to enjoy it."

Gina turned to look at Keeta's thin frame that today was decked out in lime-green designer sweatpants, a matching white T-shirt with lime trimming, and expensive walking shoes, and she fairly hooted with laughter.

"You've got to be kidding me," she said. "What do you weigh? Like 90 pounds sopping wet? If you walk too much you might just disappear."

"I weigh 115, thank you very much, and I know it sounds silly now," Keeta said, "but I was chubby all through high school and college, and I don't want to go back to that. I was miserable. And that leads me to why I wanted to talk to you without anyone else around. Larry told me he talked to you about my, um, history last night."

"Yes, he did," Gina said. She couldn't think of anything else to say beyond that, and she couldn't imagine what might come next. Surely there couldn't be any more to the story.

"I'm glad you know, that's all. It's part of who I am, and I want you to know me. I want to know you. I know I must seem shallow and silly to someone like you who is an engineer and helps run a farm and a business, but I do at least have a heart. I love Larry and Dex, and I'm really excited to have an actual sister. I wished for a sibling the whole time I was growing up, but as you know, I was adopted when I was nine. My mom couldn't have children, and she and Dad just put all their love and attention into me. I was spoiled and happy -- who wouldn't be? -- but I was also lonely. I'm glad we're family, and I want us to be friends. There. I guess that's the big speech I wanted to give."

"Keeta," Gina began, and then she clapped her hand across her mouth. "Crap! I mean Marqueeta."

Marqueeta laughed out loud, and this time the whinny didn't sound so shrill.

"Larry told me you had that nickname for me. I like it. Nobody's ever given me a nickname before. My mom even wanted the teachers to call me by my full name -- Marqueeta Nadine. That's a whole lot of name for a little kid to have to live up to."

"It's pretty, though."

"Do you have a middle name?"

"Marie. Mom was in her Catholic years when I was born, and so I got the whole treatment. Regina means 'queen,' so my name quite literally means 'Queen Mary.' Talk about embarrassing when you're a little kid in Catholic school!"

"But it's pretty."

"I guess. At least for anybody who doesn't know Latin."

She laughed, but Keeta didn't seem to get the joke. "So anyway, let's get back to your weight. I can't imagine you were ever heavy, but it's something I struggle with all the time."

"I'm sorry," Keeta said. "I wasn't even thinking when I said that. I think you're really attractive."

"That's nice of you to say, but I could stand to lose about 30 pounds. How did you get it off?"

"By doing the stuff everybody talks about but nobody actually does -- diet and exercise. I had been dumpy and unattractive for so long, and I was sick of it and disgusted with myself every time I looked in the mirror. I never had a real boyfriend in college. I was always the friend with the good personality who got fixed up with the geeks by my cuter friends and their cuter boyfriends. I never had a real relationship. And honestly," here she took a big sigh, "I probably didn't want one. Because of my childhood, I was terrified of men. When I was a kid we had a housekeeper who knew what had happened and felt sorry for me, and she was always giving me treats she made, like apple pie and ice cream or a big piece of chocolate cake every day when I got home from school. When I got to college my parents bought me a little fridge for my dorm room, and when everyone else was out at parties, I was sitting in my bed eating cheese curls and reading movie magazines."

"Wow! That's hard to believe. So what happened? You looked incredible when I first met you, and you still do, even after having a baby."

"I wanted to be on my own, and like everyone else in this city, I thought I was going to be an actress, but you can't get anywhere in L.A. if you don't look positively anorexic. So I moved down here and was living with some friends in an apartment. One of them really was anorexic, and I learned from her the joys of eating whatever you wanted and then puking it back up into the toilet. At first I thought it was a great idea, but considering I was already on meds for depression and with all the baggage I was carrying with me, I got myself into a real mess. I mean I was really sick. My roommates called my mom, and she flew down and marched me back home to her doctor. I started seeing a shrink, and he's the one who suggested walking and eating the right food, and here I am."

"Do you still go to a gym, too?"

"I go to a gym in the winter when it rains and I can't be outside, but I like seeing everything up close and noticing little things -- like watching the flowers in someone's garden bloom or following the progress when someone has work done on their house. And I like seeing people that I can say hello to. The same group walks here, and any time I'm out I'm likely to see someone familiar. So we say hi and sometimes things like 'Happy New Year,' and then we keep on walking. I'm connected but not obligated to do things like invite them to dinner or say I'll watch their kids. When Dex was a baby I'd push him in a carriage when I went for my walks so he could get to sleep."

"Interesting. I'm not kidding. That's really interesting."

"Well, it has worked. I can pretty much eat what I want, and as long as I take my walks, I can still get into my clothes. Larry has a treadmill, and if I can't get to the gym or walk outside, I use that."

Gina laughed. "Yeah, I'd need one of those. Where I live it gets down to below zero in the winter, and the ground is usually frozen and covered with ice and snow."

As if Keeta had conjured her up, a tanned, white-haired woman passed them on the sidewalk.

"Great day, isn't it?" the woman sang out. "And I see you have a friend to walk with. How nice!" She stepped off the curb to pass them and kept walking.

"Keeta, about what happened to you when you were a little girl. I don't want to pry, and I know it must be so uncomfortable for you, but do you remember it? Do you know why men freak you out?"

Keeta shook her head and looked down at her feet, examining them too carefully, as if watching to make sure they would lift up and set down again in an orderly and timely fashion to get her where she wanted to go.

"Not really. I know I was beaten when I misbehaved, but my psychiatrist thinks I've blocked out the rest. My 'parts' didn't become an issue again until I started dating Larry and wanted to go on birth-control pills. The first doctor who gave me a pelvic exam freaked me out pretty badly. I still take a tranquilizer before I go for my checkup. My psychiatrist does some hypnosis to regress patients to other times in their lives, and when I first started going to him, he wanted to try it with me. I told him I knew it was something bad and that was enough for me. The last thing I want is to relive something awful."

"Even if it might mean you and Larry could have a ... well, a more ... you know what I mean."

"No. We do okay, I think."

Gina saw her visibly stiffen.

You so don't, she thought, but she had said all she was willing to say in an effort to help get her brother's marriage to a better place. That part of his life wasn't really any of her business, and any more meddling could cause this fragile new relationship to disintegrate before it could even be explored. Keeta was right. It would be fun to have a sister.

CHAPTER FOURTEEN

When they got back to the house, Marqueeta disappeared to her bedroom upstairs and finally came back downstairs while they were having a drink before dinner. Lupe had rolled a portable minibar outside to the deck and placed a platter of bruschetta and one of cheese and fruit on the table beside it. Larry had poured scotch for himself and Steve, and Gina had helped herself to a glass of chardonnay, anxiously checking her watch as she took the first sip. The sun was on course for its daily disappearance into the sea, and Steve and the girls had already been up several more hours than the rest of them. She hoped dinner, which had already been postponed twice, would be ready soon so they could get the bedtime routine started before it got much later and the girls' good behavior disintegrated into exhausted tears. To Gina's mild annoyance, nobody else seemed to consider the three-hour time difference a problem. She longed to go into the kitchen and offer to help, but she had figured out that this was Lupe's domain, that plans were in place to entertain her and her family, and that in the upside-down world of the rich and coastal such an overture would somehow have been perceived as rude.

The children were playing in Dexter's room. Despite the difference in their ages and genders, the three of them had greeted each other like refugees on a new planet and disappeared to check out Dexter's remarkable collection of toys. Earlier, when Larry had brought the three of them to the guesthouse, the girls had shrieked with delight at their fairy-encrusted bedspreads and the welcoming banner.

"Stephy!" Stephanie had sung out, and worried that Larry's feelings might be hurt, Gina had quickly whispered, "I know, honey, but don't ..."

"I love it! I've never had a nickname before."

"We call you 'Steph' all the time," Gina reminded her.

"I know, but that's just short for Stephanie. It isn't cool, like something I'd write on my notebook. I'm going to use it all the time."

"That was Aunt Marqueeta's idea," Larry said. "She's been busy getting things ready for your visit, which is why she's tired-out today and needed to have a rest before you got here. She's really looking forward to seeing you later."

He was obviously well-practiced in the art of spinning such tales to cover for Marqueeta's absences.

"Aunt Marqueeta is so pretty," Stephanie said to her sister in a reverential tone Gina also found less irritating than she would have before the walk with her sister-in-law. "I got to be in the wedding, but you were just a baby." Danielle pulled a face, but her sister ignored it, too enchanted with this wonderful place and her idyllic memories to let her childish little sister ruin it for her. "She wears fingernail polish and high heels and bracelets."

Gina felt suddenly self-conscious in her flip-flops, her nails short and clean, her tanned arms bare.

And now, here she was, stunning Marqueeta, more beautiful in illness than most people in the bloom of health. She said she'd taken a nap after their walk, but she still looked delicate and vulnerable, her face pale, the blue patches of exhaustion visible beneath her eyes. She wore tailored jeans with a simple white cotton blouse, the collar turned up in the back. Her long bangs were caught in a barrette on the back of her head, and the sides fell loosely to her shoulders. Even Steve, who barely knew her and didn't much like what he knew, was silenced by her entrance. He had been in the middle of telling Larry an anecdote about the store, but then here was a woman who looked like a movie star coming toward him with her arms open, obviously about to embrace him. He gamely hugged back with one arm while he kept the other extended to avoid pouring scotch down her back. Then she hugged Gina again, as if she, too, were just arriving. She seemed calm and low-key -- probably, Gina decided, medicated.

"I'm sorry again about today," she said to Gina. "I loved our walk, but it would have been fun for us to have lunch and go shopping. I was hoping I wouldn't have any episodes while you were here."

"You know what, I had the best day ever," Gina responded. "I loved the time I had with Dexter, and I really enjoyed our walk."

"Really?" Marqueeta looked as if she found that hard to believe.

"Really. I do like to eat, which is obvious, but I'm not much of a shopper."

Had Larry still not told her anything about them? Did Keeta not realize that she couldn't afford to shop at the mall in Bedford, let alone at the designer stores in Malibu?

At that moment the three children emerged from the house, clamoring for food, and Lupe at the same time called out that dinner was ready.

Breakfast the next morning was what Gina had been hoping for the day before. She cautiously kept her family at the guesthouse until Lupe called down to tell them breakfast was nearly ready, not wanting to risk a repeat performance of the day before, this time amplified with the arrival of three extra people. But today the scene was completely different. Larry, looking relaxed in a pair of gray sweatpants and a plain white T-shirt, was manning a griddle covered with blueberry pancakes. Lupe poured orange juice into glasses at a table set with bright pink napkins as if for a party and decorated with a low bowl of yellow roses.

"Go ahead and sit down, everybody," Larry said. "Marqueeta's on her way down now." He slid the browned pancakes onto a plate and poured more batter onto the griddle, causing it to make a sizzling sound.

Gina wondered if Keeta was really on her way or if their family idyll might still be ruined by her lack of sleep or medication or mood swings. She realized this must be what Larry woke up to every morning -- the question of whether his day would be pleasant or chaotic, whether Keeta would be able to manage her life or he and Lupe would have to set aside their own plans and do it for her.

But now here she was, a bright smile on her face, her hair in a ponytail, her legs encased in jodhpurs and tall boots. Stephanie and Danielle snapped to attention as if royalty had entered the room.

"Hey, do you girls like horses?" she asked without saying good morning, as if they'd been up for hours and already dispensed with the niceties associated with the first encounter of the day.

Their eyes widened and they nodded their heads in vigorous affirmatives, looking first at each other and then back at their aunt to see what she had in mind. Marqueeta poured herself a cup of coffee and sat down across from them at the table.

"The reason I ask is that Uncle Larry and I have a friend who has some horses, and he's invited us over to ride this morning. What do you think?"

She winked conspiratorially at Gina, whose first thought was that she should have checked with her and Steve before extending such an offer. How big were the horses? Did the owners provide helmets? Would their limited health insurance plan cover them out here?

"Whoa! How cool is that?" Steve said. "Are you the luckiest kids in all of California or what?"

The girls were so excited they could barely eat. Gina imposed her "no snacks later if you don't clean your plates" rule, but nobody heard or cared as they wolfed down what they could and carried the rest to the sink to be scraped into the disposal. Stephanie, with her arm around Marqueeta's waist, and Danielle, pulling on her aunt's shirt sleeve, pelted her with questions as if no one else were in the room. What would they wear? What color were the horses? What were their names? How long would it take to get there?

An hour later Stephanie was seated astride a sleek chestnut mare and Danielle a bay. The friend turned out to be a television sitcom star who hugged Marqueeta and shook hands with Gina and Steve before turning them over to Arturo, his stable hand, and disappearing down the winding driveway in a Ferrari.

"Have you ridden before?" Arturo asked them.

The girls shook their heads slowly, their eyes telegraphing to their aunt and their parents the fear that this might get in the way of their being able to do it today.

"No problem," Arturo said. "I'll teach you."

"Arturo sometimes helps us at the studio when we're filming movies that have horses in them," Larry told them. "He's no ordinary stable boy."

Arturo flashed him an appreciative smile and nodded.

"Thank you, Señor Langley," he said. Then he motioned for Stephanie to follow him to a stall where the chestnut, Daisy, waited. Two stalls down was the bay, Mr. D, that would be Danielle's. Marqueeta picked up an apple from a basket that sat on a stack of hay bales and fed it to a black Arabian stallion in a stall across from where Arturo was helping the girls up onto their mounts. Larry and Steve helped with the girls. Gina followed her sister-in-law.

"You seem to know your way around horses," she said. "My first clue was that you had the proper clothes for it."

"I started riding lessons when I was just a little older than they are," she said. "I loved it, and eventually my parents bought me my own horse. Since we lived in San Francisco we stabled her at a farm in the East Bay. I had her until she died of old age. I was inconsolable and said I didn't ever want another horse. Then when Larry and I moved out here, and it turned out he knew Chad and Arturo, I started riding again. I still enjoy it, but I don't get to do it as much as I used to, now that I have Dexter."

Gina couldn't see how that would affect Marqueeta's free time since she didn't seem to spend much of it with her son, but instead of saying anything, she gave an understanding nod and let it go.

"Do you want to ride?" Marqueeta asked now, suddenly realizing she hadn't made the offer to Gina.

"No, no, no. I'm good," Gina said. "I'm just happy to watch you and the girls. I do like horses, though. Steve's family has kept some in the past. They don't have any now, of course. With the money problems they've had, they don't have any luxuries."

"I'm sorry," Marqueeta almost whispered, and Gina realized that once again she had embarrassed her with references to the difference in their economic situations.

"No, no, I didn't mean anything by that," she said. "I was just remembering that when Steve and I were dating I went home with him for weekends and holidays sometimes, and we'd always take the horses out and ride around the farm. They had a lot of land then, and we'd pack a picnic lunch and be gone for hours."

She smiled to herself at the memory of Steve's spreading out a red plaid saddle blanket on a pile of golden autumn leaves during one of those outings and their first time having taken place in a thicket of nearly naked trees on an unseasonably warm October

Saturday afternoon when she'd come home with him for the wedding of a family friend.

"Sounds like a lot of fun," Marqueeta said. She hoisted a western saddle up onto the back of the horse and reached underneath his ribcage for the cinch.

"It was. In fact ... oh, nothing. It's just going to sound like more whining, and I don't want to do that. We're having such a good time, I don't want to spoil it."

Now Marqueeta turned to face her, forgetting the horse and saddle for a moment and putting a hand on Gina's arm.

"No, please, go ahead. I understand now about your money troubles. Larry told me the whole story last night. I wish I had known before. He tries too hard to protect me from anything upsetting, and sometimes the result is I feel totally left out of the loop. Like I said yesterday, you're my family now, too."

"Thank you," Gina said. "I appreciate that. It's just that before we lost our farm, one of our dreams had been to turn it into a stable where people could board their horses. A lot of people who live in Indianapolis and Chicago have farms around Bedford that they come to for weekends and vacations, but they're closed up the rest of the year. I know some of them would like to have horses, especially the ones with children and grandchildren, but they can't because there's no place to keep them when they're not around. We knew we weren't going to be able to make enough money growing crops, so that seemed like a good way to make the farm pay for itself again, and since we have children who love horses, it seemed like a perfect idea."

"So why didn't you do that?"

"We just didn't have enough money. We'd used up every dime trying to keep the farm afloat. We would have had to convert the barns, hire a trainer and, oh yes, buy the horses, which aren't cheap. We were so overextended -- Steve's whole family was -- that there wasn't a bank in the world that would have given us any more credit. But it would have worked. I know it would have. We even wrote a business plan that showed how profitable it could be, but the one banker we showed it to said there was no way."

"So now Steve runs a hardware and feed store and you help out, right?"

"Right. The banker we talked to was part owner of a store, and he was looking for a new partner when his former partner died, so something good did come out of the whole thing. We have a perfectly fine life, but I know it's hard for Steve to spend his days selling seeds and feed and fencing and giving advice to people who are in the very business he loves and wishes he were in."

Arturo opened the gate to Stephanie's stall and led her and Daisy gently outside the stable. He handed Larry the reins and went back for Danielle and Mr. D. Marqueeta rode out on her stallion, Magic, looking like the heroine of a movie riding in to save the day. Soon the three of them were walking around the track outside the stable, Arturo holding onto the reins of both girls' horses, Marqueeta trotting on ahead and Steve recording the whole thing on a camcorder he had borrowed from one of his brothers for the trip. After they had warmed up, Arturo took them out to an enclosed pasture to teach them to trot.

"This is really wonderful," Gina said to her brother as they watched them ride off into the distance. "The girls are having a ball." She couldn't help thinking when she turned to face him that the sunglasses he was wearing probably cost more than all the clothes she and her family were wearing combined.

"It was all Marqueeta's idea," he said. "I told you, in some ways she's still a little girl. Despite her fears about caring for Dexter, she's happy to play with him for hours if someone else is around to handle any emergencies. And girls -- she's crazy about girls. I guess because she was one. She talked at one point about trying to have another child, but I'm against it. With all the problems she has, I think responsibility for still another person could drive her over the edge. I'm around as much as I can be, but it's my job that pays for the lifestyle she also enjoys -- not to mention for the hours Lupe puts in."

"I'm really enjoying getting to know her. All I've had to go on was the way she behaved at the wedding and the night we were leaving Dennis MacDonald's office and she wanted you to abandon me and get straight to some party."

"It's like I said. She has a really good heart. She's a lovable person, and strange as it seems, I do love her. But she can't handle anything that deviates from her plans. The word 'flexible' isn't even in her vocabulary."

They were walking slowly toward the pasture from which they could hear shrieks of excitement. The sun, now directly overhead, warmed Gina's back and arms.

"She's brought up our money situation a couple of times, and I've talked to her pretty openly about it," she said.

Larry glanced at her with a look that was clearly panic.

"No, not about that. But if we're going to be a part of each other's lives, she needs to know why I don't wear designer jeans and that I can't run to Malibu for a shopping trip."

Larry's features relaxed visibly.

"She says you try too hard to protect her from things that might be upsetting. Is that why you've never told her about what happened to us?"

"I suppose that's been part of it."

"And the rest?"

He was silent for several seconds, obviously mulling over what he should say next and choosing his words carefully. He stopped on the path and bent over to pick a dandelion, then tossed it away and began walking again.

"I haven't talked much about you at all to Marqueeta," he said finally. "You and I haven't been big players in each other's lives for a long time, you know."

"And whose fault has that been?"

"Well, I blame you. You went off with your fancy scholarship and got your big-deal degree and became an engineer. Then you married into a family that had nothing in common with ours and adopted them as if they were your own. Even Mom says she misses you. You never come out here, and if she wants to see you she has to go there. It's like there's no connection anymore, like you don't want to be a part of us. You don't write, you don't call. Even with e-mail as easy as it is, I never hear from you. I thought it would get better when you came out for my wedding, but instead you were bossing everyone around and trying to run things your way. I never got the feeling that you were here for me. It was all about what your family needed and when they needed it. The girls needed to eat, Steve wanted to get to bed, yadda, yadda. You've even stopped sending us Christmas cards."

Gina could not have been more surprised and hurt if he had slapped her. Tears burned her eyes and started down her cheeks before she could stop them. Instinctively, she tipped her head back. Once waiting for a doctor's appointment she had read in a magazine article titled "How Not to Cry at the Office" that if you imagined the tears running backward into your eyes, they would stop. Something else that would work would be drinking a liquid at the wrong temperature, like warm soda or cold coffee, but there was none of that in the offing out here in the middle of this meadow.

"You have got to be fucking kidding me!" she said through a liquid fog. The technique had not worked; the tears were still coming, and now her nose was running, too. She groped in her jeans pocket for a tissue. "You're the one who thinks you're so special with your Hollywood career and your big house on the ocean. I wrote you plenty of letters that you never answered when I was in college, and when you did, it was because you were in study hall and bored."

"I was a kid, Gina. I'm talking about since we've been grown-ups."

"And of course I was concerned about my family when we came out for your wedding. You were completely oblivious to anyone except yourself and Marqueeta."

"It was my wedding day, for Christ's sake. Isn't that supposed to be the idea?"

"I had children, Larry. You didn't know anything about that yet, but now that you have Dex, you should realize that kids get hungry and tired. You can't march a baby and a four-year-old all over San Francisco just so the photographer can get the right shot and not expect them to be cranky at some point. And Steve was exhausted. We still had the farm then, and you have no idea what it took for him to be able to be away for two days. He was up all night before we got on the plane. Then our stay turned into three days because Marqueeta's mother decided to have a brunch at the last minute with no thought whatsoever to anyone else's plans."

"How would I know any of this? At what point did you tell me about any of this? All you had to do was say you had to get back. You didn't have to stay for the brunch the day after the wedding."

"I didn't want to let you down. Distant that we may have been -- and obviously still are -- I am the only sibling you have, and I didn't want to leave if you wanted me to be there."

Now she gave up the battle and buried her face in her hands. Larry tried to put an arm around her shoulders, but she pulled away.

"I don't think I'm a hotshot because of my job, Gina," he said quietly. "I think I'm about the luckiest guy in the world. Do you know how many musicians -- good musicians -- there are out there, especially in this town? People wait their whole lives for a break like I got, and it just fell into my lap."

"Not really," she said. She blew her nose and looked up at him. "You worked hard, always playing the piano and practicing with the band. If you hadn't been good, believe me, that opportunity would not have come your way. You got your job because you're good at what you do."

"And as to my house, sure I like it, and I know it's nice. But it's all Marqueeta's idea. I was happy back in a condo, but Evan and Sylvia are wealthy, and she'd grown up having everything she ever wanted given to her. We could afford it, so why not? But I don't take any of it for granted. I'm grateful every day for what I have, flawed though it is."

"The Christmas cards didn't stop until you turned me down for the money," Gina said, picking up on a different thread in their conversation. Now she stopped walking. They were approaching the meadow where the girls were now galloping on the horses, and she didn't want them to see what she knew were red, swollen eyes. "After that, what could I say to you. I was, in every sense of the word, your poor relation who had come to you with my hand out for money. And yes, I do love Steve's family. They have taken me in as one of their own, and I can't imagine my life without them. But I know they're uneducated and nothing like the background we came from."

"I'm uneducated, Gina, which is what has always made me feel like you think I'm inferior."

"Well, my education hasn't really paid off, has it?"

"You've had choices to make, and two of them are right over there riding on those horses. You can't possibly have any regrets about not leaving them to go back to work."

"Just that if I had -- and if you had been willing or able to help -- we might still have our own farm. Steve might still be doing the work he loves instead of selling the equipment to someone else so that they can do it."

"Do you know what I'd give to have the kind of relationship you have with Steve?" Larry said now.

"What could you possibly know about our relationship?" she asked.

"Maybe not much, but I saw him pat your ass as you two were walking back to the guesthouse last night and the little kiss you reached up and gave him and how you held hands the rest of the way. It was none of my business and not for anyone else's eyes, I knew that. But I couldn't stop watching and wishing I could be that easy and comfortable with Marqueeta. I guess my point is that I have everything money can buy, and you have everything it can't. I don't think either of us is an asshole. We've just played the cards we've been dealt. That's all anybody can do."

The girls saw them now and rode their horses to where they were standing.

"Mommy, look," squealed Stephanie. "We've already learned to trot. I love this horse. I so wish I could have one of my own."

And there it was. Another tantalizing dream that couldn't come true, another experience waved in front of them like red flags in a bull ring to remind them of all it wasn't possible for them to have.

"You know, honey," Gina said, "Aunt Marqueeta doesn't have her own horse, either. That's why we had to drive here in the car. She's just lucky enough to have a friend who will let her ride his horses."

"These girls are naturals," Arturo interjected. "I didn't expect that they'd get this far in one lesson. I was just going to let them walk around, and now here they are, running around the pasture like cowgirls! Maybe you can find a stable where they can ride when you get back home?"

Before Gina could answer, he gave Danielle's horse a smack on the flank that set it off back toward the meadow from which they had come. Stephanie's horse followed, and Arturo trotted dutifully after them on foot. Marqueeta, who had ridden up behind them, dismounted and walked to where Gina and her husband were standing.

"If I didn't know better, I'd say you'd been crying," she said.

"Allergies ...," Gina began, but her brother shook his head.

"Yes, she has been crying. We've been talking about our family stuff. It's dug up some bad feelings."

"But the girls are having a great time, don't you think?" Marqueeta asked hopefully.

"Yes, yes of course they are," Gina answered. "How could they not? This is so generous of Chad -- and of you to set it up."

"Do you think there's a chance they could have riding lessons when they get home?" Marqueeta went on. "I understand that owning horses is out of the question, but maybe just riding once a month or so at a stable in Bedford?"

"That's kind of the point," Gina said, feeling the tears coming again and struggling to unwind a dry corner from her saturated tissue. "There isn't anything like that in Bedford. That's why we thought it could be a profitable business. There are lots of families with kids who could afford riding lessons even if they couldn't afford their own horses, and there are lots of wealthy families who live in cities and have weekend farms near us who would own horses if there was a place to board them when they're not in town. We thought we could serve both of those needs and our own kids would get to learn, too. It might even have been a business they'd want to run when they got older. But ..."

The tears started again, and she tossed her head back angrily in an attempt to make them go away.

"Ignore me, please," she said, laughing in embarrassment. "I'm not usually a great big crybaby. I don't know what's wrong with me."

"I'm guessing you haven't talked about all of this in a while," Larry said, "and I can see why bringing you here would bring it all up again. Maybe it wasn't such a good idea, after all."

Marqueeta looked crestfallen, as if she were about to cry, too.

"No, it was a wonderful idea, and the girls are having such a good time. I hope you have half this much fun when you come out to see us. Like I said, just ignore me."

Marqueeta turned to walk her horse back to the stable and Gina started to follow her, but Larry caught her arm.

"I'll talk to her this afternoon. You're right. I need to treat her like an adult, and if we're going to be a family, she needs to know it all."

Back at the house Lupe served lunch on the deck -- a curried chicken salad for the adults and peanut butter sandwiches for the children with lemonade all around. After that she took Dexter to his room for a nap while Larry worked in his office and Marqueeta surprised the girls with a Barbie camper and new Barbie dolls of their own that she promised to ship to them after they'd gone home. Gina and Steve watched from the playroom door as their sister-in-law sat cross-legged on the floor with her nieces and began talking in a high voice on behalf of an older Original Teenage Barbie doll she was dressing in cutoffs and a poncho.

"Hey, guys," she squealed, "do you want to go up the coast in my new camper?"

Stephanie ripped the cellophane off the box that held her new Snow White Barbie, deliberately waiting to answer until she had freed the doll from the cardboard box and plastic twist-ties that imprisoned her.

"Sure," she said finally. "Can we have a picnic at the beach on the way?"

And before Marqueeta's doll could answer, Danielle's Cinderella Barbie piped up, "Can we have s'mores?"

"Too bad she doesn't know how to play with boys," Gina whispered.

Unnoticed, she and Steve backed away from the door and dashed through the kitchen on the way to the guest cottage. They were kissing before the door was closed and a half-hour later had made love for the second time in less than twenty-four hours.

"Geez! What is up with us?" Gina gasped when Steve had rolled to his side of the bed.

"I don't know, but I think I want to stay in this cottage forever. Do you think your brother would let us just move in?"

Through the window they could see the marine layer gathering over the ocean and rolling in toward them, the scrub through which Gina had hiked with Dexter the day before disappearing in the mist. They wrapped themselves in the duvet and slept.

Lupe had the night off for her cousin's wedding, but before she left she made a pot of spaghetti sauce and set the table simply -- black plates against woven-wood mats with stark white napkins, a simple bowl of white roses in the center of the table and votive candles that set the dusky twilight gleaming. After dinner, the adults put the worn-out children to bed with the promise of a trip to Disneyland the next day, and then they regrouped around the table for another glass of wine. When one of the candles flickered wildly and then guttered out, Marqueeta quickly replaced it with a fresh one, unwilling for the evening to come to an end, for the fragile intimacy they had finally achieved to dissipate as they went their separate ways and got ready for bed.

Larry opened a second bottle of the pinot noir they had served with the pasta and reached around the table to each of their glasses, looking thoughtful as he poured.

"Just for grins," he said, "what would it cost to start up an operation like you're talking about, the stable thing?"

"Oh, Larry, it's been such a great day, let's not ..." Gina began, but he interrupted her.

"I think one of the best things about this time we've had together is that the elephant in the room has finally been unleashed -- or slain or put to rest or whatever the metaphor is. We've talked about what happened. I know why you've been angry with me, and now Marqueeta is up to speed, too. And you know why I felt I couldn't do anything at the time. Now let's talk about the future. Surely you haven't given up dreaming just because you've hit a rough patch."

"Larry, honestly ..." Gina ran her fingers through her hair and then threw her hands up in the air in a gesture of total futility. "A rough patch? Is that what you think this has been?"

"Sorry. What do you want me to call it?"

"It doesn't seem like a big deal to you because what you don't understand is that things don't happen for most people like they do for you. You even said that yourself earlier. You're talented and you're lucky. You dream about a career in music in Hollywood, and then you get it. I'm not saying you don't deserve it, you do. I'm just saying that dreaming of opening a stable full of horses when you can't even afford rent is a big waste of everybody's time."

"But Mom is giving you -- us -- all this money. Won't that make a difference?"

"She's giving us $56,000 a year, Larry. That's a lot of money, and we're grateful to have it, but it isn't enough to start a business."

"Just humor me a little bit. Isn't land a lot less expensive back there than it is here?"

"Yes, of course. You know it is."

"So what would a few acres with a house and a barn and a stable on it cost?"

Now Steve entered the conversation.

"We have some neighbors who put their farm on the market a couple of months ago. They've got 20 acres, a house, a barn and some outbuildings -- no real stable -- and a 5-acre stand of timber. They're asking three hundred thousand. They'll probably never get it. They haven't been able to make it pay, and the next guy won't be able to, either."

Larry looked thoughtful.

"Wow. That would cost a couple million out here."

"It might as well be a couple million there," Gina said. "It's still out of our reach."

"What would the down payment on a farm like that be?"

"Probably fifty thousand, if you didn't want the mortgage to last until you're an old man," Steve said.

"So Mom gives your fifty-six this year and ..."

"For God's sake, Larry," Gina said, "we've already got that money spent. The girls need school clothes, Steve's truck had to be repaired, and we're setting most of it aside so that if the owners of the farm where we live should decide to sell, we'd be able to pay rent somewhere else. That's the best part about getting this money. At least now I don't lie awake nights wondering if we're going to be homeless -- and I mean that literally."

"I'd never let you be homeless, and neither would Mom."

"Whatever," she said, verbally underlining the individual syllables and sounding like a petulant teenager, even to herself, but not caring.

He ignored her sarcasm.

"OK, what else? What else would you need to start up? You said you'd written a business plan to show the bank, so you must have some idea."

"At least another hundred thou, maybe more," Steve said, sounding as defeated as Gina felt. "We're talking horses, feed, equipment, liability insurance."

"But you'd do the work yourselves, so you wouldn't have a lot of employees to pay and give benefits to."

"We'd have to have a trainer if we wanted to give lessons," Steve said. "We'd know about feeding them and raising them, but we'd need a teacher."

"It was a pipe dream that didn't work out," Gina said, finishing her wine and pushing the empty glass away in a gesture of finality. "Maybe we can think about it someday when the economy is better. And when the girls are older, we can move to a city and I can go back to work. There are options, but they're not open to us right now, and we're a lot happier when we don't sit around thinking about what we don't have."

Then abruptly she stood up and said, "Goodnight, everybody. I'm going to bed."

CHAPTER FIFTEEN

September had always been Gina's favorite month. As a child she had loved going back to school at the end of the summer. For someone growing up in San Diego, it had been, along with the winter holidays and spring break, one of the few demarcations of the seasons.

"We have two seasons in San Diego," Jay had always joked when they had company from out of the state, "early spring and late spring."

But it seemed to her that even seventy-degree, cerulean-sky San Diego got serious after Labor Day. Adults went back to work with a renewed sense of interest in their jobs after the holiday weekend, and children stuffed their backpacks with new textbooks, pristine tablets, and freshly sharpened pencils that were ready to record all the possibilities that at this moment lay in their futures.

She grew to love the month even more once she moved to Indiana. Here there really was a change of seasons, a dip in the early morning temperatures, a shortening of the days, a pronounced changing of the colors of the foliage, as if Mother Nature had flipped over her calendar and realized she'd had just about enough of summer.

This morning there had been a sobering change when Stephanie, who now wanted to be called Stephy exclusively, climbed onto the bus headed for the Stoneridge Middle School. It was the same bus she'd always ridden, and she still boarded with her sister, just as she had last year and the years before. But now everything was somehow different. The classes would be more demanding, the peer pressure more crushing, the girl herself firmly situated on the inevitable path toward being a teenager and then an adult with no chance of her turning back, the toddler and the little girl she had been gone forever.

Over the summer there had been other changes, too. Just before Stephy turned twelve in July, she had started her period, and now she was using underarm deodorant and shampooing her hair more frequently. She cried over silly misunderstandings and shut the bedroom door against her little sister, only to have her mother humiliate her further by demanding that she open up and reminding her that it was Danielle's room, too.

"What does a person have to do to get a little privacy around here?" she had wailed only last night when her sister had teased her about spending the entire evening deciding what to wear on this significant first day. She had tried on outfit after outfit before finally deciding on the jeans, yellow camisole, and blue-and-purple plaid blouse she'd bought with her mother at Penney's in Indianapolis and carefully hanging them on the doorknob. A pair of navy high-top sneakers sat waiting for morning beneath the ensemble. Even these she had tried both with laces tied and laces fashionably but dangerously dangling.

Gina had waited at home until she saw the bus stop at the end of the lane, the door open, and her daughters disappear through it. She watched their shadowy selves move along the aisle and settle into different seats with their own friends. She would like to have walked with them to the bus stop and kissed them good-bye when they boarded. Instead, not wanting to embarrass them, she settled for looking out from behind the draperies at the living room window. Then she packed up her own briefcase and drove to the store.

It wasn't the career she wanted or even a job she liked, she thought as she drove into town, crossed the railroad tracks, and turned left at the stoplight in the direction of the store, but it was what she needed to do right now to help keep her family out of real poverty. And despite the circumstances that had put her here, she couldn't help but feel the excitement of it being the day after Labor Day, the sense of new beginnings, the idea that something wonderful might be lurking just around the corner.

She parked her old silver Hyundai in a space marked "Employees Only," and waved to Steve, who was already at work rolling dollies filled with boxes out onto the loading dock. "You can't be the boss until you know how to do everyone's job," he had told her once, and she felt a fierce surge of pride seeing him out there like that, his shirt sleeves rolled up, a flash of white T-shirt visible at the open neck. Then she walked through the back door and up the stairs to the ancient office. She flipped on the light and surveyed the damage. On the days she didn't come in to work, the rest of the staff piled her desk with invoices, mail, and notes asking for days off or reminding her they had been picked for jury duty. She would spend most of the morning sorting through the stack and seeing what needed urgent attention, and then she would fire up the cumbersome old desktop computer and pray it would churn out one more set of payroll numbers.

Everything in the office was old. When she came here it was as if she had walked through a rift in time, leaving the twenty-first century behind and landing squarely in the 1950s. One entire wall of the small room was filled with filing cabinets holding dusty manila folders crammed with invoices dating almost that far back. She seldom had occasion to open the drawers, and when she did she wondered if the people who had purchased the wheelbarrow or bags of seeds or "men's work gloves, one pair" were even still alive. She longed to spend a weekend in here tossing and cleaning, but Steve was a pack rat, and every time she brought up the idea, he looked like he might throw up. It was, after all, his domain.

Even the telephone was an antique, the handset attached to it with a spiraling cord. Gina was forever forgetting that it wasn't a cordless phone like the one they had at home and starting across the room with the receiver, only to be stopped in her tracks like a character in a comic strip when the cord to the wall grew taut and the base clattered to the floor behind her. She had priced replacing the whole system, but even the few hundred dollars it would have cost was too much. Every penny counted here, just like it did at home, where they squeezed the last crusty globs out of the toothpaste tube and swished water around the ketchup bottle to make it go just a little farther. As long as the phones worked and the computer still fluttered to life, that's what they would continue to use.

Still, she loved this little office. On cold winter days it was warmer than the rest of the store, and surrounded by the files and papers, almanacs, and ring binders filled with farming reports she felt safe and insulated, like she thought a mouse might feel when it snuggled into the cottony nest it had assembled with shredded papers, a piece of ribbon, a shoelace, or a length of dental floss that had failed to make it into the wastebasket under the bathroom sink. A bank of windows allowed her to look out over the store below, as if she were the captain of a ship. From here she could see who came in to shop and which employees were taking breaks. Once she had seen the school superintendent's son slip a padlock into his pocket without paying for it on the way out. The security arrangement here was as out of date as the phone system and the computer. The little electronic chips that would have sounded an alarm as customers passed through armed gates if they hadn't been disabled were too expensive even to make it to the wish list.

Below her she noticed that Betty Burns was working today, at the moment demonstrating an electric edger to a woman in a flowered dress. Larry Hart, wearing overalls, was driving a forklift loaded with bags of seeds through the big garage doors at the back. Two men in suits came through the front doors, and Steve appeared to shake their hands. Then the phone rang.

"Good morning. Chambers Farm and Feed," she said automatically, groping through papers as she did in search of a pencil and notepad.

"Hello, my darling!" her mother's voice sang through the line.

"Hey, Mom, where are you this time?"

"Bavaria. I'm working on some old German castles. Everything from here on out will be in Europe."

"Tough work, but somebody's gotta do it, huh?"

"It's gorgeous here. I wish you could see it. Green everywhere, trees and mountains and the Danube. And they've got me staying in an adorable little cottage that's right out of *Heidi*."

"That was in Switzerland, Mom."

"Yes, but you know what I mean. It's all gingerbready and cozy. I'm going to paint it while I'm here, too. It'll be great on note cards."

"Well, you sound wonderful, and it's great to hear your voice, but why are you calling me? Is anything wrong?"

Even when someone else was paying she couldn't help but worry about the cost, and besides, she and her mother had communicated by e-mail the whole time Anita had been traveling.

"Because I've got news that absolutely can't wait, and I wanted to tell you myself."

Gina couldn't imagine what it would be. With Anita you could never tell. Even when she and Larry had been children, they'd known their mother wasn't typical. She'd always had a job, and while the other mothers volunteered in the classroom and made cupcakes for school parties, she was more likely to crash in at the last minute, grabbing the last seat in the house for the Christmas pageant or an awards ceremony, a grocery store bag of Oreos peeking out from an oversized handbag. But while she might not have been traditional, she was always there, and Gina couldn't have imagined being anyone else's daughter. She missed her mom now, not just because she was traveling and so far away but because Anita was different in other ways, too. Her life had changed for the better, there was no question about that, but as happy as Gina was for her, that new life had also stolen the mother who had visited more often and cooked her favorite childhood foods and had time for walks and talking. Since Jay's death she had built a kind of shell around herself. She was impervious, an exotic beetle, wrapped in silk, always with an airline ticket in her tapestry bag, always with someplace else to go. Until Larry had told her about Mr. Wu and the two of them had found the photo with Dennis MacDonald in Hawaii, Gina believed her mother had never had so much as one date after she was widowed. She'd been asked out on several occasions, but she always turned down the potential suitor, telling Gina that two marriages were enough and she didn't want to be greedy.

"I'll give the other girls a chance," she always said, laughing at herself and then changing the subject. She had embraced her painting like a new lover, and maybe that was enough. You could never tell what was going on in someone else's head, even if it was your own mother.

"So shoot. What's the big news?" Gina asked now.

"I need to have you do some work with me."

"What kind of work? And where? You're a million miles away."

"Watercolors. Gardens. Scenes for stationery and designs for wallpapers."

"Mom, I haven't painted in years and ..."

"Not true," her mother interrupted. "I saw the painting you did of my garden. It was gorgeous. I had forgotten what a talent you are, and it turns out I need some help. I've got to stay focused on this book, but I have a contract with another company that calls for me to submit new designs for next year's greeting card collections. I showed your painting to my agent, and he showed it to the company where I have the contract, and they like it, too. You'll have your own signature line, but they'll bill you as my daughter in the promotional materials. If you say yes, you'll need to get started right away. They've got a contract ready to FedEx to you the minute I give them the word. Please say yes."

For a moment Gina was silent, struggling to fit the pieces together and figure out what her mother was saying. She had left the watercolor of her mother's garden on an easel in her studio in La Jolla as a surprise. Anita wouldn't be home for months yet, and she couldn't possibly have seen it.

"Mom ..." she said slowly, "how do you know about that painting? I purposely left it at your house as a surprise for you to find when you got home."

Her mind raced with possibilities. Had her mother come home after Asia and before Europe? But it would have made no sense to do that, and Larry would have told her. In the weeks since their return from California she had been e-mailing with her brother almost daily. He surely would have seen Anita if she'd been in California and told her.

"Your brother is the culprit. He and Marqueeta went down to check on my place just a few days ago. He took the painting back to his studio, and they scanned it and e-mailed it to me. As it happened, I had just gotten off the phone with Alice, my agent, who said the greeting card people were nipping at her heels about my pieces for next year. She told them I didn't have anything finished yet to show them. The fact is, I don't even have anything started. This year has been all about the book."

"Can't you use some of the pictures you're doing for that?"

"No, everybody wants exclusive rights, at least for a while. A year or so after the book comes out the publisher will probably be willing to release second rights to me, but they don't want to put all of this money into a hardback book when people could just as easily buy the same thing in a box of birthday cards."

"But, Mom, I'm not set up to do any of that. I don't have a studio or paints, and I don't travel to exotic places or visit beautiful homes, and you forget that I have a husband and two kids and I work here at the store. I don't exactly sit around watching soap operas and eating bonbons."

"You wouldn't need much, honey," Anita said, ignoring the edge to Gina's voice, "just a drawing table, an easel, some paints and good brushes, some good, heavy cold-pressed paper, a few ..."

"But that's what I'm saying, Mom. I don't have any of that stuff, and if I did have, I wouldn't have any place to put it. The girls already share a room, and I don't have a guest room that I can convert like you did."

"What about that nice big window in your living room? The light would be good."

"That's where my sofa is, Mom. And the living room is where we do everything as a family and have people over."

"OK, what about renting a little place? That might be the best idea anyway. You could get away from all the other stuff you have to do and really concentrate for a few hours each day."

"Mo-om!" she said, much like her fifteen-year-old self had done when Anita had refused to let her have her hair frosted and wear a strapless dress to the spring formal. "Everything you're talking about costs a lot of money that I don't have."

"I can advance you some money," Anita said now. "That's not a problem. Do you think you can find a little studio somewhere there in Bedford?"

Gina recalled walking down Main Street just the week before and wondering what was in the rooms above all of the old storefronts. The one above the Walgreens drugstore had a "For Rent" sign in the window. The economy being what it was, it would probably only cost a few hundred dollars a month, but it was a few hundred she didn't have, and the last thing she wanted to do was borrow from her mother. If Steve had been willing for her to do that, she might have asked when they were about to lose the farm, when they really needed it, and things would be different now.

"I'm sure I could, Mom, but ..."

"Don't say but, Gina. This is an incredible opportunity. It's a chance for you to build on something I've already established, and if it all goes well, when I'm out of the picture, you can take over the whole shebang -- like Dear Abby's daughter took over her column. I'm really excited. I had no idea you still had an interest in painting, and there's no one else to ask for help while I'm busy with this other project."

"It was one painting, Mom."

"That you did in one morning, according to your brother, and he said you were delighted with it."

"It was fun, yes. I had forgotten how much I liked doing that. I used to watercolor some of my architectural drawings just for the heck of it."

She didn't let her mother hear how much she wished she could say yes to everything she was offering.

"We're talking about doing something you love and making a whole lot of money, Gina. It could be a big boost for you and Steve and your family."

Aha. There it was. She could imagine the conversation Anita and Larry must have had after the trip to Hong Kong, both of them clucking about poor Gina and trying to figure out how they could help now that it was too late and then their relief when this chance came up for her mother to throw a little work her way.

"We're fine, Mom. You and Larry don't need to try and fix us. We're making it on our own."

Her mother's ebullient tone changed, and even from thousands of miles away, Gina could tell she was annoyed.

"You've got to stop looking back, Gina. I'm so sorry about what happened. I feel just awful, and I would have helped you then if you had just confided in me. Larry's sorry, too. But the past is what it is, and what I'm talking about is the future. And just for the record, when I e-mailed Larry to thank him for sending the painting and tell him my idea, he was absolutely thrilled, but he never once mentioned your financial situation -- just that he thought you'd love to do it. You have got to stop feeling sorry for yourself about that damn farm. What happened was terrible, and yes, you do have a chance here to make things better."

Gina bit her lip. She knew the clock was ticking and that this call from her mother's cell phone in Germany must be getting expensive, but for a few seconds she couldn't speak. She knew there was some truth in what her mother said, and against her will, she felt her whole being warm to the idea of painting for a living.

"I don't travel as much as you do," she said finally. "Assuming I have a studio and an easel and paint, where are these gardens and rooms you want me to create?"

"Exactly where mine are -- in my imagination. You look everywhere. You read books about gardens, you walk around town and look at people's yards, you take your camera wherever you go, and somewhere along the line the pieces all find their way into your paintings -- a flowerpot here, a eucalyptus tree there, a picnic blanket -- it all comes together. It could be a table set for lunch on a patio, a gate to a meadow, like that. Vignettes."

"And the money? What exactly are we talking about? I guess I need to know that before I make a decision. That's the first thing Steve will ask me when I tell him. Doing this would take up a lot of my time, and that might mean fewer hours here at the store."

"I understand that. They pay $1,000 per painting, and they need forty a year -- twenty for the spring and twenty for the fall. The one you've already done will count as the first one, but they won't buy that one unless you agree to do the others. With a greeting card line, the same artist has to do all the work."

"Wow. I had no idea. That's $40,000 a year."

"Yes, but it will come to a lot more than that. The contract will also entitle you to a certain amount of the royalties, so every time a card sells, you get a few cents. It's not much, but it adds up. And then once you're comfortable there, I'll ease you into other aspects of the business. You could eventually be doing a book like the one I'm doing now."

"You're assuming a lot -- like that I have some kind of talent that even comes close to yours. You may be overselling me to these people."

"They've seen the painting, Gina. I didn't oversell anything."

"I'll have to talk to Steve."

"I understand that, honey. But don't wait too long to let me know. They'd need the first batch by January to start production."

"Thanks, Mom. I really mean it. This is overwhelming. I'm excited about it, but I'm also scared. I don't want to let you down. I just don't know."

"Think about it. Talk to Steve. And then send me an e-mail. I'll be waiting."

Gina hung up the phone and buried her face in her hands. She had not seen that call coming here on this September morning of new beginnings. And here was Larry, a little late, maybe, but coming to her rescue all the same. She would call him, but not until she had talked to Steve and made a decision. It might not work out. But even as all the reasons why she couldn't do it ran through her mind, she imagined herself in the room above the Walgreens, her drawing table pushed up against the window that looked out over the courthouse square. She saw herself sitting at the table and on it the picture of an inviting green door with a brass knocker and a terra-cotta pot filled with red geraniums just next to it. At Christmastime the same door would have a wreath hanging on it and in the fall pumpkins and gourds stacked on a nearby hay bale. Or maybe a country mailbox with daisies spilling out or a picnic table with a red-checked tablecloth and a bottle of wine with two glasses already poured or …

The door to the stairway opened, and Steve ducked into the office. Gina snapped out of her reverie and glanced at the clock. It would soon be lunchtime, and she hadn't begun the payroll yet. She had barely started sorting through the pile on her desk. She looked sheepishly at her husband, but he didn't appear to notice.

"Boy, do I have some news for you," she said. "You're not going to believe this."

"Yeah, well, I've got some news of my own," he said. "I think I just sold the store."

Fifteen minutes later they were sitting at the China Cup Diner, Steve clutching Gina's hands with his on the Formica tabletop just as he had when they'd come to this same coffee shop when they found out they had to leave the farm. The cups of coffee they had ordered as an excuse to occupy the space sat cooling and ignored.

"You might have told me about this," Gina said. "I thought the business was ours together. I thought I had a say."

"Of course you do, honey," Steve pleaded. "I haven't signed the papers yet. That's why I need to talk to you now."

"And what about George?"

"He's absolutely on board. It's good business. He sees that. The point is, Gina, that we don't really have a choice. We already knew the Handy Man chain was building a superstore out on the bypass. They'll run us out of business within a week. Their location will be better, and because they're part of a big chain, they can afford to have grand-opening sales that would cripple us."

"So why don't they just do that?" she asked miserably.

"Because they have a good public relations department. They don't want to come into town on a sour note because they've put us out of business. If they buy us and we have a good opinion of them, the customers will easily transition over to them."

"The customers won't have a choice. There won't be anyplace else to go for what they need." She shook her head sadly and withdrew her hands to take a sip of her coffee. "So when would all of this happen?"

"Next spring, when the store is finished. We'll stay open until just a couple of weeks before they open. They don't want there to be a big enough gap that customers find someplace else out of town to go. They're going to put a big countdown sign on the building site so that people know they're coming, and when customers come into our store, we'll tell them they're giving us a fair price and we're happy to be working with them. Like I said, it's all about PR."

Gina blew out a long breath of defeat.

"It's not the way it used to be," she said finally.

"Nothing is, babe."

"And once our little windfall is spent, what then? I know it might sound like a lot of money now, but it won't last forever, especially if we end up having to move and pay rent somewhere."

Now it was Steve's turn to look defeated.

"They've also offered me a job," he said.

"Managing the store?"

"Managing the garden department."

"Isn't that a good thing? You do a lot of that now, don't you?"

"I'm used to selling seeds and equipment to farmers, but they've already got that covered. I'd be selling ferns and African violets and little bags of potting soil to housewives."

The bitterness in his voice was palpable, the set to his jaw almost frightening. He picked up the cold coffee mug from the side opposite the handle and swallowed it down as if it had been whiskey.

"So what did you tell them?"

"I said I needed to think about their offer and talk it over with you, but I've got to take it. George is jumping up and down he's so happy, and he is, after all, the bigger partner. At the end of the day, I have to do what he wants, and the job will keep us going. It's all that's out there for me right now. We've got to live."

Finally it was her turn.

"When you came into the office, I told you I had some news."

He had been slouched in the booth, one foot up on the vinyl seat, staring out the window at the people walking in from the parking lot, the empty cup still gripped so tightly in his hand that Gina half expected it to shatter.

"Oh, yeah. Geez, I'm sorry, honey. What was that about?"

"I've got an opportunity to do some work that would make us $40,000 a year, maybe more."

Now she had his attention. He straightened in his seat and faced her directly.

"It wouldn't cover everything, but if we get some money from the sale and you have this job with Handy Man and I do this, we could make ends meet."

"Well, yeah, I know your mom's sending us $56,000..."

"Yes, we'll have that, too, but I'm talking about work. Real work. That I'd do."

"What kind of work? Engineering, I'm assuming. With someone here in town or does Meyercorp want you back? You're not thinking of going back to Indianapolis, are you, because we already ..."

This made her laugh.

"Could I talk, please?"

He set down the cup and rolled his open palm toward her in a signal for her to go on.

"No, it isn't Meyercorp, and I'm not going to Indianapolis. The employer would sort of be my mother."

Steve continued listening, but his eyebrows knit together in a frown and he shook his head slowly from side to side.

"I see where this is coming from," he said. "More charity from your mom for the poor Chambers family."

"No. That's what I thought, too, at first, but Mom convinced me that it has nothing to do with that. When Larry and I were at her house last month, I got up early one morning and painted a picture in her backyard. It wasn't a big deal. I just did it because he wasn't up yet and I had kind of gotten the urge to paint again while we were sorting through her studio. But it turned out pretty well, so I decided to leave it on an easel in her studio as a little surprise for when she got home. What happened was that Larry and Keeta went down to check on her house, and he saw it again and decided to e-mail it to Mom. About the same time, she was being pressured by a greeting card company she works with to send them some new paintings. She's busy with the book, so she sent them mine and suggested that they do a contract with me. They've agreed to hire me for forty paintings. The one I already did would count as one."

"That sounds like a lot of work."

"They're small, and they're not that hard to do, and honestly, I had forgotten how good it can feel to do something until that morning when I was out there painting."

"But it's not engineering, any more than my selling flowerpots is farming."

"It's still creating something where there was nothing -- taking a blank page and putting something on it that makes people want to own it. It's exciting."

"So what did you tell her?"

"That I wanted to talk to you. It would mean some changes in our lives. I was concerned that I'd have to spend less time at the store, but I guess that won't be an issue for much longer. It would also mean finding a place to work. Mom's talking about advancing me enough money to rent a studio."

"A studio?" He said this in disbelief, as if it were a word not to be used in a diner in Bedford, Indiana. "And where would you find this studio?"

"A room, Steve. There's no space at home. I don't want to clutter up our whole house with easels and paints, and the light's not really all that good anyway. There are some rooms to rent over other businesses on the courthouse square. I'm thinking of looking into one of those."

"Won't that be expensive?"

"No, I don't think so. With the economy the way it is and all the empty real estate in this town, I can negotiate something. Besides, Mom says the contract includes my getting royalties, so once the cards begin to sell, there will actually be more money."

"You sound pretty jazzed about this."

"I am. I really am. It seems almost too good to be true -- to do something that's fun and get paid for it."

"Then you're going to say yes, just like I am to the Handy Man people."

CHAPTER SIXTEEN

The view out the window of Gina's second-floor corner studio on the courthouse square wasn't New York City or San Francisco or Paris, but it had its charms, especially now, with the leaves bright red and gold against a bright blue October sky. The tree across the street at the corner of 12th Avenue and Main undulated with the slight breeze that had picked up during the morning. It was completely green on one side -- deep hooker's green, she thought, with a drop of ultramarine -- while the other side sported graduating waves of raw sienna, lemon yellow, and cadmium red with just a hint of alizarin right at the top.

The busy downtown Steve described from his childhood had disappeared when the businesses migrated to the mall at the west edge of town, and now doctors' and lawyers' offices, locally owned boutiques, bars and cafes filled the storefronts where there were once hardware stores and dress shops. Directly across the street was the square where a modern courthouse still contained the wall of one erected in 1872 and a memorial paid silent tribute to the pioneers who had settled in the area and to Lawrence County's wartime dead. The windows that looked out over the side street revealed a fabric store, a religious bookstore, and a shoe repair shop, the owners of which couldn't afford the move to a better location.

Just down the block and out of Gina's view was the columned Masonic temple, its architecture causing it to look at once out of place and yet strangely at home, nestled as it was between other old buildings that now housed offices, stores, or empty rooms where the remnants of failed businesses mingled with piles of dirt and dust that had been hastily swept up at the last minute with nowhere to go. Gina had stopped one day to look inside one of these empty spaces, and having moved from the farm not that long ago, she imagined a grieving shopkeeper doing the last, right thing by sweeping up, and then, realizing that the trash cans had already been packed and driven away, simply giving up, exhausted, and walking away from the heap.

Below her a woman pushed a stroller, presumably containing a baby, although she couldn't see it because of a protective canopy. Two men wearing suits carried cardboard cups of coffee and walked quickly, their heads tilted toward one another, apparently deep in conversation.

She smiled to herself. My studio, she thought. My studio. At first the idea had seemed far-fetched and pretentious, out of her league, but once she'd claimed the space and moved her painting things in, it seemed exactly right, like the Masonic temple, strangely hers. The room -- actually one of two plus a bathroom, having once been half of an apartment long since divided up for commercial purposes -- delighted her more than she could have imagined it would. It was spacious with high ceilings and a bank of north-facing windows that on sunny days provided her with a perfect quality of light -- neither the optimistic blaze of orange sunrise nor the flaming farewell of a purple sunset but instead steady, accommodating beams throughout most of the day. The suite, as the rental agent had euphemistically called it, cost $400 per month,

including utilities. It sounded like a lot to Gina, given their circumstances, but at $1,000 per picture, which she would still have a hard
time believing if she hadn't already completed two and gotten her
first paycheck, it had already paid for itself.

As her mother had pointed out, having a studio was absolutely
essential and not the luxury Gina had at first argued it was. Home
provided too many distractions, even though she had scoured all
the rooms and even the garage to look for a space she could appropriate for her painting. Their bedroom was too full of furniture and filing cabinets that had been in their office at the other
house. The kitchen was too busy and cluttered. She might possibly
have been able to work at the table, but that would have meant
clearing away her paints after every session and virtually having to
start from scratch the next day. The garage was dark and cold and
smelled of motor oil and freshly cut wood; the living room was the
only room in the house that had any sense of order and the only
place where they could watch TV together or occasionally have
people over.

The space over an insurance office -- the Walgreens rooms having already been spoken for -- had been vacant for at least five
years. The surfaces had been coated with dust the first day she and
Steve had come to look at it, and they had choked and coughed
when they turned over a faded piece of carpeting that had been
left by former tenants years ago and sent a cloud of dust and sharp
particles of dirt into the air. There was also a stale smell that dissipated when the agent -- with some difficulty and a crowbar from
the trunk of his car -- pried open one of the windows. The bathroom sink was dirty, the mirror splattered, the toilet bowl blackened by years of disuse. Faded, curling blue flowered wallpaper
that had probably been more cheerful in its heyday covered the
walls. Steve had shaken his head and said he thought they ought
to keep looking.

"We can do better than this," he told her.

But Gina could see the possibilities even then.

"All it needs is a mop and some hot water, some scouring powder in the bathroom, and a gallon of paint," she said, her eyes shining with more excitement than he'd seen in them for a long time. "And it's just for a year. When I get this first set of paintings done, Mom's publisher might not even want me anymore."

Steve laughed.

"It's your decision, honey," he said. "Lease it for a year and see what happens. It's my guess that they're going to love you, and the only reason you won't renew a year from now is that you'll need a bigger, better place."

He was as impressed by his wife's talent as her brother and her mother had been. He had seen some of the drawings to which she had added watercolor in her work, but he didn't know she had this capacity for choosing one detail and building an entire scene around it from her imagination. "A vignette," she had corrected him when he said as much. First it was his grandmother's bread bowl, which his mother now kept filled with fruit on the dining room table. The second one had grown out of a lamp she had seen in an antique store and photographed with her phone. The final image hadn't looked anything like the picture, but the picture had served its purpose to start her down a path at the end of which lay the beginnings of financial freedom. With his job at the new store and her paintings, the money they'd get from selling the store and from her mother, and especially not having to pay rent, they might be able to start putting money into a college fund for the girls, might be able to someday own their own place again.

Gina credited Lindsay with the way the place had turned out. As a widow, she had learned new skills she never knew she had before -- like how to fix broken doorknobs and paint ceilings, install faucets and replace light fixtures. She had been as enthusiastic as Gina was when she saw the place, and two weekends later, while Steve met with the managers of the new store and Sid and Maryanne took the girls for an overnight stay, she and Gina had transformed the bleak rooms into an atelier. They stripped off the ugly wallpaper and painted the actual workroom, probably a bedroom in an earlier incarnation, a warm cream color so as to make the best use of light. Thanks to a visit to a second-hand store and some garage sales, a stool, straight-backed chair, and painting table were now positioned near the windows, much as they had been in Gina's imagination. Gina's paints and brushes were fanned out across another table that sat against an adjoining wall, and as a studio-warming gift, her mother had sent a cabinet like her own for storing blocks of paper and tubes of paint. It sat in a corner across the room, at this point still unused. Gina had developed an appreciation for why her mother's studio had seemed in such disarray. She didn't want to store her paints and brushes away, preferring to have them available for use whenever she needed them, and like her mother, too, she had already begun to pin up photographs and sketches on the corkboard that adorned the wall where there were no windows.

The other room was transformed, at Lindsay's urging, into a reception area.

"And who exactly will I be receiving?" Gina had hooted.

"You'll be surprised," Lindsay said. "Eventually you'll want to display what you're doing and bring people up here so they can see. You might even want to do a little show and sell some of your pictures locally."

In warming up for doing the paintings for which she had been contracted, Gina had produced several pieces that depicted places around Bedford -- the band shell at the park, a patch of wildflowers behind Lindsay's barn, and even a small portrait of Casey on his tricycle that now hung over an easy chair in Lindsay's living room -- all from her kitchen table. Because they had turned out so well, she acceded to Lindsay's plan. With the loan from her mother, they were able to get a fake Turkish carpet that filled the center of the room, leaving just enough hardwood, now gleaming, around the edges to show what the apartment must have looked like in the 1930s when the building had been new. They had found two cast-off chairs from the Goodwill store, recovered them in deep-green paisley, and set a small table between them. Across the room a folding metal table waited to be covered with a white tablecloth and set with wineglasses and cheese plates. Lindsay had insisted in all seriousness that Gina be prepared for her first opening.

"You've heard about the law of attraction," she said as she stood back to look at the placement of the table. "If you get ready to have a show, you'll have one. You put glasses out for people to drink wine from, they'll come and drink it."

Gina had snorted with laughter and called her a New Age kook, but she hadn't put up an argument. What could it hurt?

Now she glanced at her watch. Three hours until Larry and his family would arrive. Any other day that would have been time enough to get some work done, but not today. She was only here to make sure the studio looked its best, dusting and rearranging even though nothing was dirty and she had already placed the brushes and paints as artfully as the ones on a recent cover of the art catalog from which she had gotten the idea. Larry had told her by text from the airport that he was eager to see where she worked, and she was as nervous as if she were showing off her home, which he'd also never seen. She'd brought in the vacuum cleaner to run over the carpet and a cooler into which she put some cheap champagne and bottles of cold water since they said that they wanted to come here first.

She and Steve had offered to meet the plane in Indianapolis, but Larry assured them it would be just as easy if they rented a car and drove down.

"There wouldn't be room for all of us," he'd said when Gina brought up the idea during a phone call. "And besides, you don't want to be running us back and forth to the hotel."

That made her wince even now, even with the plans in place and everyone seeming satisfied and Larry, Dexter, and Keeta stowing their tray tables in a plane getting ready to land just a few minutes from now. Her mother thought it was just as important for Larry to see her way of life as it had been for her to see his in California, but the staggering differences in their lifestyles took her breath away. In Malibu there had been room for all of them, and she and Steve had been able to enjoy Larry's home and all the luxuries and spoiling that came with it. Here it would be glaringly obvious that the haves were coming to visit the have-nots. For starters, they would not be staying in Gina's home but rather at the seedy Hotel LaSalle downtown. The leather sofas in its lobby were ancient, the elevator slow and undependable. The beds and dressers in the rooms looked as if they had been delivered in the 1940s, as they very well might have been. The pipes in the bathroom made noise, and there was no room service or TV. When she had offered Larry the choice of that or a chain motel outside of town, he had said quickly and with great enthusiasm that they wanted something that was emblematic of Bedford, something that had character. Try making a movie out of this, she had thought to herself when she walked into the lobby late one afternoon to book the room. Maybe *Psycho*. Even making the reservation had given her pause. She hadn't asked Larry how many rooms they wanted, so she booked two, just in case, with a rollaway for Dexter. They could apportion the space any way they wanted. That was for sure none of her business.

Even making the grocery list had been stressful. How could she compete with Lupe's elaborate concoctions, especially on a budget that only allowed for beef once a week and in a place where jicama and cilantro were only occasionally available in the upscale market across town and sometimes not even there. Had Dexter gotten any better at eating what was put before him, or would he throw his breakfast on the floor and demand something different while his mother looked confused and her own mind rang with the cash-register sound of cha-ching? And how would they arrange the meals, anyway? Would Larry and Keeta be willing to drive to her house every morning for breakfast, especially with a hungry three-year-old in the backseat clamoring to be fed? And where would they all sit? Mentally she counted: there would be the two extra dining room chairs that were stored in the barn and the desk chair from the girls' room. But Dexter had still been in a highchair when they'd been to Malibu two months earlier. What would she do about that? Could they put the booster seat from the car on the desk chair and make it work?

Lindsay once again saved the day by bringing over Casey's highchair, which she said she hadn't been able to part with, and her mother's recipe for a root vegetable stew along with a crisp white tureen with shiny yellow sunflowers on the lid in which to serve it. She also typed up a list of affordable restaurants and places they could go to sightsee so that Gina could keep painting and meet the next deadline before her guests arrived. This morning she had driven to the hotel with two baskets of mums from her garden that she asked to have placed in the Langleys' bedrooms, and now she would be arriving shortly with a plate of sandwiches and a fruit salad so that they could kick off the visit with a festive lunch.

"How cool will that be?" she said to Gina when they were making the plans, laughing as she imagined the scenario. "It's not everybody who starts a visit with lunch in an artist's atelier."

Gina shook her head, but she couldn't help smiling.

"Nice try, sweetie, but for starters, I wouldn't even be working as an artist if it weren't for my brother, at least not yet. And you forget that if he had taken me to his workplace, we would have had lunch with movie stars in the executive dining room. I'm not sure my little studio is going to blow anybody away."

"Still, it's interesting. You're interesting. Look at what you've done since all of this started back in the spring. You've been to Hong Kong, you've been to Malibu and La Jolla, and the long silence with your brother is over. That's a lot to celebrate. Maybe I should bring balloons."

And bring them she did, arriving just before Steve with a bouquet of them in shimmering Mylar red, blue, and green, the blue one with "Welcome" emblazoned across it. Their long strings were attached to a weight so that she could position the arrangement to fill up an empty corner near the door to the workroom. She had hoped to be gone before the family arrived and was taking the cellophane off the sandwiches and setting out paper plates and napkins on the little table between the chairs when they heard footsteps on the stairs and Dexter's shrill little voice telling his mother repeatedly that he wanted to see Stephy. Lindsay knelt to pull some glasses out from a box under the table while Gina flung open the door and embraced Larry, who was ahead of everyone else and carrying a bottle of expensive Veuve Clicquot champagne. Then she went partway down the stairs to hug her sister-in-law and reach for Dexter's hand.

"You look great," Keeta exclaimed. "Have you lost weight?"

Gina had hoped she would notice.

"Thanks to you, yes," she said. "I've been walking three miles a day since we got back from visiting you. It has only been a couple of months, but I've knocked off about 15 pounds."

"Can we walk while I'm here?"

"I'm way ahead of you, sister. I've already got us a couple of different routes scoped out."

"The reason I ask is that walking seems to help stave off my episodes."

"Sure," Gina said. She had hoped Keeta would have the fond memories of their Malibu walks that she had, but once again it seemed to be all about her.

"Where's Stephy?" Dexter wailed.

"She's at school, honey," Gina said, pulling him along up the stairs behind her. "We're going to have a little lunch here, and then we'll go to my house, and you'll be able to watch for the girls to come home on the bus. I'll walk down the lane with you when it's time. They're excited to see you, too. They told me so just this morning."

That was a little bit of an exaggeration. In fact, the girls had been wondering how they were going to keep a spoiled little boy entertained and grumbling about having to stay home from a hayride to which they had been invited.

"Not fair," Stephanie had complained, and her sister had chimed in, "She's right, Mom. They're coming to see you and Dad, not us. Why should we have to give up our plans?"

"Did you see how they treated you in Malibu? Do you think Keeta was whining when she put those fancy bedspreads on your beds and made the welcoming poster? I'm asking you to play with your cousin for a couple of days. You can take him outside and push him on the swing and show him the cows. We'll be doing other stuff, too, so it won't just be you three trapped in your bedroom the whole time. And besides, you know he's crazy about you guys."

The girls finally grudgingly agreed, and they had even seemed to have fun digging through the boxes of their old toys Steve brought down from the attic over the weekend.

When she entered the reception room with Dexter, Steve had already taken Larry into the studio proper and was pointing out the window and telling him about the stores that had been there before the mall was built. Keeta halted awkwardly in the middle of the reception room as if she had just entered a party where she didn't know anyone. Lindsay gave the champagne flutes one more polish with a towel and was just turning around to tell Gina everything was ready when the men came back into the room. And that was the tableau Gina would always remember -- herself caught in the crossfire of Larry's and Lindsay's first glimpse of one another. She felt the barometer change as if the air had been charged with electricity and the oxygen sucked out of the room. The look was followed by a few critical moments of silence during which she thought she could hear everyone's heart beating, during which she struggled with what to say next, how to handle the situation. And then it was over.

"Lindsay, this is my infamous brother, Larry, and his wife, Marqueeta." She managed to stumble over both women's names in the introduction as if they were completely new to her and had their roots in some other language.

Lindsay put her hand out toward Marqueeta, clearly overreacting when it seemed to Gina obvious that she would rather be touching Larry.

"Lindsay is my best friend, and she's been a huge help in getting the studio into shape. You should have seen it before we redecorated it. I can show you some pictures."

She was talking too fast and about nothing to fill the awkward gap.

"Oh," Keeta said in surprise. "I thought you were the caterer," which explained why she hadn't made any overtures to Lindsay when she entered the room. Even knowing her error, she couldn't get past the idea of Lindsay as a servant. "The food looks very nice," she said weakly.

"It's nice to meet you both," Lindsay said, still ignoring Larry as if he weren't even in the room. "I was just about to leave. In fact, I hadn't meant to be here when you arrived at all. In a way I am the caterer. I just came over to bring the lunch and make sure Gina had everything she needed for your visit."

She picked up the handbag she had left on a chair and put it over her shoulder.

"Please don't go," Larry said, fairly barking, the words much louder and sharper than they should have been, and again Gina had the sense that she was in the middle of some kind of shift in the atmosphere, like Lindsay and Larry were Maria and Tony from *West Side Story*, facing each other in the spotlight on an otherwise darkened stage and maybe about to burst into song. "I mean, do you have to? If you're Gina's best friend, I'd, I mean we'd like to get to know you, too."

Lindsay looked at the oversized watch on her wrist, her husband's, she had once admitted to Gina.

"No, I guess I could stay for a little bit. I have a little boy, and I need to be home when the school bus comes, but I've got a couple of hours before then."

"What's his name?" piped up Dexter, oblivious to what else was going on around him.

"Casey," Lindsay said, and she knelt down beside him so that she could look him squarely in the eyes. "He's a little bit older than you are, but I think he'd love to have you come over and play while you're here."

"You'd like that, wouldn't you, Bud?" Larry asked, now kneeling next to Lindsay and looking at her as he asked his son the question.

Lindsay stood quickly and said, "Gina, why don't we serve lunch, and then you can show everybody around."

Glad to have a reason to be busy, Gina turned to the table with a flourish as if it were a lavish buffet instead of a plate of sandwiches and a tray of fruit.

"Larry and Keeta, you're the guests of honor. Why don't you start. Honey, would you pour the champagne?"

It turned out that Lindsay, not thinking she would be a part of the party, had only brought four flutes in the cooler."

"Where's yours?" Larry asked her when Steve had poured and was handing the glasses around.

"I'm fine," she said, seeming flustered by the very fact that he had spoken to her. "I think there are some paper cups in the bathroom. I'll grab one of those."

Larry proffered his own glass to her so quickly that foam sloshed over the edge and dripped down the stem and onto the carpet. "I'll find a cup," he said. "You have mine."

Gina wondered if she were the only one who noticed that his ears were red and that he had bolted in the wrong direction for the bathroom with all the grace of a newborn colt. He opened a closet door and then closed it sheepishly, looking around to see if anyone had noticed his mistake.

Steve saved the day by saying matter-of-factly, "The bathroom's there to your left, just inside the other room. I've done the same thing," although he never had.

When the awkward lunch was over and Gina had given a tour of the space to people she was pretty certain weren't listening -- Keeta had pecked on her phone the whole time -- Lindsay repacked the cooler and picked it up to carry it down to her car.

"Here, let me help you with that," Larry said, again seeming to bleat out the words.

"I'm fine, really," Lindsay said, laughing. "When you're a farm girl, you have to carry heavy things all the time. I don't even think about it."

"But surely your husband helps you at home."

"Uh, no, I'm not married. I'm actually a widow."

Now Keeta's interest was piqued.

"You're so young," she said, looking as if she were grief-stricken herself. "What happened?"

"A tractor accident," Lindsay said, smiling briefly, painfully. "He was a farmer, too."

"Larry, go ahead and help her," Keeta said magnanimously, apparently believing that the widowhood of such a young woman earned her the right to receive help and would, like kryptonite, render her powerless.

Larry took the cooler from Lindsay's hands and started down the stairs. For a moment she looked as if she weren't sure quite what to do next, and then, either deeming that it would appear even more awkward not to accept or simply wanting to be with Larry as much as he wanted to be with her, she fluttered her fingertips in good-bye to the rest of the room in general and disappeared down the stairs behind him.

From the window in the studio, Gina watched Larry stow the cooler in the back of Lindsay's SUV. And then she saw them look at each other, say a few words, and then take both of one another's hands and grip them tightly, hanging on as if for dear life.

CHAPTER SEVENTEEN

G ina pulled the car into a slot marked "Visitor Parking" and turned off the engine.

"There it is," she said, her voice cracking just a bit even now. "There's my house."

Before them, across a circular driveway and a manicured lawn with hedges that spelled out "Finest Farms," was a sprawling three-story brick office building. Its many east-facing windows reflected the mid-morning sun, and the company inside seemed to be doing a brisk business. Some people passed through the massive revolving door in suits, others in jeans with plaid shirts and baseball caps. The rest of the parking lot was filled mostly with pickup trucks, and three flags flew from poles to the right of the door -- the U.S. flag, the Indiana flag, and another on a bright orange background that they couldn't make out until a breeze unfurled it and revealed "Finest Farms" yet again.

"I don't get it," Larry said. He shifted in his seat to face her, his back now to the door.

"They tore our house down -- the one Steve and his brothers built for us before we got married -- they tore it down. There's no trace of it left. They brought in heavy equipment and bulldozed everything. You can't tell where my vegetable garden was or the girls' swing set. There were some big shade trees around the house, and they took those out, too."

"Why didn't you just tell me? Why did you haul us all the way out here for this?"

She smiled bitterly.

Because I wanted you to see what you ... exactly what happened to us. You came here to find out about my life. Well, this is it. It's not like we can even drive by here and relive our nice memories. I wasn't here the day they did it. I couldn't be, but Steve couldn't stay away. That night when he came home and told me about it was the only time I've ever seen him cry. He said they started with a wrecking ball and after that they just drove over the top of it with big machines and smashed it like it was a toy forgotten in a driveway. Then they loaded all of the scrap wood onto big trucks and hauled it away -- to a dump somewhere, I suppose. I don't think they even tried to salvage any of it or even recycle anything. Sometimes I have nightmares about sections of wall covered in the wallpapers I had picked out -- blue and green plaid on two walls of our bedroom, pink bows for Stephanie, and Dora the Explorer for Danielle. I imagine them shredded but still standing straight up, like those pictures you see of the World Trade Center right after the attacks."

"But the pain coming here must cause you! I wish you had just told me what happened. I never meant to bring all this back up when I asked you do drive me past the house."

"In a way it's like chewing bubble gum on a bad toothache. You know it's going to hurt, but you can't keep yourself from doing it. And in a way it has become the symbol of strength for me -- the pain so exquisite, so distilled out from all the circumstances that led up to what happened and then preserved like in amber so that I don't ever forget. I feel like every time I drive past here I get stronger, and

I'm more determined than ever that we will climb out from under our debts and someday be financially independent again."

Larry let out a long sigh.

"And I'm one of those circumstances, aren't I?" he asked.

"Yes. Yes you are. I'd be lying if I told you otherwise."

"I'm so, so sorry, Sis. And I'm sorry for bringing you out here today. I didn't want to open these wounds again. I just wanted to see what your place looked like."

"For starters, Larry, the wound is always open, so nothing you could say or do now would make any difference. Steve and I talk about our house like it's a person who has died. It permeates everything we do. I keep trying to tell myself it was just a building and how lucky we are that we're all healthy and we have each other, and I am grateful for all of that, but I never walk into any part of the house where I live now without remembering what the other house was like. The girls each had their own rooms, and we had a dining room so that when we had company over for dinner they didn't have to sit in the middle of the mess I'd made preparing it. You saw what breakfast was like this morning."

"I thought breakfast was great. Very homey, and I loved my omelet."

"Says the man who eats every meal on an imported dining table in his fancy Malibu house with Lupe running back to the kitchen when every detail isn't perfect and you think of something else you want."

"Still. It's warm and cozy, more like when you and I were growing up, and those are feelings I seldom get in my fancy Malibu house, as you like to call it."

"That's what it is."

"Whatever."

"The other thing I wanted to point out by bringing you here was that you said you had never been out here before, but you have.

I think that speaks volumes about our relationship and how much attention you've paid to my life, even on a good day."

Larry frowned at the effort of trying to recall the experience in his memory. Finally he shook his head.

"I don't think so," he said.

"It was the night of my wedding."

"We stayed at Steve's parents' house. I distinctly remember because I was horrified to be sleeping on the sofa out in the open in their living room when everyone else was safely tucked away behind closed doors in bedrooms."

"That was the night you and Mom and Dad got in, and there was that big snow so you couldn't get to the hotel. After the wedding the next day, Steve and I left for Chicago and you guys stayed at our house before you went back to San Diego on Sunday."

Now the light was dawning.

"Oh, yeah. You had all those windows and that big front porch. Mom and Dad stayed in your room, and I stayed in a little bedroom upstairs with a slanted ceiling."

"That room eventually became Danielle's. Yep. That was the place."

The ride home was mostly silent. Gina drove him past the girls' schools, and they stopped at the store so that Steve could give Larry a tour. The office that had recently been Gina's was now occupied by Terry, a young woman just out of the technical college who shrugged her shoulders apologetically when Gina told Larry this was where she used to work.

When they were finished and walking back to the parking lot, Larry asked where Lindsay lived.

"Not far from our place. Why?"

She hoped her question would elicit a confession from her brother about the desperate clasping she had witnessed the day before, but he shrugged it off as if his interest were of no consequence.

"No particular reason, just that's she's the only person I know in Bedford besides you guys."

"We'll pass her place on the way home. If she's at home, we can stop and say hi."

When they did, Lindsay was outside struggling with one of the paving stones she had bought to make a path from the side door of her house out to her garden. The plot was filled now with brown stalks and dead leaves and among them the hopeful new blooms of two purple asters. She stood up, shading her eyes with her gloved hand, and walked through a sagging rusted metal gate to where Gina had stopped the car.

"What are you two up to?" she asked, leaning against Larry's side of the car and looking across him at Gina. "And where have you left everyone else?"

"The girls are at school, and Steve's working. Marqueeta is at home with Dex. He was more interested in the morning cartoons than in taking a ride with his dad and his aunt. I can't imagine why."

Larry had been looking through the windshield at the pavers.

"Do you need help with those? They look really heavy," he said, and again he seemed to bark out the sentence like a nervous schoolboy. Gina half expected his voice to crack and modulate up to an embarrassing tenor. Lindsay screwed up her face and nodded in a silent "Yes, please" response.

"They're heavier than they look," she said. "Steve loaded them for me when I bought them at the store, and he made it look easy. I managed to get three of them out of the car when I got home, but there are several more still to be unloaded. I've got the path dug out, but now I've got to put down some sand and get them into position and replace the sod around them. And I've got to get all this done before winter so that the path doesn't turn into a sea of mud."

"I can help with that," Larry said. "I might as well make myself useful while I'm here."

"But I've got to get home," Gina protested. "The girls will be home in another couple of hours, and Marqueeta has been alone with Dex all morning. I'm sure that's not her idea of a holiday."

"I could give you a ride when we're finished," Lindsay said, still looking at Gina as if the person to whom she was talking weren't inches away from her in the car.

"You know what," Larry said now to his sister, "we were planning to take you guys out to dinner tonight. Lindsay and her son could come with us. She could clean up here and then drive me to your place to change. Make a reservation at your favorite place. It'll be fun."

It was nearly 6:00 when the two of them arrived, and everyone else was ready to go and sitting around the kitchen table. Stephanie and Danielle were wearing the new full-skirted dresses they had worn to a friend's birthday party a few weeks earlier, identical except that Stephanie's was red and Danielle's yellow, and they passed the time by spinning around to watch their skirts flare out and running into the living room to look at themselves in the full-length mirror on the inside of the coat-closet door. Steve, who had just gotten home, said he'd go as he was, and Marqueeta had gotten Dex up into an outfit from the Gap that made him look like a miniature businessman and was herself clad in designer jeans, a leather jacket, and red heels that would be sure to get her noticed in Bedford.

Gina, who had phoned Lindsay that they had a 6:30 reservation at the Red Pagoda, looked repeatedly at the clock on the microwave over the stove and was growing increasingly annoyed.

"That should give you guys enough time to finish the path, but if we go any later we'll be running into the kids' bedtimes," she had said in her voice-mail message. Despite having called Lindsay's cell, her friend hadn't picked up.

Lindsay was uncharacteristically sober when they finally came through the door into the kitchen. She had changed out of her work clothes into khaki pants and a blue striped blouse, and her hair was damp from her recent shower. Larry was talkative and rushed.

"I'm just going to run through the shower," he said to no one in particular as he passed through the room. "I won't be a minute."

"You've got to be kidding!" Gina said, pointing to the clock. If we don't leave within the next few minutes, we're going to miss our reservation. The Red Pagoda is busy on Friday nights, so they won't hold it very long for us. You look fine. Let's just go."

What she didn't add was that he looked remarkably clean for someone who had spent the afternoon hauling stones and putting down sand and dirt for a path.

"It'll just take a minute, Sis. Chill, for Pete's sake."

"This is so typical," Gina erupted as if they were still teenagers. "He always does this. He made me late to my high school graduation because he wasn't ready. Sometimes it's like nobody else's wishes and needs even matter. I don't know how you live with him!"

This remark was directed at Keeta, who leaned against the arched doorway that led into the living room and smiled and shrugged her shoulders in resignation, as if to say what was she to do. Behind her Stephanie and Danielle continued to twirl and laugh. Lindsay, still just inside the door where they had entered, remained silent, digging into her purse as if to look for something important that she might have forgotten, checking her phone for messages and then, the possibilities for appearing busy exhausted, said she needed to call Casey, who was staying over at a friend's house. For this she stepped outside and stayed there talking until Larry reappeared.

Later, with all of them driving to the restaurant in two cars, Gina noticed as they passed Lindsay's house that while the stones had been unloaded and were stacked neatly against the foundation under her back porch, no progress on the path had been made.

On Saturday morning Steve said he had a surprise for Larry, Keeta, and Dexter, whom he openly and affectionately referred to now as "our city slickers." The time in Malibu had warmed him toward Larry's family, and he had looked forward to entertaining them when they came to Indiana. Early in the morning, before the rest were up, he had hitched a wagon to the tractor and furnished it with bales of hay. At breakfast he told them all to suit up in warm clothes that they could get dirty. Gina saw a look of panic cross Keeta's face and quickly reassured her that they could all borrow old clothes.

"Can you guess what we're going to do?" Steve asked his daughters enthusiastically as he passed a platter of pancakes to his brother-in-law.

At first they couldn't guess, and so Steve gave them a clue.

"Green gunk," he said.

"Yay!" Stephanie and Danielle cried in unison, clapping their hands, "Walnuts!"

Larry and Keeta looked equally dubious, even though Dexter was clapping his hands along with his cousins, despite not having any idea what they were so happy about.

"Green. Hands?" Keeta asked slowly, separating the words deliberately as if the very act of saying them could stain her manicured fingers. Gina would not have her husband's moment ruined.

"That's a great idea, honey," she said quickly, and then to Larry, "The whole point of this visit is to show you how we live, and this is something we do every autumn. It's a lot of fun, isn't it, girls?"

"Yes," Danielle said before her sister could speak. "We go out into the woods and find these walnuts in their big green husks. Then we bring them back home and knock the skins off with hammers so the nuts inside can dry. Dad has some rubber gloves you can wear, but even then your hands will get all green and yucky."

She shivered in delight at the prospect. Gina noticed with a tinge of regret that Stephanie, now in middle school, seemed less excited about that part of the project than she had in previous years. Dex looked from one of his parents to the other, clearly waiting to see which one of them would tell him he couldn't take part in the fun for fear of getting dirty. Again Gina read their expressions and intercepted any attempt on their part to spoil the outing.

"The girls make it seem a little worse than it actually is," she reassured them. "We wear old clothes that we put straight into the washing machine when we get back. And if you're careful, you won't get your hands dirty at all. Steve's got a whole box of latex gloves for us to wear under the work gloves. The girls just think it isn't as much fun if they don't have the stain up to their elbows when they're finished."

When breakfast was over, while Steve looked for clothes Larry could wear, Gina rifled through her closet for jeans that Keeta still had to cinch with a belt to keep up and an old plaid flannel shirt and warm jacket. Then she outfitted Dexter with a pair of Danielle's jeans that she rolled up above his sneakers and a child's sweatshirt with "Purdue" written across it. Then she packed peanut butter and jelly sandwiches for the children and ham and Swiss for the adults and filled two large thermoses with coffee and hot chocolate.

When they were climbing onto the wagon, Gina had a thought.

"Lindsay and Casey have sometimes gone with us before," she said to Steve. "Should I invite them today?"

Before Steve could answer, Larry said, "That's a really good idea. Why don't you give her a call. That would be fun, and Dex would probably like to have another boy along."

But when Gina called, Lindsay said she still had some work to do on the path.

"This good weather isn't going to last forever," she said.

"Then how about we take Casey and then you come over for dinner tonight? It's just soup and bread, but we'll have some wine, and it should be a good time."

"Casey can come along. That would be a big help to me actually, but I'll have to see about dinner," Lindsay said, and then again, "I'll just have to see how the day goes."

Minutes later she dropped her son off without getting out of the car and then drove away again as soon as she saw him disappear through the front door. Steve fired up the tractor and they set off over some deep ruts in the barnyard and then through a wide plank gate and across a jarring cattle guard into open pasture. A few of the large herd of red and white Hereford cattle looked up curiously as they chewed mouthfuls of grass and then, satisfied they were in no danger, meandered away to search for more. At the north edge of the pasture was another gate, and the dirt road disappeared into the stand of woods that separated their farm from their nearest neighbor's. Gina hopped off the wagon to open and close the gate, and when she was back on, the tractor growled ahead into relative darkness. A canopy of trees cut off the sun except for a few places where one of them had fallen and a shaft of light illuminated the forest floor. Steve drove deeper into the gloom and then turned off the tractor's engine.

"Here we are," he said, heaving himself off the seat and stepping down to the ground. "From here on out it's like an Easter-egg hunt." He leaned over and picked up what looked like a chartreuse baseball with a ruptured and blackened cover. "And this is what you're looking for." Now he produced a stack of burlap bags that had been secured under the cooler that contained the sandwiches. "There's a bag for each of us. Let's see who can find the most."

The children scattered and began at once to toss walnuts eagerly into their bags while Gina served coffee to the adults.

"How many acres is this whole place?" Larry asked.

"About 50," Steve responded. "And you saw pretty much everything there is to see on our ride out here. There's the owner's big house and yard, of course, and ours, about 15 acres of pasture and another 25 of timber."

"And the owner's house, what's it like inside?"

"Nice, real nice ..."

Gina could guess at the unspoken finish to the sentence: "... like the one where we used to live."

"Do you think we could see inside?" Larry went on.

Steve looked at Gina questioningly, as if for guidance before he spoke.

"Well, we don't usually go in there when they're away except if there's an emergency. Last year we had a real cold spell, and I went in to turn on the faucets so the lines wouldn't freeze. They usually have us over to eat when they're in town, and sometimes Gina helps them out when they have parties. Other than that ..." he trailed off dubiously.

"I don't think they'd care, honey," Gina said. "It is a beautiful place, and it's not like we're taking strangers inside."

When the burlap bags were filled and lunch was over, Steve asked if everyone was ready to head back.

"I am," Larry said. "I'd really like to have a look around that house."

Again the tractor rumbled to life, and they retraced their route back to the barn. Steve gave each of the children a hammer and demonstrated how to pound the bulky husks off the nuts and then lay them out on the burlap bag to dry. By the time they had finished, their gloves were soaked, and they chased each other out of the barn, waving their green hands and shrieking with laughter.

Gina and Keeta cycled the children through the shower and were laying out clean clothes for them when Steve called upstairs that he and Larry were leaving to go look at the main house.

"Keeta, I want you to come, too," Larry said.

"We'll all go," Gina called downstairs, "if you can just wait until we get some clothes onto these walnut-stained children."

Casey and Dexter giggled and pushed their still-green hands into each other's faces.

They left the children to play on the Greenbergs' swing set, and Steve fitted the key into the lock. The heavy wood door swung inside to reveal a home that was at once spacious and cozy. A giant fireplace dominated one wall of the living room, and across the foyer the dining table still contained the leaves that Gina had helped put in for the last dinner party. It had been Karen Greenberg's sister's birthday, and she and her family had flown in from New York for the occasion. Gina recalled the tiny bundles of chicken and vegetables, the salmon fish course, and the beef Wellington that had been the entree. Karen had told her she could go home as soon as she served dessert -- a three-tiered chocolate cake with a childhood picture of her and her sister air-brushed onto the top -- and she urged Gina to take the rest home for her family. Steve and the girls had dug in eagerly, but she had never eaten a bite.

The kitchen had been remodeled when the Greenbergs bought the property, and the copper countertops shone. A chef's range sat beneath an exhaust hood, also copper, and heavy black pans hung from a rack over a center island. Double ovens were built into the weathered brick walls.

"How many bedrooms?" Larry asked.

"Five," Steve responded. "Would you believe it? The Greenbergs have two kids, both teenagers now, and they've got two guest rooms because they have a lot of company. There's an office here on the first floor."

He led them into a room just off the kitchen that contained a built-in desk and file drawers. One whole wall was devoted to bookshelves that contained mostly medical books and nonfiction titles. Then he moved on to the stairway and directed them to follow up. At the top was a long hallway with the bedrooms opening off from it. The master suite contained a king-size bed, a massive walk-in closet that elicited a "Wow!" from Keeta, and a deep sunken bathtub and glassed-in shower with jets coming from several directions. The children's bedrooms that faced out over the front lawn had dormer windows, and the guest rooms offered amenities such as new magazines and vases waiting for fresh flowers, as if the house were a bed-and-breakfast rather than someone's home. Larry walked to one of the rear windows and looked out onto the pasture they had traversed earlier in their trek to the woods.

"I like it here," he said to Keeta. "This Greenberg is a lucky guy. He's got his job in Chicago, but he can get away from the city and relax here. I'd like that. I'd love to know there was someplace like this waiting for us when I can get away from work."

"It is a great house," Keeta agreed. "But if we had a second home, I wouldn't want it to be here. It would need to be closer, like at Lake Tahoe so we can go skiing or maybe Palm Springs or Santa Fe. I'd want a big city nearby. I'm guessing the local discount store doesn't have a personal shopper."

But her sarcastic remark fell on deaf ears. Larry was deep in thought and didn't say anything more about the big house as they walked back across the lawn to the smaller one.

"What happens now?" he said when they reached the back porch.

"Keeta and I are going for a walk," Gina told him. "You're welcome to come along, or you can stay here with Steve if you want. He'll probably put you to work in the barn."

"Actually I thought I'd take a quick shower and drive over to Lindsay's and give her a hand with the path, if that's okay with you."

"Su-re," Gina said, dividing the short word into two syllables because she felt anything but. "But I wouldn't bother showering if I were you. She's probably mucking around in sand and sod. You'll just get dirty again."

"Yeah, well, I want to get this stain off of my hands," he said.

"Sounds good," Steve, in blissful ignorance of what was happening, chimed in. "Come on upstairs to our room, and I'll get you a towel."

The sky had become overcast and the temperature had dropped. The weather report on Keeta's cell phone, which it seemed she checked every five minutes, predicted freezing rain. She and Gina changed quickly into sweatsuits and laced up their walking shoes so they could get back before it began.

"Are you going to take Casey back with you?" Gina called to her brother through the closed bathroom door.

"Nah, I don't think so. If we're going to make any progress on that path I think he might just be in the way, and besides, Dex loves having another guy here. You saw that when we were out in the woods."

She had planned to take Keeta on a route that would pass Lindsay's house and lead them on into town, but she changed her mind, turning right instead of left at the end of the driveway and walking past several neighboring farms.

That evening Larry was subdued when he came back for dinner, and he said Lindsay was exhausted and wouldn't be joining them. He said she wanted to make it an early night so that she could get up early the next morning and start working again. It was on the tip of Gina's tongue to ask what was taking so long. It was, after all, just a short path, and Lindsay had already done the hard jobs of digging out the area where it would go and bringing the stones home from the store. How long could it take to embed a dozen pavers into sand and then replace some scraps of sod on top, especially with help? But something told her not to pursue the subject. After dinner, when she drove Casey home, she noticed that only a couple more stones had been set, the rest still neatly stacked where she had seen them the evening before. Lindsay didn't come down when she walked Casey to the door.

"Thanks a lot," she called from upstairs. Wrapped in a terry-cloth robe and drying her wet hair with a towel, she came to the railing and looked down at Gina as Casey tore up the stairs, already erupting excitedly with details about his day. "You were a big help. We got a lot done without him here."

CHAPTER EIGHTEEN

"Well, the big ones are just about done," Larry said, breaking the companionable silence. He was drying the dishes they had used at breakfast while his sister, up to her elbows in soapy water, washed. The bright October sun that would have blinded them through the window over the sink was now blocked out by a shade drawn halfway down so that the kitchen was bathed in soft, warm light rather than baked in harsh glare. Yellow ochre, Gina thought, rather than lemon yellow, and then she smiled to herself. Much as she was enjoying Larry's visit -- and Dex's, too and of course Keeta's -- she was looking forward to getting back to the studio. Maybe the day would come when painting would seem like work, but so far she was having such a good time that she felt almost guilty for accepting her paychecks. She also took a newfound pleasure in disappearing into her mind, where paint colors blended and roiled even as she spoke to the clerk at the grocery store or nodded over her coffee cup to Steve. The objects that made up her family's daily life -- teapots, vases of flowers, pillows, stuffed animals, garden tools -- grew hazy around the edges, their functionality disappearing into the more exciting world of composition, starting with a delicate teapot next to a teddy bear and ending up with weathered pots and dirty work gloves piled on a red tile counter in a potting shed straight out of her imagination.

"What?" she asked Larry. Since what she had heard him say made absolutely no sense, she figured she had missed whatever had gone before it, her concentration lost again in that otherworld of her mind. Surely he wasn't talking about the relative sizes of the plates and saucers he was stacking. "I'm sorry, I zoned out there for a minute. What big ones?"

"The assignments, the reason I'm here. We've taken the foreign trip and spent time at my house and cleaned out Mom's studio. Now my family's here with yours. Most of what's left is the hokey stuff -- making a list of ten things we like about each other, doing a creative project with each other as the focus and making a scrapbook of our so-called adventures, all things we might have done in fifth grade, I might add. Now we've got to do the volunteering thing you mentioned. When does that happen?"

"Tonight, actually," Gina said. She pulled the plug, and the sink made a gurgling, sucking sound as the water swirled down into the drain. "The churches in Bedford take turns manning the local homeless shelter, and this week is our church's week. When we were planning your visit, I figured if you came now, we could kill two birds with one stone while you're here."

"Maybe even three. I've got all of my pictures on my laptop, so we can start the scrapbook if you want to." He rolled his eyes. "I've had a lot of fun hanging with you, but I still think some of Mom's little projects are silly. So anyway, tell me what we have to do."

"It's called Opportunity House because it isn't just a place for homeless people to sleep. The counselors who work there during the daytime help the people who come to stay get job interviews, find clothes for them to wear and places for them to live. The hope is that once they leave there they won't have to come back."

"And does that work out?" Larry asked. He had his doubts.

"Sometimes. Not often enough. It used to work better when the economy was in better shape. Now there aren't even low-paying jobs to help them work toward. Still, we try to make sure they go away with something, even if it's only a shirt to wear or a book about going to interviews."

"So who's there at night?"

"Just one staff member. The rest are volunteers."

"And what do they -- we -- do?"

"It actually starts now. We're going to make some spaghetti sauce and pasta and take it with us when we go for dinner. Some of the other people from church are bringing garlic bread and salad."

"We? We're going to make spaghetti sauce? I'd hate to be the poor sucker who had to eat anything I cooked."

"All right, then. Bring your laptop in here and start choosing pictures for the scrapbook, and I'll make the sauce."

"Do we just drop off the food or do we stay while they eat?"

Gina looked at her brother and laughed.

"You really are clueless, little Malibu brother," she said. "We serve the food and then we eat there with them. Part of the point is to socialize with them and acknowledge that they are real people who matter and have something to offer. Then we clean up after dinner and spend the night."

"Spend the night?" Larry's voice broke as it had when he was an adolescent. "You didn't say anything about that when we talked about it on the phone."

"Probably because I knew you'd freak out and not come."

"Is Steve going, too? And what about Marqueeta and the kids?"

"Steve and I usually take turns going. One of us has to stay at home with the girls. I've already talked to Keeta about it. I'm making a double batch of spaghetti so that I can leave some here. She and Steve and the kids can eat after we leave."

"So where do we sleep? You're right. I'm starting to get a little freaked out about this, Gina. When Mom said work on a volunteer effort together, I had in mind writing a check to the Red Cross and calling it good. I didn't know we were out to save the world."

"She wants us to have experiences together. You know that. We wouldn't learn much about each other if I just watched you write a check. I already know you can do that. And by the way, the shelter would happily accept any future checks you'd like to write. I think after you see the good they do there, you might want to."

"Couldn't I just go for dinner and then come home? They probably don't need a whole crowd. I might just be in the way."

"Nice try!" she said, punching him in the arm with a wet fist. "I signed us both up. They need two volunteers to stay over, and tonight we're it. God, you're a big baby."

He snapped at his sister's backside with the dish towel like he had when they were kids and doing the dinner dishes together, and she squealed, "Stop it, big baby," and ran out of the room laughing, just like she had then. He half expected to hear her calling, "Mom!"

The shelter was in what had been a discount clothing store. Racks crammed with empty wire hangers had been shoved up against one wall, and the "Buy one, get one free" promotion that had been the company's last attempt at solvency was still plastered on the window. The space was crudely divided with two-by-fours and unpainted drywall into rooms for each of the families. After they dropped off the pot of spaghetti sauce and the boxes of pasta in the kitchen, Gina gave Larry a tour.

"I can't show you a room where a family is staying," she explained. "We try to protect their privacy and give them a sense of dignity as much as we can." She jiggled the doorknob of a cubicle that didn't have a family's name thumb-tacked onto the door. "I think this one's vacant, though."

Inside three twin beds were shoved together against one wall, waiting for the next occupants to arrange their temporary quarters. The ticking on the bare mattresses was stained. A pillow with all of its stuffing migrated to one end of the casing lay on the one in the middle. A metal folding chair leaned against a scuffed wooden desk with one drawer missing. A bright blue gooseneck lamp without a bulb sat on the cement floor nearby.

"What about a bathroom?" he asked.

"They share," Gina said. "One of the volunteers is a plumber, and he put showers into what used to be the men's and women's rooms when the place was a store. We're slowly fixing the place up. Steve has volunteered to do some painting in a couple of weeks. Sleeping in a gray room with exposed drywall mud and tape can't be very inspiring."

In a back corner of the cavernous building where other volunteers were setting the tables, three children in parochial school uniforms played tag until Gina told them to stop running and that they should get their hands washed because it was almost time to eat. She motioned Larry to a table where the children's mother was already seated before she went back into the kitchen area to begin filling plates.

"Hi," Larry said, holding out his hand to the woman. "I'm Larry."

The woman held out her hand without looking up from the spot on the table at which she'd been gazing since before he sat down. She was heavy-set, and her short, straight hair was pulled back into a tiny ponytail that was caught in a green rubber band and stuck straight out behind her head. The remains of a weeks-old manicure colored her fingernails.

"I'm Latrelle," she said.

Gina slid plates filled with spaghetti, salad, and garlic bread in front of both of them and left to return just moments later with plastic glasses filled with water. Larry would have killed for a glass of red wine, better yet a double scotch neat, but he guessed correctly that a cabernet was not on offer and wouldn't be forthcoming.

"Well, Latrelle," he began hopefully, and then he realized he didn't have anything else to say. He couldn't ask this woman, whose children now filled out the rest of the table, what movies she'd seen or books she'd read. He couldn't even ask her what part of the city she lived in because she didn't, really. To talk about his work in Hollywood was completely out of the question. "What are your children's names?"

Latrelle pointed at each one in turn.

"There's Lucas, he's five. Warren is seven. Moesha is eleven, and LaShonda is thirteen."

"Where do you go to school?" he asked LaShonda after an awkward silence. She was just across the table from him and being the oldest seemed less intimidating to him than her unpredictable younger siblings were. When they had been playing so boisterously earlier, she had been ensconced in a worn easy chair, one knee-socked leg draped over the arm, her attention riveted on the book in her hands. Not having yet acquired the habit of averting her eyes, she flashed a big smile and answered, "The little kids go to St. Katherine's. I'm at Roosevelt Middle School."

Then, just as abruptly as she had brightened, she sobered again and began twisting strands of spaghetti around her fork.

"What was the book I saw you reading earlier?" He felt like he was badgering her, but he didn't know what else to talk about or who else to talk to.

"*I Know Why the Caged Bird Sings,*" LaShonda said. "It's by Maya ..."

"Angelou!" Larry sang out too loudly, hoping this small spark would ignite a few minutes of dialogue. "My sister read that when we were kids. I never did, but I've read some of the books she wrote later."

Warren, sitting next to him, gave his mother a furtive glance and scooted to the far side of his folding metal chair as if to get as far away from this nut job as he could.

"Did you know that Alicia Keys adapted some of the lines from the story into a song? I work in the music business in L.A., and I've run across it there, too. It's good stuff."

He heard himself talking too much, being too enthusiastic, not wanting to let go of this shred of conversation he had happened upon. When it was over, what would he do then?

Like her brother, LaShonda glanced at her mother, as if to see what she was supposed to do next. Then she turned to her sister and raised her eyebrows in a gesture that clearly said, "Right. We're having dinner in a homeless shelter with a guy who works in the music business in Los Angeles. Sure we are." Then she smiled politely at Larry, nodded her head slightly to acknowledge that she was familiar with Alicia Keys's music and returned to her food with intensified interest.

Larry figured these children must be charity cases since their mother obviously couldn't afford a private school.

"Excellent sauce," he observed.

"Yes, it is," said Latrelle.

"My sister made it. She ..." He stopped just short of saying that his sister and her husband were regular volunteers and not the new friends they were pretending to be. He finished his sentence weakly with "is a very good cook."

The small talk he had counted on was useless, freighted with judgment and condescension. He groped in his mind frantically for suitable topics and then just as quickly rejected them -- the children's grades, piano lessons, soccer practice -- and the questions he really wanted to ask: Do you have a husband? Do you have a job? Why are you here? What the hell happened? God, how he'd like a drink.

Latrelle finished eating and stood up abruptly. All four of her children followed suit as if they had been drilled like soldiers to do as she commanded.

"There's lots more," Larry said, still too brightly, like he was a radio announcer or a personal trainer. "Can I get you another plate? I think there are some cupcakes, too."

Latrelle shook her head, never yet making eye contact.

"No thank you, but we appreciated the dinner."

She collected her family's plates and stacked them on the counter to be loaded into a dishwasher by another volunteer whose eager smile was also too bright for the occasion. Then she lumbered slowly in the direction of their room with her children following along behind her like ducklings.

"Can me and Lucas have a cupcake?" Warren whispered, pulling on Larry's shirtsleeve. Larry went into the kitchen and put five of the frosted cakes onto a paper plate. They were covered with pumpkin-colored icing, and three pieces of candy corn dotted the middle of each one. But when he went back out to where he had left the boys, they had already gone, Warren throwing a wistful backward glance as his mother herded him through the door to their temporary home.

"I know," Gina said. The dishes were done and they had watched some old *Twilight Zone* episodes on DVD in the community room. Only three other people had joined them -- the shelter staff member and two men, one of whom left repeatedly at what Gina considered to be the pivotal parts of the program to go outside and smoke. The other was tall and thin and sprawled in an easy chair, a baseball cap pulled low over his eyes so that he might have been sleeping.

Now Gina and Larry were in what was called the volunteer room, stretched out in sweatpants and T-shirts on twin cots that had been covered with clean sheets and red plaid blankets. A rickety night table between them held a fake Tiffany lamp that barely put out enough light to read by and two bottles of water Gina had grabbed from the staples pantry. The only other piece of furniture was a white caned chair that looked as if it might have been a castoff from an ice-cream parlor. On the wall across from the beds was a bulletin board that contained lists of rules for working at the shelter and a calendar of which churches would staff the weeks to come. Under it a stack of a dozen or so paperback books on the floor leaned precariously against a corner.

"I've been through the same thing. I've been doing this for almost three years, and I'm still clumsy. You never get used to it. It's hard to imagine how people can lose absolutely everything. I always come away from here grateful just to have a roof over my head."

"What happens? How do they lose everything? Do you ever find out any of their backgrounds?"

"Sometimes. Like I said, the people who work at the center do everything they can to maintain the visitors' privacy and dignity. Once in a while, though, they share information with us if they think it's important to taking care of the person. And sometimes they aren't anything like you think. People typically think they're all drunks and losers."

"That's for sure what I would have guessed about those two guys who were in the TV room tonight."

"I don't know about the tall one in the baseball cap, but the other guy's story is really sad. His rickety old house burned a few months ago, and his wife died in the fire. He has a job as a janitor at one of the schools, but it doesn't pay much, and his wife was in a wheelchair, so she couldn't help with the finances. The bottom line is that they didn't have enough money for homeowners' insurance, so he's got absolutely nothing."

"Jesus. No wonder he smokes."

"And he can't sit still. He did better tonight than I've seen him do before."

"So how long has he been here?"

"Since about a month after the fire. He was proud at first and didn't want to accept charity. After he went through what savings they had on motel rooms, he finally gave in."

"Isn't there some kind of limit on how long people can stay?"

"Usually, but they made an exception for him. The director opened a savings account for him, and he turns his paycheck over to her each week. She says he can stay here until he has first month's and last month's rent and a breakage deposit saved up. Sometimes even that's too big a hurdle for people to get over."

"Are you ever afraid when you stay overnight?"

"Not really, but I do take precautions. I'm not totally naive. I know a lot of these people are desperate, so I don't bring any money with me, and I lock the door when I'm ready to go to sleep. There have been a couple of incidents when volunteers got in over their heads, but both times the people turned out to be mentally ill. They weren't so much dangerous as just disturbed. One old woman thought her parents were sleeping in here."

"Wow," Larry said. "That's all I've got. Just wow. Their lives make mine look like royalty."

"My life makes yours look like royalty, little brother," Gina said, yawning, "but I know what you mean."

She rolled over in her cot and went to sleep, but Larry was awake most of the night. Even when he dozed, every strange sound jolted him back to consciousness until finally he gave up, switched on the light, and began to make notes on a pad he found lying on the chair that had "Hope Gospel Church" printed down one side.

"You've got to use this one!" Keeta said, fishing a picture from the pile Larry had printed and slipping it down into one of the acetate sleeves she and Gina had found at the craft store. Instead of an actual scrapbook, they had selected a photo album, and they had also bought stickers with which to decorate the pages -- a pagoda and some chopsticks to represent Hong Kong, a tiny palette and paintbrushes for La Jolla, a red barn and silo for Bedford. Gina threw in some horses to illustrate the game she had played with Dex and the girls' riding experience in Malibu. Stephy and Danielle had squealed with delight at the miniatures when they helped unload the shopping bag. "Cute," they kept saying to one another while Larry rolled his eyes.

"This looks like women's work," he said. "I think maybe Steve and I will find something else to do."

"I'd like that, buddy," Steve said, his large, weathered hands holding up the brown and gold silk leaves meant to adorn the page about their trip to find walnuts, "but I think Gina has other ideas."

"Of course I have other ideas!" Gina said. "I think this project is as hokey and adolescent as you do, and I'm not doing it by myself. Besides, everything on the list is something we're supposed to do together, so wipe the 'I'm too good to do this' sneer off your face and get busy."

The picture Keeta was holding was the one they had taken of themselves at their mother's house. Funny that it looked tender and affectionate now, Gina thought, when at the time they had been stiff and uncomfortable, both of them with fakey, trying-too-hard grins spread across their faces and the space between them speaking volumes, although apparently not to anyone who hadn't actually been there.

Steve took two beers out of the refrigerator and snapped off their caps.

"This might make it a little less painful," he said, handing one to Larry and then surprising everyone by sitting down at the table and turning Larry's laptop toward himself so that he could better see all of the pictures.

"What about us?" Gina demanded. "Don't we deserve a little of that painkiller, too?"

"Well, I guess you do," Steve said, laughing as he stood back up and opened the cupboard where the wineglasses were stored. "Wine for you, right? How about you, Keeta?"

"I'm going up to bed," she said, standing up abruptly. "I'm exhausted. It's been a really long day."

Steve and Gina stole a questioning look at one another since Keeta had had a singularly uneventful day. She had taken a walk with Gina after they'd gotten home from the shelter, it was true, and gone to the craft store with her to buy the supplies for the album. But then she'd asked Gina to stop at the drugstore for magazines, which she had spent most of the afternoon flipping through. She had watched a talk show on television and then taken a nap while Gina made dinner.

"Well," Larry said in the awkward silence that followed his wife's departure, "I guess it's just the three of us, then. Steve and I'll help, Sis. It'll be fun."

Dex was already in bed, and the girls were watching a movie on television in the living room, running in during commercials to check on the progress of the album and offer suggestions. "Is Aunt Keeta coming back down?" Stephanie asked as she reached into the refrigerator for the milk carton.

"No, honey," Gina said. "She's gone to bed. We need to be quiet so she can sleep. Maybe you can turn the TV down just a little bit."

Gina had saved the original letter from Dennis MacDonald, and that's the way they decided to begin. The boarding pass from her flight to L.A. neatly filled in the field of empty stationery beneath the short missive. On the other side of that sheet they decided to put a list of all the assignments, which Larry now typed into his computer while Gina and Steve looked ahead to the Hong Kong pages.

"This is a good one," Steve said.

He held up a photo of Gina, Larry, and their mother at the Hunan restaurant that had been taken by a waiter just moments before Gina had stormed out and gone back to the hotel on her own. "It was nice that Anita could surprise you for dinner like that."

Again, Gina thought about how different the perception of someone looking at the pictures was from what had actually happened. She hadn't told Steve about leaving in anger that night. In retrospect her grandstanding seemed childish, and she had edited it out of the stories she told her family when she got home.

"Yes, it was a nice evening," she heard herself saying now, almost nonchalantly, but purposely without looking at her brother.

"Here's some more fun," Larry said now without irony. The picture he held up was of the two of them eating takeout Indian on the beach in La Jolla. That was followed by several pictures they had taken of one another in Anita's studio and then one Larry had taken of Gina's painting.

"I still can't believe you did that," she said now, "but thanks. Wow. Really, thanks."

They chose several pictures taken during the Chambers's stay in Malibu. In one Keeta was decked out in her matching track suit and running shoes; in another Lupe hugged Dex in his highchair, from which, five minutes later, he would toss his bowl of oatmeal onto the floor. Then there he was at the beach and later having the picnic with the toy horses, this time all smiles and holding one of them up for his aunt to photograph. Those pictures were a tiny bit grainy because she hadn't had her camera with her and had to resort to catching the memory with her old cell phone. The times that had mattered most -- the foggy, late-night talks with Larry -- could not be photographed at all. Neither, for that fact, could her ride back from Hong Kong in business class or his playing her favorite song on their mother's piano. What a useless exercise, she thought to herself. While the smiles in the pictures were mostly made-up, real changes had occurred between her and her brother, and those times didn't lend themselves to capture. Their mother would love this book they were making, but when she tried to find the juncture at which the ice began to melt and they began, tentatively, to lean back into one another, it wouldn't be there for her to see.

CHAPTER NINETEEN

It rained hard on Friday night, pounding down the dusty leaves that until now had clung, desperate and tenacious, to the branches from which they had come to life in the spring, provided shade in the summer, and warmed with reds and golds in the fall. They had been past their prime and ready for this storm for several days. Just the afternoon before Gina had stood at the bedroom window that looked beyond the barn and out over the pasture to the wooded hillside beyond and tried to think what color she would choose if she were to paint them. Burnt umber, maybe, but with some alizarin to lend them the hint of regal purple luxury that prevented their looking completely brown and sere. The deluge had scrubbed the corrugated tin roofs of the outbuildings clean to shining. Even the patch of concrete by the silo where Steve usually parked his truck was for this moment free of the mud and manure that would cover it again the first time the cows came in for feeding. This morning ominous gray clouds obliterated the sun and threatened another shower. The temperature had dipped considerably overnight and now registered 39 on the metal ther-mometer hanging off the back porch railing.

"Not a great day for Larry and Keeta to leave," Steve said as he poured a cup of coffee into a steel mug to drink while he drove to the store. Gina could see his long johns peeking out from the neck of his green plaid flannel shirt, a sure indication that winter had officially arrived.

"It's a few hours yet before their plane actually takes off," Gina said. She kissed him briefly and reached around him for a box of cereal, "so they can take it easy on the drive from here to Indianapolis."

"I was hoping to see them to say good-bye," he said, pushing up the cuff over his watch to check the time, "but I really can't wait anymore. We've got the big brass coming in today, and I've got to get down there before they arrive to make sure everything's ready for the meeting."

"What kind of meeting?"

"They want me to show them the books from the past few years. They're bringing in their IT people to attach our PC system to their network. They want to see how that's going to work, and they're also bringing an HR guy from the home office to evalu-ate our staff. They want to see if they need to make any changes when they move to the new location." He made quotation marks in the air around "changes" to show his distrust of the word. "I'm worried about Sam. I've kept him on after his accident so he can have insurance, but he can't do much out there in the lumberyard anymore. I wish they'd consider hiring more people, but with the way things are, I think the best thing to hope for is that nobody loses their job."

"So in other words you're teaching them to do your job so they can take over and ..."

"Don't go there, Gina," he said, holding up his palm as if physi-cally to ward off any words that could destroy his positive mood.

"We talked about this. Yes, it's true I'm not going to manage the store anymore, but now we'll have a little money in the bank that we can start to build on, and I'll have a regular paycheck. Two words keep me turning up there every morning: automatic deposit. If the economy continues to tank, it won't be my problem. Let their stockholders lose sleep instead of you and me."

She stopped the breakfast preparations she had been making and focused her attention on her husband.

"I know that's all true, but what I can't stand is that I also know your job doesn't make you happy."

"Happy schnappy," he said jokingly. He put his hands on her shoulders and pulled her to him. "It's not forever anymore, honey. With your painting money and the money from the sale and your mom's money gifts we can start to make some headway. You're right -- I'll admit I don't look forward to going to work in the mornings, but I'm luckier than most. I know guys who have taken factory jobs to keep a roof over their heads and food on the table. At least I'm still working with farmers."

"You should be farming yourself, and if it weren't for ..."

"Stop it, Gina." Now there was a real edge to his voice. "Really, I'm serious. It is what it is. You're the one who's always saying things happen for a reason. You and your brother have got a good relationship going now, as long as you can put up with Keeta." He screwed up his face when he said her name. "And that's a good thing. For whatever reason, he couldn't help when you asked him to. If everything hadn't happened as it did, you wouldn't have been at your mom's house painting that picture, and he wouldn't have shown it to her. At least one of us loves what she's doing, and for right now, that's enough. I love to see the little bounce in your step." As if to emphasize what he had just said he reached around to give her bottom a playful squeeze.

"Speaking of Larry," she said, glancing out the window over the sink, "they said they were coming for breakfast, but they're going to be pushing it to get to the airport on time if they don't get here pretty soon."

"I've got to go, but tell them I said good-bye and that I really liked having them here. Surprising as it sounds, even to me, I did. Keeta is hard to take sometimes, but Larry and Dex make up for that."

He kissed her again, grabbed the worn and cracked briefcase she'd found for him at a yard sale in one hand and his coffee in the other, and disappeared through the door. Gina heard the truck start and watched him drive up the lane toward the county road. Thanks to a ridiculous superstition that had been handed down through his family, Gina never watched him out of sight.

"Grace Davis watched her husband out of sight one day when he was going to the quarry to cut stone," her mother-in-law had told Gina with a serious face over coffee one morning early in her marriage, "and he drowned that very day. She never saw him again." Gina had the impression that Maryanne was relating this story as a cautionary tale, even though Grace Davis had been a neighbor of Steve's great-grandmother's decades ago and her husband would most likely still have drowned had his wife instead turned in the other direction when he went around the bend. Still, silly as she thought it was, she always looked away from the window when his truck got to the end of the graveled driveway and he stopped to check the traffic before turning onto the paved road.

Today, though, she saw him slow down, pull to the side of the road and then stop. A black Cadillac SUV coming from the opposite direction pulled up beside the truck and stopped, too.

"Shit!" Gina said, unfortunately just as Stephanie came down the stairs and into the kitchen.

"Mo-om!"

"Sorry, pumpkin. I've just had a surprise. It looks like the Greenbergs are here, and we didn't have any warning that they were coming. I've got Uncle Larry and Aunt Keeta and Dex coming for breakfast, and then they've got to leave soon to get to

Indianapolis to catch their plane. I just hadn't figured on having to cater to the Greenbergs, too."

"OK, you're forgiven, but you owe me a quarter."

Gina had once made a game out of charging the girls a quarter when they said rude things or used bad grammar. She had forgotten all about it until now. Stephanie opened the refrigerator and poured herself some orange juice and then looked with her mother out the window. The Greenberg vehicle still sat next to Steve's truck. The two drivers had their windows down and were talking. Then they gave each other a wave and drove on. The phone rang almost immediately. Steve would know she had been watching and would be anxious.

"What's up?" Gina asked by way of an answer. "I didn't know they were coming down, and I've got Larry and ..."

"Calm down, honey," Steve said. "That's what I'm calling to tell you. They're not technically here. Michael has some kind of meeting in town, and he's just running by the house to pick up some papers. Karen and the girls aren't with him, and he's going straight back to Chicago when he's finished."

"Wow, that's a relief. I thought it was funny that they hadn't let us know so I could open up the house and get some groceries in. They never come unannounced."

"That's all I wanted to tell you, but now I'm really late."

As Gina turned to replace the phone, it rang again in her hand. This time no name came up on the caller ID, just a 310 area code that she didn't recognize in the moment it took her to say hello. The person on the other end turned out to be Larry.

"Hey, Sis ..."

"Where are you guys?" she barked at him before he could go on. "If you don't get here pretty soon, you're not going to have time to eat breakfast before you leave for the airport. And it's going to rain some more, so the roads may be slippery. As chilly as it is, the rain could even turn to sleet."

"That's why I'm calling if you'll listen for a second." He sounded only playfully annoyed. "We've changed our flight. We're not going back until Monday."

"Why not?" Gina blurted out. It sounded accusatory, even to her. "I mean, I'm glad, but what changed your mind?" She closed her eyes and massaged her forehead with her free hand.

"I'm just not ready to go back. We've had a really good time here. Will that be a problem? We'll take everybody out to dinner tonight, so you don't have to cook. Maybe Lindsay could come, too."

It wasn't the cooking that was the problem, she wanted to tell him. What she needed to do was paint. She had a deadline in two weeks, and she wasn't going to blow the gig her mother had gotten for her. Hadn't Steve just said that her income was important, that together they were on their way to some kind of solvency again. It was time to get back to the studio. She had set aside this week for Larry's family, and she was glad for it, but now they needed to go home. Hadn't they heard the old saw about house guests and fish? Once again Larry was doing whatever Larry wanted, but it didn't make her angry as it once would have.

"Okay, fine. I'll call her and see. So are you guys coming for breakfast or not? I've got the griddle on for pancakes."

"Not today, but could we have a rain check for tomorrow? Dex was up in the night and Keeta is worn out. I think it's good if they sleep in for a while this morning. I pulled the drapes in the room, and it's like night in there."

"And what are you out doing?"

"Headed out for some coffee and then a walk around the courthouse square by myself. I've got an errand to do, too. I'll catch up with you later."

She returned the phone to its base and poured cereal for herself and the girls. Then she sprinkled a handful of blueberries into each bowl. Danielle came down the stairs, she and her sister already embroiled in one of their worn-out fights.

"You look like a sleazebag in that top," Danielle said. Stephanie was wearing a shirt that tied at the bottom and exposed her navel.

"I wouldn't talk if I were you," Stephanie countered. If you want to see a dork, just look in the mirror."

"Really?" Gina said in exasperation. "Really?"

The girls slid into their seats, glaring at one another but silenced by the tone in their mother's voice, and began eating. Gina was about to sit down at the table, too, when the phone rang again. This time it was Maryanne.

"Has your brother gone yet?" she asked when Gina answered the phone.

"No, they've decided to stay through the weekend. They're leaving Monday."

"Oh, then what I had in mind might not work out."

"Try me."

"Well, it's such a great, rainy fall day. I've got a fire going in the fireplace. I thought maybe the girls would like to come over. We could make cookies and watch a movie or whatever they'd like to do. They could even spend the night if they're not doing something special with their cousin."

"Hold on," Gina said, "I know the answer to this one, but I'll ask anyway." Then she turned toward the table where the girls were sitting. "Grandma wonders if you'd like to come over for the day," she told them. "She says you'll make cookies and watch a movie, and you can spend the night if you want."

"Yay!" They said in unison, and Gina silently chimed in, too. With everyone else occupied, she might be able to slip away to the studio for a few hours.

"I guess you heard that."

"Good," Maryanne said. "I'll pick them up about ten. Why don't you pack them a little bag in case they decided to stay over."

"Why don't we just plan on it?" Gina said. "That sounds great. They'll love it."

An hour later she pulled the kitchen door shut behind her and walked across the grass to the garage. She had cleaned up the breakfast dishes and called Lindsay. The answering machine had been on, but she had left a message saying that Larry wanted to take them all to dinner that night. It was anybody's guess what was going on there and whether she would come with them, but Gina had enough on her mind without borrowing that concern.

Minutes later she parked on Main Street and dashed through what was now a full-on downpour into the building. The wet leaves that had fallen onto the sidewalk overnight had turned it into a slippery mess, and when she got to the vestibule that led to the stairway, she stopped to stomp off the clumps of ones that had adhered themselves to her shoes. Then she ran up the stairs, as excited as if it were the first time she'd been there.

The rooms were musty from a week of disuse, so despite the chill in the air, she opened the windows just slightly. Then she filled the electric kettle with water for tea and opened her paint boxes.

She painted for three straight hours without interruption. Inspired by the frosty nip in the air, she painted a snow scene outside a window. In the distance smoke curved skyward from the chimney of a brick cottage that was situated in a stand of birch trees. Part of the room inside the window was visible -- the edge of a cozy maroon chair with a soft blue throw draped across its back next to a round table with a lamp on it whose warm yellow light would eventually illuminate an open book. The furniture was currently just a sketch. She'd paint it later, once she was sure the more difficult snow scene outside the window would work. She was using a purple and blue mix to trace shadows under the trees when her cell phone rang. It was Larry.

"Where the hell are you, Sis? I need to talk to you."

His voice sounded at once stressed and happily excited.

"I'm at the studio. Steve's mom took the girls for the day, so I decided to get some work done. What's up? Is anything wrong?"

"No, not at all." Now he laughed outright. "I've got good news, and I wanted to tell you and Steve in person. I guess I'll save it for dinner. What do you think about that Italian place out on the highway? I can make a reservation."

"Sure, we like it there. It's a little pricey, but the food's really good."

"Dinner's on me tonight. Will the girls be going with us?"

"No, they're spending the night with Sid and Maryanne."

"Too bad. The good news affects them, too. But I guess I'll get to tell it twice. Is Lindsay coming?"

"I don't know yet. I haven't heard back from her. I'll give her another call."

"That's OK. Keeta and Dex have gone to a movie. I'll just drive out there and invite her myself."

Her concentration broken, Gina put her paints away, washed out her brushes, and headed home. When she got there Michael Greenberg's SUV was parked in front of the big house, and he was just coming out. She pulled the car into the garage and then walked across the wet grass to where he was waiting to say hello to her. The rain had abated, at least temporarily.

"Hey, Michael," she said. "Steve said you had some business in town."

"Yep. I just ran down for the day. I didn't phone ahead because Karen and the girls didn't come, and I didn't need anything. I only stopped by this morning to get the papers I needed for my meeting, and I'm just here now to put them back before I head home to Chicago."

"Not a great day to be making that long drive twice," she said. "If you want to spend the night, I could run out and get you a few groceries."

He shook his head.

"Believe it or not, four hours from now Karen and I will be munching on a rubber chicken dinner at a banquet for one of her charities. I promised her I'd meet her there, so I've got to get on the road."

He opened the door and swung his considerable well-dressed bulk inside.

"Any chance you've talked to your brother today?"

"Yes, a couple of times. Why?"

"So then you know that I just sold him the farm."

Gina felt for a moment like she was going to pass out. Her head was light, and she could feel her pulse pounding in her ears. She sank onto a boulder near the driveway.

"No, I didn't know that."

"Damn. I shouldn't have told you. When you said you'd talked to him, I just naturally figured he'd discussed it with you."

"No. He didn't. He said he had something to tell us at dinner. I guess that's it."

"Are you okay, Gina?"

"Yes, I'm fine. It's just that I didn't ... why ... he couldn't ..."

"Look, please don't let on that I told you. He wanted it to be a surprise. He did tell me he was going to take you all to dinner tonight. I guess that's when he planned to talk to you about it. Damn me and my big mouth. I'm so sorry."

He glanced at his watch.

"I've got to get going or I'm going to hit rush hour in Indianapolis, and I'll never get back in time. You sure you're going to be okay? Can I help you get into the house?"

"No, I'm fine, really. This is just such a shock."

"He'll tell you all the details tonight. It'll be great to have them out here more often, won't it?"

"But what will you and Karen do?"

"You know, with our girls getting older, it was time for us to sell anyway. It was great having the farm to bring them to when they were smaller, but now with all their friends and activities in the city, we don't get down here as much as we'd like to anyway. Kim's in the school orchestra and Kathleen's looking at colleges. I'm thinking it's time for our second home to be a condo somewhere closer. We've been looking at a couple of places downtown overlooking Lake Michigan. Or maybe I'd just better put the money in the bank to pay tuition, huh?"

He laughed and then looked again at his watch.

"I've really got to get going. Enjoy your dinner with Larry tonight. He's got a lot to tell you about."

Gina didn't know how long she sat on the boulder trying to digest what Michael had just told her. Larry was buying the farm. Larry was buying the farm. Larry was buying the farm. The words didn't even seem to fit together. She even sang them to the tune of "Old MacDonald": "Larry Langley's buying the farm. E-I-E-I-O." But why? He was a Hollywood guy. His work was in L.A. His house was in Malibu, and his fancy cars would rust out the first winter he had to drive on Midwest salt and sand. Keeta's parents would have a meltdown if she moved so far away, and Keeta certainly didn't have the makings of a Midwestern farm wife. The idea of her shoveling snow or weeding a garden or canning strawberry preserves almost made Gina laugh.

But she didn't laugh. She felt panic welling up in her throat, and she wanted to scream. She and Steve had let down their guard with Larry and Keeta. They had told them about how they were beginning to see a light at the end of the tunnel, an end to their financial worries. Like pathetic fools, they had thanked him repeatedly for what he had done to bring Gina's painting to her mother's attention. But all of that depended on continuing to live rent-free on the Greenbergs' farm, and they'd told them that, too. Even if it meant Steve's working long into the evening after a day at the store, even if it meant her having to cater Karen and Michael's dinner parties, it was a home until they could manage one of their own. How many times had they lain in the dark, unable to sleep, and tried to figure out what they'd do if the Greenbergs ever decided to sell? Every move the Greenbergs made gave them cause for worry. Michael's mother had loved to come to the farm at first, but then she had died. It hadn't escaped their notice that Kim and Kathleen were growing up, either. It had been months since they'd come down with their parents, and when Steve had asked if they'd like for him to make a hayride for some of their local friends, Kim had rolled her eyes and Kathleen had pointed to her earbuds to let him know she couldn't talk right then because she was too busy listening to music.

"I'd have snatched the damn things right out of her ears if she'd been my child," he said to Gina later the night it had happened when she was brushing her teeth and he was washing his face in the sink next to her. "I'd better never see Stephy or Danny rolling their eyes at anyone who's trying to do them a favor."

She had sputtered toothpaste onto the mirror.

"Oh, honey, that ship has sailed," she had said, laughing. "They're kids, and so are Kim and Kathy. They're going through the 'everything adults say to me is boring' stage. Before you know it they'll all be grown-up, and they'll be fine."

But would Danny and Stephy really be okay? Where was her family going to live? How would they pay rent? What if the girls had to change schools?

And then another, more sickening but more likely thought came to her mind with glassy clarity. Larry was going to buy the house so that he would have a place to stay when he came out, and he expected her and Steve to continue living there and running the farm as they had for the Greenbergs. Did he really believe they would think that was a good idea? Did he really expect that he would tell Steve how to run the farm? Had he talked about this with Keeta? Did they think she would buy groceries and cook and make sure the house was ready for guests whenever Keeta called or sent a text that they were coming? How stupid did her brother think she was? What a narcissistic son of a bitch. Just like always, the fair-haired boy would somehow get credit for doing the right thing by his family and she would be the bad sister who spurned his generous gesture. She could see her mother's beaming face now. Wonderful Larry, coming through in a pinch once again. Generous Larry with a big house in the country where they could all meet for summers and have Christmases.

Finally she put her face down onto the folded arms in her lap and sobbed. The light at the end of the tunnel blinked out, a door slammed against its gleam by her own brother. How many times could he hurt her in one lifetime? How many times could he yank the rug right out from under her feet?

It started to rain again, sudden and cold, and she stood and ran for the house. Inside she pulled the cell phone from her jacket pocket and rang Steve's on speed dial. She could tell from the tone of his voice when he answered that it wasn't a good time to talk.

"What is it?" he said impatiently instead of his usual "Hi, honey."

"Hi, it sounds like you don't have time to talk."

"Nope, I sure don't. Is it anything that can't wait?"

"No. Sorry. I didn't mean to interrupt. I know you're busy."

"We'll talk tonight."

"Yes, tonight. Sorry."

Tonight seemed like light-years away. Steve hung up without saying good-bye, and she laid her phone on the kitchen table. The house was empty and silent, and despite all the times she had wished for quiet and time to herself, now the solitude was oppressive. She wanted Steve to come home immediately, but she knew it would still be hours. She wanted her girls with her, even if they were fighting and name-calling and rolling their eyes. Depression and fear settled on her like a thick, heavy, suffocating cloak. There were still breakfast dishes in the sink, but she didn't care. There was time now to do the list of chores she never got to, even time to go back to the studio and paint some more, but she didn't have the energy. She wished she could call her mother, but she didn't even know where Anita was at the moment, and if she could connect with her, someplace on the other side of the globe, her mother would have a dozen excuses ready to explain away the utterly selfish actions of her darling favorite boy.

"Explain this, Mom," she said aloud. "Explain how my loving brother has rendered us homeless so that he can have a farm two thousand miles from where he lives just because he's spent a week here and thinks the country is charming, and he's got all the money and can just buy everything he thinks he wants. He probably wants to be here because he's made goo-goo eyes at my best friend, and now I'll probably lose her, too. And all of this with my family and me living in the little house and being their servants when they come to town. Explain that, Mom."

Well, they couldn't live there, of course. So what would they do? She imagined herself and Steve and the girls at Opportunity House, not as volunteers who served meals to homeless visitors but who were homeless themselves. You could only sleep three to a room, she thought wildly. Would she and the girls be in one cubicle and Steve in the other? What could they sell? Her car! She could drive Steve to work in the mornings and then go to her studio. They could live in the studio! Yes! No. That area was zoned for business. She'd lose her studio, that's what would happen, and now she'd have to paint at home. But she wouldn't have a home. They'd rent an apartment! There would only be two bedrooms, but she would turn the living room into a studio. But how would that work when she couldn't even find a place to paint in the house she had now? She picked up her cell phone again and punched in Larry's number. He was the one she should be calling. She hated him, hated him, hated him. How could he do this to her?

She heard seven rings and then Larry's cheerful recorded voice on the line: "Larry here. Sorry I missed you, but I'll be happy to call you back."

She hung up without leaving a message and immediately tried Keeta, who also didn't answer. She looked online for the number of the hotel where they were staying and called the desk. They put her through to yet another message: "The party you are trying to reach is not answering. Please leave your message after the beep."

Was the whole frigging world too busy to talk to her? Was Larry hiding from her, afraid of what he must know was coming? Had he and Keeta turned off their phones so they didn't have to listen to the ringing, didn't want to hear the tongue-lashing they knew was coming because they so richly deserved it? Did Keeta even know what was happening, or was she just a clueless pawn in Larry's scheme? Was Lindsay involved in all of this? Did he buy the farm so he could be closer to her after knowing her for less than a week? Was that it? Were he and Keeta at this moment having it out in their hotel room? Was he telling Keeta that she could have the Malibu house and everything in it if she would give him a quiet divorce?

Now she tried Lindsay's number, but she hung up after the first ring. If her friend did have a role in this mess, Gina didn't want to know about it. She looked at the clock. Nearly 6:00. Nothing to do now but get ready to go to dinner. She wouldn't eat with Larry, she wouldn't even sit down with them. But if she couldn't reach him before then, she would tell him exactly what she thought of him at the restaurant. And then she and Steve would march out ... and do what?

CHAPTER TWENTY

Rotunda 6 was named after a restaurant with the same name in Rome, where the owners had once gone for vacation. Jimmy Comporato's family were of Italian descent, but they were not recent arrivals. His grandparents had come over from Naples and started a restaurant in Indianapolis that their three sons and a daughter had eventually taken over. Jimmy had eventually moved to Bedford and opened this restaurant. His brother had opened one with the same name in Gary. The food was decent, but the dining room was faded, its tuxedoed waiters and faux leather banquettes badly in need of updating and its wine list limited to little more than house white chablis and the house red merlot. Once Gina had ordered a whiskey sour there and had been surprised when it turned out to be pale yellow, its only resemblance to the deep amber cocktail she had been expecting the maraschino cherry and orange slice garnish threaded onto a tiny plastic sword.

Now, driving up the winding driveway toward the parking lot, she imagined the many expensive Italian restaurants Larry and Keeta must have been to, some of them even in Italy, and she winced inwardly as she passed the marquee-like sign parked on a patch of gravel near the highway that read in neon-illuminated block letters: "A tavola non si invecchia -- At a table with family and friends, you do not grow old." Then she remembered what she had come here to do and suddenly didn't care anymore if Larry and Keeta choked on their second-rate ravioli.

She wished that she and Steve could have talked about what Larry had done alone beforehand and come to the restaurant together in a united front, but his meetings had gone long, and he had texted to say he'd meet her there. She saw his blue pickup parked now alongside the building and Larry's rental car in a small, privileged flank of spaces near the door -- naturally. Had Larry ever not gotten what he wanted? Had the universe ever not opened its hands and given him the best of everything it had in its bounty? She wondered if he had told Steve the news already. Was Steve at this moment sitting blanched and sick, trying to think what to say next, what to do, how to let her and the girls know that things were getting exponentially worse just when they thought it was all getting better? He might even be fighting tears.

That thought propelled her out of her car, and she fairly bolted across the parking lot and into the restaurant to protect him from her brother. Several people waiting for tables were clustered at the front. On one end of the only available bench a teenage girl sat sideways on her boyfriend's lap, turning to kiss him just as Gina came through the door. An elderly couple huddled at the other end, turned in toward each other as if they feared catching what the teenagers had or maybe, Gina thought fleetingly, they were remembering their younger selves many years ago. A large, loud group of several couples drank from beers and cocktails they had procured from the bar, and a woman held a baby while a toddler, a girl, wrapped herself in her mother's full skirt. A thin, balding man, probably the children's father, watched the news on an overhead TV set.

Gina pushed through them all and gave her name and Larry's to the hostess.

"They're already here," the hostess said. "You're the last to arrive. Follow me."

She pulled a menu from a bin and led Gina to a large table near a window (naturally, she thought again, although she had never gotten a window table here and she'd been coming for years) where her family was assembled. Keeta was helping Dex find his way through the jungle maze on his placemat with a green crayon, and Larry and Steve both had bottles of beer in their hands and were laughing easily with one another. Apparently Larry hadn't yet lowered the boom.

"Hey, Sis, there you are." Larry stood up, ever the gentleman, always doing the right thing. "Now the party can start."

Before she could stop him, he wrapped her in an embrace from which it was impossible to free herself. She reached toward Steve with her one free hand, and he took it and squeezed it hard. Did he know yet or not? She couldn't tell if he was desperate or just having a good time and glad she was there. He took a long drink of beer from the bottle in his free hand. Was that significant? Was he drinking courage and not just alcohol?

She pulled away from her brother and glared at him. Unfazed, or simply not noticing, which was more likely the case, he kept smiling as if he had just accepted a gold medal. Well, he had, hadn't he? Wasn't he going to walk off with her home and their chance to save money and get ahead? Wasn't he robbing them of their very dreams -- again? In the casino of sibling rivalry, he had hit the jackpot.

"Larry, I'm not ..."

"Just a second, Sis."

He raised his hand and waved to a waiter, who immediately, by prearranged signal, brought a bottle of champagne and four flutes. Steve pulled out a chair and Gina had no real choice but to sit down, but she left her coat on, her hands jammed into its pockets and ready to leave as soon as she was finished. For once in her life she was going to have the upper hand and tell her brother what she thought of what he had done. In the speech she had rehearsed in the bathroom at home and in the car she told him he had been a total failure as a brother and that this was just the strawberry on the cake. But she didn't want to make a scene at dinnertime in a busy restaurant, and she didn't want any table but theirs to hear what she had to say. The waiter opened the bottle and filled each of the glasses then passed them around. For a moment their foamy heads quivered expectantly. Then Larry picked his up and raised it in her direction.

"Well," he said, "I've got some great news."

"Larry, I know what you've done," she blurted out. The least she could do for Steve's pride was cut Larry off before he made a complete fool of her husband. This new life he was forcing them to undertake would be hard on her and the girls, but it could kill Steve, with his old-fashioned masculine pride and his need to provide for his family. She would not sit through some elaborate toast and whatever Larry had to say about how great it would be to have a country place in Indiana. She would not pretend that nothing was wrong and everyone was happy. She hated her brother at the moment. She would tell him exactly what she thought of his plans and then leave. There would be no celebratory dinner with bigshot Larry picking up the tab and her and Steve groveling and thanking him for his generosity yet again. Wildly she thought of the leftover meatloaf in her refrigerator. She would make sandwiches from that when they got home -- if they even felt like eating. Maybe they would just have beers and sit at the kitchen table and try to map out what they were going to do next.

Larry frowned at her.

"What do you mean?"

"I know you've bought the farm."

"How?" To her delight he looked, for once, flummoxed. "I haven't told anyone."

"Ah, but Michael Greenberg has. He came back to the farm to drop off the papers he had taken to your meeting. I happened to be outside, and we talked for a minute. I don't know the details, but I know that you own the farm, Michael is going back to Chicago with a fist full of money, and the only people who won't be celebrating tonight are Steve and me. Just when we thought things were turning around, Larry, just when we thought we could begin to see a future again, you pull another selfish, selfish stunt with no one's interest in mind but your own. If you think we'll stay on and thank you forever for letting us live rent-free while Steve runs the farm and I cater your parties, you've got another think coming because we won't. We won't be your grateful servants. Jesus, haven't you hurt us enough? Can't you just leave us alone? To hell with Mom's assignments. She can give you all her money, and Steve and I will find a way to survive just like we always have."

Damn! She had not meant to cry. The speech she had practiced had sounded proud and noble. What had come out of her mouth had sounded whining and pathetic. Thankfully there was a wadded, linty tissue in her coat pocket, and she used it to wipe her nose. Next to her Steve sat immobile and looked as stunned as if he had just realized he had been shot. Keeta frowned at the glass of club soda sitting in front of her. Larry sat down and returned his champagne, untouched, to the table.

"May I talk now, Gina?" he said with almost eerie calm.

"Do whatever you want. That's what you always do anyway, isn't it?" She heard herself sound like a petulant ten-year-old. How many times had she said those exact words to Larry over the course of their growing up together? When they were children, they would have been cause for a fight and the inevitable punishment of time spent apart in their rooms, but this time he ignored them.

"Yes. I -- we, Keeta and I -- have bought the farm. But our plans for it are very different from what you're thinking. If you can just pat down your feathers and stop being poor self-pitying Gina for five minutes, I can tell you what they are."

She felt Steve's arm go around the back of her chair and pull her awkwardly, defensively, closer to him.

"A few years back you needed my help, and I let you guys down. I didn't realize then how bad the situation was, and I blame myself completely for getting so out of touch that I didn't even think to pick up the phone to find out what all was going on. I was busy and preoccupied with other stuff then, but that's no excuse. Then when we took the girls horseback riding when you came to visit us, I saw how much they enjoyed it and how good they just naturally seemed to be. You told us then how you had thought about turning your other farm into a stable where people could board their horses. At the time it went in one ear and out the other. But then we came here, and I saw the Greenberg farm and started having some dreams of my own."

"Right. So now you're going to ..."

"My turn, Gina. My turn. The day you took us out to pick up walnuts and I saw what the scope of the property was, I thought, hey, we could do that right here. There's plenty of pastureland, and with a little work and money, we could easily convert the barn into a stable. There's even room to build more outbuildings if you need them."

"You on a ladder? Right. I can just see that." She stood partway up, ready to storm out of the restaurant, but Steve pulled her back down.

"Let Larry talk, honey. We'll have plenty of time to ask questions, and believe me, I have a few." Steve looked levelly at Larry, as if he didn't have enough information yet to be angry but was nonetheless suspicious of everything he was saying.

"Thank you. There was a second part to this idea, too. The time we've spent together in the past few months really has made me aware of what we've been missing. For my part, at least, Mom's little game has worked. I realize I want to spend more time with my family. And now that we have Dex, I don't want him to grow up without knowing his cousins."

"So we're all going to ..."

"Really, Gina. I'm almost finished. The only roadblock was that the farm wasn't for sale. I looked at the neighboring farm that you told me was on the market, but I thought Michael's place would work out better if I could get him to sell. I called him in Chicago just to feel him out, and he said I'd caught him at exactly the right moment. He and his wife had been talking about selling because their kids are older and they've gotten busier and don't come down as much. I'd done a little research with a local realtor, so I offered him just a little more than what would be a fair asking price, and he took it without any discussion."

"OK, Larry," now Steve's temper was about to get the best of him. Gina hadn't seen it often, but she knew what it meant when she saw the bright pink of his earlobes, the hives erupting on the back of his neck, "so do I understand that you have bought the Greenberg farm, and you're going to just steal our plan and build a business that was our idea?"

"No," here Larry barked out a short but sincere laugh. "I can't imagine a stable that I would run. Gina's right about that part. I know about as much about that as you know about producing sound tracks for movies."

Now Keeta laughed, too, tentatively, as if she weren't quite sure she should and whatever Larry said next might render it inappropriate, as if she might have to recall the laugh, suck it back inside and return her eyes to their rightful place on the now-empty glass that had held her club soda.

"You, Steve. My idea was that you would convert the farm into a stable."

"Ah, yes, godlike Larry swooping in to do the right thing and make everyone grateful, so typical," Gina said, shaking her head as much as if to say she should have seen it coming all along.

"OK, yes, maybe I should have talked to you guys first, but I saw the opportunity to hand you your dream on a silver platter, and after causing you to lose your other home, I couldn't resist the chance to give you a great surprise."

"So are you moving here?" Gina asked with disbelief in her voice.

"No, no, no. My job and our home and our life are in L.A."

"So substitute L.A. for Chicago, and it will be just like before with the Greenbergs," Steve said. "I'll be doing all the work for someone else in exchange for free rent while I also hold down a job at the store."

"Jesus, you two. If you'll just let me talk, I'll tell you what my plan is. Fortunately I was able to offer Michael cash for the farm, so there won't be any mortgage or interest to contend with. It will be mine for now, but eventually it will belong to all of us, that is if you agree to it."

"Where are we ..." Gina began.

"Again, please just hear me out. The closing will be in thirty days to give the Greenbergs time to move out and make sure all of the i's are dotted and t's are crossed, then you'll move in. The house where you live now will be mine and Keeta's whenever we come to visit. It will be a family compound like Southfork or Hyannis Port."

Gina and Steve turned to each other simultaneously in question and surprise.

"The Greenbergs are interested in selling a lot of their furniture, so we'll buy some of that to furnish our place. You might want some of it, too, since you'll have more space. We won't be around much, so when we're not here, Mom can stay there when she comes out or you can use it as a guesthouse for any other company you have."

"OK, Larry, look," Steve began, "I do appreciate what you're trying to do here, I really do, but by going off half-cocked, you've missed some pretty important details. Gina and I don't have a big savings account. We're hoping her paintings and my work at the store and your mom's annual gifts will help us get ahead, but we don't have the money to go buying furniture for a great big house. You're also forgetting one other small detail -- horses. We'd have to have a few to get started. Our plan was to offer riding lessons as well as board other people's animals, and they're not cheap. We'd also need equipment and money to remodel the barn and ..."

"I haven't forgotten any of that, Steve. I have the money to take care of it."

"And I've got a job. I don't know when you think I'll remodel a barn and start a business."

"How you manage this will be your decision, of course, but my hope is that you'll let me lend you some money so that you can quit your job and concentrate on the project."

He reached under his chair for a satchel and withdrew some papers that he slid across the table to Steve and Gina.

"It's all in here. That's your copy to read and see what you think. The farm has to be in my name right now because I'm the one putting up the money and your credit rating suffered as a result of the other ordeal. But there's a payback schedule in here that starts in three years, when you've had plenty of time to get the stable business up and running and profitable. At that time you'll start making payments back to me until we're fifty-fifty owners. If you totally hate the idea, then I really have misjudged you and screwed up. All I can suggest is that you live on the farm rent-free until you get back on your feet and then I'll sell it to someone else. But I hope that's not the option you choose. I gambled that you'd want to be my business partners."

Gina opened her mouth as if to speak, but Larry shushed her one last time.

"There's one more thing I have to say that is very important. In fact it's essential if my hare-brained scheme is to work. I know I'm coming off to Gina -- and maybe both of you -- as the rich brother coming in from the coast to fix things and get lots of adulation for it. The fact is I wish I could completely take that aspect out of the equation. I feel like a real shit for what happened before, and I want to make it up to you. That much is true. But I'm not out after gratitude or Mom's approval or any of the other things you might accuse me of. If we do this thing, we will be business partners. I have the wherewithal to front the money right now, but eventually we'll be legal partners in every sense of the word. We are going into the stable business, about which I know nothing and Steve knows a great deal. I'm not doing anybody a big favor. I should have done that before, but I didn't. And I think there will be times when you'll regret ever taking me up on my offer. Starting a new business will take a lot of work, but I think it can happen and we can build something here that we can all be proud of. Lindsay says she thinks you'll have more horses to board than you'll have room for."

"Lindsay." Gina said the name as if it had just dawned on her that she knew who that person was. Now she remembered that they were going to invite her to dinner.

"Yes, Lindsay. That's what we were doing when I was over there and not getting her stepping stones laid. We were on her computer looking at property values and where the nearest stables are and how much it costs to feed a horse for a year."

"I thought she was coming to dinner tonight."

"I asked her, but she said she already had plans. She deserves to be here because she was such a big help, but now this can just be a family celebration. So what do you say?"

"This is really Gina's decision," Steve said. "After all, you're her family, and she's the one who has to deal with the emotional baggage and the anger and the sibling rivalry and whatever else goes on between you two. God knows I've got enough of that with my own brothers. But if she's in, so am I." Here he turned to his wife. "I think this idea has a lot of potential, honey," he said, "and while I'm doing the farm work, you can be painting. It really is our chance to have something again and for both of us to be doing what we like to do in the bargain."

"I guess I'm in. It's what we always wanted to do with the other place, and I can't find anything wrong with it. It's just a lot to take in right at the moment."

The champagne had warmed and its foam had disappeared, but Larry picked up his glass again and so did the others.

"To the Chambers Horse Farm!" he said.

"Shouldn't it be Langley-Chambers?" Gina asked.

"Nope. I'm the silent partner, like your banker friend with the store."

"Then I'll just say it one time," Gina said, feeling the beginnings of unwanted tears. "Thank you. And I'm sorry. Have you told Mom?"

"No, that would have been premature in case you and Steve didn't agree to the plan for any reason. And besides, I thought it would be more fun to call her together. She had no idea her little game for us would lead to this, I'm sure."

"She'll be thrilled," Gina said, still in shock but looking forward to the call.

"For now, I say we have the dinner we came here to have," Larry said, "and then go back and look at our new homes."

Two hours later Gina put her key into the lock of what had been the Greenbergs' home but would soon be hers. She had done this hundreds of times when she was getting ready for their visits, sometimes balancing bags of groceries as she did so or bouquets of flowers or once her own vacuum cleaner when theirs had quit just before they were due to arrive. She realized now that she had always done it with the metallic taste of resentment in her mouth, that much as she owed the Greenbergs and actually liked them, she was still an engineer and now an artist who had to cook and clean for people whose educations were no better than hers but whose path through life had taken them in a decidedly more lucrative direction. And Steve! An agriculture major from Purdue, for God's sake, Purdue, the Harvard or Princeton of the Midwest when it came to learning about the land. How hard it must have been to take someone else's direction about the animals and the crops and to do the work he loved after he worked all day at a store serving other farmers, exhausted and for nothing more than to be able to say he could put a roof over his family's head. She had never given voice to these thoughts before, had always pushed them far back into her mind and selected other more positive ones to get her through the day, focusing instead on how she'd arrange the flowers or set the table for the dinner party or how she needed to remember to call a plumber to get the drip in the master bathroom faucet repaired. Funny how now, tonight, when those days were apparently over, that they seeped in to threaten her joy. For one last time, she put them out of her mind, pushed open the door and stepped inside.

Larry would join them shortly. He had taken Keeta back to the hotel so that she could put Dexter to bed and turn in herself -- another tough day, she'd said -- and he said that was just as well because they'd probably want a little time to themselves.

"I probably shouldn't come over tonight at all," he had told Gina in the restaurant parking lot. Steve had already driven away in his truck, saying he had to stop for gas, and Gina had walked with Larry to his rental car en route to her own parked farther away. "I'm sure you two have a lot to talk about and you don't really need me along, but I just want to. It's a special night for me, for all of us. I want to revel in it just a little while longer."

"Of course you should come," she said, giving him a hug before he got into the car and put the window down so they could continue talking. "And you're right. Mom's going to have a cow when she hears what you've done. I think we should call her tonight!"

But Larry had been partly right. She wanted him to come, but she also wanted time alone with Steve. They needed to think this whole thing through to see if there were any loopholes that could hurt them, if there was anything Larry hadn't thought of that would render the whole thing too good to be true. Now Steve came through the door behind her, and before she could even switch on the foyer light he took her in his arms and kissed her more passionately than she could remember since before they were married. When the kiss was over he kept his arms wrapped around her and whispered into her hair, "Gina, Gina, Gina." She smiled against his shoulder in the darkness. So this is what she had to look forward to with a husband who once again had hope, who would once again be working out of doors on the land and doing what he had known was right for him to do since he was a little boy. She liked it, and as fiercely as she had hated Larry earlier, she loved him now, loved him for giving back this man who at this moment had the proverbial banana in his pocket.

"I think someone's going to get very lucky tonight," she whispered as she moved away from him, shakily, as if he had just brought her home from their first date and they had been necking in the driveway.

For the next hour they walked through the house, sometimes holding hands, and looked through the rooms as though they had never seen them before. Sometimes they were silent, taking it all in like dumbstruck children. They moved apart to examine a light fixture or open a closet, then came back to lace their fingers together as if each had newly found the other. When they spoke, they tumbled over one another's sentences in describing the changes they could make, listing the furniture they might want to buy.

"I can imagine us in this house, but I can't imagine Keeta in ours," Steve said, laughing.

"I'm betting she won't spend much time out here. I don't think Bedford is exactly her cup of tea. But in any case she won't exactly be living in ours. She told me she's already got an interior designer coming down from Indianapolis. I've got a feeling we won't recognize the old place when she gets done with it."

"Maybe we'll wish we still lived there."

"I don't think so."

Steve looked at his watch.

"It's nine-thirty," he said. "It's been an hour since we left Larry. I thought he'd be here by now. Wasn't he just going to drop Keeta and Dex off at the hotel?"

"I thought so. He said something to me about how we might want to be alone and maybe he shouldn't come, but I think he would have called if he'd changed his mind. I'll give him a call and find out."

Then, just as she located her cell phone in her purse, Larry's headlights shone through the living room window, and they heard the sound of his laughter mingled with that of a woman. It wasn't like Keeta to mess with Dex's bedtime schedule -- or to laugh for that matter -- but the sound was unmistakable. Larry rang the bell perfunctorily and then opened the door without waiting. Lindsay trailed behind him, still wearing the jeans and long-sleeved T-shirt she had been wearing all day. It didn't look like she had expected to be drawn out into the night for a celebration.

"Look who I found!" he proclaimed, as if he really meant to convince them that Lindsay had been walking aimlessly along the highway and he had serendipitously stopped to give her a ride.

She looked sheepish.

"Found, indeed! More like shanghaied. I was happily enjoying a glass of wine in front of my TV set when Larry came by to tell me he'd told you his news. I really didn't mean to barge in on your evening like this, but Larry insisted ..."

"You're a big part of tonight," Larry said. He put his arm around Lindsay and pulled her to him as easily if they had been a couple for many years. Then, addressing Steve and Gina, he went on, "There probably wouldn't have been a deal without Lindsay. She's the one who knows all the ins and outs of farming and taking care of livestock and what things cost around here. We've spent a lot of time on her computer," and then back to Lindsay, still in the loop of his arm, "haven't we?"

"Yes, we did, but I think it has really paid off. Aren't you guys happy? You're going to have the business you wanted, and you're going to have a gorgeous house and you'll both be doing work you like to do. Have you told the girls yet? They're going to flip!"

"No," Gina said. "I want to figure some things out about the house before we tell them tomorrow, like who gets which bedroom. I had enough battles over that one with Larry when we were kids that I know what's coming. Whichever room Stephy stakes out for herself is exactly the one Danny will want. And Steve and I just want to savor the surprise for a little bit before everything gets crazy, which it will in the next thirty days."

"Let's go have a look now," Larry said. He was more animated than Gina had seen him the whole visit. "Maybe we can help you decide."

We? Were they a "we"?

They walked through all of the bedrooms upstairs. Besides the master, there were four others, all with dormer windows and bookshelves built into one wall. The bedrooms that belonged to the Greenberg girls were easy to figure out -- one with green-and-brown plaid wallpaper, horse pictures on the wall, and hockey sticks in the corner, the other with pale blue striped wallpaper, ballet shoes tied around the bedpost, and a fluffy white eyelet skirt around an old-fashioned vanity. Larry tugged at Gina's arm.

"There's something else I want you to see," he said, and he pulled her down the stairs, through the kitchen, and out the back door to a screened porch. This was where the Greenbergs doffed their muddy boots, where even now their jackets hung on hooks above a bin that held mittens and scarves. She had been out here hundreds of times. In the winter it was a good place to keep food cold when the refrigerator inside was at its capacity. How many times had she ducked out here during the Greenbergs' parties to collect a fresh bottle of white wine or a plate of hors d'oeuvres made with cream cheese that shouldn't get warm. What did Larry find out here that he thought was so interesting?

"It's a porch, Larry. Why are you so excited about a porch?"

"It could be a studio," he practically crowed. "There's room to expand and make it bigger, and then you could enclose it and heat it. I know you'll still want to keep your place downtown for shows and stuff like that, but you could have a second studio here so that if the weather was bad or one of the girls was out of school sick or whatever, you'd be able to work at home. It would be like Mom's in La Jolla. Look, it even faces the same direction."

Maybe it was just that she'd had a busy day with lots of emotional ups and downs, or maybe she was overwhelmed by all that had happened in the last few hours. Or maybe it was just Larry's happy, expectant face, his generosity, and his desire to make up to her what had frozen up her emotions toward him for so many years. Whatever caused them, suddenly she couldn't hold back the tears that had surprisingly sprung to her eyes. She grabbed Larry in a giant hug in an attempt to hide them.

"You're a big, wonderful idiot," she muffled into his shirt. "I love you a lot, Malibu brother."

CHAPTER TWENTY-ONE

The palm trees at LAX were a welcome sight after digging out from the season's first snowstorm in Bedford and slipping sideways on the icy highway on the way to the Indianapolis airport. But it was snowing at Big Bear, too, Anita had told Gina the day before when they had one last phone call to coordinate plans, so they needed to bring mittens and boots anyway. It was a Sunday afternoon, so the traffic on the freeway wasn't bad, but once they got to the two-lane mountain highway, it was heavier and slower. The reason became apparent when they reached higher elevations and falling snow became a factor in their progress.

Now, just a few miles from the cabin, Gina felt suddenly anxious and unhinged. The project, her mother's assignments that had seemed so silly and childish at the outset, had become such an important part of her daily life that she wasn't ready to give them up. She had read about patients who grieved when their tumor was removed or their migraines cured. Is that what was going on with her? The projects had brought her closer to her brother and revealed an unexpected side of her mother, and they had changed her life in ways she could not have imagined. But the changes hadn't always been easy, and they had come at the price of being on an emotional roller-coaster for most of the year. In the two short months since Larry and Keeta had been to Indiana, she and Steve had moved their family into the big house, and Steve was working with a builder to draw up plans for converting the barn into a stable. As an added surprising bonus, thanks to Keeta's example, she had lost 20 pounds. And now here they all were, literally on the home stretch. The photo album she and Larry had put together was packed in her suitcase, and the list of his good qualities that Steve and the girls had helped her compile was tucked into the side pocket of her carry-on bag. That had been a surprise, too, especially when they went beyond the ten required attributes and stopped only when they got to twenty-three. She had shipped her "creative endeavor" ahead so that it wouldn't get broken in transit, and Anita had promised to bring it when she drove up from La Jolla.

"How much longer, Daddy?" Stephanie moaned. She had been texting with a girlfriend but had lost coverage out here in the woods. Danielle, wide-eyed, looked out the windows at the branches of pine trees that hung heavy with snow.

"Who cares?" she said to no one in particular. "It's beautiful."

"Just a few more minutes, girls," Gina answered. "Put your phone away, Stephanie, and get your boots on. I'm sure Gram will be waiting for you at the door."

And then they were there, like characters in a Norman Rockwell painting, over the river and through the woods, the girls bailing out of the car and running through the snow without regard to the shoveled path, both of them wanting to be the first to reach their grandmother's open arms. Behind her through the open door a Christmas tree twinkled with colored lights, and after Anita had hugged all of them, she said, "I've got two wonderful bottles of red breathing and chili on the stove. Larry and Keeta are just a few minutes behind you."

Later, when dinner was over and the children were asleep in the bunk room off the hallway that led to the kitchen, Larry wanted to get right to the lists and the pictures, but Anita held up her hand as if to slow him down.

"Let's talk in the morning," she said, rubbing her finger around the rim of a mug of mulled cider. "We've all been traveling today, and I think you're probably exhausted. I know I am. We've got a lot to talk about -- a lot to take in. I thought we'd sleep late and then have brunch. We'll talk about everything then."

Her mother was already up when Gina wandered into the kitchen, yawning, in a pair of pajama pants and a T-shirt, her hair up in a ponytail. Anita had made coffee and was checking on pans in the oven that turned out to be strudel and a cheese and egg strata. One by one everyone else emerged from their bedrooms, slow to get started even though it was after nine. Outside the bright sun glinted on the snow that covered the ground and the pine trees, and inside it laid down a buttery patchwork of light through the uncovered mullioned windows.

When they had all been served and Gina and Larry had had a mock battle over whose piece of strata was the biggest, Anita brought out a bottle of champagne and made mimosas, which she passed around the table to each of the adults. Even the children got to drink their juice in flutes.

"This is meant to be a celebration," she said. "It's been quite a year, has it not?"

"You're telling me!" Larry said, laughing and giving Gina a playful nudge. "My sister has brought me to my knees more than once."

Gina stuck her tongue out at her brother, and Danielle said, "Mommy!"

"Let's hear those lists, shall we?"

Gina pulled hers from her pocket while Larry ran back to his bedroom to get his out of the suitcase.

"Who's first?" he said when he returned to the table.

"I'll go first," Gina said before her mother could answer. "And I should tell you that, hard as it might be to believe, my family came up with twenty-three good things to say about you before I made them quit. But here are the top ten. Number one, you love me, and now my family."

"Well, doesn't that go without ..."

"No, it doesn't. Before, you loved me because I was your sister and you had to, but now I feel like you know me and you love me anyway."

"Thank you for not saying half-sister."

She gave him the raspberries.

"No, really." He was suddenly serious. "I mean it, too."

"Number two, you're incredibly talented. Just last week Steve and I went to the movies and saw your name on the credits, and I was so proud of you. I even pointed it out to the strangers sitting next to us, who probably thought I was a lunatic and making it up, but I couldn't help myself. And now you've got us all paying more attention to the music in the movies we see and trying to figure out why you or the person at another studio picked what you did and talking about if we would have done anything differently. Number three, you're a good dad. I've watched you with Dex, and I can see that he adores you and you him. Number four, you're funny. You make me laugh. Number five, you're thoughtful when I least expect it. Like scanning my painting and sending it to Mom. You make me want to be a better person, too. Number six, you're cute."

At this Larry snorted and everyone laughed.

"No, seriously, all of these are serious. When we first started doing the assignments, I was resentful because I thought you wasted a lot of money on image. Now that I've spent a little time in L.A., I see that it's important to look the part, and I appreciate that you're well-dressed and attractive. Number seven, you married someone who showed me how to finally get off the weight I've been struggling with for the past few years."

Keeta smiled, then immediately looked down at the floor, obviously not expecting to be included in the list and not knowing quite how to react.

"Number eight, you're generous. I was a horse's ass about the flight to Hong Kong, but I really appreciated flying back in business class, and 'grateful' doesn't even begin to tell you how I feel about your buying the farm, but we've been all through that. Number nine, you're smart. I see the wheels turning behind your eyes all the time. I love how you put together the idea of a movie set in Hong Kong and bought all that Chinese music when we were there."

"And number ten?" Larry used his fingers to make a drum roll on the tablecloth, as if the tenth point would somehow have more weight than the other nine.

"You're a good son. You've taken much better care of Mom than I have since Jay died."

"I'm not exactly at death's door, you know," Anita said with mock indignation. "I don't actually need to be 'taken care of,' as you so delicately put it."

"You know what she means, Mom," Larry said, and then back to Gina, "I live closer, so it just makes sense that I'd be the one to look after her house while she was away."

"It goes deeper than that. You keep in closer touch. You know her better. It was you who made sure she got back to Mr. Wu's house the night I stormed off in a snit in Hong Kong."

Anita, sitting closer to Larry than to her daughter, gave his arm a squeeze.

"You're both wonderful children," she said.

"I'm just saying I plan to do better," Gina went on, "and I'm hoping that now that we have more room and Larry and his family will be spending some time in Indiana, maybe you will, too. We can actually all do some family holidays and birthday parties together there. I'd like for my girls to get to know their grandmother better, and you won't have to be alone so much."

"I'd like that," Anita said, a tiny smile playing around her lips that Gina would look back on later and realize was significant.

Gina handed Larry the list of thirteen more good attributes.

"You can read the others sometime when you're having a bad day, but right now I want to hear what you have to say about me, little bro."

Larry unfolded a piece of yellow legal paper and started reading without ceremony.

"Number one, you're a great sister. Just that. I wouldn't trade you for anyone else, even when you make me crazy."

"Wow," Gina whispered. "Just wow."

"Two, you're a wonderful aunt. I love watching you with Dex. He really responds to you, you know? I like how you explain things to him and how you can stop his tantrums and dole out consequences and still let him know that your love for him never changes, no matter what. So then, number three naturally follows: I think you're a wonderful mom. You've produced two beautiful, smart daughters whom I'm proud to call my nieces."

Stephanie and Danielle rolled their eyes theatrically and then burst simultaneously into laughter, thoroughly delighted with what their uncle had said.

"Number four, I like how you've made me see that there is life east of L.A. I loved the day we went out looking for walnuts and the way the trees change colors and the way neighbors help out neighbors and wave to each other on the road even if they don't know one another. Number five, I think you're a gifted artist. I'm so glad that you're working now at doing something you love and that it's profitable for you, and I selfishly like knowing that I had a small part to play in that happening. Number six, I like how you take charge of situations. When we were kids I would have called that being bossy. Now that I'm grown up, I see what an important quality it is to plan ahead and to be able to make decisions and act on them. Number seven, I like that you married a great guy. I wish

I had made the effort to get to know you better, Steve, but now that we'll have the stables, I think we're going to make a great team. I'm glad that now I also have a brother."

Steve nodded in acknowledgment. "Right back atcha, buddy," he said.

"Number eight, I think you're pretty."

Now Gina coughed nervously and didn't know where to look.

"A guy doesn't often look at his sister as any more than just an omnipresent nemesis, but since we've been doing these assignments, I've tried to step outside myself and see you the way other people see you. You've always been attractive, and losing some weight has made you seem to kind of glow, like you're really happy, and that makes you really beautiful. Number nine, I think you're a fabulous cook. When we were together in the fall, I think I may have put on all the weight you've since lost. I couldn't believe the meal you made after we went to the farmers market and the things you were able to do with the tomatoes and peppers from your own garden."

Now it was Gina's turn to drum her fingers on the table.

"And number ten?"

"Number ten: I really love the fudge you used to send us at Christmastime, and I hope you like me enough now to start sending it again."

Everyone laughed. It was the perfect comic ending to what had been a serious conversation. Now he handed her his paper.

"I stopped at ten," he said, "but I could have gone on, too. You're a hell of a sister, and I'm glad I found that out before I was an old man and we had lost all of the time together that we're going to be able to take advantage of now."

Anita leaned over the table to hug both of her children.

"I couldn't have said it better," she said, her eyes shiny with tears, and everyone clapped and cheered in honor of the woman who had made it all happen so that they were sitting here together today.

Anita disappeared into the kitchen and returned shortly with a tray on which were stacked several coffee mugs.

"How can I help, Mom?" Gina asked. She felt a harmony with her mother that she had never had as an adult. So this was what mothers and daughters who spent time together did. Life wasn't all family drama. Sometimes it was just helping each other with simple chores, like pouring a cup of coffee.

"You can bring in the coffee pot, honey," Anita said, obviously also feeling the closeness of the moment. And there's a pot of hot water, too, for tea and hot chocolate. Stephy, you can bring the marshmallows for your cocoa."

When they had settled again, Anita said, "OK, let's see the creative projects. This is the moment I've waited for since I dreamed up this idea. Gina, yours is in the closet in my bedroom. I hid it there so Larry wouldn't see it too soon."

Gina left and came back with a large flat box that was packed tightly with foam peanuts and taped securely at both ends with plastic tape. She used the paring knife her mother handed her to slice it open and then pulled out a flat object that was wrapped in brown paper. Before she pulled off the paper, she ran back to her bedroom and brought out the photo album she and Larry had created.

"For you to understand this painting, we'll need this, too," she said.

She opened the book to the pages of pictures they had taken at Anita's house in La Jolla. Then she slid the framed painting from its wrapping and held it up for her family to see. They all murmured their appreciation and then applauded. To a casual observer, the piece would have looked like a portrait of two smiling people, but now Larry was the one with tears in his eyes. He pulled his sister to him as he studied the painting.

"You have to look at the picture to know why this is so important," he said hoarsely.

He pointed to the photograph in the album that was nearly -- but not quite -- the painting's twin. They had used a tripod to take it of themselves that night in La Jolla when they had finished organizing Anita's paints. In the actual photo they were sitting on chairs with space between them and their smiles had been phony, an attempt to please their mother when they eventually presented the album. In the painting, they were seated together on a sofa, Larry's left arm draped casually around Gina's shoulders, Gina making a fist and pretending to give him a friendly punch. In this version they were looking at each other and their smiles were real.

"Oh, Gina," her mother gasped, tears now in her eyes. "It's incredible."

"I'm glad you like it," Gina said. "I'm usually not all that good with painting people, but this just came together somehow."

Larry carried the picture from place to place around the room, holding it up first over the fireplace and then against the opposite wall.

"Where are you going to hang it, Mom?" he asked.

"Not here, I don't think," she said. "Although ... no, never mind. I think I'll take it home with me and hang it there. That's where the moment happened, and that's where I spend most of my time. I don't get up here as much as I'd like to, so I'd seldom get to see it. I want it with me every day."

Gina squeezed her mother's shoulders.

"Thanks, Mom," she said.

"And now, Larry, what do you have?" his mother asked.

"Gina's a tough act to follow," he said, "but I'll give you what I've got."

He sat down at the old upright piano that sat in the narrow alcove between the dining area and the living room. It was the one on which he had learned to play that had been supplanted by the spinet in La Jolla. Now he ran through a series of scales to make sure his mother had gotten it tuned as he requested, and she had. With

Stephanie and Danielle sitting on the floor near him and the rest of the family settled on the sofas around the corner, he began to play. The introduction sounded very much like "Through the Eyes of Love," Gina's favorite song, and each of the adults in the living room frowned slightly in question. The project was supposed to have been original. Then he began to sing.

"Gina, sister, sister true,/how could I not know you,/how could I let the years go by,/many days without you, angry words about you,/now that I know you,/I'll be a real brother now."

He went on for three more verses that covered experiences they'd had during the course of Anita's assignments, always coming back to this chorus. In the living room Gina groped for a tissue in her pocket, no longer trying to hide the fact that she was openly crying. Anita, also misty, moved to the arm of the sofa where Gina was sitting and rubbed her arm gently. Steve hummed along with the melody, and Keeta awkwardly picked just that moment to say she needed to check on Dexter. On the floor near the piano, Stephanie whispered to Danielle that they had the coolest uncle who ever lived.

When the song ended, Larry came back into the living room and took an elaborate bow to effusive applause.

"And now," Anita said, looking at her watch, I've got a surprise for the children. There's a holiday movie playing in the village. Steve, I've bought passes for all of you. I wonder if you and Keeta would be good enough to drive them down so that I could have some time alone with Larry and Gina."

Steve all but sprang to his feet, obviously relieved to have an excuse to get away from the emotional scene that had just played out. Gina kissed him on the cheek.

"Thanks, honey."

"Hey, I'm happy to leave you California people with all your mushy stuff. I appreciate the sentiments, but I think some fresh air and a movie will be good for this Indiana farm boy."

When they had gone, Anita motioned them back to the table and opened a second bottle of champagne.

"We're going to need this for courage," she said, her smile tight and too bright. "But then, if all goes well, we'll use it to celebrate."

"Mom," Gina blurted before her mother could say anything more. "Are you all right? I've wondered all along if your plan to bring Larry and me closer didn't have something to do with your health."

Now Anita laughed.

"No, honey. I'm fine. I promise. I'm glad to know that when I eventually leave this planet you and Larry will have one another, but my plans are to stick around for many, many more years before that happens."

She sobered.

"But I do have some things I want to talk to you about. I've given a lot of thought to how to do this -- about where I'd tell you and when. I hoped that having you do the assignments would have exactly the result it has and that maybe when you were closer to each other, it would be easier to hear. In some ways it's good news for you. In other ways, well, I just don't know."

She threw up her hands as if in exasperation.

"Holy crap, Mom, just spit it out," Larry said. "Whatever it is can't be as bad as what we're imagining."

"I'm going to tell you the whole story, start to finish, so please just bear with me. I'll answer any questions you have, but if you just let me talk without interrupting me, you probably won't have any."

She took a sip of her champagne and laughed nervously.

"I really wasn't kidding about needing the liquid courage."

Gina realized she was sitting perfectly erect and on the edge of the dining room chair, as if posture and attention were the catalysts that could cause her mother's words to tumble out faster.

"Davey Calhoun was the love of my life," Anita began after what seemed like hours. She wasn't looking at either of them now, instead toying with the raveled edge of a blue plaid cloth napkin left over from brunch.

"But ..." Larry began. Anita held up a hand to stop him.

"No interruptions, please. I'll make everything as clear as I possibly can. Jay Langley was the love of my life, too. That may be hard for the two of you to understand, but it's a fact of my life. Davey made my hair catch on fire. I know, I know, children never want to think of their parents as being madly in love, but I truly fell in love with him at first sight. I hadn't even met him, but I told the girlfriend I was with that I was going to marry him. She and I had taken a shortcut through the music building on campus because we were late to a class, and his band was practicing in the auditorium. When I looked up on that stage and saw him ... Well, I never made it to class that day. My friend went on, and I just sank down into one of the seats and watched him play. For all I knew, he was the only one on the stage, in the building, in the world. Happily for me, the feeling was pretty much mutual. When they finished their rehearsal and the other guys were packing up their instruments, he walked back toward where I was sitting, but I didn't even wait for him to get there. I started walking toward him. 'What's your name, little bird?' he asked me. We were all about the British invasion then, and girls were all 'birds.' I told him, and he asked would I wait for him while he packed up his guitar and the sound equipment. We left together and were never very far apart after that. And the girl who had laughed when I told her I was going to marry him was the maid of honor in my wedding. It was small, just my parents and a few friends. Davey's parents were both dead by that time -- his dad in an accident and his mom of heart disease, very young. You've never seen any pictures of it because there weren't any.

"My parents never did approve of him, and in many ways they were right. He may have been crazy about me, but his real love was music, and wherever it took him, he followed like a rat after the

Pied Piper. When the band actually made it big, he just couldn't handle all that came with even a little bit of fame -- the women, the drugs, the rock-god attitude. My love for him never faltered, but I couldn't keep looking the other way like it didn't matter. People always shake their heads and act like they can't understand it when someone like Elvis Presley or Janis Joplin or Michael Jackson goes around the bend. I know exactly how it is. They get to a point where they just implode. When I found out Davey was dead, my heart shattered into about ten million pieces, but I wasn't surprised. And I had you, Gina, I had another love that filled up my heart and took away my attention. He loved you and liked showing you off to his friends, but not enough to miss a practice when you were sick and I had to work and not enough to be home for Christmas when there was a Christmas Eve party they could play. He kept saying he was doing it for you, for us, for our little family. But I knew why he was doing it. He had to. He had no real choice, and neither did I. Once I became a mother, baby Gina came first. I wanted to save money so you could have cute clothes and go to college someday. I wanted to stay home nights and take care of you and not haul you all over the country sitting in dressing rooms and waiting back-stage for the adoring women to finally let him go. But if we weren't with him, sometimes they didn't let him go at all. I couldn't stand it, and I filed for divorce."

Anita took a deep breath and poured more champagne into their three glasses.

"A couple of years later I met Jay. Against all the odds, I had finished college and had a good job at the design firm. I was the low woman on the totem pole, but I was in and the other designers were teaching me so much and giving me more and more respon-sibility. And now that I wasn't with Davey anymore, my mother agreed to help watch Gina. Well, you both know this story. One afternoon I was measuring for curtains in a house we were doing, and when I went into the den, there was Jay. He was the couple's stockbroker, and they were going over some papers he needed them to sign. I said I'd wait until they were finished, but the designer I was with had to get back to the office for an appointment. Jay said he was driving back that direction when they finished, and he'd drop me off. I wasn't looking for a boyfriend certainly, and he was a little bit older than I was, so I didn't think about having a relationship with him, and I wasn't trying to make a good impression or anything. I just needed a ride. By the time they finished with their papers and I got the measurements I needed, it was time for my office to close. We were having a nice talk in the car, and Jay said could he take me to dinner by way of apologizing to me for using up so much of my time. I called my mother, and she said she'd give you dinner and put you to bed, so off I went. We began dating pretty steadily, and then one night he told me he loved me. I couldn't say it back at first. I liked him. I thought he was smart and handsome, and he was always good to me, but Davey was always in the back of my mind. Jay asked me on about our second date when my birthday was and what my favorite flowers were and my favorite color, and he never forgot. There were bouquets of zinnias whenever they were in season. 'Just because,' he would say. And he never forgot my birthday or our anniversary. He let me know he appreciated everything I did -- whether it was a dinner I cooked or his dry-cleaning that I had picked up, he never took me for granted. And he knew how important you were to me, Gina, and then later on Larry. He adored you both and couldn't have treated you better if ..."

Her voice shook, and Gina said, "Mom, if this is too ..." Anita shook her head violently. "No, let me get this said. So anyway, he was the opposite of Davey, and in the same way Davey made my hair catch fire, he gave me a sense, down deep inside, of what real love could be like. It was like Davey was a teenager and Jay was a grown-up, and I wanted a grown-up. I needed a grown-up. I said yes when he asked me to marry him, even though I still hadn't told him I loved him. 'I don't want to say it until I really feel it,' I told him, 'but I know that one day soon I will.' And I did. I told him the day we got married. I meant it then, and it only got better and deeper as the years went on. He was the best husband a woman could ever have."

"So you loved both of your husbands differently," Larry said, perplexed. "That's probably true of anyone who has ever been married more than once. Surely that's not the big news you wanted to tell us."

"No, Larry, it isn't." Her tone was suddenly severe, and Gina was glad she wasn't the one who had asked the question, even though it had sprung to her mind, too.

"For all the years we've been coming to this cabin I let you believe Jay and I bought it, but the fact is I inherited it from Davey."

Now Gina frowned, and the words popped out of her mouth before she could stop them.

"But by the time ..."

"Let me finish, please, Gina. I know it sounds like I'm rambling, but you'll see how all of the pieces fit together, I promise. The cabin had belonged to Davey's parents, and he had inherited it when his mother died. We used to come up here all the time together. Once things started to get crazy, it was the only place where our life seemed to make any kind of sense anymore. I even said that to him one time. 'Maybe this is our real home,' he said then."

She took another deep breath and looked down into her lap at the napkin that now was wadded into a ball. She looked suddenly older than the globe-trotting, champagne-pouring mother with whom they had had brunch just an hour before.

"For the most part, I didn't see Davey again after I married Jay," she went on. "It just didn't come up. Jay and I had our life with you, Gina, and Davey was traveling with the band. But one time the band came back to San Diego to play for a New Year's party.

After that they took a little hiatus, and Davey called me and said he was at the cabin and wanted to talk to me. Of course a part of me still loved him. You don't get over someone like him just because you've married someone else. So I said yes. He wanted me to bring Gina, but I said no. Jay was the only father you had ever known, and I thought it would be too confusing for you. You were just a toddler."

Her voice broke again, and this time her shoulders heaved with sobs. Larry and Gina looked at one another helplessly.

"Jay had gone to San Francisco on business," Anita said finally. "So I didn't have to explain to him where I was going. I told my mother I was going to see a friend, which was kind of the truth."

She took another deep breath, another sip of the champagne.

"It started out to be a day very much like today -- with snow on the ground and sunshine making everything sparkle, but as the day wore on, the clouds rolled in and in the late afternoon it started to snow heavily. I knew I should have left and gotten down the mountain before the snow got too deep, but we were all alone, and it was like there was no one else on earth. We sat in the window together and watched the snow cover my car. I called my mom and told her I was snowed in at my friend's cabin, and I stayed. It was like old times, when we'd been crazy about each other before any of the bad stuff started to happen."

She pressed her lips tightly together and closed her eyes momentarily.

"Well, like I said, I know children don't want to think about their parents having sex, so I'll draw the curtain there. But not long after that I found out I was pregnant, and that baby was you, Larry. What I'm trying to tell you is that you are Davey's son. You and Gina are one hundred percent biological brother and sister."

"But how do you know that?" Larry blurted out, forgetting his mother's admonition not to question her until the end. "They didn't have all the tests back then, and surely you and Dad, uh, ..."

"Yes, Jay and I were very close, but the thing was that he had too low a sperm count. He couldn't have children."

"So how did you fool him?" Larry's voice was growing louder with frustration and an irrational anger at his mother on his father's -- or whatever he was -- defense. "Or was he in on the big lie, too?"

"It wasn't a lie," Anita said. "He was in every way that counts your father. You've seen the Father's Day cards that say it's easy to be a father, but it takes something special to be a dad. Davey was your father, but we never saw each other again after you were conceived, and he never knew I was pregnant. He died before you were born, not that I ever would have told him anyway."

"But Dad ..."

"Your dad very much wanted to have his own children, so when month after month came and I still wasn't pregnant, he decided to get a checkup. We knew the problem didn't lie with me because I'd already had Gina. At that time there weren't all the privacy laws we have now, so when the results of the test came back, the doctor called and left the bad news on our answering machine. I had just found out I was pregnant, so I erased the message before Jay came home from work and told him the doctor had left a message saying that his sperm count was low but that a baby wouldn't be impossible. The timing was extraordinarily convenient. A couple of weeks later I told him I was pregnant, and we lived happily ever after. You've always resembled me more than Davey, so Jay had no reason to question who your parents were. He was so happy when I told him, and he loved you so much. He loved you both."

"But wasn't there a good chance that the doctor would talk to Dad about it in a later visit? Weren't you worried about being found out?"

Anita shook her head.

"They did talk. The doctor and his wife were actually good friends of ours, and he and your dad even played golf together once in a while. He was one of the first people Jay called after I told him the news, and he was thrilled for us. He said it was like couples who adopt because they think they can't have a baby and then find out they're pregnant. He chalked my pregnancy up to our being more relaxed about the whole thing, and he always called you our miracle baby. I kept my past deliberately murky so that in case you turned out to be blond and fair like Gina, no one would think to connect you with my first husband. It seems the only thing you got from him was his musical ability."

She was silent then, like the mannequin that tells fortunes at carnivals falls silent in her booth when a quarter's worth of time has run out.

"So why tell us now?" Larry asked when he realized her story was over. "You could have fooled us, too."

"I don't want to fool you, au contraire. I want you to know who you are, and I want you to know your genetics for your sake and your children's. You're not predisposed to get the disease that killed Jay. That's good news, isn't it?"

"So that's what the assignments have been about," Larry said, more to himself than to anyone else in the room.

"The assignments were probably a crazy idea, but I could see you and Gina drifting farther and farther apart, and I wanted you to know each other and care about each other before I told you that you were brother and sister. You were both Davey's biological children and both Jay's children psychologically and spiritually."

"You've got to admit it has been fun, Larry," Gina chastised him.

"It has been. I'm not saying it hasn't," Larry said, with a trace of anger still in his voice. "But you didn't just find out that your father isn't who you thought he was your whole life, Gina. It's going to take some time for this to soak in."

"What you have just found out is that you had two fathers, just like me," Gina said quietly. "Davey Calhoun didn't know you existed, but he did know about me, and at the end he elected not to have anything to do with me. Which of us has the bigger load to carry, do you think?"

"That's not quite true," Anita said. "He wanted to see you that day when I went to the cabin. He wanted me to bring you, and I'm the one who said no because he hadn't been a real father to you."

"You were right to say no, Mom," Gina said. "Wanting to see what I looked like and wanting to be a parent to me are two entirely different things. Jay was my dad, period."

"And if I had taken you with me, the day might have gone very differently. And if that had been the case, you might never have been born, Larry. I might not have been able to give Jay the child that he wanted so much. Believe me, I've played all this over in my head a thousand times. I'm not trying to say it was okay that I was unfaithful to Jay, even just that once. He deserved better than that. But because I slipped that one time with someone who had once been my husband, I have you and Jay had you. And Gina had a brother instead of being an only child like I was. Everyone benefitted and nobody was hurt."

Gina reached out for Larry's hand.

"I wouldn't have said this before we did the assignments," she said, "but I'm glad, too. We'll probably always make each other crazy from time to time, but I can't imagine my life without you."

"Me, either, Sis. Me, either."

CHAPTER TWENTY-TWO

B y 4:30 in the afternoon it was practically dark. Much like on the long-ago afternoon Anita had described to her children, leaden clouds obscured the earlier sunshine, and the dense, snow-covered pines that surrounded the cabin blocked out the meager light that was left. Now the lamps inside the house were casting splotches of light outside onto the piles of old snow that were quickly being covered with feathery new flakes.

Anita had put an apple pie into the oven that was beginning to fill the cabin with the aroma of cinnamon. Gina, who had spent much of the afternoon sketching parts of her mother's cabin to work up into paintings later on, was now buttering slices of bread for grilled-cheese sandwiches. Larry had gone for a walk into the village, saying he needed to think about everything his mother had told him, and then sacked out in his room for a nap. The moviegoers had just returned, and Keeta was upstairs changing Dex out of his snow pants and into warm pajamas. Stephanie and Danielle, their cheeks pink, munched on the cinnamon-sugar piecrust their grandmother had made for them and argued over whether Santa could find them in California. Stephanie was no longer a believer, but she played along to humor her sister and winked broadly at her mother over Danielle's head to make sure she was getting the credit she deserved. Sisters, Gina thought. Siblings. They were rivals who could be lethal and mean and hurt you in a way no one else could, but when the chips were down, they had each other's backs. Steve was busy placing the gifts they had shipped ahead to Anita under the Christmas tree. Anita carried in a stack of plates, atop which a nesting of silverware chattered gently. While they had all been busy with their individual pursuits, she had added leaves to the dining table and covered it with a green linen tablecloth and red napkins. With the sandwiches ready to go onto the griddle and the accompanying pot of tomato soup simmering, Gina now joined her mother in the dining room.

"Beautiful," she said. "How can I help?"

"You can put out the silverware after I've set the plates around. And we'll need candles. I've bought new ones. They're in the drawer of the sideboard."

By the time Gina retrieved the candles, her mother had finished with the plates and started on the silverware herself. Gina counted the places and frowned.

"Mom, I think you've got too many places set. There are only eight of us -- Steve, the two girls, and me," three in Larry's family and you."

The smile she had seen earlier once again played around her mother's lips.

"I've invited someone to join us," Anita said, flushing a little bit, Gina thought, although it could just have been the heat from the kitchen. "He'll be here in about an hour."

Anita returned to the kitchen and busied herself unnecessarily with checking the pie repeatedly and folding and refolding the dish towels. Gina followed her.

"He? Ooh-la-la!" she said.

"We'll talk about it later, before he gets here. I might as well tell all of you about him at the same time."

"Larry, Steve, Keeta!" Gina shouted.

"Shhhh!" Anita hissed. "I think Larry's still asleep."

"Not with Keeta and Dex up there with him, and besides, they all need to come down soon for dinner."

"Be there in a minute," Steve called from the living room. He stood up and surveyed his work before he followed his wife's voice into the kitchen. He had arranged the presents that spilled out from under the tree and into the room so that each person would naturally get a gift as they handed them out in rounds.

Larry grumbled down the stairs, his clothes rumpled and his spiked hair for once disheveled, looking put-upon and very much like he had as a teenager when his mother had repeatedly yelled at him to come to breakfast, her voice getting higher and louder with each subsequent call.

"What's the big deal?" he asked. "Why is everybody yelling?"

Keeta was behind him carrying Dex, and the girls huddled under the tree, reading the cards and guessing what was in each of the packages.

"I think Mom has something she wants to tell us about," Gina said archly. "Or make that someone."

"It could have waited, it's not that big a ... well, yes, it is a big deal. Steve, could you open another bottle of champagne. This has been a champagne kind of day, hasn't it?"

"Jesus, are you going to lay another one on us like you did earlier?" Larry asked. "If that's the case, I need a double scotch instead of a glass of champagne."

Steve poured champagne into the flutes that were still sitting in the drying rack on the kitchen counter, not yet put away from when they had used them earlier. Then Gina helped him carry them into the dining room and pass them around.

"Oh, sit down, everyone. Please!" Anita said. "You all look as if you're prisoners waiting for the verdict at a trial. I think what I have to tell you is good news."

The adults sat down at the table as quickly as if they were contestants in a game of musical chairs. Stephanie and Danielle abandoned the Christmas tree and stood together between their parents' seats, looking at each other nervously. Dex climbed onto Keeta's lap, oblivious to anything except the Elmo puppet he had been given as an early Christmas present from his other grandparents.

"Watching you do my assignments, even from a distance, has been one of the greatest joys of my life," Anita began. "I know they seemed silly to you when you first learned about them and started to do them, but they have meant a great deal more to me than you can imagine. I regret now that I tied them to money in the beginning, but I wasn't sure you'd do them otherwise, and it was so important to me that the two of you get closer again. My mother and her sister were estranged for thirty years and only made up when Aunt Betty came to see Mom in the hospital when she was dying. I was there when it happened, and I remember Aunt Betty putting her face into her hands and sobbing. They couldn't even remember what their argument all those years ago had been about. I wasn't going to let that happen to the two of you. But surely you knew that I'd give you whatever you needed and that you would share whatever I leave behind when I'm gone."

Gina looked at Larry, eyes wide, and telegraphed, "I told you so. She's sick. Something awful is about to happen, and she's putting her usual positive spin on it." He shrugged his shoulders in an expression of "Who knows?"

"And it has been all of you -- not just Gina and Larry. Keeta and Steve and the children have all been involved with getting to know one another, too. I got so much more from my plan than I had bargained for. A year ago, Larry and Gina were barely speaking to each other, and as I learned only today, you," here she looked pointedly at Gina, "had even stopped sending the Christmas fudge. That's just sad."

Here everyone laughed but still a little hesitantly, not sure what was coming next.

"But today, here we are," she continued, "the family we should have been for all the years we've missed being together. I wish Jay were here. He loved both of you so much, and he would love seeing your families together. But the funny thing about this project we've been doing is that I'm the one who learned and changed the most. I learned about you and your families and your childhood memories and what makes you tick. But I learned something more. Watching my two children and their partners has made me realize what I have been missing since Dad has been gone. I want to be a part of your lives, and heaven knows I have been this year, even when I was halfway around the world."

Again nervous laughter as they wondered what all this was leading up to. They had a sense of being in the third act, the ninth inning.

"But I'm more than a mother and a grandmother, and I selfishly want more from my life, too. Don't get me wrong -- I'm happy just as I am. I love the travel and the painting and my house and living near the beach -- I am the luckiest person I know. But something else I've discovered is that I'm lonely. I want what you both have -- a partner to talk to about my day while we cook dinner together, someone to share my excitement about my work, to hold hands with under an airline blanket as we explore the world. And I think I've found him. I know I have. And I've asked him to come up to spend Christmas with us. That's who will be sitting at the ninth place, Gina. He should be here any time now. And I think he'll be at the ninth place from now on because he has asked me to marry him."

She retreated to the kitchen and came back with the champagne bottle to refresh their glasses. Larry looked at Gina and mouthed with confidence, "Mr. Wu!" Gina immediately began imagining what family holidays would be like back in Hong Kong. Since she had no idea what Mr. Wu looked like, all she could imagine were years of expensive airline tickets and piles of unusual foods her daughters wouldn't eat.

Just then they saw car lights glance off the snowy trees along the driveway and then they heard the engine turn off and the thunk of a car door followed by another of what must have been the trunk. That was followed by the stomping of snow off boots and the ringing of the doorbell.

"I'll get it," shrieked Stephanie, obviously eager to be the first to discover the identity of the mystery guest. Her sister followed closely behind her.

She yanked open the door, and Dennis MacDonald stepped into the room, pulling off a knit cap and ducking his head sheepishly when he saw the small, speechless crowd waiting to greet him. He carried a shopping bag filled with wrapped gifts that he set down beside the door.

"Hello," he said awkwardly.

"I've told them everything," Anita said as she kissed him briefly and took his coat to hang in the hall closet.

"I guess you were pretty surprised, huh?" he asked them. "Well, me, too. I've tried for a long time to get your mother to say yes."

"We were just having some champagne," Gina said. She was the first to regain her composure. "I hope you'll join us. After all, we do have something to celebrate."

"You bet," he said. "Yes, we sure do."

Later, when they had finished the soup and sandwiches, they opened their gifts, as they had done since Gina and Larry were children and Anita had done before that as a child with her parents. Santa would come in the morning, but tonight was about family gifts to one other. Anita had shipped hers back from places she had visited around the world -- sweaters from Ireland, a kilt in his family tartan for Dennis from Scotland, soaps from France, a stuffed koala for Dex from Australia. Dennis brought toys that were too young for Stephanie and Danielle -- picture books with talking animals and puzzles with giant pieces -- but they squealed with delight and thanked him as if that were exactly what they had hoped for. Since Dennis had no children of his own, his cluelessness was endearing. For Anita he brought the wedding rings the two of them had picked out during a trip to Santa Fe -- turquoise and silver instead of traditional diamonds and gold.

"I offered your mom diamonds, but you know how she is," he said in mock frustration, smiling at Anita as he spoke, obviously completely content with exactly how she was.

The last gift under the tree was labeled "To Larry from Gina." It was a square box that he recognized immediately -- Indiana fudge. He opened it at his spot on the floor by the fireplace and then walked on his knees to the sofa to give his sister a hug.

For a while they savored sitting in the colorful confetti of shredded wrapping paper and ribbons ripped off and discarded in abandon. Christmas music played softly in the background, and the candles on the table still flickered and filled the room with the scent of pine and bayberry. They would have to sift through the piles later on to make sure nothing was lost, but no one minded.

When Anita went into the kitchen to make hot chocolate, Larry followed her.

"I honestly thought you were going to tell us your mystery man was Mr. Wu," Larry whispered when they were out of earshot so that Dennis wouldn't hear. "So did Gina."

"Really?" Anita said, stunned to immobility as she reached for sugar and cocoa in a cupboard near the stove.

"Well, yeah, really. When he was waiting up for you in his bathrobe and pretty eager for me to leave that night in Hong Kong, I figured something was going on."

Now Anita laughed and gave his arm an affectionate squeeze.

"Jan Wu is a wonderful man and a good friend, but the reason he was in a hurry the night you took me back there was because he does, in fact, have a lady friend, and she had come to spend the evening. I think he wanted to get rid of you so that he could give me the obligatory nightcap and send me on my way, too. And besides, while I like Jan very much, I don't feel about him the way you need to feel about someone to marry him."

"But you do feel that way about Dennis?"

"Yes, honey, I do. He's not Davey and he's not Jay, but I love him from a whole new place. I am not a little old lady marrying for companionship, if that's what you were wondering."

"Good. I'm happy for you. I really am. He seems like a good guy, and he's obviously crazy about you."

"As I am about him."

Minutes later they returned to the living room. Larry was carrying a tray that held fat red mugs of hot chocolate. A marshmallow lay melting atop each one.

"So, Mom," Gina said, settling in against Steve on the sofa and drawing her knees up amid a pile of tissue and bows, her hands wrapped around the warm cup, "do you guys have wedding plans?"

Anita and Dennis smiled conspiratorially at one another.

"Yes, we do," Anita said. "We're getting married tomorrow."

"You're kidding, right?" asked Gina.

"No, darling, we're not," Anita said, laughing. "I have all of the people I love most in this room. Dennis and I both have a lot of friends, and if we start making lists, they will be endless. Then there will be the expense of everyone traveling and staying in hotel rooms and thinking they need to bring us presents -- no. We'll have a little cocktail reception after the first of the year and invite all the people who might have come to a wedding. It will be more casual -- much better."

"I have a friend who is a judge, and he happens to have a cabin up here, too," Dennis said, picking up where Anita left off. "Tomorrow afternoon he'll come over and do the ceremony here."

"But it would have been nice to ..." Gina began, and then almost immediately she realized that what they were doing was exactly right.

There would not be the crush and anxiety and expense of a wedding, and what could be better than a Christmas Day anniversary. "Never mind," she said, interrupting herself and laughing. "It's just me taking charge and being bossy again." With this she gave her brother a significant look. "This all sounds great. But where are you going to live? You just said a little while ago how much you love your house."

"We're going to keep both of our places," Anita said. "Dennis has a condo in a beautiful old neighborhood in Pasadena, so he'll be there during the week and with me on weekends. We've both been on our own long enough to know that we need some space. That way we'll both get some work done."

"And I don't mean to practice full-time forever," Dennis said. "I'm old enough to retire now, but I like my work, and I've got some long-term cases that I need to wrap up. After that we want a chance to do some traveling together, so when I do finally hang it up, we'll probably sell my place and live in La Jolla all the time."

Larry stood up and extended his hand to Dennis.

"Welcome to the family," he said. "When I woke up this morning I had one father. Now I seem to have three. There's a sentence I never thought I'd hear coming out of my mouth."

There was laughter all around, and Anita looked relieved. She had lain awake for nights on end, wondering how to tell Larry the truth, knowing she had to but feeling like she was somehow letting Jay down if she did. It could have gone a very different way, but it hadn't. And she thought they'd be happy about Dennis, but there was no guarantee of that, either.

Then Steve echoed Larry's sentiment, and Gina gave Dennis a hug.

"Now!" said Anita. "I hate to spoil this Norman Rockwell moment, but I think we need to clean up this mess so Santa can find our tree in the morning."

She caught Stephanie's eye and winked.

EPILOGUE

The calendar that hung in Gina's studio was no longer a give-away from Chambers Farm and Feed but instead displayed scenes of Hong Kong -- a birthday present from Larry. The May page at which she was looking featured a picture of the famous floating restaurant, and under it he had scrawled, "Thanks for making this tourist go here." It had been a year almost exactly since the letters from Dennis MacDonald had arrived. He had been a stranger then, and now he was their stepfather, strange as it seemed to call him that at this age. And that wasn't all that had changed.

The studio was no longer downtown but in a sunny remodeled room that had been the back porch, a perfect spot -- just as Larry had said it would be.

"We're going to have builders out here working on the stables anyway," Steve had said one night when they had the architect's blueprints spread out on the dining room table in the big house. "I think Larry's idea is a good one. Why don't you use some of your mom's money and have exactly the place you want? You could design it so the light is just right and you'd have room for all of your paints and equipment."

She felt a twinge of regret. It sounded like a good idea, but she would miss the windows that looked out over the small but busy downtown, miss running up the stairs with a paper cup of coffee and ideas buzzing her head. She would miss the ridiculous, heady sense of living as artists did in cities like New York and Paris. Work had filled her up as she had never been filled when she was calculating how big a load a balcony off a bedroom could hold. Even if she had gone on to work on high-rise buildings and bay-spanning bridges, she didn't think the thrill could match putting paint to paper and watching a whole new world materialize. And it seemed to her that her muse lived in the grubby little rooms she and Lindsay had fixed up so she could have a place that was just hers in which to paint. What if there were too many distractions on the farm? What if she couldn't paint anymore? And people surely wouldn't drive all the way out here to see her work.

She had been about to tell Steve no when a small art gallery had opened downtown, and the new owners called her before she even knew they were moving in. For a reasonable commission they would include her in their advertising, show her paintings, and handle her sales, leaving her free just to paint and do the greeting cards and calendars to which she was gratefully and happily committed. Maybe that was the sign she needed. There had never been a real art gallery in town before, and just when she needed one, there it was.

Now she worked in a space that was almost embarrassingly state-of-the-art. She would never be mistaken for a starving artist here, inside this room that was designed to her specifications -- her work table and stool exactly the height she needed, the windows on three sides fitted with shades she could draw when the sun was too bright, a built-in shadowbox for arranging still-life props, a tea kettle and a hotel-size refrigerator so she could take a break or have lunch and keep right on working without the distractions that might lie in wait in the rest of the house. Bookshelves under two windows held all of her art books, and a soft throw was tossed over the back of a comfortable chair with an ottoman in case she wanted to curl up and read.

From the western windows she could see across the pasture -- now enclosed to make a corral -- to where Stephanie led a frisky Appaloosa from the stable to meet an excited girl and her mother who had just arrived for a lesson, and Steve, who had been tinkering with a belligerent tractor in the other side of the barn, ran out to join them. They were booked solid for summer lessons, and they already had two families who permanently boarded their horses at the Chambers Horse Farm. After worrying about money for so long, Gina couldn't stop tallying up the income they were earning and comparing it -- always favorably now -- with the overhead. They had already been able to start making payments to Larry.

"We'll be like the people on *Dallas*," he had joked. "Maybe I'll talk to the studio about a movie called *Bedford!*"

Danielle had gone into town with Keeta and Dex to pick up groceries. Larry's family had been staying in the guesthouse for a week, and Anita and Dennis were coming in a few days for the long Memorial Day weekend. They hadn't been here since just before the remodeling began, and Gina could hardly wait for them to see how the whole place had been transformed.

She left the studio and stood outside in the yard to look at the house -- the big house, her house -- where Larry now sat on the front porch, his feet crossed on the railing and tapping up into the air to keep time with whatever music was playing in the earbuds that sprouted from his ears, a clipboard in his lap, his eyes closed, seeming to lead an invisible orchestra with the pencil he held in his hand. Apart from the family get-together, he had come to work on a new soundtrack, much of this one to be made up of his own compositions.

For the most part all of their lives had improved, it seemed, and it all led back, at least indirectly, to Anita's assignments that had seemed so ridiculous in the beginning. But there had been one big disappointment in Gina's life and, she was to discover, Larry's.

Not long after the night at Rotunda 6 when he had made the announcement that he was buying the farm a "For Sale" sign had appeared in Lindsay's front yard. Gina almost missed it as she was driving past, focused as she was on the pile of paving stones that still leaned against the house and wondering what had actually taken place between her brother and her friend. She only noticed it when she was already past the entrance to the driveway, but then she slammed on the brakes and put the truck she was driving into reverse so she could turn in. She heard the thud and felt the vibration of the groceries in the bed of the truck as they fell over and then the rumble of apples scattering from their bag, but this was more important. She jumped out, ran up to the back porch and pounded on the screen door as hard as she could.

"What the hell?" Lindsay asked as she came through the back door drying her hands on a kitchen towel, but she laughed when she saw Gina, knowing immediately the source of the noisy outrage.

"That's exactly what I was going to say to you -- what the hell? You put your house up for sale and you don't even bother to tell your best friend? What are you doing? And why didn't you talk to me and where are you going?"

"Do you have time for coffee?"

Gina glanced at her watch. It was 4:15 in the afternoon.

"No, but I've got time for wine," she said. "I think I'm going to need a drink to hear this story."

Lindsay disappeared into the dining room to get stemmed glasses from her grandmother's china cabinet and then took an already-open bottle of pinot grigio from the refrigerator. She filled the two glasses and then clinked hers against Gina's.

"Cheers," she said.

"Really? Cheers? Really?" Gina responded. "That's all you've got?"

"Okay, here's what's happening. This farm is really too much for me to handle on my own. You know I've got nobody here, and ..."

"Nobody?"

"You know what I mean. I love you and Steve and the girls, you know that, and I know you'd do anything to help me that you could. But you've got this busy new life, and I can't be calling you every time I need the lawnmower fixed or the dryer goes on the blink."

"But what about Casey? This is the only home he's ever known."

"Casey is going to be fine. I have an aunt in Louisville who lives in a big old house overlooking the Ohio River. I'm her only living relative, and one of these days I'll inherit the place. She's in great health now, but she's starting to need some help running her business."

"What kind of business?"

"Real estate. She also owns a couple of condo complexes, so somebody has to make sure the toilets get fixed and the units get painted and recarpeted when they change hands."

"So you're going there to do something for her that you're leaving here because you can't handle doing? That makes no sense."

"I'll be the property manager, so I'll be hiring people to do those jobs. I won't be doing them myself. And I think I might also look into getting my own realtor's license."

"Is this place in the country?"

"Not really. More like the edge of the city."

"So Casey is going to be a city boy after growing up his whole life on a farm?"

Lindsay grew serious.

"He's going to be a boy with a lot of opportunities he would never have had here. Think of the art and music and museums ..."

"Take him to Indianapolis, for God's sake. We could do that together. We could take all the kids. Stephy and Danielle would love that kind of stuff. We could even ..."

Lindsay smiled sadly and shook her head.

"Thanks for trying, but it's no use, sweetie. I've told my aunt I'm coming, and I've already had two couples come to walk through the house. The realtor says she thinks the second people were really interested. Whatever happens I'll stay here until the closing, and then I'm gone. Aunt Lydia is even paying for the movers to pack my stuff. She's really eager for me to get there."

"But I'll miss you so much," Gina said, feeling tears welling up and her face contorting. "And there's Larry. He and Keeta are going to be coming out here a lot and you know he would ..."

And there it was -- a look in Lindsay's eyes so fleeting that she would have wondered if she'd imagined it if Lindsay hadn't also bitten her lip and looked down at the floor as if instinctively protecting her emotions from being discovered.

"Linds ..."

Lindsay shook her head violently, tears also now springing to her eyes that she didn't want seen and didn't want to talk about.

"I can't live near Larry."

"I thought you and he hit it off and ..."

Lindsay looked at her quizzically, still fighting tears, as if to ask if she were really that dense.

"Oh."

"Yes. Oh."

"So what happened here? I thought you were spending all the time you should have been laying pavers helping him do research about buying the farm."

"I did."

Now Lindsay nodded her head as vehemently as she had shaken it before, tears visibly running down her face. She stretched to reach a tissue from a box on the counter behind her.

"We did do some of that. Mostly we talked. It happened that first day when I met him at your studio. I felt like he was the other half of me that I had been waiting my whole life to meet. It was like I was full of electricity, like my hair was on fire."

There was that expression again. Anita had felt that way about Davey Calhoun.

"I saw you out the window that day. I saw the two of you holding each other's hands."

"We were just saying, 'Oh my God, oh my God, oh my God,' over and over again. We both felt it."

"You know, he and Keeta don't have a very ..."

Lindsay held up a hand to ward off the words.

"I know. He told me all about Marqueeta and her problems. We talked about everything. We talked a little bit about what life would be like if he left her to be with me, but we both knew that wasn't going to happen. She needs him, and in a weird, screwed-up kind of way he loves her. They have a whole life out in L.A. He certainly isn't going to give up his career for me, and the last time I looked there weren't many movie studios in Bedford. But it's not even that. There's Dex and there's just doing the right thing. From everything you ever told me about Larry, I thought he was the world's biggest jerk, but now I know he's not."

"And so do I," Gina said softly, as much to herself as to her friend.

"Right? Imagine if I told you that I was going to take part in wrecking that family? I wouldn't be your best friend for very long, would I?"

"Yes, you would. I don't think Larry's marriage brings him much joy. If you could, I'd be all for it. But even if he stays married to her, you're both grown-ups. Surely you can handle your emotions long enough to be around him during the few times he's going to come out here each year."

"No. No, Gina. I can't. And he can't. That's what I'm trying to tell you. If he came here, we would not be able to stay apart. We would need to be together, and everybody would be hurt -- everybody."

Now she was sobbing.

"Oh," Gina said again. "So you didn't just talk."

"No. I feel like a shit, and so does he." She paused and blew her nose noisily. "But honestly if we were to see each other again, it would happen again. I know it would. I didn't know what I was going to do. I thought I would just have to live with it and try to be out of town whenever I heard he was coming out here, and then my aunt came up with this idea of us moving in with her, and it seemed like it came at just the right moment, like it was some kind of message that getting out of here and staying away from him was the right thing to do. It's hard enough to even be with you, to be in your house and see pictures of him and his family and listen to you talk about them."

"I thought now that you knew them you'd be interested," Gina said lamely.

"Too interested. Desperate to hear anything you want to say about him. Desperate to have a reason to say his name. Larry, Larry, Larry."

Gina put her arms around her friend.

"I love you, and I respect what you're doing, but I hate it. Can I at least come and see you?"

"Of course. I'd be mad if you didn't! And you know, it's also not so bad that I'm going to make a new start somewhere else. This farm was more Kevin's dream than mine. And maybe I won't ever meet someone who hits me like lightning again, but there might be someone. You never know. I have to allow for that possibility, and in a city I'll have a better chance of meeting people. If I stayed here, it would be like I was grieving for Kevin and now Larry, too. I don't think my head could handle all that sorrow, and I don't want to waste my life moping over what might have been."

Gina's chance to talk to Larry came the next day, while Keeta and Dex were napping and Steve was working in the stables with the girls. It was a warm, sunny afternoon, with the last of the daffodils still in bloom under the kitchen window and a blue jay violently bathing himself in the newly filled birdbath.

"Feel like a walk?" she asked her brother.

"Sure," he said. "Where to?"

"Maybe back up into the woods. It might be warm enough for the morels to be out, and I can teach you how to hunt for mushrooms. I'll take a bag just in case."

Minutes later they entered the cool shade of the forest and skipped, one after the other, across a rocky stream.

"Did you know that Lindsay is selling her house and moving to Louisville?" she asked by way of opening the conversation. She was behind him and not able to see his face. He jammed his fists into his pockets and remained silent.

"I'll take that for a yes, but I didn't know until I saw the sign in her yard yesterday. I felt awful that she hadn't talked to me about it, and I stopped to ask her why. At first she just gave me the routine about her aunt's house and what a good opportunity for Casey and blah, blah, blah. But then your name came up, and I saw her reaction. She tried to hide it, but suddenly the lightbulb turned on in my head and everything fell into place -- the paving stones, her silence when you were around, the ..."

"Well, nothing is going to change," he said, interrupting her. "She must have told you that, too. Nobody is going to be hurt unless you decide to repeat what you know."

"You know I won't, but that's why I wanted to talk to you. It's not really any of my business ..."

"No, it sure isn't."

She hadn't heard that tone of voice since Larry had been a sullen teenager.

"Except that you're my brother and she's my best friend and I love you both," she said, running ahead of him and then turning to look up into his face. "What I want to say is that I think what you're doing is very noble and brave, but if you wanted this story to end another way, I would support you. Do you understand what I'm saying?

His lips were pressed hard together in a thin line, and he looked out over her head at some point behind her that she sensed he didn't actually see. For a long moment she thought he wasn't going to speak at all, and she was determined not to fill the space between them with needless chatter.

"Yes, I do know what you mean," he said bitterly. "I can't tell you how many sleepless hours I've spent thinking about what life might be like if I could live it with Lindsay. But Keeta needs me, and Dex needs me, and I am grateful for the way things have turned out between our two families. And who knows what would have happened if Lindsay and I had made the decision to be together. Maybe we'd be like country mouse and city mouse and bore each other beyond belief."

He laughed shakily, like he was making a bad joke, and Gina said, "You don't really believe that, do you?"

"No. I don't. She's everything I've ever wanted in a woman. Stable, fun, pretty, nice, lots of energy, wicked sense of humor. But it was more than that. The first time I saw her, I knew. I fell really in love, maybe for the first time ever. I never believed in love at first sight. I thought that stuff just happened in the movies, but now I know it's real."

Now he couldn't stop talking. He had kept the secret for months without being able to let it out and share the burden with someone else.

"Then maybe you should ..."

He shook his head vehemently no, just as Lindsay had.

"I'm sorry that Lindsay is going to move. I had hoped I would be able to see her just once in a while. You know, just take her in. Like maybe she'd come to dinner, and I could just touch her fingers when I passed her the salt shaker. I told her that. I told her I wanted her to stay so that we could breathe the same air once in a while, but she said she couldn't stand that, and I realized what a selfish bastard I was being. At the end of the day, I'd be with Keeta and she'd go home alone. She needs to be somewhere that she can move on. She'll meet somebody in Louisville..." Here he took a deep breath. "And she'll start the new life she deserves. She's been through a lot. She's got so much ... I don't know, fortitude, I guess. She's fearless."

Gina could think of nothing to say. They walked for a few minutes, deeper into the woods, kicking at May apple plants and the rotten stumps of fallen trees as if they really were looking for mushrooms.

"Do what's right for you, little brother," she said at last. "I don't have a clue what that might be. I just want you to be happy."

"Then believe that I'm doing the right thing and let it go."

They walked on in silence, making a loop through the woods and then recrossing the stream and popping back out into the sunlight on the same path where they had entered. Ahead Gina could see the trainer they had hired giving a lesson to Stephanie and Danielle in the corral, and beyond them the house she had always dreamed of owning and the studio where she now spent some of the happiest hours of her days.

So much was different from last year at this time. When she had written in her Christmas letter that it had been a year of changes, she hadn't been kidding. Her relationships with her mother and her brother and now her sister-in-law -- flawed and difficult as she might be -- and her nephew were starting all over again, fresh and shiny and new. Her daughters had grown up and changed with these new people in their lives. Yes, her best friend was moving away, but even that might hold some surprises. She would go to visit and discover Louisville and new places to paint, and she would support Lindsay as new opportunities came into her life. Louisville was only a couple of hours away. It wasn't like she'd never see Lindsay again. In a few months she would be traveling to England with her mother to meet the publisher there, and that would change things again.

Just then the stable door opened and Steve stepped out into the sunlight. He smiled when he saw them coming and started running in their direction. When he reached them he picked his wife up and swung her around in pure happiness, and in that moment Gina felt her hair catch fire.

www.ingramcontent.com/pod-product-compliance
Lightning Source LLC
Chambersburg PA
CBHW060351260626
47160CB00006B/2278